JUL 3 1 2007

W9-BNW-792

MAIN

insatiable

insatiable

the rise of a porn star

Heather Hunter

with Michelle Valentine

St. Martin's Press

New York

This is a work of fiction. All of the characters, organizations, and events portrayed in this novel are either products of the author's imagination or are used fictitiously.

www.stmartins.com

Chapters 15, 17, 18, 19 23, 26, 31, 32, 33, and 34 photos courtesy of Global Media International Films; chapters 10, 28, 29, and 30 photos courtesy of Heather Hunter; chapters 1, 3, 4, 5, 7, 8, 11, 14, 16, 20, 22, 24, and 25 photos courtesy of Vivid Entertainment, LLC; chapters 2 and 6 photos by Susan Randall; chapters 9, 21, and 27 photos by Brian Moss; chapters 12 and 13 photos courtesy of Getty Images

Library of Congress Cataloging-in-Publication Data

Hunter, Heather.
    Insatiable : the rise of a porn star / Heather Hunter with Michelle Valentine. — 1st ed.
    p. cm.
    ISBN-13: 978-0-312-36884-5
    ISBN-10: 0-312-36884-4
  1. Erotic films—Fiction.   2. Motion picture actors and actresses—United States—Fiction.
I. Valentine, Michelle.   II. Title.

PS3608.U5928I57   2007
813'.6—dc22

                                                                2007011841

First Edition: July 2007

10 9 8 7 6 5 4 3 2 1

To my higher being, for giving me the creative talents to express myself. To my family, and true friends, thank you for showing me unconditional love and support through this journey of life!

acknowledgments

Special thanks to my mother and father; my sisters and brother, Michael; step-mother, Marie Hunter; my manager, Dave Copeland; Janet Jacme, Alonzo Brown, Jo Schuetz, Wyclef Jean, Silver Narvarro, Giles Francis, Markus Carr, Hassan Johnson, Goldie, Evan Smith, Sonya Pruneda, Demetrius. B, Kool Aid, Bassment Beats, Gina Harrison, Akinelye Adams, Adam Tripps, Andrew G, D.J Premier, Claudette Warfield, Kitty Kat, Rahsun, Ms. Shaun, Cerene, Cousin Bill and family, Cousin Deeja, my idol Prince, Tony Core and Core DJs, Scott Storch, Freedom Lyles, Teflon, Madison Taylor, Miss Sig, Gerard Dure, Michael Lesser, Steven Lewis, Bill Maher, Carlos Narcisse, James Weber, Brian Moss, Michael Williams, Leomarys, Malcom Jamal Warner, Madina, Gbenga, Jo Jo and K.C., Monifa, Kwame, Fantom of the Beat, Timbaland, Cardian, Babs Bunny, Lil Kim, and to all the female M.C.'s, much respect to you, and the hip-hop industry, Ralph McDaniels, X Clan, Crazy Legs, MC Lyte, Big Daddy Kane, Uncle Luke, BET, HBO, Black Spot, Myra, Treach, Special K & Teddy Ted, Wendy Williams, Steven Hirsch and the Vivid Team, Robyn Byrd, Kobei Tai, Mr. Marcus, Sean Michaels, Jenna Jameson, Tori Welles, Timothy Greenfield Sanders, RIP George Jackson, RIP Hurley Hunter—I'm still your wild flower!—my book agent, Mannie Barron, Michelle Valentine, Monique Patterson, and St. Martin's Press, thank you for believing in me! And to my fans, you mean the world to me! And to those who I did not mention . . . I love you all!

Forever Shine!

5

4

3

2

action . . .

September 1992

I am not focused on the people who are watching the decadent scene, of which I am a part, unfold. Instead, I am focused on my job and the massive chocolate dick I have sliding smoothly across my eager tongue, taking in every single inch of its splendor as my mocha-complexioned stud moans in ecstasy, enjoying a professional blow job as only I can give it—licking his glistening shaft up to its base and along its muscular, veined external walls. But as the tick of the camera rolling behind me resonates throughout the atmosphere, amid my partner's animalistic grunts, I hear a melody.

What was the hook to that sappy song by that chick, Deborah Cox?

"How did you get here?"

Yeah. That's the melody I heard in my head like a never-ending stream.

As I allow more saliva to drip from my succulent, crimson-colored lips upon the head of his throbbing member, the words to the song grow louder in my head, as if someone has turned up the volume on the Bose speakers playing crisply within the crevices of my mind.

"How did you get here?"

There it goes again . . .

I'm not ashamed to answer. So if you really wanna know, I'll tell you. . . .

one

a taste

The story of my life . . . While it's not so spectacular to me, when compared to the average person, I guess it is rather unique.

Like all little girls, I played with my dolls, rode my bike, and cried for my mommy when I skinned my knee. But somewhere along the way those similarities began to change and I became different from my peers. I think it all started with my insatiable desire to be someone special, someone famous, and my craving to be loved. And if you ask anybody who knows, craving to be loved is dangerous because you are willing to compromise everything else you may desire to attain it.

Like many young people, at age eighteen I thought I knew it all, including the specific direction in which I wanted my life to go, and I thought I knew everything I needed to know to get there. Nobody could tell me a damn thing. Not even my mother. And boy did she try! But my mother's way was not the fastest road to accomplish anything, never mind achieving stardom. And while my mom was relentless in her attempts to redirect my course, what she soon realized was that I was just as relentless in my passion to make it all the way to the top in the easiest and least time-consuming way possible. Unfortunately for me, tired from struggling, working, and probably just life itself, Mom eventually threw her hands up in the air and let me do my own thing, after warning me that I would have to learn the hard way.

A single, divorced mother of two, Francine Young worked three jobs to provide for my older sister, Regina, and me and to maintain the three-bedroom house left to her by our grandmother. When her marriage to our father was coming to an end, Mom decided that it was time for Dad to go, but it took everything out of her to maintain the lifestyle that we were used to living. Between paying for dance classes for me and living expenses, Mom was forced to give up her dream of owning her own hair salon in an effort to make ends meet and take care of us. Sometimes she was gone sixteen hours a day, seven days a week, which obviously didn't leave much time for her to spend with us. So we were pretty much forced to raise ourselves. By the time I'd turned thirteen, I began finding it difficult to focus. As puberty took over, I started feeling emotions and desires I had never felt before, and things like ballet class were no longer at the top of my priority list. Besides, since Mom was always working, it was up to me to get myself to class, and the streets were starting to call my name—loudly. I wanted to see what they had to offer. Ballet, music, and art just weren't as exciting as the local weed spot, and I eventually stopped going to class. When Mom caught wind of all my absences, relieved not to have to pay the bill anymore, she simply let me drop out. Of course, this only lead to trouble, because anybody who knows can tell you that boredom, lack of focus, and puberty are the three ingredients that make the most troublesome stew. With our dad MIA and Mom gone most of the time, Regina and I knew this recipe all too well. I started getting into trouble and doing plenty of shit I knew was wrong. Right around this time, hip-hop was born and I quickly became mesmerized by the culture. Rapping and graffiti art was far more interesting to me than anything I was learning in a classroom, and cutting school became my favorite pastime.

Since drawing was one of my passions, when I met Ding, one of the best graffiti taggers in my neighborhood, I would do any and everything to be around him. With his adventurous spirit, he quickly became my idol, and he was more than willing to teach me the art of tagging. The adrenaline rush I would get when we'd jump down onto the tracks in the subway station was indescribable. The distinct smell of old and new piss that permeated the dark, rat-infested tunnels made for a wild and creepy danger-filled experience. The police were also always on our heels, ready to arrest us for defacing New York City property, which made the thrill that much more exciting. I always knew that we had to get in and out quickly or risk being caught and jailed or worse—turned over to my mother. Still, on any given school-day afternoon, Ding and I would run through those scary tunnels to the train yard, where we'd find paradise. Clean, vacant trains seemed to rest there, just waiting to be tagged, and we happily obliged. My name was Tasty and I carried a knapsack filled to the brim with every color spray paint you could imagine, and the bulk of it sometimes made it difficult to run. On one occasion, I was forced to drop my bag as I heard the weighty footsteps of the cops approaching in the darkness. Ding went one way while I went another, knowing that if we separated, they'd never get us both. In an effort to save my own ass, I made the split-second decision to jump over the third rail onto the platform where I then ran up the stairs as if my life depended on it—which in a way it did. As I arrived on the uptown side, a D train was about to leave the station. In the nick of time, I forcefully thrust through the closing doors and dropped, panting, into a seat. When I looked up, all eyes were on my paint-covered face and clothes. But I was safe. I don't remember what happened to Ding that day; the only thing I cared about was that I had won the game.

When I wasn't cutting school and tagging my name all over the city, my other beloved pastime was hanging with my homegirls. They were my homies from around the way. We probably got along so well because we had much in common. It was like the blind leading the blind. They were pretty much in the same boat I was: clueless and searching. With her mom strung out on crack, Ebony had no choice but to live with her eighty-year-old grandmother, who did her best but who was definitely no match for this overly boy-crazy teen with low self-esteem and raging hormones. Jessie, on the other hand, lived with her mother, but Ms. Faye always found her much younger boyfriends far more interesting than her teenage daughter. Then there was my girl Carmen, who I'd met when I was fifteen during a ninety-day stint I was forced to do at the St. Rose Catholic Reform School after my mom got tired of reporting me to the cops for truancy. Now, Carmen was a ride-or-die chick to the bone—a five-foot-seven Puerto Rican beauty with pretty almond-shaped eyes and thick black lashes to complement them. Sexually frisky and mischievous, Carmen was known as the hot, freak-me-all-week girl, with long black curly hair that bounced seductively around her angelic face—a misleading feature since she was really a devil in disguise. Carm had perfected the art of using her assets to entice what she wanted out of anybody she set her sights upon, and both men and women lusted after the juiciness she had to offer. Just a few months from completing her sentence when I met her, she was in for being a chronic runaway. While on the surface it looked like she simply didn't want to abide by her mother's rules, she secretly told me that her stepfather had been molesting her since the age of eight, and on her thirteenth birthday she'd finally gotten the balls to take flight. She'd run away so many times that the local cops knew her by name. But each time they'd catch her and bring her home, the abuse would start all over again. Within days, she'd run again. By the time Carm turned fifteen, her mom had grown tired of having her brought home by the police and signed the papers for her to be admitted to St. Rose's. She refused to believe Carm's story about the molestation and just wanted her daughter out of her hair. St. Rose's was the easiest solution.

Carmen was tough and I looked up to her. In a way, she ran St. Rose's, garnering respect from the kids and adults alike. It was rumored that she possessed this incredibly freaky and promiscuous side, but truth be told, I never saw it. She got good grades and nobody fucked with her, and I wanted to align myself with that. Sure, her life was a never-ending saga, but my girl was a master at making the sweetest lemonade out of the most sour lemons. Connected through our dreams of becoming famous, Carmen and I became fast friends, watching each other's back and helping each other get through our stint any way we could.

Since my own sister and I didn't see eye to eye on too many things, I was elated to have some sister/friends who I could count on and call my own. They gave me the feeling that I belonged somewhere, because while I loved my older sister dearly, she was just too weak for me. Whenever I looked at her, I promised myself that I would never be anything like her. Even though we both started out with big dreams, Regina had given up all her power to a guy whose sole purpose in life was to use and abuse her. I, on the other hand, was determined to make my own happiness and my own money, and to maintain my own power. I had my own opinions and ideas about how things should go down in my life and had no intention of putting in work for which I did not reap the full benefits. What I saw in her was a scared woman with low self-esteem and even lower self-worth. I guess our father's absence had manifested itself that way for her, but *that could never be me*, I often told myself. I craved the good life—flyy clothes, blinding jewels, fast cars, and unlimited cash, and I wanted to be among those who craved the same things. But first, I knew, I had to get out of my momma's house and up from under her rules.

Hanging out was my way to escape. While I'd party every night if I could, Friday was the night that I always found my way into some underground spot hoping to meet someone who could help jump-start me toward my goal. Basement parties, house parties, block parties—if it was a party and there were

lots of people, I was there. Like Lotto, ya gotta be in it to win it, and this particular Friday was no different.

Carmen, who I spoke with on the phone frequently but rarely saw these
days, had called me the night before and invited me to hang out at a club called
the Vision with her and a new group of friends she had recently made. Needless to say, I was more than excited. I was tired of coming up empty at the local
spots in my neighborhood, and the Vision was one of the premier nightclubs in
New York City. The club had a velvet rope so thick that it metaphorically resembled a steel wall that no one was permitted beyond without a special pass.
The only way you could get in was to be invited by somebody who *was* somebody. And even then, the bouncers looked you up and down and made the decision on whether you were cool enough to walk beyond its privileged doors.
So I figured that whoever Carmen was rolling with must have been somebody
pretty big for her to invite me there, and I couldn't believe that little old me was
going to be partying in one of the hottest celebrity hangouts in the city. And
knowing Carm like I did, I knew I was in for a night filled with lessons and
tests. School was always in session when I was with her and I was the anxious
student, eager and willing to participate in an evening I would never forget.

A light spring breeze gently rustled my perfectly styled hair as I walked up
the block toward the club; my heart raced with excitement as I wondered
what kind of celebrities I might meet on the other side of the Vision doors.
As I approached the establishment, I saw a crowd anxiously waiting to gain
entry and wondered if I would be able to get in. During our conversation the
night before, Carmen had told me to go to the rope, ask for Mylo, and tell
him my name, and I would be granted immediate entry. While those directions had sounded fine on the phone twenty-four hours earlier, at that moment they suddenly didn't seem like they were going to work. Still, I
managed to make my way to the front of the mob with hopes that Mylo
would be available to slide the rope aside for me.

As I walked toward the thick burgundy twine that separated the
wannabes from the already-weres, I spotted a large, dark-skinned Shaquille
O'Neal lookalike brotha with a glossy bald head. Standing nearly seven feet
tall, he had a shiny gold hoop in his left ear and teeth that were as white as
freshly fallen snow. When our eyes met, he made his way over to where I
stood and before I could ask him anything, he spoke:

"Simone?"

"Yes," I stuttered, shocked that he already knew who I was.

"Mylo," he announced, his voice as smooth as Log Cabin maple syrup. "Carmen's waiting for you in the VIP lounge," he continued as he peeled back the rope for me to enter. After clamping a neon pink plastic bracelet upon my wrist, Mylo nodded in the direction of the door and smiled, again revealing the pearliest whites I had ever seen in my life. With my eyes wide open, I was amazed at the ease with which I was granted entry to one of New York's hottest clubs and wondered who on earth my girl Carmen was hanging with to not only obtain VIP status for herself but for me as well. While I was no stranger to the club scene, the places where I'd partied had been filled with raunch and grime—basement parties, poorly lit gymnasiums, or an occasional function at the Black-Top, a ghetto-fabulous spot located at the tip of Harlem, frequented by local 'hood rich drug dealers. With its glitz, glam, and extraordinary people, the Vision was a far cry from the one-room cardboard boxes I was used to.

Amazed, I slid past security, winking at the doorman as I glided into the club. Once I was inside, the music surged through my body as I walked through beautiful burgundy-and-gold curtains that hung throughout the massive room. To say that I was completely mesmerized would be an understatement. I had certainly never been to a place as grand as this before, but it was all that I imagined it to be and more. Of course, I was in heaven.

As I maneuvered through the crowd, weaving in and out and between the people to get across the club, I was spellbound by the atmosphere. The club's lights flashed to the beat, and as the bass permeated my veins, I really wanted to dance. I knew I was a good dancer, but being in such a huge and hip place made me feel a bit self-conscious. Eagerly trying to find Carmen, I looked around the smoky club, bouncing up and down on my tiptoes. I diligently searched the dance floor but my friend was nowhere to be found. I knew she had to be in there somewhere, or else Mylo wouldn't have been so willing to let me in. But for the life of me, I couldn't find her anywhere. As sweat formed in little droplets upon my forehead, I decided to head toward the ladies' room to freshen up. I definitely wanted to look my best when I finally found Carmen and her important friends.

Eager to dab my face with a wet paper towel, I swiftly pushed the swinging door and stepped into the hazy tiled room. However, I stopped short just at the entryway, wondering if I should turn around and go back out when I spotted two girls taking a hit of coke off the bathroom sink. They looked up as I walked in and I did my best not to make eye contact, trying to act like it was nothing. Figuring it was best that I make a beeline toward one of the stalls, I headed to the one at the farthest end of the room, ensuring them some privacy. But when I pushed open the metal door, unlike the drug scene I had just witnessed, the scene that greeted me had me frozen to the floor. Like a live porno flick before my very eyes, there was a couple fucking right there in the stall. A sexy black guy was sitting on the toilet lid with this Asian hottie straddling his cock, riding him like a bull.

"Oh my God, excuse me!" I exclaimed. I was embarrassed, but my eyes were locked, watching the girl's pussy slide up and down his massive two-toned dick. It was as if I fell into a trance. As my nipples tingled and hardened beneath my purple halter, I stood there paralyzed, staring at them.

Suddenly sensing my presence, the guy looked up.

"You want some next?" Sexy snapped. Catching an unexpected case of laryngitis, I was unable to reply.

"If not, close the door, bitch," he continued.

I snapped out of my daze and backed up, letting the door close. When I looked around the foggy room, it seemed like all eyes were on me. Still refusing to make eye contact with anybody, I made a quick exit and followed my nose out of the bathroom and back into the crowd.

No sooner had I escaped the restroom when a very butch-looking female bumped into me, stopping me from returning out into the club. Standing about five-foot-ten, she had a low-cut bleached-blond Caesar and a pack of cigarettes rolled in the left strap of her gray wife-beater. As if I were a well-seasoned piece of filet mignon, the butch pulled the toothpick she'd been gnawing on from her mouth and licked her ashy lips.

"You must be looking for someone to fuck. I can fuck you so good, you wouldn't never think about dick again," she told me.

"No, I'm okay," I hesitantly replied. "I'm just looking for my friend."

"Well, if you don't find your friend, baby girl, I'll take you home and pound that pussy right. Ya hear?"

She put the wooden stick back in her mouth and eyed me up and down before moving out of the way to let me pass. I had only been in the club thirty minutes and had encountered more craziness than I had ever experienced in my whole life. The Vision clearly lived up to its reputation and so much more in so many ways. I had always wondered what it would be like to party there, but I never expected it to be so wild.

As I made my way back out into the club, I noticed a section covered by heavy drapes. From the way it looked, it seemed that only certain people were allowed in, so I figured it must be the VIP room. As I made my way over to peep through, a very tall person pulled the curtain aside. I wasn't sure if the individual was a man or a woman, but given all the unusual sights I had witnessed since entering the club, I was not surprised by its presence.

"We've been waiting for you, Miss Simone!" He/she grinned.

"How do you know my name?" I asked incredulously.

"Come on in. Carmen is over there, boo," he/she replied, dismissing my inquiry. I looked to where he/she was pointing, but I didn't see my friend. All I saw was a room jam-packed with glamorous people.

"Get on in there, girl! They're waiting for you!" he/she said with a snap in the air before stepping aside for me to enter.

"And tell 'em Miss Diva Divine sent you!" she called from behind.

A six-foot-four drag queen, Miss Diva Divine wore killer stilettos and a hot-pink satin pantsuit with a black-and-pink-striped waist pouch to match. She was really working that VIP door, if the bulge of tips in her small bag was any indication.

Trying hard not to stare, I couldn't help but notice that the smoke-filled room was overrun with rappers, managers, agents, and all sorts of celebrities, hobnobbing and socializing. Hiding my awe, I meandered around in the direction Miss Divine had pointed me, scanning the room until I finally spotted my friend sitting in a corner booth. No stranger to Carmen's freakish ways, I was still a little taken aback when I saw her lips tightly locked with those of a very beautiful and sophisticated-looking woman. They were completely engrossed in each other's mouths, seemingly oblivious to the very fine-looking dark-skinned Italian man who was seated across from them. Although I could barely take my eyes off Carmen and her chick, I could not help but notice that he appeared to be in his early fifties, worldly, and extremely wealthy.

As I watched my friend kiss another woman, something inside of me began to burn and I started feeling sensations I had never felt before. Ignoring the tingle between my legs, I calmly walked over to the booth where they were sitting and patiently waited for them to come up for air. After about a minute's time, Carmen reluctantly pulled away, wiping the corners of her mouth before she looked up.

"Simone!" she exclaimed, excited to see me and jumping up to give me a big hug. "You look faaaabulous! You turned out to be a sexy little momma after all!" she continued as I laughed heartily, hugging her back.

Turning to her buddies on the couch, she said, "Let me introduce you to my associates." She smiled, pointing to a very leggy gorgeous dark-haired woman with the bluest eyes I had ever seen. "This is Vicca. She's a big-time model from Germany, and since she's only in town for one more night, I figured we could end this night with a bang—give her some memories to take back overseas with her." Carmen laughed. Vicca seductively smiled at me while swinging her lovely crossed legs beneath the table.

"And this," Carmen continued, "is George Luca Santini. He's a high-fashion photographer from SoHo. He's photographed all the big ones—you know, Beverly, Iman, Christie—you know, the superstars."

"Hi." I smiled, reaching over to shake their hands.

Without hesitation, Vicca came straight out and, with a heavy German accent, inquired, "Do you do coke? Because I would love for you to lick some off my nipples."

"No," I nervously replied.

Carmen sat back down upon the plush sofa and motioned for me to sit beside her. As if she'd never been interrupted, Carmen resumed making out with her German friend while George remained quiet and engrossed, openly lusting after me and checking out my supple young body.

A perfect erotic vision sitting there in her strapless black dress, Vicca seductively sipped a glass of red wine. Her expression said that she was enjoying the attention she was getting from Carmen, who had begun to gently place deep red passion marks up and down her pale neck as her hands were busy between Vicca's legs. Although I knew Carmen was the epitome of the Latin hottie, I still never expected to observe her in such an explicit display of sexual exchange. After all, she was my girl and we had shared a room. You think I would have known about her bisexuality. Surprisingly, though, it didn't turn me off. In fact, it aroused me in a way I had never been aroused before. As I quietly watched the action taking place in front of me, I became increasingly hot. Carmen slowly slid her hand out from between Vicca's legs and stuck her finger into George's mouth. He sucked on it hard and I inconspicuously noticed his dick swelling beneath the expensive suit he wore. Now that George was part of the scene, I shifted in my seat and attempted to clear my throat. There were at least fifty other people in the lounge, yet I seemed to be the only one watching their show; everyone else seemed to be completely oblivious to what was going on on our sofa. Much to my own surprise, part of me wanted to lay Vicca out on the table right then and there and lick her forbidden fruit while George fucked her with his stiff cock from behind and Carmen watched.

"Um," I began, clearing my throat again. "So what's been up?" I asked in an attempt to cover up my awkwardness.

Carmen winked playfully at me. "You know. Same ol' shit. In a minute we're gonna go to George's studio. He wants to take some pictures of me. Is that cool?"

"Yeah, sure." I shrugged, gathering myself and preparing to exit. It had already been a wild night for me. From the moment I had entered the Vision, the things I had experienced beyond its massive front doors were all new to me. From the scene in the bathroom to watching my friend get busy with another woman, I had clearly entered the twilight zone. All I needed was for Rod Serling to buy me a drink.

As we left the VIP section, heading through the club and out onto the street, my heart beat with excitement and anxiety. If the three of them were getting it on in the VIP lounge in front of perfect strangers, I could only imagine what was about to go down in private.

The limo ride to George's studio was like a continuation of the scene in the lounge. Carmen and I sat next to each other as we watched Vicca and George engage in some pretty heavy petting. I became confused as I watched Carmen and Vicca, Vicca and George, and George and Carmen all engage sexually with one another. Who really wanted who? I had been thrust into the middle of an erotic free-for-all.

As Vicca stroked George's crotch through his designer slacks, he intently fondled her perky breasts, gently stroking her nipples until they became so hard they resembled little mountains of fuchsia-colored steel. I loved watching their performance and I relished the moment and the scene as it played out before me. And while Carmen was definitely more advanced than I was, my own sexual curiosity began to grow, making me want to experience the power it could have over others.

While he continued to fondle Vicca, I looked deep into George's dark eyes and could see that he had some of the power I craved. He had to, I reasoned, in order to be able to manipulate Vicca in such a way that brought the freak out of her in front of a complete stranger. When Vicca finally caught my eye, she opened her legs wide enough to give me a whiff and a clear view of her pussy glistening with moisture, which only increased my desire to taste what she had to offer.

When the limo stopped, we got out and stood in front of what looked like some kind of showroom gallery. George unlocked the iron gate and then an inner door, holding it open for us to enter. I was amazed at the atmosphere beyond the threshold. While from the outside it didn't look like much, on the inside it was totally grand. One look around and anyone could see that George had money. The look on Carmen's face said she saw it, too, and wanted as much of it as she could get.

As if she had been there many times before, Vicca kicked off her heels and made herself comfortable on an exquisite deep blue suede and sandalwood couch. George handed Vicca a crystal flute filled to the brim with champagne from his well-stocked bar.

"Carmen, Simone, would you like a drink?"

"You have Hennessey?" Carmen asked.

"Um, I'm not really a drinker," I replied, very naive to what was about to go down inside these four walls. "Do you have Pepsi?"

"No Pepsi, but plenty of *coke!*" George laughed, as did everyone else in the room.

He poured some creamy dark-colored liquid into a short crystal glass. "How about some Kahlúa?" he offered.

"OK, I guess." I softly smiled.

Slowly walking around the room, I gazed at the bevy of erotic photographs hanging on the salmon-colored textured walls. Carmen was right. George had photographed everybody who was anybody, and I recognized most of the gorgeous women from the covers of *Vogue* and other high-fashion magazines.

With the ease of a snake, Carmen slithered over and sat on the couch with Vicca before sliding the bottom of Vicca's dress up around her hips. She then slowly glided the fabric up over her head, throwing it aside and exposing Vicca's well-toned body for all of us to lust after. With the same effortlessness,

Carmen began sucking on Vicca's nipples and rolling her tongue down her lean German stomach, pulling down her g-string with her teeth. Then, turning her around, Carmen bent Vicca over the back of the couch and gently spread her legs apart. She gently massaged Vicca's firm buttocks for a few seconds and then proceeded to finger-pop her as she simultaneously licked her Brazilian waxed pussy. New to all of this, things were happening a little too fast for me and I was frozen beneath a huge portrait of two women masturbating. Breaking the silence of the scene, Vicca began to moan loudly before she roared, *"Eat me, you sexy bitch, eat me! Yes!"*

Alerted by Vicca's cries, George came running from the next room. With a drink in one hand, he whipped out his dick with the other, just in time to witness Vicca's climax.

"I'm not too fond of strangers, but oh, I could get used to you, honey." Vicca grinned before crumpling down at the corner of the couch. She then stroked the side of Carmen's face appreciatively with her freshly manicured fingertips before they both turned their lusty eyes on George and crawled over to his heavy cock, which hung nearly eight inches below his balls. George had a museum dick. The kind you could just stare at and wanted to show to your friends, as if it were an exquisite piece of art. It was thick and long and perfectly tanned, as if it had been strategically placed on an Italian beach at high noon.

Once Carmen and Vicca reached the seasoned artifact, they started sucking and licking on it at the same time like it was a piece of licorice candy. I watched intently, hoping to learn a thing or two as their lips glided up and down his shaft, giving him the blow job of his life.

They had barely lifted their lips from his member when George grabbed his camera off the coffee table and started snapping shots of the two women paying homage to his manhood. Sweat quickly dripped from his forehead onto the camera, and I silently backed up against the wall, eager to watch the scene play out. Oddly enough, George seemed to be more interested in taking photos than getting blown. For him, this seemed to be the photo shoot of a lifetime. After snapping away for what felt like an eternity, he finally told Vicca to lie down and pose spread-eagle before instructing Carmen to tongue-fuck her once again.

"Vicca, make love to the camera, baby. I want to see it in your eyes," he moaned. Vicca made a hungry look for the camera. I have to admit, the shot was making me incredibly hot. Following George's instructions, Carmen ate her like a starved animal that couldn't get enough, until her face was completely smothered with Vicca's pussy juice.

After the camera had stopped flashing, George got down on his knees behind Carmen and began vigorously rubbing her ass. She had taken off all her clothes except for her thong, and her pretty tanned butt was raised up in the air while her face remained buried between Vicca's long, smoothly shaven legs. George slid his nimble fingers beneath the fabric of the thong, stroking her kitty-kat and getting it primed for his throbbing cock. He then rubbed some of her sex juices on his dick, lubing himself up for action. He pulled the thong to the side and spread her lips apart with his thumbs before plunging in deeply. My seat granted me a perfect view of Carmen's pink internal flesh as George strategically worked it with his dick, taking his time and gripping her hips to hold her in place.

"Yeah, baby, take all this cock. . . . That's a good little girl, Carmen," he muttered. Like a fly on the wall, I quietly enjoyed the show, becoming extremely horny and wet from watching the three of them go at it. Since I wasn't brave enough to join in, unable to stand it much longer, I decided to slip away. Because the place was so huge, it took me a minute before I finally found what I believed to be the master bedroom. As I stepped through the entryway, my mind was in a haze, for I could not believe what was going on just feet away. My head was spinning from the Kahlúa, so I laid my burning body down on the king-sized sleigh bed that sat in the middle of the room and reached for a pillow. Feeling the liquor pumping through my veins, I slid the black satin cushion up between my thighs and began masturbating on it. I couldn't believe how wet I was! The sound of flesh smacking flesh and the moans that echoed in the distance excited me beyond belief. Wishing I had been bold enough to join in on the festivities, I let my imagination run wild and envisioned being fucked and pleasured by Carmen, Vicca, and George all at the same time. After about three minutes, a wonderful, warm sensation flowed through the walls of my pussy and I came like never before.

"Oh my God . . ." I moaned as I gripped the bedsheets and bit down on the pillow. I was having the orgasm of my life, and as my body spasmed, I realized that I was drenched in sweat. When I finally exhaled, I passed out with my hand between my legs and my skirt hoisted up around my waist.

two

peep the game

I was awakened by the light of the rising sun, which glared brightly upon my eyelids. I groggily opened them to see that it was morning. Slightly disoriented, confused, and not quite sure that the previous night had indeed been reality, I quickly looked around the spacious room. The black satin pillow that had given me such pleasure just a few hours earlier rested beside me, and beneath my body, still clad in my wrinkled clothing, was the same sleigh bed that I had tossed myself upon the night before.

"That shit was real . . ." I whispered to myself. Beyond the door of the room I could hear the sounds of the others. They were evidently already up and about. I straightened myself up and crept to the bedroom door, peeping out to see what was happening. Carmen and George were in the kitchen standing beside a glass breakfast table. Carmen smiled coyly as George placed a neatly folded stack of crisp hundred-dollar bills into her hand before my friend counted each of them individually upon the tabletop. They then shook hands as if they were closing some sort of deal and she gave him a tiny peck on his right cheek. When she headed down the hall toward the bedroom, I stepped out.

"Hey, girl, let's bounce!" she instructed.

Without a word I followed her lead, and as we made our exit, I gently waved good-bye to George. He winked back at me and called from behind, "Simone, if you ever want to have a good time, name your price!"

Out on the street, I looked around and realized that we were in SoHo, a trendy historic district in New York City, famous for its quaint artistic edge. The narrow streets and limestone buildings glistened beneath the morning sunlight as Carmen and I strolled along the cobblestone sidewalk. It was early and all was calm—at least in this neighborhood. I listened as the birds chirped loudly above our heads, knowing they would soon be drowned out as its residents awoke and the galleries and boutiques opened for business.

"He's an asshole, but he pays well. Real well," Carmen said into the silence. Hearing my friend's words stunned me. I had known that Carmen was a freak, but I had no idea that she was a prostitute. I didn't quite know what to say, but as if she had just hit the Lotto, Carmen was all smiles.

"What?" she laughed, noticing the look on my face. "I *know* you don't think those people are *friends* of mine." She shook her head. "No, baby. That was business.

"Damn, girl, didn't I teach you anything while we were at St. Rose?" she continued, tugging on my arm and leading me in the direction she wanted to go.

"Come on. Let's get some grub. I don't know about you, but I'm starving. And while I'm fillin' my belly, I'm gonna school you on how to hustle anyone you want with what you've got. 'Cause if you wanna survive, you gotta learn the game, baby."

We headed toward the main street to this posh little spot that served brunch all day. The waitress sat us at a cozy booth by the front window and we ordered omelets loaded with veggies and cheese, as well as smoked salmon with cream cheese and bagels.

"We'll start with two hot cups of coffee," Carmen informed the waitress. Once she walked away with our order, dying to know all the details, I zeroed in on my friend and began an interrogation that would have put Sherlock Holmes to shame.

"So where did you meet George? Have you known him long? How much did he pay you? What about Vicca? Did he pay her, too?" I eagerly questioned.

Carmen laughed like a mother does when her small child turns up the curiosity to the highest volume. She then sipped the coffee that was placed in front of her before answering.

"I met him at a party 'bout a month ago. Why?" She shrugged.

"Oh, you know me—always looking for that *in* to get my music and acting career started. Do you think he may know someone who can give me an audition or an interview? Or maybe he can give me some tips on how I can get my foot in the door," I said. I thought Carmen would have been eager to answer all my questions, being that she had brought me there with the intention of schooling me to the game. But instead she looked out of the window at the passing traffic and said nothing. After a few moments, the waitress brought our food and asked if we needed anything else.

"No, we're cool, thanks," I answered, waving her off, eager to continue our conversation. "You know I'm ready to get out on my own. I wanna get my own place." I paused long enough to take a bite of my omelet. "Me and my homegirls have been looking for a place for the three of us to rent together. If I had a job, I could move out and start working on my career. Hey, maybe you could move in with us. What do you think?"

But the response I got was silence.

"Carmen, Carmen!" I snapped my fingers trying to get her attention.

"Huh, what?"

"I *said* . . ." I sarcastically began, but stopped. It was obvious that Carmen hadn't heard a thing I'd said. Something pretty heavy seemed to be on her mind, and knowing her, there was no telling what it was. I was used to my friend zoning out sometimes, though. We'd been friends for a while and I knew and accepted most of her ways. Even when we didn't see each other for a while, when we would get together, it'd be like we hadn't missed a beat. That's why I was so taken aback when I saw the transaction between her and George. As cool as we were, I really had no idea that Carmen got down like that, but I definitely wanted to know more. As afraid as I was to partake, I could not deny the fact that I was ultra curious.

Carmen had lived a life that was crazy—always getting into something and always willing to do anything for a thrill. She lived with her mom and spent most of her money on weed and flyy clothes just to keep a smile on her face. All she seemed to care about was getting paid, and that was all she ever talked about. Well, that and sex. But at that moment, as I watched her staring beyond the glass pane that separated us from the rest of the world, it dawned on me that Carmen must have issues deeper than I imagined.

"Hey, what's up? You barely said two words since we walked in here," I said, putting my interrogation on the back burner for a moment.

"Oh, I'm just thinking and listening to you. I can hear the hype in your voice. It sounds nice," she replied.

I paused, not knowing what to say. Then she gave me her undivided attention once again.

"So listen, baby girl. I'm atell you how to get your hustle on without getting hustled. How to run the game, but not let the game run you," Carmen said, using her fork like a conductor's baton for emphasis. Like a new person, Carmen switched gears quickly, perking right up and eating hungrily as she schooled me on the game of life.

"First rule, always stay in control. That means making your own decisions and not letting someone else make them for you. If you do all the work, you keep all the money. Second rule—and real important—never kiss and tell. A girl who keeps her mouth shut keeps friends. People learn real quick who's a big mouth and who can keep their business to themselves. And you never know when you might need a favor from somebody. And third, you gotta make them burn for more. The reason I pull such a high fee is 'cause I give 'em what they want and then some. I'm their fantasy. Someone they'll dream about and remember."

"So, how'd you become such an expert on all of this? Where'd you learn all of this? Did George teach you or were you just born with it?" I asked. Carmen laughed heartily.

"George?" she bellowed. "Puullleeeze. If anything, I taught *him* a thing or two. That's why he's willing to pay me so much."

"How much did he pay you?" I asked with a raised brow.

"Eh eh eh . . ." she answered, shaking her head. "Business is business and that's confidential. But what I will tell you is that I learned the hard way. I had to teach myself and got a lot of bumps and bruises along the way. But one day I finally got it right. And since you my girl, I'ma do my best to make the process easier for you."

The waitress returned to the table and refilled our cups before speeding away to her other customers.

"All right, what do you mean that you learned the hard way? What happened?" I asked. Despite the fact that she didn't answer my question, I wanted to hear more.

"I'll spare you all the gory details, but I will tell you this: once my mom shipped me off to St. Rose, I was all alone. I had no friends . . . until you came. Guess all the girls were jealous of me or something. But I had no money and was forced to take care of myself. Life inside there wasn't no picnic. But I don't need to tell you that. And until you got there, I had to watch my back from the dykes and the dudes. Now, I like to get my boots knocked as much as

the next chick, but *I* choose who I fuck. Not the other way around. So anyway, my first year in, I spent most of it making enemies and building a rep for
myself so I wouldn't get fucked with, which is the reason I never studied and
couldn't pass my classes. I didn't trust nobody. When I failed my first year and
had to repeat the tenth grade, I was desperate. So something had to give. And at
the rate I was going I was never gonna get outta there. I didn't want to be
locked up with those nuns until I was legal, which is what would have happened if I didn't figure out a way to pass my classes."

"So what did you do?" I questioned, visualizing how it must have been
for her before we met and became a team. Carmen stirred her coffee as she
went into the story of the beginning of her life, as she called it.

"Let's just say that I figured out that everybody has a price and a weakness. And *everybody* can be bought. What I learned to do was find a person's
weakness and capitalize on it by charging them my price to satisfy it. And
I tell you, it works every time."

"It can't be that simple." I rolled my eyes, feeling like she was holding back.

"Well, it's as simple or as hard as you—the vendor—make it."

"And what's that supposed to mean?"

"Damn! Are you really that green, Young?" she huffed. "Look, you're the
vendor. That means you can charge whatever price you want for your shit because you're in control of your merchandise, which means people who want
what you got have to come to you—and only you—for *your* shit, whatever
that *shit* may be."

Finally realizing what she was talking about, I shook my head and pushed
my plate away. I was not about to stroll my ass along the West Side Highway
looking for someone to buy my pussy like some two-dollar whore. I was not
my sister.

Sensing my discomfort with her suggestion, Carmen softened her tone,
"Look, I'm not saying you gotta go put on a vinyl micro mini with no panties and do the ho stroll like some Hunt's Point hooker. All I'm saying is that
you're young, beautiful, and smart. There's a lot of people who will pay to be
around that and you should capitalize on it before you lose it. That is, if you
really wanna make it."

"I wanna make it but not like that."

"Look, there's a lot of ways to use what you got to get what you want
without laying on your back, ya know."

"Well, I didn't hear you say nothin' else."

"What I said was that you're young, beautiful, and smart. That could mean a lot of things. That could mean using your youth or using your beauty. Using your smarts. That's all."

Carmen paused to take the last bite of her bagel. The authoritativeness was back in her voice and she looked me dead in the eye.

"Did I look like I was having fun last night with George and Vicca?"

"Yeah."

"Well, I was. Did I look like I was feeling good?"

"Yeah," I answered, wondering where she was going with this.

"I was. But nothing in life is free, and since they wanted my youth and beauty, they had to pay to play. I made two thousand dollars for a couple of hours of fun and feeling good. Now, do I look like a Hunt's Point hooker?"

My jaw hit the table as the total number of what George had handed Carmen made its way to my ears. Two thousand dollars?! Two grand?! Two zero zero zero? To get fucked and sucked like that? Was she serious?

"Are you serious?" I asked.

"As a heart attack." Carmen smiled.

"All I'm saying is that sometimes you're in the right place at the right time and an opportunity may present itself. If you're smart you'll take advantage of it. That's using your smarts. Once you're in it, if the situation calls for other things, that's when your beauty and youth kick in. It's up to you to decide if you're gonna go there," she further explained. "Catching the coach at St. Rose's getting a serious head job from the school freak was the beginning of me using what I had to get what I wanted."

"Coach Mike?!" I exclaimed. The coach at St. Rose's was just about the only decent adult who worked there—or so I thought. I had no idea what he did behind closed doors. Now I knew.

"That would be the one. Well, sometimes shit just happens, and it's up to you to capitalize on an opportunity. And good old Coach Mike just *happened* to like himself some little hot-ass juvenile delinquent pussy and I just *happened* to be in the gym one quiet afternoon when he was getting slurped off real good by Tanya Smith and I just *happened* to have a camera in my gym bag. So he just *happened* to make sure that I passed all my classes with flying colors!"

"Get outta here!! Why didn't you ever tell me?"

"Remember rule number two? Never kiss and tell. Or in this case, never blackmail somebody and tell another soul. You'll lose your leverage."

I shook my head in disbelief. I had always wondered how Carmen had managed to get straight A's when I was never even sure if she ever went to class. I sure was learning a lot in that diner that day. As I listened to her talk, I was completely mesmerized by the words that fell from her lips, and with my mouth half open in awe, I mentally took down a list of points that I knew might be useful to me in the future. I never knew how diabolical my friend really was, and at that moment, I wanted to be just like her when I grew up.

"See, Simone, Tanya ain't know how to use her power. She ain't have control, the coach did. He was getting his rocks off and she was satisfied with getting nothing. But I knew that my picture snatched his power and made it mine, 'cause he had way more to lose than any student would. Shit, man, he could have lost his job, gotten arrested, ruined his family and his reputation with the church. Oh no, I could smell right away that he was shittin' in his pants, 'cause he knew from the look in my eyes that I wasn't playing and that I wasn't no fool like that stupidass Tanya," Carmen went on theatrically, as if she was reenacting the entire scene in her head. I was so caught up in the picture Carmen was painting that I barely noticed the waitress clearing away the plates of partially eaten food.

"Wow," I finally managed to say. "Just like that you saw an in—a chance to make your life better at St. Rose—and you took it. You went for it, full steam ahead. You took control."

"Exactly! And that's what I mean when I say 'use what you got to get what you want!' " she said.

"Well, that's what I want, Carm, and that's what I'm gonna do—find my *in* so I can take control and make my own future and live the life I want!"

Interrupting our conversation, the waitress came back to the table with the check, shaking us both back into reality.

"Can I get you girls anything else?" she asked.

"No, we're done," Carmen smiled, reaching for the ticket. "I got it, baby girl. After all, only one of us worked last night."

Carmen dropped some cash on the table and the two of us quickly gathered our belongings before rising from the table. With a slightly raised brow, I shook my finger at my friend. "I knew your ass was bold, but I never knew you were built like this!"

"Girl, for the right price, *anything* goes."

"I cannot believe you made two grand last night," I said, shaking my head in awe.

"Girl, that wasn't shit. Hang with me and you'll be blowing two grand in one day on nothing."

"So why didn't you teach me all this when we were at St. Rose's?" I questioned, wondering if I might have been further along in my life if she had.

"You can't go to college without a high school diploma. A student can't learn before they're ready."

"And I'm ready now?"

"Coming to the club was junior high. The way you *acted* at the club was high school. The look in your eye as you watched the scene at George's was your college entrance exam and the fact that you even took the test says that you're ready." She laughed.

Feeling up-beat and rejuvenated, I was totally not ready for the scene I walked in on when I opened the front door to my house.

"Oh my God, what happened?" I exclaimed as I dropped my bag in the middle of the floor and hurried into the living room. Mom was tending to my sister, who was holding a balled-up bloody rag to her face. Blood dripped from Regina's nose and mouth, her left eye was swollen, and she had black and blue bruises on her neck.

"Mom?!" I frantically screamed. "Did he do this to her again?!"

"Yes!" Mom angrily replied before starting in on her elder daughter. "I told you to leave him alone! He's gonna kill you one day! Or is that what you want?!"

Regina gave our mother an incredulous look before talking through a swollen split lip.

"Is that all you can say?" she sobbed. "I told you we had a misunderstanding. All couples fight, but I love him and he really does love me!"

Mom stared at my sister in disbelief, then dropped the rag in her lap.

"You keep thinking that!" Mom snapped in disgust. She then turned her attention toward me and spat, "And don't think you're off the hook, either. If you're grown enough to stay out all night, then you're grown enough to get a job and start paying some bills around here. But I'll deal with you later."

Mom left the room in a huff and stormed down the hall. I watched her go and kept staring after her until the sound of her bedroom door slamming jarred me back to Regina. I went over and sat down on the couch beside my sister. I picked up the rag, dabbing at her face to wipe away the blood.

"I'm sorry, Gina," I softly stated. Regina and I had our differences, but I hated seeing her broken and despondent. I think hearing me call her by the pet name I used when we were kids touched her because she started to cry again. Once the river of tears slowed, she looked me squarely in the face. Through wet sniffs and heavy sighs, she managed to speak in a serious tone.

"Whatever you do, Simone, don't be like me. Learn from me and do better," she whispered.

Words could not express how much I hated seeing my sister in pain and my mother acting so cold. I knew Mom was tired of sounding like a broken record when it came to Regina's boyfriend, Rolondo, and while I knew she cared, I just wished that one time she would offer consolation instead of disdain. I guess I might have acted the same way if I were in her position, though. After all, it was a monthly ritual. It seemed like every couple of weeks, Rolondo would beat Regina to a bloody pulp only to apologize a few days later. Of course she would go right back to him and the same thing would happen all over again a few weeks later. So while I clearly understood my mother's position, I still wished that somehow she could find it within herself to be a shoulder to cry on instead of turning her back on Regina. As I quietly watched my sister, who had fallen asleep from emotional and physical exhaustion, I thought back to when we were girls and remembered how much I had once looked up to her. There was a time when I thought she was so beautiful and smart. I had wanted to be just like her. But those days were long gone and all that was left was a wish that Regina would wake up and realize that she deserved better.

Later that evening, I settled down in my room thumbing through the want ads in the *Daily News*. There wasn't much there, but I circled anything I found remotely interesting. As I marked my third prospect, I heard Mom leave for work. She didn't even say good-bye.

three

sugar and spice

A few days later, things at my house were back to normal. As expected, Regina went back to Rolondo and I had the house to myself after Mom left for work.

After diligently searching the want ads for several days straight, I finally found a job that I felt was perfect for me. The ad said, *Ladies only! Open call for music video dancers! All types wanted. Auditions at the G Spot. Friday night, midnight.*

I immediately got on the phone with my friend Tony, who had connects at every club in town. Tony told me that the G Spot was the first and only hip-hop club in Manhattan. He also informed me that D.J. Red Alert, one of New York's most popular disk jockeys, was looking for some dancers to be part of his show. Knowing the dynamics of the club, Tony warned me that it would be hard to get in but offered to help. He knew the head bouncer but told me that I needed to make sure that I was there before 11:30 P.M.

Anxious and excited, I quickly got on the phone with my girls and told them to be at my house by nine so we could get ready. I needed them there for moral support and constructive criticism. Hoping that Mom would be proud of me for trying to do something with my life, I told her about the opportunity and secretly craved her approval.

"Simone, that's not a real job," Mom snapped. "And do you know how much competition there will be? You have a slim-to-none chance of getting it. Honey, you need something reliable and steady. Like answering phones or being an office assistant. But the first thing you need to do is get your GED."

In a rare moment, Mom put her hand up to my face and caressed my cheek with her thumb.

"My sweet Simone. Such a pretty girl, but you need an education to go along with those good looks. Looks don't last. Education does. What kind of future do you think is waiting for you without a high school diploma?"

Happy to get her attention but disappointed in her words, I looked down at my freshly polished toenails to hide my true feelings. It was obvious that my own mother had no confidence in my talents. She honestly didn't think I could make it.

"School is just not on the path I'm trying to take right now, Mom," I replied. "I'd really like to take an acting class or something like that, but I know it costs money."

"Then start looking for a job that lasts for more than a day or a season. Everyone wants to be a star, Simone. The welfare line is full of pretty girls who want to be stars. You really need to start being practical and think long term," Mom huffed as she headed out the door to work.

When I heard the door close tightly, I retreated back to my room, my bubble temporarily busted by my mom's negative attitude. I was beginning to have second thoughts when the doorbell rang. When I opened the door, my two best friends, Jessie and Ebony, stood firmly on the stoop.

"Hey, bitch. We waited around the corner until we saw your mom leave. When is she gonna fix the name on your mailbox? The *Y* is missing, and when I'm high all these damn houses look the same!" Ebony loudly questioned, in her own way telling me that she already started the party without us.

"Shhh, come in, before the neighbors hear you two and tell my mom I was partying in the house again," I hissed, closing the door before tightly hugging them both. It had only been two weeks since they were over last, but I'd missed them just the same. As we started up the stairs, the doorbell rang again. I turned and went back to answer it as they headed up to my room.

"Hi, kitten!" Carmen smiled, stepping across the threshold. "So you got a gig of your own to go to. I think our little talk at the diner did you well. I'm impressed. If it doesn't work out, of course you know you can always roll with me and make some *real* money."

"Yeah, I know, but 'escorting' is not my thing. That's yours." I smirked.

"Don't knock it till you try it, mama. Actually, I do get to do some acting and modeling every now and then, ya know." Carmen winked at me mischievously, knowing how I had a hard-on to be an actress and star in films.

"You guys remember my old roomy?" I announced as Carmen and I entered my bedroom.

"Yeah, hey, what's up?" Ebony said.

"Hey," Carmen gave them both hugs and found a comfortable spot on my full-sized bed to relax. Without a word of warning, Jessie produced a blunt from her bag and lit up.

"Wait. We gotta burn some incense," I said. "It'll be my neck if my mom smells anything funny in this house."

I reached for the stash of incense that I kept hidden behind my bottom dresser drawer and set them around my room before stuffing the crack beneath my door with a thick white towel. Meanwhile, Jessie took a long drag on the blunt, then passed it to Ebony, who was sitting up against the headboard. After lighting the incense, I grabbed my throw pillows and made a mound to lounge on at the foot of my bed. It wasn't long before the entire room was engulfed in a smoky haze of weed and musk-scented fragrances. Carmen took a hit from the blunt, then passed it to me. Sitting up on my elbow, I took a long pull and almost immediately started coughing. My friends laughed and patted me on the back, thinking they were helping. Once I had calmed down and caught my breath, I felt serene, like I was floating on clouds.

Breaking the silence, Ebony put on her intellectual face and like a seasoned librarian informed us, "I heard if you hold the smoke in long enough you'll cum in your panties."

"Girl, shut up. You're high," I giggled, stating the obvious. Once we had smoked down half the blunt, for some reason the girls started swapping stories about their sexual escapades. It seemed apropos, considering the smoky euphoric dreamlike state that engulfed the atmosphere. After inhaling an inferno of smoke, Jessie tightly closed her eyes as if she were envisioning the scene all over again in her mind.

"OK," she began. "So, one night I got outta bed, hornier than a mutha, dying for some dick. I think I was dreaming about getting some or something and just woke up wanting it. So I call this dude, Troy—me and him sometimes kick it just on some physical shit, so I knew he'd be wit' it. So anyway, I get outta my bed—it was like two A.M.—and decide to head to the Bronx where he lives. His mother is a nurse and she works the night shift so she ain't never home till the morning, which gives us more than enough time to get our groove on. Anyway, I got on the train and of course it was pretty empty, being that it was the middle of the night and all, but I saw this fine-ass dude sitting at the end of the car. It was just me and him in the car. He was one of them light-skinned Al B Sure pretty-boy types. He had a curly jet black hair and I just wanted to run my fingers through that shit, he was so sexy. So, he was rocking with his Walkman, bopping his head to the beat, when he caught me staring him down. He checked me out for a second but went back to his music, ignoring me like. Well, you know I wasn't having that, 'cause ain't no brotha ever blown me off like that. So I strutted over to where he was sitting and slowly walked passed him and winked. Then I signaled for him to follow me down to the end of the car where the doors are, ya know. Of course, he looked at me like I was crazy, but after I stuck my finger in my mouth he jumped up and fell in line. So there we were—standing between the cars, just staring at each other. When I stuck my tongue out and licked it across my lips, he grabbed me in a lip lock and we started at it." Ebony and I looked at Jessie in amazement, wondering how she and the guy stayed steady in between a moving train. "And let me tell you. It was on. I was wearing a mini skirt with no panties for easy access for Troy, but this nigga pumped his iron up in me and I rode him like a stallion before I could even get my horny ass to the Bronx!" she cackled.

"Yeah, yeah, yeah," Ebony chimed in with a chuckle. "But I can top that one. One night," she began, pausing to take another pull, then exhaling ringlets of smoke through her mouth, showing off like she was Rizzo from *Grease* or something. "An old girlfriend of mine was mad at her parents for grounding her. So she calls me up and says, 'Let's take a ride. I'm outside your house.' She's like, 'I took my father's car.' It was like one in the morning and, of course, she had plenty of weed, so we lit up lovely before we even got to the main road. Anyway, after about an hour of smoking and listening to her complain about her folks, you know, we got hungry. And I don't know about ya'all, but when I'm high and hungry, I get horny—I call it the three-H syndrome."

We all laughed, nodding our heads in agreement at what we all understood only too well.

"So we go to this twenty-four-hour Micky D's to satisfy our munchies. And when we roll up to the window to place our order, this deep, sexy, Barry White voice comes over the intercom—'Can I take your order?'" she mimicked. "I was like, 'Hell yeah. Um, we'd like two cheeseburger Happy Meals and your dick!'"

We all started laughing out of control, trying to breathe and gasping for air through our hazy tears. "Then I added, 'Puleeeze?'" Ebony continued. "It probably wasn't even that funny now that I think about it, but you had to be there . . . anyway, we pulled up to the next window and we're hoping that he looked as hot as he sounded. So when he steps up to the window, me and my girl are thinking we hit the jackpot. He was definitely a cutie. So now I'm like, 'Wow you sure are fine, baby. You all alone in there tonight?' We could tell he was nervous but he was wit' it so he answered, 'Yeah, I'm alone! Would you like some ketchup with those fries?' and my girl goes, 'Only if we can lick it off your dick!' Then we bust out laughing hysterically. But I'm serious, 'cause I'm so fucked up—and I ask him if me and my homegirl could come inside and serve him for a change. After that, we parked around the back and ran inside, damn near stripping our clothes off in the parking lot. I guess he shut down the drive-through window 'cause we had barely got inside before he started touching on me, rubbing my boobs and shit. Then we followed him to the back of the restaurant into the manager's office and he took off his apron and whipped the monster out. We put ketchup on his dick and mustard on his balls—my girl squirted and I sucked. We had the wildest threesome. It smelled like French fries, cum, and warm after-sex when we were done. You had to be there. . . ."

Laughing, shaking our heads, and flying high as kites, we each looked at Ebony like she was crazy before finishing off the spliff. Carmen held the smoke in, trying to get as much out of it as she could before she took center stage.

"You're both amateurs," she announced, rising from her spot as if she were about to put on a live performance. "If you truly wanna be a freak, be a real one!" Carmen snapped, leaning in toward us, holding our attention with an escapade of her own.

"Picture it . . ." she began, raising her hands to paint the canvas vividly. "First day of classes at St. Rose. End of third period. Lunchtime. And I didn't eat their nasty-ass food, so I head back to my room to take a little private break of my own. But in order to get to my room I gotta pass the boy's dormitory. When I look up there's these three guys standing by an open window. Of course, they started whistling and hooting and shit 'cause most of the chicks there are straight-up dykes and I'm one of the few pretty ones there. Well, I hadn't had none in awhile 'cause it was hard to get your shit off with all their crazy-ass rules and regulations and shit, but this day it seemed like nobody was around, so I decided to take advantage of the moment, and since all three of 'em were cute and I was horny and feeling really nasty, I hollered up, 'You fellas wanna have some fun?' Seconds later they were downstairs holding open the back door, gesturing for me to hurry in before anyone saw. They snuck me inside and I followed them up to their room. I walked in, closed the door, and locked it, 'cause I wasn't trying to get caught up in there. Anyway, they were all even cuter up close—two black guys and one sexy dark Latino cat—so I decided to really have some fun wit' it. I sashayed my overheated body in between the beds and slowly started to undress, doing a little striptease. By this time they had all stripped down to their boxers and sat there watching me with tents over their crotches. Anxious and moist between my legs, I was ready, so I took my bra off and threw it in the face of the Latino boy. Then I reached up under my skirt and pulled down my panties and threw them at the other two. One of them snatched them out of midair and started sniffing them. He had this intense look on his face. The other two hooted and hollered, egging me on. Their eyes were transfixed on my boobs and they were salivating, waiting for me to drop my skirt. I did, and then, butt-ass naked, I walked over to them and started checking out their packages. 'Not bad,' I said to the first as I felt up his crotch. Then I moved over to the next one and was like, 'Umm . . . you're nice and meaty.' But when I felt up the third one, I was like damn! That kid had the biggest balls I had ever seen!" We all laughed, envisioning the scene as she painted it before our very eyes. Motioning the same way she must have done that day in the boys' room, Carmen seductively swayed her body and continued.

"Then I slowly licked my lips and said, 'I'm going to love fucking you boys, one by one and all at the same time!' When they pulled their boxers down, their dicks were hard as torpedoes, pointing straight up toward the ceiling, throbbing like they were calling my name, which I don't even think they knew. But they waited for me to make the first move. So I went over and sat on the lap of one of them. Then I spread my legs open for the other two to get a full view. I put my hand down between my legs and spread my kitty-kat open, showing them my pretty clit. I was getting hotter by the second. The boy I was sitting on was rubbing his hands all over my boobs and squeezing my nipples. I told them they had to get me ready so I would last for all of them. So one of the black guys got up from the other bed and knelt down between my legs and started eating my pussy like a pro. I leaned back against the one I was sitting on, grinding up against his dick. I motioned for the other one to come over and stand beside me. He put one knee up on the bed, behind my back. I turned my head and his cock was ready and aimed at my lips. I started sucking on him and he instantly started pumping in and out of my mouth. The other fine brotha was licking my kitten real good and the one I was sitting on started squeezing my boobs harder. I could feel the head of his penis sliding up and down the small of my back in his own pre-cum juice. I was rubbing the balls of the one ramming his joystick in and out of my mouth. All four of us were in some sort of sex-crazed frenzy. Then, when I couldn't take it anymore, I let them fill up every hole in my body they could get in. We musta went at it for like an hour—cumming and fucking over and over again until we were all exhausted. When they finally all passed out, I got up and got dressed, leaving the three of them lying naked across the beds. Let me tell you, I had the biggest orgasm of my life!" Carmen started laughing as she remembered. We all chimed in, wondering what it must have felt like to have three dicks in us at once.

As each of my friends put periods at the end of their final sentences, I was really shocked to hear the girls' stories and a little embarrassed that I was so inexperienced. Unlike them, I had no juicy story to tell, only fantasies in my head. When everyone had calmed down from laughing, they all turned to me to see what I was going to hit them with. But I just sat there with a dumb look on my face and nervously smirked. "I don't kiss and tell! Isn't that rule number two?"

"Yeah, bitch. But you can tell *us*!" Carmen snapped.

"Maybe you don't kiss and tell because you don't have shit *to* tell!" Jessie howled.

"It's that knocked-up phobia she has," Ebony added.

"You ain't gonna get pregnant! Take your ass down to the clinic and get on the pill. Stop being scared to get pregnant. It's ruining all your fun!" Carmen snapped.

"And if you do get pregnant, you can take your ass to the clinic for that, too!" Jessie threw in.

"Yeah, 'cuz lawd knows they know Jess on a first-name basis down at Planned Parenthood!" Ebony joked as Jessie flipped her the bird. We were all talking at the same time, high as kites, laughing at me and one another. While I adamantly denied my inexperience, my girls knew I was still a virgin of sorts and made friendly fun of me about it, promising to help me get rid of that problem sooner rather than later. They were right, though. I was terrified of either hooking up with some dude like the cats my sister got dominated by or getting pregnant, and that fear was enough to make me keep my legs tighter than I wanted to. Don't get me wrong. I liked to feel good, but I couldn't help remembering what had happened to my sister when she told my mom that she thought she was pregnant. Mom kicked her ass so bad that I didn't recognize her for a week. It was the first and last time I'd ever seen my mother lose her entire mind. Turned out Regina wasn't even knocked up. But the beat-down I witnessed was enough to have me shook for years to come. On the other hand, as I silently observed my sister's life, it seemed that after a guy "got some," in his mind you were now his personal property, and I wasn't with that at all.

four

the hot spot

Me and my girls rounded the corner onto Broadway to see one of the longest lines I had ever seen in my life. The block was jam-packed with people trying to get into the hottest hip-hop spot in the city. Scantily clad chicks, b-boys, b-girls, and model types all jockeyed for position as they eagerly waited to be chosen to enter the popular club. Through the mounds of people, I could barely see anything other than a sea of heads as I managed to make my way toward the front doors. While my "excuse me's" were met with plenty of rolling eyes and teeth sucking, my girls and I pushed our way to the front of the crowd in desperate search of Tony. After ten minutes, I finally spotted my homeboy up by the door and yelled out to him. He stood talking with a group of guys and smiled when he saw me before motioning for us to come over. When we finally reached him, we hugged and he called his boy over to the ropes.

"Yo Regg, can you slide me and my crew in?" he asked a short, well-toned man with a young-looking face. Although we had never met, I figured the dude was Tony's friend Reggie Bell, head of security at the G Spot and one of the biggest party promoters in New York. I made a mental note that Reg was definitely someone I wanted on my team.

"I don't know, man." Reggie looked around and shrugged. "It's kinda crowded tonight. How many you got with you?"

"Three of my boys and, oh yeah, sexy little Simone here and her friends." Tony motioned for us to step forward. I pushed my way up on the red-carpeted step so Reggie could get a look at me, hoping he'd see something he liked. Just as I'd hoped, Reggie's face melted, obviously spellbound by my innocent good-looks. He opened the ropes for us without another word and even hooked us up with drink tickets. As I walked by, Reggie grabbed my hand and smiled. I paused for a moment as our eyes met and had an entire conversation of their own. When he released his grasp, he tilted his head to the side and with a gleam in his eye warned, "Don't get too bombarded by all the rappers and players in there to have time to speak to me before you leave."

Not knowing what to say, I simply nodded my head as if to say "OK." He then gently kissed my hand, told me to have a good time, and went back to his post at the door. With Reggie's words echoing through my psyche, I entered the club gushing with confidence, gassed at the fact that the guy who had the power to deny or grant entry into the hottest club in New York was smitten with me.

As my girls and I walked through the club, we were now surrounded by lots of fine, tall, African-American b-boys. Brushing elbows and squeezing through the throngs of talented and sexy rockers started an incredible feeling of arousal and self-awareness within me. The sensation fluttered low inside my belly, but then somehow managed to swell and seep down between my legs. It tingled, feeling like pins and needles at the warm spot in the center of my panties. The admiring looks I received from both men and women made me feel desirable, as it seemed like everyone in the place was on the prowl and I was the female in heat they'd all be willing to fight over.

Rob Base and D.J. E-Z Rock's "It Takes Two" pounded in my chest as I stood beneath a huge speaker watching the crowd as the bass drove the smoke-filled club into a complete frenzy. As the high-pitched "woo yeah" met my eardrums, I looked up at the deejay booth and could see the infamous Kool D.J. Red Alert mixing and scratching on two turntables. He was incredible and I was honored to be in his presence. I wanted to shake his hand and let him know that I wouldn't disappoint him if he chose me to be one of his dancers.

Captivated by the strong beat in the song, I could feel the effect of the drum as I instinctively hit the dance floor to show off my style of the latest dances, the smurf and the wop. Little did I realize that alongside me was Crazy Legs from the Rock Steady Crew, break-dancing and doing his fly thing. In awe of his skills, a crowd formed a circle, giving him additional room for his already blazing fire.

The club was packed to capacity and every girl was flyyer than the one before as they pranced around with their tight bodies and pretty faces. But even though I seemed to blend in with the crowd, I knew I was different. I knew that I had more to offer than my competition, and I was determined to make others know it, too. I also knew that what I may have lacked in experience, I more than made up for in determination, which was what I believed was far more than what my peers could say. So in an effort to be seen, I threw my hands up into the air and shook myself wildly. Sweat began to cover my body as I swung my bouncy mane back and forth trying to get someone to notice my uniqueness. For some strange reason, I felt extra confident and sexy, not caring that I was dancing alone and not even realizing that my girls had headed off in different directions within the club. But while I had asked them to be there, I was actually glad they had disappeared, as it would give me an opportunity to step out of their shadows. I knew that if I played my cards right, I could be a force to be reckoned with in my own right.

Because of the auditions taking place that night, there were many famous dance and hip-hop crews in the club. The most popular ones were the Rock Steady Crew, the IOU Dancers, Grandmaster Flash's crew, Africa Bambatta's crew, and Red Alert's team. It was hip-hop heaven and I had always admired all of them from the street. The only thing I wanted to do in life more than act was dance, and that night, I knew I was among the best.

As the lights flashed to the beat of the music, I instinctively gyrated and dipped my hips in synch. I had never been in the presence of so many talented dancers before, and was a little intimidated being in such a melting pot of natural-born stars. Although my dancing skills were pretty good, I secretly wondered if I could truly compete. However, the music definitely had me feeling myself, and when the moment was right, I decided to go for it, flipping a spin and jumping into the circle with Crazy Legs himself. He cracked a smile at me and then busted out with his own up-rock move that blew my mind, panicking me for a second because I knew I was in no way half as good as he was. Not trying to play myself by getting spanked on the dance floor by Crazy Legs, I tried to walk away but stopped when he reached out and grabbed my arm.

"Hey, where you going, sexy? I know you ain't giving up that easy!" he said. Flattered that he was willing to give me his attention, I remained fixated, eager to learn whatever he was willing to teach.

"Come here and let me show you how we do this." He smiled, then showed me some moves. It wasn't long before I was all over the floor, making new friends and dancing with the best. On a natural high, I felt as though I had finally found my place.

Without warning, the lights dimmed and the emcee announced the start of the auditions. The crowd pushed back a little and the upper dance floor was cleared. A spotlight beamed down and the crowd started screaming. In the center of the spotlight, demanding our attention, was D.J. Red Alert. He waved to the crowd and threw up the peace sign as he sat authoritatively in a large, red velvet up-back chair that resembled a throne. Then, with a snap of his fingers, the parade of girls began. I decided to stand back and watch for a while to see what the competition was like. But after about a half hour of watching, I became bored and disappointed. It seemed like all the chicks were doing more jocking than dancing, walking around him smiling and tossing booty. A few of them even gave him lap dances. With all the simulated sex acts going on, I didn't think I had a chance in hell of actually getting my chance to show him what I was working with. Disillusioned, I headed back out into the club to look for my friends. After searching for what felt like an eternity, I figured the night was a waste and headed toward the doors of the club. I didn't find my girls, but knew they'd have to pass by me to leave. When I approached the entrance, I saw Reggie and smiled, hoping that some part of the night could still be salvaged.

"Excuse me," I began. "Do you think I can hang out here for a second to get some air? It's like a sauna in there."

He turned around, ready to say no, until he saw who had made the request. A big grin then spread across his handsome face.

"Sure, sexy. As long as you stay close." He smiled.

"No problem," I replied in the most pleasant voice I could muster.

The sidewalk on the other side of the rope was just as insane as it was inside the club, and although it was late, I couldn't believe people were still trying to get in. Being on the inside of the ropes felt good, but the reality was that I hadn't gotten a chance to dance for Red Alert. Still, as I stood near Reggie, I felt cool and powerful and although I had not accomplished my goal, I enjoyed sharing Reggie's clout. With one point of his finger or a nod of his head, a hopeful wannabe was either in or not. And as I watched him do his thing, I wished I had a smooth job like that.

After denying three nerdy-looking cats entrance, Reggie turned to me and questioned, "So, how come I never seen you here before?"

"I came out for the auditions, but it's so crazy in there, I never even got my chance," I replied.

"Well, if it's up to me, you'll be partying here from now on." He smiled.

A cracked voice interrupted our conversation, causing my head of luscious black curls to swing around in search of its source.

"Well, it's actually up to *me*, but he's right. A pretty young lady like you is welcome in my club anytime," stated a very distinguished-looking older white man. As the man got closer, Reggie and the rest of security suddenly became more alert and stiff spined.

"Excuse me, Mr. Walton. You're so right," a suddenly uncomfortable Reggie replied after clearing his throat. He then politely excused himself and walked over to where the other security guy was checking ID, leaving me and the man standing together.

"Jimmy Walton," he introduced himself with a firm handshake. "I own this place," he announced with a nod of his head. A short, stumpy gentleman with thick dark hair and lots of teeth, Jimmy Walton looked like a well-seasoned businessman who had experimented with many business ventures before finding one as lucrative as the G Spot.

"Oh." I smiled, now understanding why Reggie had removed himself so quickly.

"Your beauty is diverting the attention of my staff, and while I can understand why, their job is to watch the door and monitor who's going in and out of my club. But instead, I catch my head guy watching you, and that's not what I'm paying him to do," Jimmy chuckled.

"Oh, please don't blame him, Mr. Walton. It was really my fault for distracting him," I explained, not wanting to get Reggie into any trouble.

"I pay him very well not to be distracted by anyone or any*thing* . . . but again, I guess I can understand," Jimmy continued with a small laugh. "And please, call me Jimmy."

"Simone Young," I replied, my hand still in his grasp. "And I'm sorry if I look a little shocked, but I never thought the owner of a place like this would look like you."

"And what do you mean by that?" he asked, knowing he probably heard that all the time. Without beating around the bush, I was clear and to the point,

"Well, you're white, and I never seen a white man run a black club before. But that's some cool shit!" I laughed, as my eyes twinkled like the stars in that old nursery rhyme. Quickly infected, Jimmy laughed, too.

"You're young and you're cute. A little rough around the edges, but you have the balls to say what you feel and I like that, which means I like you. You got cojones, kid," he replied.

As I chatted with Jimmy, my body language went from playing it cool to a mode of seduction, which didn't go unnoticed. But refusing to go there, Jimmy shook his head at me and smiled.

"I know what you're trying to do," he began. "And while you are definitely sexy, you're way too young for me. I been out here a long time and it doesn't take a Ph.D. to know you're dangerous."

"And how do you know that?" I coyly asked.

"Trust me, I know these things. Everything about you screams 'fresh meat.' And everything about you says you're barely legal, including your name, *Miss Young*. So since you've already been inside my club, I'm glad I don't see you with a drink in your hand." I could not help letting a laugh out myself. The old man was funny and had a certain charm about him in a quirky Hugh Hefner kind of way.

"Everything about you also says that you want something. So without trying to fuck me, why don't you tell me what I can do for you," Jimmy said.

Feeling a little silly and embarrassed that my intentions were so easily read, I bowed my head. I wanted so much to be like my girls, to have a story to tell the next time we puffed a little weed, that I was trying too hard to be sexy and it really wasn't working.

"Sorry." I blushed, my cheeks turning the color of sweet cherries. "I'm out here in front of your club making a fool of myself. Excuse me. I think I'm gonna go back inside, if that's OK with you." I winked. Jimmy took my hand and led me back into the sweltering heat, passing Reggie on the way.

"Miss Young, it was a pleasure talking to you," Jimmy chuckled, turning to his top security man. "Reggie, take care of her anytime she comes in, but don't let her drink and don't let her distract you from doing your job."

"Thank you," I shyly replied, still a bit embarrassed.

"Maybe one day you'll share with me what it is you want for yourself. But until next time, good night, Miss Young. And watch out for the predators.

Fresh meat is their favorite delicacy." Jimmy smirked before leaving us at the entryway.

Without hesitation, Reggie approached me with a large grin plastered on his face.

"You made a big impression on my boss. And he doesn't like too many people," he stated as he began handing out flyers to people as they left. Feeling useless, I began helping, sliding the cardboard announcements into the hands of everyone who passed me by, as if I worked there.

As people began to pile out of the club, I glanced down at my watch and noticed that it was nearly four A.M. I also realized that I had not seen my girls the entire evening. As the club closed down and the last partygoers filed out, I finally saw my friends heading toward the exit, with Carmen leading the way.

"Damn, girl. We been looking all over for you!" she bellowed as she grabbed my arm for balance. Keeping my focus on my friends, I quickly said good-bye to Reggie before joining them and heading down the concrete toward the subway station. Clearly tipsy, it was evident that my girls had spent most of the night hanging out at the bar. By the time the train left the station, they were all nodding off in a drunken stupor. I, on the other hand, hadn't had one drink and was still full of energy, my mind replaying the events of the evening. When I arrived home, the sun was rising behind me and I anxiously jumped into a hot shower to rid myself of the thick coat of perspiration that covered my body. As the water forcefully hit the back of my neck, I closed my eyes and flashed back to the faces I had seen and the music I had heard. I was still disappointed that I hadn't gotten chosen to be one of Red Alert's dancers, but something told me that I had gotten so much more.

Maybe one day you'll share with me what it is you want for yourself, Jimmy's voice echoed in my mind.

"I sure will," I said aloud, enjoying the gentle pulse of the water. When I finally laid my head down upon the softness of my pillow, the sun's rays were shining brilliantly over the horizon full blast. I felt really good about what was to come, and before I drifted off to sleep, I strategically planned my next visit to the G Spot. After all, I now had an *in.*

five

the price is right

Two weeks had flown by since I had made my "debut" at the G Spot nightclub, and after diligently pounding the pavement in search of a job, I was still empty-handed. While I wanted to go back to the club, the stress of finding a job began to consume my every waking moment, making me unable to focus on much of anything else. Mom had turned up the pressure extra hard, and even told me that she would put me out if I didn't start contributing to the household bills. To make matters worse, Jessie and Ebony had found the perfect apartment and were threatening to give my spot to one of their other homegirls if I could not come up with my part of the deposit. Life seemed to be moving forward for everyone but me, and I was at my wit's end as to what to do. My mind raced as I realized that I didn't have any more time to waste if I was going to break out on my own and start living the life I not only wanted but *needed* to live. Hearing my mom's disapproving voice was starting to really get to me, and I knew that if I lost my spot in the apartment with Jessie and Ebony, there would be no telling how long it would be before I would get out from under my mother's roof. I knew that once I became a success, Mom would forgive all and be happy for me, but at that moment, my most urgent matter were my finances, and Carmen was the only person I knew who could make money appear like magic. Broke and desperate, with no pending opportunities, I reached out to my friend, who I hadn't spoken to since I had waved good-bye to her that day at the G Spot.

"Speak," Carmen answered on the first ring.

"Hey girl, it's me," I began. "What's been up?"

"Hey, baby girl. I'm cool. You ready to party again?"

"Yeah, if there's money involved. I need cash bad."

Carmen paused for a second.

"Oh," she chuckled. "So you ready to use what you got to get what you want?"

"I guess. I'm just thinking about getting paid right now."

"OK. Well, I'll see what I can hook up. Start looking for something sexy to wear and call me back at eight."

"OK, bye," I replied, hanging up the phone and heading straight to my closet. I moved the hangers of clothes aside in search of something to wear when I stopped for a moment and stepped back. It suddenly dawned on me that I was turning to Carmen to get money, and while I was definitely fascinated by the game, I knew that I didn't want to get in too deeply. So as I pulled out a tight, strappy, silver top and a black-and-silver miniskirt that didn't leave much to the imagination, I told myself, "One time ain't gonna hurt."

As planned, I spoke to Carmen at eight o'clock. She gave me the address to her friend George's studio in SoHo and told me that he would be expecting me around nine. I was feeling good when I arrived in front of his place but hoped that I didn't look as nervous as I felt. While I had tried to look older, I wondered if all I had accomplished was to look young and fast.

As I approached the door, I hesitated for a second before ringing the bell. It was dark and looked as though no one was there, but when I was about to ring it, I noticed that the door was slightly ajar, so I slowly walked in and pushed the door closed behind me. The living area was dark and all I could see was a red light coming from under a door. Apprehensive, I stood still before I heard the sound of the front door being locked behind me. Startling me, a voice came out of the darkness.

"Are you ready to get nasty?" the sultry voice asked. I nearly jumped out of my skin before I realized it was Carmen.

"Carmen . . . ooh, girl, you crazy! You tryin' to get me horny or scared out of my mind?" I exclaimed.

"Don't be afraid," my friend whispered in my ear, her warm minty breath laced with the scent of cognac. "You've come this far. Now you're halfway to crossing over to the other side. Just relax and enjoy yourself. It's all about feeling incredible pleasure. Reaching your sexual high. I promise it won't hurt," she giggled, almost sinisterly. I nervously smiled as my eyes finally adjusted to the darkness.

"Okay, but please be gentle," I said sarcastically.

Carmen began gently removing my clothing, which softly dropped onto the hardwood floor as I stood paralyzed in the center of the room.

"You won't be needing these. Follow me and I will lead the way to complete ecstasy," she said. We walked hand in hand toward the red light and Carmen started to giggle.

"Where are we going? Girl, are you high? This is some freaky shit!" I whispered loudly.

"Relax and close your eyes. Don't you trust me?" Carmen asked as she turned and blindfolded me with a red silk scarf before leading me up a flight of stairs. Butt naked from head to toe, I was simultaneously frightened and intrigued as gentle warm breezes engulfed my body. We climbed higher and higher until we finally pushed open a door where the sensation of the warm spring air assaulted my senses, making me feel sensual yet innocent. My senses told me we were outside, on the roof, as I could hear the traffic passing by below. Being in the open air aroused me beyond words as the breeze made love to me, caressed every crevice of my naked body. Although my temperature was clearly rising, I involuntarily shivered, and with every forward step, I felt as though I was elevating to orgasm. Still blindfolded, I heard soft music playing in the background and I burned with curiosity, desperate to snatch the scarf from my face and take in my surroundings.

Once we had walked a little deeper into the area, Carmen removed the fabric and let me have a look around.

"Well, what do you think?" my friend asked. I was speechless.

"It's so beautiful!" I managed to say. There was a mahogany four-post pedestal king-sized bed made up in ivory-colored satin sheets with deep red rose petals gingerly tossed across its splendid surface. Scarlet-hued chiffon drapes were wrapped around each post, and strategically placed at each base large cream-colored scented candles burned. The backdrop of the New York City skyline added a celestial touch that could only be created by a heavenly being, adding to the surrealism of the entire scene. As I soaked in all the view had to offer, I could not wait to climb aboard the bed and meet the pleasure that awaited me.

Then I noticed the wound-up electrical cords and the propped-up camera equipment.

"Where's George?" I asked, still preoccupied with the atmosphere.

As if on cue, with a camera in hand, George emerged from behind an elaborate Oriental silk screen, scantily clad in black satin boxers; the wild hair that sprouted from his chest reminded me of King Kong.

"Ah, the lovely Ms. Simone. You have a beauty that could stimulate any man to premature ejaculation. There's so much I want to do to you—just name your price!" George said.

Not really knowing how to respond, I stood silent, feeling vulnerable. I was ready for a quick romp in the sack, but I didn't know if I was too comfortable with being photographed. The attention George bestowed upon me, however, made me feel special and bolstered my confidence to a level it had never seen. The fact that he found me pretty and sexy translated into a form of love I had never known. So without saying a word, I walked over to the fantastic mammoth-sized bed and climbed on. Following my lead for a change, Carmen joined me before leaning over and giving me a tender kiss on the lips. Taken aback, as I had never been touched that way by another woman, my body melted and an indescribable surge of electricity throbbed between my legs like never before. I watched as Carmen crawled around like a tigress wearing nothing but a pair of red high-heeled pumps while George snapped away with his camera.

"*Si, buono,*" he moaned, his Italian turning me on even more. "Talk to me with your body, Simone. Smile. Let yourself go. You are safe here. You can trust us. . . ."

I slowly lay back on the pillows and let my body do its own thing, posing in positions that felt natural to me. The contrast of my long wavy black locks spread out against the backdrop of the ivory sheets was electrifying, and George's camera was catching every bit of my splendor. As Carmen eased herself onto the bed behind me, she rested on her side, propped up on her elbow. She smiled and looked hungrily at my body before slowly licking her full red lips in delight.

"Together. I want you to pose together. I want you to explore each other," George instructed. Following his orders, I leaned back against Carmen's stomach, looking into the camera with heated anticipation. For something so new to me, it seemed incredibly right, and I was surprised at the level of comfort I felt. In silence, my friend gazed dreamily down at me and stroked the side of my face. She then slowly dragged her finger down between my ripened breasts, following their shape and contour as she outlined my hardened nipples as if she were tracing them upon a piece of paper. Surprisingly, the presence of the camera seemed to elevate my arousal, as the animal magnetism between Carmen and me emanated from the bed.

"*Si,* Carmen, *la voglia* . . . show me your desire," George uttered as he changed lenses and snapped photos from as many angles as he could. We were clearly better than amateurs and George was prepared to take full advantage of that, capturing all of our lust and sensuality with his camera.

In full view of the lens, Carmen knelt down sensuously behind me, resting her chin on my shoulders and draping her arms down over my erect tits. Instinctively, I reached both of my arms back to embrace her supple body, arching my back and shyly looking directly into the camera.

"Carmen, I want you to spread Simone's lips open with your fingers. Show me her pussy," George coached as he crouched down and zoomed in on Carmen's freshly polished nails holding my throbbing split apart.

"*Buono.* Now slowly move around and taste her candy. Make it *caldo* . . . hot," he begged.

As if I had smoked a dozen joints, I was lost in the euphoric state of the moment. For the first time in my life, I felt truly beautiful, desired, and loved. The soft silky feel of the rose petals and sheets against my bare skin took me to another realm. Just as I had imagined from witnessing her exchange with Vicca, Carmen knew how to lick pussy superbly. She sucked on my clit and softly spat on my anxious flesh to get that extra wetness. Totally prepped and primed, my body was more than ready to complete the sensuous part of the experience and get the freaky part rolling. I wanted to let go and rub my heated pussy all over Carmen's face until I came.

Concentrating on my own pleasure, I couldn't help noticing that George was equally distracted, as he kept rubbing himself in between our repositioning. It was obvious that he was having trouble focusing on the pictures he was taking as he restrained himself from joining in the frame. But his tongue slowly emerged from his mouth as he flicked it back and forth in the air while he snapped dozens of erotic shots. He was focused and excited. As he reloaded the film, he instructed us to move into a sixty-nine position, and as we moaned and licked each other's curly brown bushes, he couldn't contain his arousal any longer. He elevated himself upon a wooden stool and began shooting directly over us, his hardened dick poking the back of my head as I was positioned between Carmen's thighs.

When the fast clicking of the camera ceased, I raised my head up to see what was going on only to see George's colossal dick aimed straight at my open lips, slippery and ready. I impulsively stuck my tongue out and licked away at his pre-cum juice. Not wanting to be left out, Carmen crawled over and shoved my head down on his monumental cock, almost making me gag. She then joined in on the licking from the other side, pumping her head up and down until saliva dripped down from the sides of her mouth. Effortlessly, she peeled herself from George's dick and backed her bountiful ass up onto it so he could ride her doggy style.

Trying to get in where I fit in, I went beneath where their bodies connected and licked his fleshy balls as they vigorously smacked up against Carmen's saturated pussy. His skin felt smooth and tight against my tongue, and the sensation of barreling his dick inside tight wet pussy while getting his balls licked at the same time caused him to groan in ecstasy, making me secretly wonder if the sounds of us fucking could be heard out on the street below.

When I finally came up from my testicular feast, I forcefully stuck my tongue into George's gaping mouth. I pushed my firm young tits up against his face, smothering him in lust. George kept hold of Carmen's round butt as he pounded her, while he stuck his thumb inside her tight little asshole. She moaned loudly, her muscles tightening up and contracting. Then without warning, she came hard all over his dick. Her pussy was so wet and juicy, it splashed profusely upon his tanned flesh and her body uncontrollably jerked as if she was having an epileptic seizure. I watched intently, rubbing my hands across George's hairy chest and pinching his nipples. I could see his cock pulsating uncontrollably, evidence that he was ready to burst. Without warning, Carmen popped off his dick, flipped around, grabbed it, and began stroking it, hard and fast.

I slid down below once again and stuck my tongue out under the base of his fat dick, flicking it back and forth across his balls. The instant George felt my moist tongue, he exploded like a rocket and came all over my face, a shot of cum just missing my eyes. His white cream was thick and sweet like Reddi-Wip and I lapped it up, making a slimy mess upon my own face. With a girly giggle, Carmen licked the remnants of George's cum from my cheeks and nose before he reached for his camera and began snapping once again. Still horny, I watched as George stood before us butt naked, saying all the right things to keep me and Carmen going. Caught up and turned out, I was open, to anything at that point, and with George Luca Santini's words in my head, I was posing like a natural-born professional freak.

I smiled as George continued to snap explicit photos of me and Carmen pleasuring each other until exhaustion took over and ended the hype. As we lay there in a sticky pool of cum, the full moon glistened above our roofless heads and an unobstructed view of the sky blanketed the earth. When we finally caught our breath, the three of us headed downstairs to cool down. George offered us plenty of weed and expensive alcohol to aid the process, but as I tried to make small talk with him, I noticed that Carmen had very little to say.

"Man, this is the first time I actually got high from weed. I guess you *are* supposed to hold it in!" I giggled, my head engulfed in smoke.

After taking a long drag, George laughed, "You are cute and funny. I like you! You picked a good one this time, Carmen."

Seeing little humor in our exchange, Carmen abruptly interrupted, "We gotta go, George. You got the money?"

"Yes, of course. But did I say something wrong?" he asked, noticing the attitude. Carmen said nothing, but replied by rolling her eyes, sucking her teeth, and holding out her hand. Confused, George got up from the table.

"Wait here. I will go and get the money," he said.

Not quite ready to leave and puzzled by her response, I turned to my friend and asked, "What's your problem?"

"My problem? *You're* the one getting too close to the trick, Simone!" Carmen scolded. Baffled, I stared at her.

"Damn, I barely said five words to the man!" I said.

"That's five words too many," she snapped.

"Well, he may be a trick to you, but I was kinda hoping that he'd be a new friend who might be able to help me out," I muttered, adjusting my wrinkled skirt.

Looking me up and down, Carmen barked, "You have a lot to learn. Remember, *I'm* the one who brought you here, not the other way around!"

"I know, but—" I began, only to be interrupted by George's return. He handed Carmen a wad of cash, which she quickly counted. She then gave me a portion of the money before shoving the remaining bills into her designer bag. Without a word, my friend stormed out the door, leaving me standing there alone with George, looking stupid.

"That girl is crazy. She does too many drugs, ya know," he chuckled.

"And you don't?" I sarcastically stated.

"Yeah, but I can afford them!" he laughed heartily.

I swiftly counted the money that Carmen had given me and realized that I had just been paid to partake in the best sexual experience I had ever had in my life. My eyes lit up and I suddenly became hot beneath the collar once again. The crisp feeling of the new bills as they rested in the palm of my hand gave me a sexual surge that I had not expected.

"Eight hundred dollars!" I exclaimed.

"Yeah, and there's more where that came from if you wanna keep on having a good time. Just name your price."

Stunned that I actually had the potential to make sixteen hundred dollars in a mere two hours, I folded the money and grabbed my purse, preparing to leave.

"Do you have to leave right now?" George asked, rising from his seat. "I like your company. Have another drink, hmmm?"

I smiled at him, happy that he seemed to be taking a personal interest in me, but before I could say yes, he slyly winked.

"I'll give you another three hundred if you hang out for a bit."

Obviously he just wanted to see more of my pussy. I'd thought George might actually want to get to know me. A sudden iciness came over me as I realized there was simply no room for emotions in this game. Still, if my body was what he wanted, then my body was what he was going to get—at *my* price and on *my* terms, of course. If she hadn't left pissed, Carmen would have been proud of me.

In an unexpected metamorphosis, I suddenly grew a new layer of skin and smiled.

"Four-fifty."

He thought a second, then replied, "Four-fifty it is. You're a negotiator. I like that."

With the extra money in hand, I hung out with George for a while longer. At his urging, I took some more pictures before enjoying his museum dick a few more times. He fucked me and licked my pussy in his kitchen and in his living room upon the same deep blue suede and sandalwood sofa on which he had screwed Vicca and Carmen weeks before. While I was having a good time with my new acquaintance, I mentally added a new rule of my own to Carmen's list: Never take any man who's connected to a dollar seriously.

As once again the sun rose before I had a chance to close my eyes, I figured it was time for me to bring the night's events to a close. George had gotten his money's worth and then some, and I was over twelve hundred dollars richer than I was when I arrived. Thus, it had been a good night for all of us.

Physically exhausted, I finally headed toward the front door of George's studio. With a slightly raised brow and a gleam in his dark eyes, he bid me a kind farewell and smiled.

"I had a wonderful time, Ms. Simone. I hope to see you again. Just—"

"Name my price," I said, finishing his sentence with his own infamous proposition.

"Here's my card. Call me." He laughed before I crossed the threshold. I tucked the card away without looking at him and waved good-bye, all the while thinking I had finally hit the jackpot.

hip-hop honey

I awoke late the next day in my own bed, groggy and still dazed from the previous night's events. Unable to move, my burning eyes scanned the ceiling watching the fan above my head spin to its own rhythm. Even in my hungover state, I couldn't help thinking back over the events of the previous night— what I did and how it had made me feel. Just thinking about it sent a slight surge of electricity between my legs. I had been risqué and was now dipping way in on the wild side, doing things I never thought I would do. Yet while I had essentially pimped myself for money, I convinced myself that at least it had been my decision. After all, everything I had earned had come home with me. Plus, I'd had the thrill of a lifetime making it. I just hoped that Carmen wasn't still angry. I was happy with my decision and proud of myself for going the extra step with George, securing my position with him directly and cutting out the middleman. After all, I had made a new friend whom I hoped would become a regular source of income for me if I needed it.

When I eventually pulled myself from the bed, I was greeted by a message on my answering machine from Ebony. She wanted to give me one last chance at the spot in the apartment with her and Jessie before offering it to her cousin. I immediately called her to secure my position, as there was no way I was going to miss out on that opportunity now that I had a pocketful of cash. I now had more than enough to cover my portion and then some.

Overcome with excitement, I wished Mom was home so I could share the good news. At only eighteen years old, I was actually getting my own place. Now all I needed to do was lock down steady employment. Replaying Mr. Walton's offer in my mind, I decided to go back to the G Spot to see if he would make good on his promise to help me.

A few days later, I went with my girls to look at the apartment and turn in the deposit. But it really didn't matter what the apartment looked like. The important thing was that I would finally be away from my mother's rules and on my way to living my own life. That was really all that counted. Of course, it helped that at $840 a month, the place was a three-bedroom duplex in Harlem with one and a half baths and lots of windows, making my move all the more exciting and wonderful.

After turning in the first and last month's rent to the landlord, Jess, Ebony, and I happily parted ways, anxious to pack and move into our own place two weeks later. As I headed back to my mom's house, I envisioned hanging my clothes up in my new closet and relaxing on my bed, gazing out my own window. I desperately wanted to rush over to the G Spot to speak to Mr. Walton, but it was only one o'clock in the afternoon and I didn't think he would be there, so I opted to wait until that evening to catch him. Now that I had my own place, I was determined more than ever to get a job.

As my cab turned the corner and pulled up in front of the club, I started to get a little nervous and excited at the same time. When I got out of the taxi, the first person I saw was Mr. Walton hollering at a bunch of people on the line. I noticed that his door host was not around and Reggie was working the ticket booth. They looked short-staffed. I somehow maneuvered my way through the insane crowd up to the front where he stood flustered.

"Jimmy! It's Simone. Remember me?" I hopefully asked.

"Not now, kid!" he snapped, barely looking at me and making me feel stupid. After a moment of feeling like he had sold me a pipe dream, Mr. Walton suddenly turned in my direction and asked, "Hey, kid, do you think you can watch the ticket booth? I have to bring Reggie out here to work the door before things get outta hand!"

I eagerly nodded my head as if to say yes, speechless and stunned that I was suddenly getting the opportunity I wanted without even asking. If I proved to him that I could do the job, how could he possibly refuse me when I asked to be hired?

"Now kid! Get in here quick! There's a fight breaking out in the back!" Jimmy lifted the rope for me and we ran inside as Reggie headed over toward us.

"Reggie, I need you to go out front and work the door! It's a madhouse out there!" Jimmy began, out of breath as if he himself had just broken up a fight.

"Simone, you stay here and hold down the ticket booth till I get back! Can you do that?"

"Yes!" I answered without hesitation. I could not believe my stroke of good luck. Who would have thought that I would have simply *walked* into a job, and while I had never worked a ticket booth before, I knew that it wasn't rocket science.

"Good, I'm counting on you. I'll be back!" he told me as he ran through the club with the rest of his security. Within a minute Red Alert had shut the music down and all that could be heard was loud screaming. Thrilled by all the excitement, I casually remained in the small glass booth as though nothing unusual was happening.

When security stormed through the front lobby, pushing and dragging some guys out of the club, I kept leaning over the booth trying to see the action.

"Yo, get your hands off me, man! I'll kill your ass! You know who you fuckin' wit, man?!" I heard one cat holler.

"Shut the fuck up! This my club, bitch! Now get the fuck out!" Reggie barked like a raging lunatic. Within seconds, security had physically thrown their troublemaking asses out onto the concrete. Intrigued by the drama, I continued to lean over the booth, when someone tapped me on the shoulder.

"Are you still watching the booth like you're supposed to?" Mr. Walton questioned, catching me off guard.

"Oh, yeah! I was just—" I replied.

"Being nosy. And that, kid, can get you fired. Remember that," he informed me with a fatherly disposition.

"Sorry," I apologized, once again embarrassed.

"I think I can take over now, kid. Thanks for watching the booth. You didn't take any money, did you?" Jimmy asked with a silly look on his face, trying to be funny.

Slightly insulted, I answered him in all seriousness. "No. Because if I wanted to, I could make more than this in two hours!" I exclaimed, obviously feeling myself.

He chuckled at my suggestion, obviously not believing me.

"I'm just joking with you, kid. If I didn't think I could trust you, I woulda chosen someone else." He smiled.

"Go 'head in and have a good time," he continued. "Since you're underage, get yourself some soda from the bar and I'll chat with you later. I might even have a job for you if you're interested. Reggie speaks very highly of you."

I cracked a wide grin. "Thanks! I'll be on the dance floor working up a sweat."

I tingled with excitement as I hurried off but before I got two steps, I doubled back and gave him a big hug.

"What's that for?" he asked nervously.

"Just for being a cool guy. Thanks again." I beamed, happy that I had secured a job without even trying.

Inside the club, the dance floor was packed. Everyone was having a great time and it was like the fight never happened. People kept right on partying hard. I walked over to the bar and got a Coke before heading out to the middle of the dance floor, which was where all the real dancers hung out.

Optically drawn to the deejay booth, I couldn't help looking up while I danced. I was hoping to make eye contact with Red Alert and wave hello, but he was so engrossed in his turntables, he didn't even notice me staring at him.

"Is Brooklyn in the house?" Red Alert finally shouted into the mic.

"Hell yeah!" the crowd answered him back.

"Look, we gotta keep the bullshit outta here! Don't make me have to shut this beat down again! Now, *are y'all ready to party?*" he yelled.

As the answer and response continued, I took in the scene around me. The crowd was going bananas and people started booing and yelling at the thought of the music being turned off.

"Turn it up, turn it up, turn it up!" the crowd hollered.

Red Alert hit the mic again, "We got some hot shit for y'all tonight! Y'all get ready, 'cause Public Enemy is in the house!"

I couldn't believe my ears. I had no idea that artists actually performed at the G Spot, as if the club wasn't already hot enough. Thinking maybe I had heard wrong, I turned to the guy next to me and asked, "Did he say Public Enemy?"

"For sure!" The guy smiled at me, also excited. Without hesitation, I flew over to the stage, hoping to get a good spot close up.

Smoke covered the stage like a foggy mist. Then, through the cloudy haze, out came the infamous "Security of the First World," brothers in black military outfits who stepped in a cadence like American soldiers. The crowd went wild as the speakers pumped the heavy bass. Out of nowhere, Flavor

Flav, the group's infamous hype man, ran out onto the stage, a huge clock hanging around his neck and a Dr. Seuss hat covering his head. It was maniacal! By the time the group's front man, Chuck D, stepped out, the place was uncontrollable and beyond the point of return. In a hip-hop trance, Chuck D had the crowd screaming.

"Don't believe the hype! Don't believe the hype!"

Hypnotized by the group's lyrics and beats, I followed his instructions while continuing to dance to the infectious melody. As I swung my hips and waved my hands in the air, I heard someone call my name.

"Mr. Walton wants to see you in his office," Reggie said, tapping me from behind.

"OK," I replied, slightly nervous about the impromptu meeting. As we walked toward the private area of the club, Reggie leaned in close, so he didn't have to yell above the noise and music.

"You're about to get hooked up. I think he's going to offer you a job."

Hearing his words, I put a pep in my step. I was about to get put on in the best way and could barely contain myself. We hurried through the club, squeezing our way between the throngs of hot sweaty bodies. When we slipped through a side door and up a narrow dark stairway, I could hear the faded muffled music behind me as Reggie banged on the door.

We entered the medium-sized room to see Mr. Walton sitting behind a messy, dented steel desk piled high with papers. A black phone sat to his right and two plain chairs were positioned on the other side. It surely wasn't what I was expecting to see, as I had imagined Jimmy's office to be glamorous and elegant, with cherrywood accents and plush carpet. But in spite of how it looked, I could smell the money he was making there and I definitely wanted to be down with it in any way possible.

"So, kid. You any good at answering phones? I need some help in that department. The phone rings nonstop in here. I need someone responsible to take messages for me and keep this place organized," he began, without looking up from his *Billboard* magazine.

"Talking on the phone is my specialty. I can definitely handle that," I told him before he impatiently cut me off.

"Listen, this is serious. I get very important calls coming through here, so you can't fuck up. If you do, you're out of here. Are we clear?"

I smiled with confidence.

"I got it, Mr. Walton. You don't have to worry about a thing," I assured him.

He started shuffling through the mound of papers on his desk. "Okay, now get out of here. Enjoy what's left of tonight and be here Monday at ten A.M."

Reggie and I left the office in a half walk, half running pace, excited as we headed back downstairs to get our groove on for the remaining minutes of the night. As we approached the dance floor, Reggie stopped me suddenly and asked,

"Can I get the last dance of the night?"

"You don't have to ask." I smiled, leading my buddy out onto the dance floor. As we got into the music and each other, I could feel the eyes of strangers glaring at us. Reggie was an incredible dancer, and as the disco ball's sparkling stars glimmered across my face, I danced so hard I was starting to get totally turned on. Seeing Reggie more like a brother than a lover, my mind raced as I tried to think of someone who might be able to satisfy my sexual needs. I'd never really had a boyfriend and was still a virgin. I mean, I had done a lot with George, but it had been oral and I had never allowed him to actually penetrate me. I realized that my overwhelming fear of being controlled or becoming pregnant had stifled my sexual exploration in so many ways. But that night, I wanted to cross the line into womanhood, exploring my sexuality on a level other than a monetary one. My pussy was hot and womanhood refused to wait another minute.

As I racked my brain for someone to call, the image of this hot and sexy West Indian cat I'd met at a rockers party a few weeks back entered my mind. I'd only called him once or twice and didn't really know him, but that was a good thing. I figured that giving my cherry to a stranger was safe. After all, if he started to trip, I'd simply cut him off like it never happened. And since he didn't have my number, I was in control of whether or not we'd fuck again. With that in mind, I felt powerful and in control, which was exactly what I needed.

After dancing with Reggie, I went to use the pay phone in the ladies' room. I dug around in my purse for a torn piece of paper and pulled out Rastaman's number. Standing about six-foot-three, Chris looked like a roughneck with a sexy five o'clock shadow and dark thick dreads that he pulled back tightly in one big ponytail. The phone rang six times and I was just about to hang up when someone finally picked up.

"Ello?" a deep voice answered.

"May I speak to Chris?" I asked, holding my breath. Although I knew he was definitely diggin' me when we met, I was scared that he might not remember me.

"Who dis?" he questioned, his sexy Jamaican accent turning up the heat in my veins.

"Simone. We met a while back. Do you remember?"

"Ow could I forget? What's up wit' chu? Thought you wasn't gonna call."

"Been kinda busy lately, but the first moment I got free, I'm reaching out," I lied.

"Well, why don't you come see a nucca?"

"Just tell me where to meet you and I'm there!" I grinned, surprised at how easy the exchange was.

"Take the train to Nostrand Avenue and meet me at the token booth," he suggested.

"Okay, I'm on my way," I told him, hanging up the phone.

I headed back out into the club to say good-bye to Reggie before I hustled to the subway.

"Hey," I said, before leaving. "Thanks for taking me up to Jimmy, Reggie. I really needed this job." I swung my arm around him and embraced him tightly.

"Don't sweat it." He smiled.

An hour later I was standing next to the token booth in Bed-Stuy, Brooklyn, waiting for my late-night booty call. After a half hour of repeatedly checking my watch, I was ready to give up on him. But just as I was about to turn and leave, Chris came running down the subway stairs toward me. My face lit up as soon as I spotted my sexy thug and I walked to him and gave him a big hug. His eyes were already bloodshot and the distinct odor of weed lingered in his clothes and hair, making me smile to myself, knowing that we were gonna have an "in the zone" humpin' good time.

"What up, baby? Sorry I'm late. I had to handle some last-minute business for the night. But now, I'm all yours," he promised.

"Good. 'Cause that's what I want—all of you!" I stated, giving him a wicked naughty look.

He grinned back at me and we quickly headed out of the smelly subway station. Once out on the street, we walked swiftly to his apartment. When we arrived at the dilapidated building, Chris flipped his keys out and unlocked his door, then stepped aside like a gentleman for me to enter first. Surprisingly, his place was set up nicely. It was a small but cozy one-room studio with candles in the corners and the scent of Black Love incense in the air. The music of Teddy Pendergrass played softly in the background, creating a romantic atmosphere. As I looked around, Chris sat down and lit up a big spliff. When he called me over to the sofa, I dropped my purse and fell into his strong, muscular arms.

"Wow, you did all this for me?" I asked in awe. He didn't answer. I could tell he wasn't much for words, but when he started kissing me gently, that's all he needed to say. Overwhelmed by the events I had recently experienced, his tenderness prompted emotion and I began to talk.

"There's something I should tell you," I began. "I'm not really very experienced in the sex department."

From the look on his face, I could tell he was shocked. He took a long drag on the blunt and then passed it to me as I snuggled up under his arm.

"So you're a virgin. You sure don't act like one," he stated.

"I ain't saying all that. I'm what you could call a foreplay queen. But I think I'm ready to explore."

"Would you like to explore with me tonight?"

I tried to inhale the smoke of the blunt and hold it in, but it was too strong and I began to cough and sputter, breaking the flow of our conversation. Chris chuckled and took the thick Philly from my hand before I could drop it or burn a hole in his sofa.

"Here, let me help you, mommi," he offered, taking another hit, then pulling my lips toward his and giving me a "shotgun." This time I inhaled slowly and as I exhaled, I relaxed back into the warm crook of his arm, succumbing willingly to the euphoric feeling. After a few more hits, I was feeling sexier than ever, taking it upon myself to walk over to his bed. Once there, something came over me and I slowly began to strip to the rhythm of the music. Once naked, I climbed upon the bed and stretched my hand out to him, motioning for him to join me.

"I'm ready," I moaned in a soft whisper.

Chris headed toward me, shedding his clothing as he got closer to my gold. He liked the way I'd moved my tongue over on the couch and was eager to see what else I was working with. As he approached me, his dick stood erect at least ten inches from his body and I became nervous. From the look in his eye, I knew Chris was about to fuck the shit out of me. He was hung like a stallion, having one of the biggest dicks I'd ever seen—even bigger than George. Thus, the thought of his hard cock invading my tiny tight pussy made me cringe. But I was at the point of no return and was feeling like he had put some sort of Jamaican mojo on me.

I reached for the enormous muscle between his thighs and pulled him close, wrapping my small manicured hand around his swollen member. As I vigorously stroked, he immediately responded to my touch with a deep moan. I then sat up and knelt down in front of him so that I could stuff all of his thickness into my mouth. I involuntarily gagged on his monstrous weapon while I slid my hand up and down his shaft. Saliva dribbled from the corners of my mouth as I continued to suck. While I slurped in all of his lusciousness, Chris's eyes rolled back into his head and he moaned my name, caressed my cheeks, and ran his fingers through my messy hair. The music, the aroma, and the ganja definitely had us in the zone.

Abandoning his wood briefly, I continued stroking the shaft up and down with my fingertips, as I let my tongue venture down upon his balls. I licked them gently at first, then sucked on each fleshy sac, slurping them into my mouth and licking up the dripping spittle. My lips hesitantly left his jewels and I looked up at him, still squeezing tightly on his balls. When he could no longer stand it, he snatched me up and laid me down on my back. My pussy was extremely wet and ready with anticipation, as my sticky inner thighs glistened from my dripping juices.

Interrupting the sensual sounds of our encounter, in a husky voice Chris let me know that he was taking over.

"Open your legs for me," he instructed.

Before I knew what he had in mind, he dove in headfirst and licked at the silvery cream smeared on my inner thighs. His tongue licked and sucked on my vigorously pulsating clit and he devoured my pussy righteously for what seemed like an entire hour. When he finally came up for air, it was evident that I was in ecstasy and ready for his big black Jamaican dick. He kissed me passionately on the mouth, giving me a taste of my own sweet honey. When he felt the time was right, Chris mounted his body on top of mine, sliding his dick against my pussy before whispering in my ear,

"You ready for me?"

Barely able to speak, I somehow managed to say the word *yes*, giving him the green light to reach for the condom he had on his nightstand. Without further adieu, he slipped it on seconds before he grabbed his throbbing pipe and slid it slowly inside of me, causing my body to tremble. The head of his dick was so plump that my pussy kept pushing it out. Determined, he continuously nudged his way inside my treasure chest. Finally, unable to control his lust any longer, Chris reared back and rammed his steel deep inside me, making me scream out in a pain that hurt so good. My feminine walls spasmed and then relaxed, opening up to release a spray of creamy nectar that came bursting from my ripened peach.

For almost an hour, Chris put me in positions I would have never guessed possible. His eyes looked at me longingly as if I was a priceless gem and I definitely could not have imagined a more perfect "first time" than this. As I held my breath to increase my light-headedness, Chris's body began to jerk quickly as he gently sped up and pumped in and out of my loins. It was obvious that he wanted to please me, as he seemed to be genuinely making love and not fucking.

"Ah, ahh, I'm cummin'! I'm cummin'! Aaaahhh, uuurrgh!" he finally yelled. He pulled his dick out and in one swift motion, slid the rubber off, shooting the rest of his cum onto my flat stomach. With a possessed look in his eye, once the last drop was squeezed out, he fell lifelessly on top of me.

"Damn, that pussy was good!" he sighed, before passing out.

As the soft sounds of Luther Vandross gently whispered throughout the scented room, I lay there, looking up at the ceiling with a big smile on my face. I now finally had a story to share with the girls. I had joined their ranks and was finally a woman!

seven

wicked wonderland

After a few weeks had passed, I was fully acclimated as one of Mr. Walton's employees, answering his phones, taking his messages, and organizing all his files and contacts. My girls and I had moved into our new home and were clearly enjoying our newfound independence. Our place was becoming a regular weekend hangout pad for Ebony and Jessie's boyfriends of the week, and of course, my freaky best buddy, Carmen, who had seemingly forgotten all about what had happened on George's rooftop.

One particular Sunday morning I was awakened by the smell of fried potatoes and bacon. As I stretched and yawned happily like a Cheshire cat, I began to stir, before I realized that there was a warm body lying beside me. I froze and looked down, before a smile gradually spread across my face as I realized that it was Carmen. I didn't remember getting up to let her in, but knew that anything was possible since we had partied pretty hard the night before.

"Mornin', Carm. Time to get up!" I sang, shaking her.

Carmen groaned and pulled the pillow over her head.

"Still tired," she cried.

With a chuckle, I climbed over her to get out of the bed. I shook my head before putting on my robe and heading downstairs. I followed the delicious aroma that resonated from the kitchen and found Jessie standing at the stove preparing a feast.

When all the goodies were ready and served, I joined Jess, Ebony, and their male companions, at the breakfast table. As I chomped on a strip of perfectly crisp bacon, my mind began to drift away from the idle chitchat of the others.

Eight months had passed and I was still wandering around trying to find my niche. While I was happy to be out on my own doing my thing, living off my salary from the G Spot just wasn't cutting it. Mr. Walton wasn't paying me as much as I thought he would have, and I hadn't had the nerve to participate in another George-like scenario. Although Carmen had fully introduced me to the world of erotica, I was hesitant to jump into it with both feet. Still, she and I partied every night, meeting many different types of people, each one more fabulous than the one before. Rolling with her, I met entertainers, politicians, directors, and photographers, anybody and everybody, and anybody who was anybody. And while I had gotten a peek at the elite social scene, I still wasn't really part of it.

"Simone!" Jessie yelled, tossing a piece of toast at me.

"Huh?" I replied, looking up from my plate to see everyone staring at me.

"I asked what you're doing tonight. The four of us are gonna have a smoke out and rent some movies. You game? Why don't you invite your Rasta friend?" Jess suggested.

"Nah, I've got to go down to the club for a minute, then I've got a party to get ready for," I told her.

"OK, well, you go do your thang. We know you're on a mission," Ebony encouraged as she got up and began to clear the table. "Who knows. Maybe tonight will be the night you meet someone who really can help you get where you're going."

A couple of hours later, I strutted into the G Spot and headed toward Mr. Walton's office. Although it was my day off, I had wanted to stop by and chat with him about my future. While I was grateful for the opportunity he had given me, I hated being cooped up in the office all day. Bigger than that, my shyness seemed to be preventing me from meeting the people I needed to meet who could help jump-start my career, and I was starting to feel like I was wasting time. Respecting his wisdom and worldliness, I wanted to ask Jimmy if he had any suggestions about what I should do to expedite the process.

I knocked on the office door but no one answered. Just as I was about to leave, a big shadow moved across the wall in front of me and I spun around to see who was behind me.

"Boo!" the shadow shouted. I let out a sigh of relief and started to laugh as I realized that it was Ben, one of Reggie's security team.

"You scared the shit outta me!" I said, giving him a playful smack on his arm.

With a chuckle, he asked, "You hanging out with Reggie and me tonight?"

"Nah, not tonight. I got plans."

"Too bad."

"What are you doing lurking around corners and shit?"

"Is that what I'm doing?" he laughed. "I thought I was securing the joint."

"I mean, you are, but it's creepy in this place when the club's not jumpin'. Does Mr. Walton realize how big this place is? And there's all these dark passageways and doors. If somebody was trying to stick this place up, how could you catch him?"

"Oh, I'd catch him . . ." Ben assured me with a nod of his head and a mean look on his face. Ben lowered his voice. "But lemme tell you a secret. There's some legendary ghost stories about this joint. Want me to take you around for a tour?"

Looking around, his words did not surprise me. Being in the club sometimes, alone during the day, I had already felt an unexplainable presence within the surrounding walls. Now that Ben was talking about "ghost stories," I knew that the spirits I felt were probably those ghosts—if I believed in that sort of thing, which I wasn't sure that I did. Still in all, just to be on the safe side, I never dared venture past Jimmy's office. Spotting Reggie headed our way, I replied, "I'll go if Reggie comes with us."

"Comes with you where?" he asked.

"I was just about to take little Simone here on the G Spot tour," Ben informed him with a wink.

"You've never done the tour? Well, you're in for a treat. This place is cool when it's empty. The ghosts come out." Reggie made a quick side glance at Ben and widened his eyes.

"There you go with that ghost shit again," I snapped but stood strong. "Well, if you think I'm scared, you got the wrong girl. Let's go!"

The three of us walked toward the back of the club. Ben stopped at a door that was hidden behind a black silk drape. On the surface of the door in bold letters was a sign that read "Do not enter!"

Ben reached for his keys and finagled the silver ring to find the right one.

When he opened the door, dust and cobwebs blew out at us. I coughed, waving my hand back and forth in front of my face. It obviously hadn't been opened in a long time. Ben hit the light switch on the wall and headed up a narrow staircase as Reggie and I followed closely behind him. My curiosity began to rise and I was interested in seeing what was ahead of us on the other floors.

"Simone, watch your step. These stairs are tricky," Reggie warned, just as the lights went out, leaving us in complete darkness and causing me to let out a loud shriek.

"Yo, chill out!" Ben snapped. We all stopped, afraid to take a breath as we stood very still in total blackness. "You hear that?" Ben nervously whispered. Stifled with fear, neither Regg nor I could reply.

"I'm just messing with you," Ben broke out into a wicked laugh and popped on his flashlight. "There's something wrong with the wiring in that switch. I think there's a short. It did it to me before."

My heart felt like it had fallen through my stomach.

"That's not funny! You both are full of shit!" I scolded. Ben pointed the light in my faced and laughed,

"I'm full of shit, huh? You better watch your mouth, kid. Respect your elders!" When we finally reached the top of the landing, we both stopped behind Ben, who began to narrate his little tour.

"Now, Little Miss Know It All," he began. "Let me hit you with some history."

He clicked off the flashlight, and like an optical illusion, a warm pink light appeared. He then altered the tone of his voice as he spun the tale of the mysterious, beautiful room that was in the attic on the top floor of the G Spot.

"Enter," Ben directed, in a voice unlike his own. Reggie walked in first and lifted a dust-covered drop cloth from a beautiful antique love seat. Captivated, I stood silently in amazement.

"It's like we opened a treasure chest," I said in awe, blinking hard to make sure I wasn't dreaming. The windowless room looked like a clandestine love nest. Expensive gold-framed paintings were mounted on every wall. In one area of the room, there were Italian sofas appointed with velvet burgundy and gold trim while matching drapes wrapped around nearby columns. Without Ben telling me, I assumed that in the old days, this room would have been a secret hideaway for the elite and discreet. Socialites who had left their spirits behind, spirits that were so strong you could almost hear their voices. When my curiosity surpassed my fear, I walked to the far end of the room and turned the corner. My mouth nearly dropped to the floor and I couldn't believe my eyes.

"Reggie, come here!" I called excitedly.

Together we stared at the beautiful plush, heart-shaped bed that stood high on a platform, its little heart-shaped pillows and soft satin sheets covered in a thick layer of dust. Above our heads were paneled mirrors, reflecting down our own murky images. The room was the color of vintage Merlot that looked eerie and sensuous at the same time in the foggy shadow. It seemed as if the room hadn't been disturbed in fifty years, and although the bed was partially covered with a large white cloth in an attempt to keep it clean, the dirt and dust had found their way beneath it. Ben walked over to us and began, "Now listen closely and I will tell you the story of this room."

We took a step back and listened intently as Ben paced around the cobwebbed room as he told the story.

"The G Spot has many famous legends," Ben began. "And since I've been here for a long time, I know many of them. Back in the day, a lot of nightclubs had secret rooms for the wealthy and famous. This was one of those rooms. I was told that *Playboy* magazine used to shoot some of their layouts right here on that bed. Back then it was considered taboo to express yourself sexually, so this was a place for private members to have their fun, without fear of it leaking to the press."

"Maybe that's why I felt so much sexual energy when I walked in here. But it also feels cold and sad," I said.

"Can we go now?" Reggie asked, obviously starting to get freaked out.

"Good observation, young lady," Ben continued like an experienced tour guide, ignoring Reggie's request. "The cold sadness might be coming from the famous singer who died in this room between performances many years ago. They say that even to this day, the sultry songstress still haunts the G Spot—with many patrons claiming to see her reflection in the mirrors of the restrooms and at the bar right before closing. As legend tells it, the starlet wants to finish her set. And no lie—there's some strange shit that goes on in here when the club is closed."

Having heard enough twilight zone shit for one day, I immediately headed toward the door.

"Well, fellas, I think I've had enough for today. Gotta go," I snapped, storming toward the exit and running down the stairs so fast that I left my two comrades behind. In the distance behind me I could hear their laughter, causing me to wonder if they had been pulling my leg. Whatever the case, I didn't have time for their silly games and ghost stories. I had my own game to play and I was nowhere near winning.

The notorious Johnny-Jism was the porn industry's top male star. A true bona fide sex freak, he had a reputation for throwing the most elaborate off-the-chain parties, just to see how many new girls he could recruit and turn out. He was also a close friend of George Santini's. So when Carmen told me that we had been invited to such a party, there was no way I would have missed it.

Agreeing to meet Carmen there, I arrived at the corner of 59th Street and 3rd Avenue around eleven o'clock. I eagerly walked into the building, announced my name, and was escorted up to the penthouse suite by one of the party attendants. On the elevator, I silently hoped this would be the night that I finally became part of the elite crowd that would help me get closer to achieving my dream.

With the confidence that I had psyched myself into having, I entered the party room looking smashing and all eyes turned to me. I'd used my entire paycheck from the G Spot to splurge on a new designer outfit from Saks and had convinced the girl at the Estée Lauder counter to use my face as a canvas for her most expensive products. With all that work put in, I knew I looked good. Of course, I didn't know how I was going to pay my share of the rent that month, but I hoped the answer would be found at Johnny's party.

A topless waitress came over with a tray of champagne and offered me a glass. I accepted, and as I took a sip of the bubbly, I scanned the room to see if I could locate George or Carmen. Unable to find either of them, I observed in amazement who was in attendance. Given the party's honoree, I had expected the room to be filled with people from the porn industry, but was pleasantly surprised to find myself in a melting pot of politicians, directors, famous photographers, and celebrities. You name him, he was there.

Like a fly on the wall, I sipped my champagne and watched everybody engage in wild and freaky activity for a while before taking it upon myself to mingle. I was beginning to feel pretty freaky myself after watching women dancing around half and totally naked, chatting with drinks in their hands, as if their nudity was nothing unusual. Then there were those who weren't doing much talking at all. In fact, over in one of the dimly lit corners, a woman was getting fucked by two muscle-bound men as casually as if they were playing a game of checkers. My blood was heating up by the second. As I sipped the last of my champagne, I stopped short of the final swallow to watch a sexy blonde take it up the ass from one guy while she diligently sucked on the cock of another. Spectators stood around masturbating and I figured it was time for me to get a refill.

Over at the fully stocked bar, I finally spotted George talking with Johnny-Jism, surrounded by a bunch of dancing sexy women. I knew Johnny's face from the movies Carmen had shown me. Relieved to find my friend, I walked up to George and gave him a kiss on each cheek before he made a formal introduction.

"Wow, you are hot! Madam, I'm transfixed," Johnny exclaimed, laying it on thick as he bowed and kissed the back of my hand. "Are you a porn star?" he asked.

"No!" I said defensively.

"Well, you certainly could be," he said.

I giggled shyly, slightly flattered, "I don't think so."

"You got the look, baby. Come. Let me show you my world," he offered. With George's blessing, Johnny took me by the hand and led me up the spiral staircase. My curiosity made me follow him in silence to a set of elaborately carved double wooden doors. When we stopped, the unexpected loud clap of his hands startled me, but not half as much as what was waiting for us on the other side. What I saw caused my eyes to light up like firecrackers on the Fourth of July.

Inside the ornately decorated room was an orgy of about thirty people taking place on a grand, gold-leafed, California king–sized bed. I followed Johnny in, as my brain went into overdrive. There was a multitude of pussies and cocks dancing to the rhythm of lust as a glistening sheen of sexual juices covered their beautiful bodies.

To my right, one woman was treating three studs to a simultaneous oral sucking train. She sat on a velvet stool as the men stood above her in a semicircle with their dicks aimed at her face. As she sucked and stroked them with her hands, the men guided her lips onto their cocks, shoving two in at the same time and stretching her mouth to its limit. Another woman was down on all fours with one guy in between her legs licking her pussy while yet another guy lined himself up right behind her, grabbed her by the hips as he began hitting it fiercely. Everything was so out of control that the woman had to hold on to the legs of the stool to keep her balance.

As a natural response to what I was watching, my pussy twitched uncontrollably, and I didn't know whether to join in or continue being a spectator.

"Isn't this beautiful?" Johnny asked, interrupting my trance. "I have to say one of my best masterpieces."

I was unable to reply when all of a sudden, without looking my way, Johnny ripped his clothes off and stood there looking sexy with his superstar cock up and ready to go.

"Please join us . . ." he invited, tugging at my arm.

"Oh no no no!" I said, pulling away.

"Well then, go back down to the party. I'm going to stay here and fuck all the women in this room. It was nice meeting you! Enjoy!" he exclaimed before he dove onto the bed and I backed out of the room without turning around.

Moments after I reentered the main living room, a man walked up to me with a smile, and with authority in his deep voice said, "Hello, my name is Wellington, and you are?"

"Simone Young," I replied.

"Are you in the industry?" he inquired.

"Nooo . . ." I stressed with a chuckle.

"Well, what do you do for a living?"

This man was beginning to get on my nerves. Why was he asking me all of these personal questions five minutes after meeting me?

"Well, I mean, I have a small job. But why are you asking me all these questions?" I asked, visibly annoyed.

"I'm not trying to pry. But I might have a job for a pretty girl like you, if you're in the market."

Now he had my attention, and I turned to face him. I looked him up and down speculatively. He was a tall and lanky educated-looking fellow, with skin the color of creamy milk chocolate. Horn-rimmed glasses sat on his keen nose, adding to his intellectual appearance.

"What kind of job?" I asked suspiciously.

"I own an escort massage parlor called Magic Hands. Do you know what an escort business is?"

"Of course I do," I replied.

He took a step back and got a better look at me.

"You are over nineteen, aren't you?" he asked.

"Well, actually I'm eighteen."

He looked disappointed and like he was ready to walk away, but he had my curiosity peaked and I wanted to know more. Eighteen/nineteen, what difference did it really make? I was old enough to fight for my country.

"Wait," I told him, causing him to stop dead in his tracks.

"I may be eighteen, but I'm sure I can do escorting, massaging, or whatever you've got going as long as it pays. I need a good-paying job, and preferably, one that makes money quick. Does your job pay well?" I questioned. Skeptical, Wellington looked me up and down and hesitantly spoke.

"Tell you what. Why don't you come by my parlor tomorrow, I'll explain to you exactly what we do and how we do it, and we'll take it from there. How does that sound?"

"That sounds great!"

"Here's my card. The address and phone number are on it. Come by around one o'clock."

I readily took the card and shook his hand. Then I watched him as he maneuvered his way through the throng of people and out the front door.

After meeting Wellington, I decided that I'd had enough voyeuristic excitement for one night so I headed back to Harlem. I never did see Carmen, who was the reason I had gone to the party in the first place, but I had gotten something much more valuable than simply hanging out with my girlfriend—another job opportunity that hopefully would pay better than the G Spot.

When I walked into the Magic Hands massage parlor, I was greeted by two very sexy ladies. The place was erotic and inviting, decorated like some type of royal harem, with richly colored drapes and sheer muslin tapestries hanging around fake pillars. Obviously expecting me, the ladies led me to Wellington's office, where he was seated behind a very impressive-looking desk, just finishing up a phone call. He motioned for me to sit in one of the chairs and went straight into business mode.

"Glad you could make it," he began. "Well, Simone. Let's get down to logistics. An escort business is one where men and women are provided with companionship—escorts for the afternoon or evening, to accompany them to social and political functions, for however long the client wishes, at a premium hourly rate. I say premium, because I hire only the most professional and beautiful variety of female and male escorts. I also run a massage parlor here that charges top dollar as well. My masseuses are top-notch and absolutely fantastic with their hands. Did you know that there's actually a spot in the small of your back that if you touch it the right way, with the right pressure, for the right length of time, it can bring you to the ultimate orgasm?"

"No," I replied, frowning with doubt.

"Well, anyway, what I need from you is to answer the phones, screen the clients, and book appointments for me. Do you think you can do that?"

"Yeah, I can do that, but I was really hoping for something a little more exciting. How much do the escorts make?" I asked.

"The split is sixty/forty. I take in sixty percent for setting up the dates and housing the business. Obviously, since you're doing administrative work, you'll be given a flat rate. So, do you want the job?"

I hesitated, my mind spinning with another plan. Seeing the look in my eye, Wellington seemed to know what I was thinking.

"Look, I'd love to send you out on dates, but I think you're too young for our clientele. You definitely have what it takes in the looks department, so that's not the problem. I just have a feeling you wouldn't be a popular request for companionship. My clients like their escorts to be inconspicuous, to blend in. Someone as young as you would stick out like a sore thumb in many of the more sophisticated environments."

"Well, how much will I make answering the phones and booking the appointments?" I asked, disappointed. I wanted to be out and about, meeting and greeting, not stuck behind in some stuffy office, talking to faceless people over the telephone. I had already done that at the G Spot. It was time for me to step it up.

"I'll pay you a hundred dollars a day. Until you're older, that's about all I can offer. Can you settle with that?"

Although I was still not satisfied with being a glorified secretary, I was happy with his proposition. If I worked at Magic Hands five days a week, I could take home two g's a month, which was nearly twice as much as I was making at the G Spot.

"Yes, I can settle with that." I smiled. "Just don't try any freaky shit with me or I'll break out!"

"Oh, you don't have to worry about me. You're not my type." Wellington laughed, handing me a hundred-dollar bill.

"Then it's all set. You can start today. Let's get you set up."

Wellington motioned for me to come around to his side of the desk.

"Pull up a chair. Watch, listen and learn," he instructed.

I sat at the desk with Wellington as he answered the lines and took appointments for his new and VIP clients, catching on quickly. In just a few short hours, I had learned how to entice potential customers and reel them in with a calm assured voice, seducing them into booking larger packages and spending more than they wanted to. Quirky as he was, Wellington turned out to be pretty cool and I could see that he was pleased with my first day's performance. All I had to do now was figure out how I was going to tell Mr. Walton that, like *The Jeffersons,* I was movin' on up.

eight

the magic touch

Soon after I started my new job at the Magic Hands massage parlor, I broke the news to Mr. Walton. The G Spot had served its purpose and now that I had been offered more money, it was time for me to move on. To my surprise, Jimmy was gracious, telling me that his door was always open, which I definitely appreciated. Though I still wasn't any closer to starting my career, I had learned many invaluable lessons about the power of sex while working at the parlor.

Not satisfied with simply answering phones, I managed to figure out a way to make each day at the parlor an unexpected erotic voyage. While there was plenty for me to do on my eight-hour shift, I still managed to periodically sneak a peek beyond the heavy curtains that separated the real world from the planet of lustful fantasies that lurked just steps away from my desk. The images I was often presented with were a lot kinkier than I had imagined, ranging from dominatrix scenarios to straight-up orgies, making the job perks even more than I had bargained for. When the phones were slow, I sometimes doubled as a parlor attendant, stocking the rooms with fresh towels, lotions, and massage oils. I liked doing attendant duties because it gave me the opportunity to feed my newfound voyeuristic curiosity, and for certain customers, the "therapists" would sometimes ask me to help with exhibition-ism requests. This would require watching a session and pretending to evaluate and inspect the masseuses' work as they created reality from fantasy. There were also times they would have me place shackles on the customers' ankles and tie them down to the massage tables with ropes. I learned a lot about myself, including the fact that handcuffing was a favorite of mine. And while I never spoke, it was exciting to silently watch and learn how to please the clientele. Making the deal even sweeter, the ladies would always tip me for a job well done, adding an unexpected extra bonus to my already adequate salary.

After one particularly busy afternoon, with hopes of getting out at a decent hour, I checked the appointment log and noticed that my boss's name was written in the eight o'clock slot. Being that we usually took our last client around seven, Wellington must have made his own appointment in the VIP section for a duo treatment with Tanya and Tami, our after-hours treatment specialists.

"Hey, Simone. Today was hectic, wasn't it?" Tami, one of our clients' most favored boodilicious, honey-blond masseuses stated, shaking her head as she stood above my desk.

"Yeah, I'm about to head home. That is, if you, Tanya, and Wellington don't need me here during your eight o'clock appointment," I replied with a raised brow.

"Oh shit, I forgot it's Tuesday. Wellington has his usual massage and rubdown tonight, but this time he's bringing an important business partner with him. Some investor. Damn!" she sighed, obviously wanting to follow my lead out the door. I knew she was probably tired from such a crazy day, but VIPs tipped very well and it was in her best interest to make that money.

"What's wrong, girl?" I asked, gathering my belongings.

"I didn't realize it was Tuesday and I told Tanya she could leave about thirty minutes ago! She said she had a headache or something. Wellington will hit the fuckin' roof if there's nobody available for a VIP double!" she hesitated for a moment but suddenly had a look in her eye like she had just come up with the best idea in the world.

"Simone, do you think you could be a doll and help me out? Just this once, pullleaseeee . . ." Tami turned to me with an earnest plea.

"Me? Girl, I don't know how to give a massage!" I exclaimed, knowing that what she did to make those men cum was totally on some other level.

"You won't have to give a *real massage,* silly," she giggled. "You and Tanya are about the same complexion and size, and since you'll be wearing a mask, no one will even know!"

"I don't know." I hesitated.

"I'll split the fee with you fifty/fifty!" she tried to convince me.

The mention of making money gave me the green light I needed to forge ahead.

"Fifty/fifty? Say no more, I'm in," I told her.

"Great! Let's go get you ready."

"Wait. What about Wellington? Won't he be mad that I'm working with the clients?"

"You won't be. You'll be doing him. I'll take the client. And the phones shut down at seven, anyway. He'll think you went home. With the mask on, you'll look just like Tanya. Come on, we gotta get you in costume!"

Tami hurried around the desk and grabbed my arm, pulling me into the masseuses' dressing lounge. She tossed me a black Lycra mask that resembled what someone might wear to a stickup. She then sat me before the lighted mirror as she grabbed a nearby brush and gathered my lengthy tresses up into a braided ponytail on top of my head with a red satin scrunchie. The mask felt like a do-rag, fitting snuggly across my face and head, with cutouts existing for my heavily mascaraed eyes. Tami swiftly pulled my braid out through the top hole and smoothed the mask down over the bridge of my nose, revealing only the bottom third of my face before assuring me,

"Now, we'll just put some lipstick on, strip you naked, and you're ready to go. Trust me, Wellington won't have a clue."

I got up and checked myself out in the full-length mirror. The bright cherry red lipstick illuminated my flawless complexion, creating a sun-kissed glow that could stop any man in his tracks. In awe of myself, I studied my reflection before pulling my braid around my neck and letting it fall down over my perky ripe melons.

"This could work," I spoke with confidence as I tried out several different seductive poses and expressions with my mouth.

"Of course it will. Wellington won't really be looking at you anyway, so relax," Tami continued, tossing me a pair of high-heeled black boots and a leather braided horsewhip.

"Okay, lemme look at you," Tami asked as she scanned me from head to toe.

"Perfect!" She grinned, clearly pleased. "Listen, all you have to do is follow my lead and seduce them with your body and your hands. You say you're an actress, right?" she asked. I nodded.

"If I didn't know any better, I'd swear you were Tanya under there! But just to be on the safe side, lemme do all the talking so you won't give yourself away," she suggested.

"Okay, but what exactly am I supposed to do?" I asked, my nervousness kicking in.

"Whatever comes natural. Don't underestimate yourself. It's not as hard as you think. Wellington likes to be smacked around a bit and if he gets on your nerves as much as he gets on mine, I'm sure that'll make it a whole lot easier!"

We burst out laughing, slapping high-fives, but quickly sobered up when we heard the door chimes ringing and two male voices up front. Tami used the adjoining door between the dressing room and the couples' suite to usher me in quickly before dimming the lights. In the couples' suite were two massage tables, one couch, a small counter with a sink, and a rolling supply cart that was stocked with a lot more than towels. Upon its surface sat an array of sweet-smelling body oils, creams, and scrubs; a thick velvet rope; and a pair of shiny silver handcuffs. Tami trickled a few drops of oil into an incense burner and turned the knob on the wall beside the light switch that controlled the music volume in the room.

"Stay here and get comfy. I'll go get our clients," she coached.

I sat patiently and seductively on the arm of the couch as I waited for Tami to return with the two men. Wellington looked a little stiff and tired as he disrobed. His business associate was pumped and ready to go once Tami dropped her robe to the floor and guided him over to the table. She ordered him to get undressed and then to lie down on his stomach. Then she placed a warm hand towel over his squishy backside. When Tami gave me the cue, I stood up and cracked my whip, pointing it at the other table. Then I followed Tami and covered my boss's butt with a towel from the warmer. When both men were prepped and ready, Tami poured warm oil into the palms of her hands and passed the bottle to me so I could do the same. I continued to follow her lead, sliding my hands down the muscles in Wellington's neck and back and onto his legs and feet. I inconspicuously teased him, letting my fingers slide beneath the towel to massage his derriere. I watched how Tami lifted the towel and instructed her customer to roll over onto his back, before dropping it back in place over his bulging crotch.

The men talked business as we caressed their flesh, but once they flipped over, all shoptalk died down. When Wellington turned over, my eyes bugged wide. His cock had more than doubled in size. His thick member lay attractively slumped over his left thigh, slowly moving counterclockwise until it was stiff and pointing straight up toward his navel. I'd had no clue that he would be so well endowed, and my eyes were fixated between his legs. Instead of covering him up, I got some more warm oil and proceeded to give him a hand job while Tami did the same to her client. The sound of oil and flesh being smacked and whacked started to turn me on and I was getting an itch between my legs, aching for something long and hard to scratch it. As my hands continued their duty, Wellington's balls began to draw up and I knew he was about to burst. Anxiously, I leaned over and took the entire length of him into my mouth, slurping up and down his pulsating shaft.

Remembering Tami's advice about Wellington liking pain, I tightly squeezed his balls with my free hand, only to be startled when he bucked like a wild steer, thrusting up into my mouth, practically choking me. In an instant, he grabbed my head and held me down as he shot his load off into my throat. His business partner began to follow suit, grunting and moaning, obviously stimulated by the primal noises coming from our table.

Once Wellington loosened his grip on my head, I wiped the cum from my mouth with a nearby towel and went over to position myself upon the back edge of the couch. I rested one foot up on the arm of the sofa, opened my legs wide and leaned back to give him a clear view of the main course.

"How's that pussy, man?" Wellington asked his colleague as he lay on his back staring up at the ceiling, reveling in the after sensations. "Didn't I tell you it was just right? Nice and tight!"

"I haven't gotten to the pussy yet, man, but she sucks dick like a pro!" the man replied.

I looked over to see Tami kneeling between her client's legs, bopping up and down on his cock while he fondled her breasts. He grabbed a hold of her golden blond locks and wrapped the strands around his hands to push her back and forth. After about two minutes, he popped his dick out of her mouth and slapped it across her face. Tami then turned around and positioned her butt over his dick. Wellington's business partner began licking his lips and squeezing Tami's ass, smacking her butt cheeks with his dick and his hands. When he was ready, the man wet his finger in her pussy juice before pulling her down upon his throbbing cock. He thrust up in her pussy, gyrating around a few times before commenting to my boss,

"You're right, man. This pussy is incredible!"

Tami started riding him hard and fast before she twisted around to look at him and lick her lips. Just a few feet away, I winked at Wellington and slid my hand down between my legs to spread my pussy lips apart, giving him the perfect view of my moist pink flesh. Thoroughly into it, I took my forefinger and slid it inside myself, pulling it out covered in my own creamy milkshake. Then I slowly started to finger-fuck myself, before calling him over with my other index finger. Wellington charged at me and beat his cock on my clit as he cooed, "Ooh . . . that's it!"

I continued to encourage him in a lusty whisper as I glanced over at Tami and smiled. Tami nodded her head in approval. Before I knew it, Wellington grabbed me by my hips and pulled me violently down onto his dick. The shock of the invasion made me gasp, as I wasn't expecting to be stretched open so wide. I held on to the back of the couch for support and didn't dare move out of fear of being hurt as he pounded away inside of me like a wild man. Amazed at the amount of force he was using, I felt like I was being fucked by a horse.

"Aghh! I'm about to cum in your face!" Wellington screamed. He then pulled out of me and moved around to the side of the couch. In response, I arched my head back over the arm so he could rub his balls back and forth across my cheeks. He squeezed my titties together and slid his dick between my perky tits. With every passing moment, it seemed as though his cock grew bigger and harder. Just as he was about to cum, he bent his head down and started licking my clit. When he suddenly came up, he started pumping his dick furiously through my breasts once again, squeezing them even tighter. Just before he bust his nut, he backed up and jerked off, shooting his ammunition vehemently into my face.

"Ahhh, yeahhhh. Um, umm!"

He jerked a couple more times and flicked the last of his joy juice off into the air before rubbing the head of his dick around in his own cum and spreading it all over my face.

A couple of feet away, his partner made indescribable sounds as if he were hypnotized by Tami's unbelievable sexual prowess. When all was done, the men chuckled at the fact that they'd hit their climax one behind the other. With a whisper, Tami signaled me and we inconspicuously made our hasty exit from the room.

Back in the dressing lounge, Tami thanked me and gave me a big hug and kiss, then went over to her makeup table and pulled an envelope out of the top drawer. There was a wad of cash inside and she gave half of it to me.

"This is yours, girl. Five hundred dollars. Not bad for a newbie. Didn't know you had it in you." Tami kissed me on the mouth and handed me the money. Stunned, I kissed her back, enjoying her soft, warm lips.

"You'd better go before I make you my bitch," she warned.

We waited for our subjects to enter the shower before cleaning ourselves up, and when I snapped out of my erotic trance and said good night, I headed home on the subway with a pocketful of quick-and-easy cash. Words could not describe how much I'd enjoyed the control I'd had over my boss, making it all the better that he hadn't had a clue. I was finally getting a taste of what it felt like to really have power and control over others, and I liked it. It was at that moment that I knew there would be no turning back. My fancy had been tickled and my palate was anxious to try a full-course meal.

nine

erotic city

With all the hours I started putting in at Magic Hands, my dream of becoming an actress seemed to keep getting pushed farther and farther out of my reach. Hooked on the money I was making at the parlor, there was no time for me to go on auditions. Although I was making a lot of cash, my financial situation was still unstable. Never knowing the definition of the word *budget,* I had a bad habit of spending money faster than I made it. If I had a good week, with lots of extra duties and tips, I did OK. But if we were slow or I only did what I was hired to do, I ran into problems. While the parlor paid well, my appetite for designer clothing, fine restaurants, and expensive things had reached an all-time high. I had also acquired a marijuana addiction that had me spending money on several dime bags a day. That being the case, when the first of the month crept up on me, I often found myself scrambling to put together my portion of the household bills.

After being unable to reach my pal George one time too many, I decided to pick up a copy of the *Village Voice* in hopes that it would have some listings that would allow me to make some quick extra cash. While I didn't want to get a new job, I definitely needed a second gig to help me come up with my share of the monthly household funds.

Nestling deeply into my newly purchased Ralph Lauren down comforter and matching throw pillows, I cruised through the ads of the paper. At first glance, I really didn't see anything that I could do, and there certainly weren't many jobs that paid daily. But as I flicked through to the back, there on the final page was a big bold ad that read: "Exotic Dancers Wanted. Make Top Dollar Up to $300.00 Day Shift/$500.00 Nights. Earn $1000.00 Minimum Weekly!"

I stared at the ad, contemplating whether I had what it took to be an exotic dancer—a stripper.

"Could I do that?" I asked myself out loud.

I walked over to my full-length mirror, took my clothes off, and stared at my body, twisting this way and that. Pleased at the reflection that stared back at me, I ran over to the dresser and turned on my boom box to see if I could dance sexy and exotically. Fixated on my own eyes, I struck provocative poses and smiled, and once I got more comfortable with my own reflection, I began twirling around the room like a pro. I jumped on the bed in a heated frenzy and started to grind, arching back on my legs and thrusting my hips upward. Then I flipped over onto my hands and knees and started grinding over an imaginary man. I thought of Jennifer Beals in the movie *Flashdance* and told myself that I was better than she was. After all, I was a born dancer, and if she could do it, so could I.

"Ha, ha, ha, yes! I can do this!" I laughed, lighthearted and hopeful again. I quickly grabbed my clothes off the floor and put them on, then ripped the ad out of the newspaper and ran to the phone. I dialed the number and asked for the contact name when a mature-sounding voice answered.

"This is Jack Woods. How can I help you?" the voice said.

"Hi. My name is Simone and I saw your ad in the *Village Voice*. Are you having auditions for exotic dancers?" I inquired hopefully.

"Yes, if you're pretty, young, and in good shape. You ever dance before?" he asked.

"Well, not nude . . ." I hesitated, wondering if I should lie. "But people tell me all the time how good I look. And I know I'm a great dancer!"

"OK. Well then, let's set up an appointment. Are you eighteen or older?"

"Yes."

"Then when can you come in?"

"How about right now?"

"Wow, you don't waste any time. But I like that." He then gave me the address. "It's suite number twenty-four F."

"I'm on my way," I replied, jotting down the information on a nearby scrap of paper. When I hung up, I hurried to pick out something sexy to wear and headed out the door. Scared and excited, I hoped I was ready for whatever the exotic dancing world had to offer.

When I arrived at the address, I was in awe of the thirty-story posh office building. I walked into the gold-accented lobby and was greeted by a smiling uniform-clad doorman who eagerly pointed me in the direction of the elevators after announcing my arrival to the resident in Suite 24F.

Once upstairs, I nervously walked down the long marble hall toward the door. I took a glimpse at myself in the shiny chrome between the panels that separated the elevators. When I finally reached the end of the hall and saw the sign that read "The Jack Wood's Agency," I turned the doorknob and slowly entered. A melodious bell chimed to alert those inside that a visitor had arrived, and from what I assumed was a back office, a middle-aged man emerged.

"Simone?" the tall, pasty-complexioned, goofy-looking man with a crooked smile and chipped front tooth asked.

"Yes?" I asked.

"Jack Woods," he announced, gripping my hand tightly. "Sit down, make yourself comfortable."

He seemed a little seedy but had a nice aura about him. From the looks of the place, I could see that his business was booming. The office was plush, with hot new art deco furniture and strikingly bold-colored walls, which created a dazzling high-powered atmosphere. Still the office didn't match the man, which sort of threw me off, since Jack looked so nerdy.

"You got a very nice place. I love your taste." I smiled.

"Thank you. I have a lot of help around here," he replied, looking me up and down. "So let me take a good look at you."

He approached me, slowly walking around where I stood.

"Take your jacket off so I can see your figure," he said, standing directly in front of me and lifting my chin. He then tilted my head to both sides and looked deeply into my eyes. I momentarily felt like a fertile slave on an auction block in Mississippi, but quickly shook the feeling, knowing that it was his duty to fully inspect his goods.

"Doesn't look like you do heavy drugs. Ever snort or shoot up?" he asked.

I screwed up my face and answered emphatically, "No!"

"Relax, relax," he chuckled. "I have to ask these questions."

"OK . . ." I replied, calming down.

"Well, you are pretty. But I have to warn you. It is harder for an Afro-American girl on the road. But then again, you may get some of the best gigs because of your color. Some guys actually have what I like to call a jungle-fever fetish. I don't make the rules but I do think we can make it work if you are willing to give it a try. You're fresh out of the box and you say you can dance, so hopefully your race won't be an issue." He shrugged.

"Well, I've never had a problem so far," I informed him, a little insulted.

"And I hope you never do," he retorted. "Very well. Why don't you go into the bathroom—no, on second thought, why don't you do a little something for me right here? And if you're as good as you say you are, I'll give you a shot."

I raised an eyebrow, hoping that he wasn't some sort of freak using the agency as a front to lust over naked girls, but decided to take a chance anyway. If I really wanted to make the kind of cash the ad promised, I knew I had to be fearless and bold, and not worry about what would or could go wrong in any given situation. From the look on his face, I could tell that Jack was a bit skeptical about me and probably thought I was shy, but he was in for a shocking surprise. I was determined to give him the thrill of his life and in full Carmen mode, I purred, "Turn the music up . . ."

Jack walked over to the stereo and cranked up the volume. I instinctively moved behind him and pushed him down into his black leather egg-shaped chair. Then I spun around and jumped on top of him straddling his lap and swinging my head from left to right, swooping my long wavy hair all over his face like I was riding a bull in a rodeo. As his eyes popped, I jumped up and spun around on the floor, ripping my clothes off like a wild woman. Like a seasoned stripper, I swung my clothes around like a lasso high above my head before throwing them his way. Once I was totally naked, I started making love to the floor, seductively thrusting my hips around, bouncing from spilt to spilt, giving him a side view and a back view as he sat in awe of the fact that I was able to remain perfectly in rhythm with the music.

Jack sat watching me, totally engrossed, and judging by the growing bulge in his pants, mesmerized and excited. As the heavily bassed music set the tone of the atmosphere, I was in a trance, captivated by its hypnotic beat. The cool breeze from the air conditioner caressed my nipples, making them hard and alert, perched upon my firm titties as they softly jiggled up and down, which seemed to add to Jack's delight. Sensing his excitement, I proceeded to back my round plump ass up onto his lap and rubbed back and forth across his hard cock, barely touching him at times, teasing him and making him yearn for more.

My lap dance drove Jack absolutely crazy, but I still wanted to push the meter further and show him that I was down for whatever and not about to let my skin color stop me in any way. So I spun around and knelt down in front of him and in one swift motion, started stroking his dick through his jeans with a devilish look in my eyes. Slightly embarrassed, since he hadn't expected me to touch him, Jack turned red and involuntarily began jerking as he bust a nut right in his pants. After his climax, I let go of his pants and twirled up from the floor just as the song ended. I curtsied like a cute ballerina who had just performed in *The Nutcracker Suite*, which in a way, I had.

"Wow! You have a gift!" he sighed, clapping exhaustedly as if I had zapped all of his energy.

"Forget everything I said before," he told me. "You're going to be big, Simone Young. *Really* big! And this is what we are going to do. I'm going to call you later and I'm sure I'll have a gig for you. Let me take some Polaroids of you and I'll work my magic."

"OK!" I exclaimed, proud of a job well done. Once he had snapped the pictures, I grabbed my clothes and ran to the bathroom. When the door closed behind me, I jumped up and down with joy. I had impressed another asshole and I knew I was good! As I caught my breath, I got dressed and fixed my hair in the mirror before exiting the bathroom with a confident smile on my face. Hoping that I had done a well enough job for him to believe in me, I decided to push the meter just a little more and make a final request before I headed on my way.

"Hey Jack, thanks a lot. But, could I ask you a little favor?" I began.

"Sure."

"It's the beginning of the month and my rent's due. Do you think you could spot me some money until you get me my first job? I'll pay you back out of my first check."

Jack stood up and smiled.

"I don't usually do this, but I got a feeling you're gonna make me a lot of money, so here's something to hold you over. I'm pretty sure I can get you on this tour that's leaving tomorrow."

"A tour? How exciting!" I exclaimed.

"Yeah. We send our girls all over the world. The Fiji Islands, Turks and Cacaos, you name it. We supply the most superb girls to fulfill many exotic fantasies."

"Do I have to sign something?"

"I don't deal with all that legal mumbo-jumbo stuff. I get you work. They pay me, I pay you. As long as I like you and you like me, we can play together. If either of us stops having fun, the game is over. So go home and pack. I'll give you a call later with the details," he said as he reached into his wallet and handed me a wad of twenties.

"Thanks!" I exclaimed, not expecting it to happen that fast or easy.

When I arrived home, I was too excited for words. I immediately started packing my things and sat by the phone waiting for it to ring. I daydreamed about what it was going to be like being on tour as an exotic dancer. I could only imagine how many interesting people I was going to meet and how much money I was going to make traveling to tropical lands. I was a little sad about leaving Magic Hands, but I was very eager to see what was ahead. I figured I would call Wellington from the road so that he couldn't talk me out of my decision, and hoped that he'd forgive me for leaving the parlor without notice.

Since I had no idea what to put in my bags, I decided to pack everything that was important to me. I didn't know what to expect and wanted to be ready for anything the adventure had to offer. As I forced the lid of my Louis Vuitton suitcase closed, I heard the phone ring and leaped across the room to get it.

"Hello?"

"Simone Young please," Jack Woods began.

"Hi, Jack. It's me."

"Well, Ms. Lady, I hope you're packed and ready to go to the fabulous city of Atlanta!" he exclaimed like Bob Barker on *The Price Is Right*.

I stared at the phone like he was crazy. Atlanta? There was nothing exotic about Georgia.

"Atlanta? That's not exotic or international!" I frowned as if I had tasted sour milk.

"For your information, little girl, Atlanta happens to be one of the world's wealthiest cities and it has a mecca of strip joints. I have a close relationship with the owner of one of the city's hottest clubs, so you'll be in safe hands. They're good people down there. In fact, it's a black-owned spot so you'll fit in just fine. And they'll also cover your room and board. They keep a house for all the out-of-town girls. You can work part-time or full-time shifts, six days a week for three weeks. And the best thing about this is that you can make up to eight thousand dollars if you stay for the duration." He hadn't had my full attention until the payout left his lips.

"Say what?" I asked, damn near dropping the phone.

"Eight grand, for twenty-one days of work," he reiterated.

"So what do I got to do?" I asked, slightly skeptical, since it sounded too good to be true. I was praying that he wasn't gonna tell me that I had to fuck any chickens or anything crazy like that.

"Exactly what you did in my office," Jack told me. He informed me that there would be a ticket waiting for me at the Delta counter at Kennedy Airport at nine A.M. the next day. He gave me my flight number and departure time before reassuring me that once I landed, someone from the club would be there to meet me.

"There'll be two other girls going with you, so hopefully the three of you will get to know each other during the flight," Jack said in conclusion. When I placed the receiver back into its cradle, my heart raced with anticipation. A new chapter in my life was about to unfold and I was more than ready for it. And while Atlanta, Georgia, wasn't one of the glamorous places I yearned to visit, the bank damn sure was.

I arrived early at the airport armed with all of my most-prized possessions—my Louis duffel bag, my makeup case, and my trusty backpack that I carried at all times filled with all of my most treasured stuff. Not realizing how I must have looked to strangers, I even had my little brown teddy bear dangling beneath my arm. Tick Tock was my good-luck bear and I'd had him since I was a baby. He was one of the few things that had survived my childhood and that's how I knew he was lucky. We both were.

I was glad my flight was in the morning because it didn't give me time to get sad and misty-eyed about saying good-bye to my roomies. Ebony and Jessie had gotten up to see me off but we had not actually discussed what I was going to do. All they knew was that I had a dancing gig in Atlanta.

Physically strong and tough for my petite frame, without a care in the world, I carried all of my bags through the spacious terminal. The airport was crowded with people scurrying to get to their destinations. Since I had never flown before, this was a new experience for me. When I finally made my way through the mob, I obtained my ticket and checked all of my bags except for my knapsack. Then with a sigh of relief, I dropped down into one of the hard plastic seats, hoping to catch my breath before I boarded the plane. As I focused on the activity around me, I felt a gentle tap on my shoulder. When I turned around, standing behind me were two sexy young girls, about my age, holding hands and smiling. I looked them up and down and before I could say a word, the taller one spoke.

"Are you Simone?" she asked. She was a pretty dark-skinned Latina with thick flowing hair and boobs that resembled fresh ripe cantaloupes.

"Yeah. You two must be the other girls Jack told me about. How'd you know who I was?" I questioned, glad to have some company.

This time the other chick, fair-skinned with long red locks, replied, "Honey, you look and smell like a stripper in training!" She reached out a long manicured finger and ran her fake nail down the center of my V-neck T-shirt. A little embarrassed, I really didn't want to look like I just fell off the cabbage truck.

"Is it that obvious?" I asked.

"Don't worry. We all had to start somewhere. I'm Precious and this is my girl, Diamond," she announced, pulling her friend aggressively to her side and giving her a wet and juicy French kiss. I shook my head, thinking, *Look at these two tonguing each other down in the middle of the airport.*

They certainly weren't amateurs and seemed to know exactly what they were doing. People glanced—some in delight, some in disgust—as they watched Precious and Diamond go at it.

"Ah, excuse me . . ." I snapped.

"Oh, we're sorry! We just make each other so horny! We're a team act, ya know. We dance together. The guys seem to like it when we bend over and shake our asses in the air at the same time." They looked at each other and burst out laughing.

"I bet they do!" I smirked.

"Well, we hope you enjoy your stay in Atlanta. We live there but we travel all the time. You one of Jack's girls?" Diamond stated.

"Yeah. You, too?" I asked.

"Sometimes. His commission is too high, though. So the job has really gotta pay for it to be worth our while," she continued, still focused on me.

Hoping they would be seated somewhere far away from me, as I wasn't in the mood to be embarrassed by these two freaky girls who couldn't keep their hands off each other, I was disappointed to see that we were all seated in the same row. I didn't mind doing my thing behind closed doors, but I wasn't big on public spectacles, which they seemed to enjoy. Once on board, they made a scene in the narrow aisle, and as much as I tried to act like I wasn't with them, it was evident that we were all together. I did my best to ignore them and concentrate on my thoughts. My mind raced with expectations and I closed my eyes to think about all the things I was going to do with my eight thousand dollars. I also thought about Diamond's words, wondering how much Jack was getting if I was walking away with eight grand. I had never thought about asking him what the split was going to be. All I knew was that eight thousand dollars was more money than I had ever seen in my life!

I could feel the motion of the plane as it took off down the runway and then lifted. I could also hear Precious and Diamond beside me, kissing and rubbing on each other. When I took a peek on the sly, Precious and Diamond were nose to nose, giggling and whispering to each other as if they were in their own little world.

As I tried hard not to concentrate on what was happening, I suddenly saw the flight attendant out of the corner of my eye approaching our seats. Oblivious, Precious and Diamond remained fixated on each other. As the stone-faced, missile-breasted stewardess reached us, Diamond suddenly came so hard that all of her juices squirted out onto the fabric-covered seat. With a quickness, we all straightened up in our seats and tried to act like nothing was going on.

"Is there a problem?" the attendant asked with an attitude, not quite certain if she had seen what she thought she saw.

They giggled softly before Precious decided to answer, "Ah, yes! I was wondering if you had another blanket."

The flight attendant said nothing but walked off in a huff, rolling her eyes. Speechless, I looked at my two new friends.

"You two are crazy!" I laughed.

"You ain't seen nothin' yet, *chica*! We're just having a little fun!"

The flight went by quickly, and before I knew it, we were landing in the state known for its plump ripe peaches. As the lights in the cabin came on, I opened my eyes and stretched, ready to start collecting my cash.

In silence, the three of us exited the aircraft and headed down to baggage claim. As I looked through the sea of people, there were folks waiting, holding up signs that said "Welcome Home" and things of that nature. However, none of them had our names posted, making me a little nervous. Sensing my concern, Diamond assured me,

"Don't worry. Kareem will be here to pick us up. He's usually a little late, but he always shows up."

Just as she had promised, after we had gotten our luggage, a smooth-looking cat in a black pinstripe suit approached us with a devilish grin splashed upon his face. He was a cool-looking brotha' with smooth chocolate skin and light brown eyes. He was a little rough around the edges, but that only added to his sexiness. He had a cocky but humorous way about him, but he also looked like if you crossed him, he'd take care of you in the worst way.

Both Diamond and Precious hugged Kareem tightly before they handed him their bags and made a formal introduction.

"Kareem, this is Simone. She's a new jack so go easy on her," Precious told him with a wink.

"Easy is as easy does," Kareem said slyly as he looked me up and down, licking his lips, before reaching out his hand for a shake.

With my knapsack firmly in place upon my back, we headed toward the parking lot, where we piled into Kareem's black SUV. Precious and Diamond jumped into the rear seats where they got comfortable and got back into their signature petting and necking. I, on the other hand, relaxed as I cozied into the plush leather seat ready to have a friendly chat with Kareem.

As we cruised along North Terminal Parkway, I fervently soaked in the warm Georgia sunshine and clear blue sky. It was an absolutely picture-perfect day—perfect for a new career, perfect for a new life, and perfect for me to take up official residency in the land of anything goes.

ten

from the pole to riches

As we approached my new place of employment, I felt like we had landed in Vegas instead of Atlanta. Kareem pulled in to his VIP parking spot and I was immediately told that Vanity was the hottest gentlemen's club in the country.

"Chicks come from near and far trying to get a chance to dance here. But only a few are chosen," he told me.

On the outside of the club, like some sort of big-budget Hollywood movie premier, bright lights beamed out from every angle, even though it was only two in the afternoon. The brilliant colors sparkled up and down the block drawing attention to the building as if it were silently extending an invitation to anyone with a pocketful of cash. As we crossed the threshold, Precious and Diamond left me in the dust as they headed off in different directions. I, on the other hand, walked apprehensively into the establishment, greeted by the sounds of Big Daddy Kane's "Raw" thumping in sync with the palpitations that fluttered in my chest.

"Simone, let's go to my office so I can go over the rules of the club with you. After that, I'll show you around. Then I'll take you to the house where you'll be staying with the rest of the out-of-town girls." Kareem looked at me and hesitated at the door. He must have seen the look of reservation on my face. My insecurities had kicked in and I wondered if I was truly ready for prime time. I thought I would be starting my career in some small after-hours spot with cheap liquor and a tiny stage. I had no idea that my first gig would be in a five-thousand-square-foot multimillion-dollar club where nothing but ballas and wannabe ballas freely roamed with their anxious dicks and hefty wallets.

"Hey, kid," Kareem said soothingly. "Don't worry. You're in good hands.

I know this is your first time out, but trust me, you'll do fine. You wouldn't be here if we didn't believe that."

I'd heard *that* one before. I knew from experience that I could never really trust someone when they said "Trust me." Both my sister's pimp and my father's absence had taught me that. But my journey had forced my skin to thicken and my back to straighten. And even if I was terrified, it was nobody's business.

Fear is a sign of weakness that gives predators the green light to devour you, I told myself. I had read that somewhere. Or maybe I saw it in a *Rocky* movie? Whatever. I needed something to get me to the next level. Mind over matter.

I strolled deeper into the club with a sweet sex appeal that came out of nowhere, psyching myself out and telling myself that I was ready.

Kareem took me around back and through a narrow kitchen. The smell of chicken wings and pizza mixed with alcohol lingered in the air. We walked through the kitchen and out a door that put us beside the main bar. I had to hustle to keep up with him or else I would have gotten left behind yet again. With pep in my step, I followed him around the corner, watching as he ignored the buxom female who hounded him as he got to the door of his office. He entered the security code that unlocked the door and stepped aside for me to enter.

"Chyna, not now," he scolded the thickly built caramel-complexioned girl with long golden braids. "I got business to take care of. Simone here is a new girl and I'm setting her up. Get your ass out there and make some money. Don't let me have to tell you twice! Now bounce!"

"Fuck that bitch!" Chyna snarled.

Hyped from the thump in my chest and anxious to establish myself in my new environment, I snapped my head around and barked, "I got your bitch, *bitch!*"

"OK, OK! Chill! Chyna get back to work; Simone, have a seat," Kareem instructed. I did as I was told but not before rolling my eyes and sucking my teeth in defiance. Kareem's office was cluttered with papers and boxes of T-shirts with the club's logo on them. Along the wall were autographed pictures of celebrities and adult movie stars who had been featured at the club. I stared at the photos while Kareem answered questions and gave quick orders to the rest of the passersby before rushing them away from his door.

"My bad. Some of these girls in here like trouble, so make sure you watch your back. Chyna is a real hater. She especially doesn't like new girls who come in and try and take her paper. The only reason I don't fire her ass is because most of her regulars are big spenders," he said, partly in warning.

"Thanks for the heads-up, but I think I can handle myself. I know how to tame a bitch!" I replied, no stranger to handling the antics of jealous heffas on the streets of Brooklyn. Chyna was the least of my concerns as I became engrossed in the bevy of glamorous shots plastered around Kareem's office. And instead of thinking about Chyna's envy, I was far more interested in how to get my own picture up on that wall.

"Have all these adult stars performed here?" I asked, observing all the naked lusciousness staring back at me from the walls.

"Yeah. We get a new one in every week. It's a good arrangement for the club because it brings in new clientele. But back to business. Are you ready for the rules?"

"Yeah. Shoot," I replied, now paying attention.

"As you know, this is a nude club. Not a topless bar. So you strip till you're bare-ass naked. You're not allowed to touch the customers and they can't touch you. You get fifteen minutes on the stage and then you work the crowd and do table dances for another fifteen. After that, you take a break for thirty, then you're back up on the stage for your next dance. You do six sets per night and then your shift is done. That's considered the part-time shift. So if you wanna work full-time, you dance twelve sets but that's up to you. I must stress that you wear a garter to collect your money. The garter must be on your leg 'cause that's the law. And lastly, no fraternizing with the customers or the staff. You got it?"

I looked at Kareem with a baffled look on my face.

"That's a lot to remember. You got the Cliff Notes version of that?" I asked.

"I hope you are kidding," Kareem drily replied.

"Yeah, I'm kidding." I chuckled, trying to play it off.

"Cool," he laughed in return. "So, you got a stage name?"

"Yeah, Simone Young," I answered, not about to start calling myself some sort of silly moniker like Peachy or Pumpkin.

"That's all right for now, but you should think about one. You might not want customers walking up to you on the street yelling out your government name." He was right.

"Now, I need you to sign some paperwork and then I'll take you to the house so you can settle in and meet the other girls. Your main salary goes to Jack but you get to keep your tips each night. Oh, by the way, you have to tip the deejay and pay the house forty dollars every night. That's a small price to pay for all the loot you'll be making from table dances and doing your set."

I continued to smile and nod my head like I was totally clear on it all. I knew I'd have to take baby steps before I got the hang of how things really operated, but thank God I was a fast learner. After I had signed my life away, Kareem opened his bottom desk draw and pulled out a Polaroid camera.

"Let's see what you got." He smiled.

"You waste no time," I tensely giggled.

"I need a picture to put in your file. That's all. You ain't got shit I ain't seen before, trust me," he explained. There was that phrase again. I knew he was full of shit but since I was in a playful mood, I decided to go along with his request. After all, I couldn't exactly get shy now.

"You got any dollar bills? Ha ha hmm," I asked, holding out my hand.

"Smile for the camera, little lady," he answered, ignoring my question.

I stood in the middle of Kareem's office and seductively removed my pants to the low sound of the music that played in the distance. Then I took off my bra and swung it around in the air like a lasso. With a twinkle in my eye, I offered him the cutest and most genuine smile that I had, hoping he would melt and be excited at the thought of my overwhelming potential. When I was done, Kareem peeped over the camera and stared at me, rubbing his crotch as if to tame his quickly rising manhood.

"Jack was right. You're gonna do good in this biz." He grinned.

His words were like music to my ears, boosting my confidence level up ten notches. As I began to put my clothes back on, there was a knock at the door before a cute honey-complexioned girl wearing two bouncy ponytails with pink satin ribbons walked in. She smiled at me as she passed and walked over to the other side of Kareem's desk, dropping to her knees.

"Simone, go check out the club. I'll meet you outside in about ten minutes. I have some business to take care of," he stated.

"Sure," I replied.

Knowing what was about to go down in my new boss's office, I headed out into the dimly lit club as the blasting music hit my eardrums and made the floors vibrate. I strutted my stuff over to the bar, passing other dancers and customers, and could feel everyone staring at me. As I walked like a peacock among pigeons, guys tried to touch me and ask me to dance but I kept walking, remembering what Kareem had said about fraternizing with the customers. At the bar, in an effort to calm my nerves, I bummed a cigarette from the bartender, although I wished I'd had a joint. I then ordered a Corona with lime before turning to watch the girls swing around the poles on the main stage. Their slick bodies seemed to glow beneath the hazy red lights. Smoke blew from fog machines across the stage creating a mystical glow, as bikini tops and g-strings came off with ease and were tossed into the air. Then I realized that none of the girls were actually dancing. They just walked up and down the stage grinding their hips back and forth up and down the pole, shaking their asses to the beat. And truth be told, Vanity had some of the hottest asses I had ever seen in my life. While I was definitely no slouch, I had a tiny butt compared to the moneymakers on that stage. But for the first time, I felt comfortable about dancing because I knew I could outdance any bitch in that place. I smiled to myself in anticipation and couldn't wait to show my stuff. I planned on becoming one of the biggest moneymakers Vanity had ever seen—without the enormous ass.

Disrupting my train of thought, several customers approached me as I sat at the bar and said hello. I invited them all to come by and see me dance the next day, as I sipped my brew and smiled like Miss America. I had just taken the final puff on my Newport when that queen bitch, Chyna, walked up to me and cut her eyes.

"So, new bitch," she began with a deep Georgian drawl as she leaned against the bar. "I can tell you think you're hot and whatnot, but I'ma tell you once and only once. Stay the fuck outta my way and we'll be cool. Step on my toes and cut in on my profit and you'll wish you never walked the fuck up in this bitch!" she barked.

I looked her up and down. She stood about five feet eight inches and weighed in at around 165. She was a thick biscuit-and-gravy-eating Southern bitch with a triple-D bra, ass for days, and one of the tiniest waists I had ever laid eyes on. Her microscopic golden-colored braids gently swept across the crack of her rotund behind and her eyes were slanted like she was some distant kin to Bruce Lee. If she hadn't been such a bitch, she mighta been fine. But as her warning rang in my ears, I had to refrain from punching her right in her face. I wasn't about to let her end my career before it started. She was clearly going to be a problem, but I was way too smart to let her get me fired, which was what I'm sure she was going to try to do. Still, I had to show this bitch that I was not one to be fucked with. Rising from the bar stool, I positioned myself directly in her face and with the coolness of a cucumber said, "Fuck with me if you want to, bitch. But if your shit was so tight around here, you wouldn't be sweating my new jack ass. So all you really saying is that you know you could never be on my level. So stop trying to climb!"

Just as old girl was about to go off, Kareem walked up—and not a minute too soon—and interrupted what might have been a brawl.

"You ready?" he asked me.

"More than you know," I answered, still not taking my eye off the enemy.

On the way out, I turned to wave good-bye to the bartender and gave Chyna the finger. As Kareem and I headed over to my new home, I dismissed the thought of her jealous ass and kept my eye on my eight-thousand-dollar prize.

I was overly impressed by the gated community that housed the condo where I would be staying for the next three weeks. The grounds were impeccably manicured with freshly mowed lawns and perfectly groomed trees.

We parked in a spot directly in front of the corner unit and Kareem led me inside. The condo was large, elegant, and inviting, with an expensive, modern cream-colored leather sectional sitting smack dead in the center of the living room. The powder-blue carpet was so thick, my feet sank three inches into its depth, and the walls were adorned with exquisite original gallery-quality prints. From the looks of the place, I knew I would be very comfortable during my temporary stay. I only hoped my new roommates weren't as nasty as Chyna.

"What's up, ladies? This is your new roommate, Simone," Kareem announced as he dropped my bag in the foyer.

"Hey Simone!" the girls happily greeted me in unison.

"This is Maria, Candee, and Peaches," he said, making the introductions.

Maria, the mother of the house, was a mature Spanish woman who had aged well and still had her good looks. Candee, a bouncing, big-busted light-skinned chick with thick strawberry blond tresses that fell upon her delicate shoulders, was dressed in pink from head to toe; while Peaches, a cute, brown-skinned girl with deep sexy dimples and an "onion" booty, smiled and offered a friendly wave before grabbing my bags and heading up the stairs.

"Come on, girl. We're gonna get you set up!" Peaches said excitedly.

"You are so cute, like a little black Barbie doll. You mind if I play with you some time?" Candee coyly asked, not wasting any time letting her desires be known.

The girls giggled their way down the hall to show me my room. I was so happy that they were welcoming and nice, making me feel like I had entered some sort of *Facts of Life* dormitory. Before I heard the door slam downstairs, Kareem shouted up, "Simone, I'll be back to pick you up tomorrow at eleven A.M. Your shift starts at noon."

"Yeah, yeah, she'll be ready," Maria huffed in her heavy Hispanic accent, thick with slurs. "Now don't you worry. Go! Leave the girls to get acquainted," Maria snapped, as she shooed Kareem out the door.

"You'll be sharing a room with me," Candee stated, a little too happily.

"Cool," I smiled, scanning the spacious area. There were two beds lined up at two separate ends of the room with enough space between them to do three cartwheels. On the walls were cool psychedelic posters and pretty brightly colored, freshly cut flowers on both adjacent nightstands. Blue scarves were draped over the lampshades, creating warm sapphire hues that cascaded around the room. I felt relaxed, at ease, and at home. The atmosphere was girlie and romantic, the perfect setting for three pretty girls to explore themselves—and each other.

"We're gonna have fun being roomies!" Peaches exclaimed.

I placed my backpack on the vacant bed beside the window and claimed it as my own. "I like this," I announced.

"Before the night is over you'll be liking me, too." Candee slyly grinned. She was relentless, but Peaches quickly came to my rescue.

"Stop messing with her, Candee. Simone, you'll have to watch her. She loves to turn girls out," she warned.

"Tell you what. I'll let you know if I'm interested. But for now you stay on your side of the room," I said with a smile.

As the evening progressed, we got to know one another as we shared personal stories about ourselves and how we ended up in Atlanta and dancing at Club Vanity. They also filled me in on some of the rumors they had heard about the club in the streets.

"I hear they actually pay off the county police to make sure they aren't hassled," Maria, who was by far the most knowledgeable of our bunch, stated informatively. According to the girls, Club Vanity was a moneymaking cow. More than a hundred thousand dollars came through its doors every week thanks to all the high rollers who frequented the club. But they warned me to be careful of the vultures who would come in and try to take advantage of the girls' dreams with promises they would never fulfill.

"They'll seduce you with big promises, when all they really want is to have a piece of ego-boosting eye candy on their arm and personal entertainment for the themselves and their friends," Candee warned.

"That is, until they get tired of you and toss you back out into the real world," Peaches added as if she was speaking from experience.

The hands on the clock moved swiftly and as I listened to all their tales of wisdom and caution, my eyes became heavy. When Maria and Peaches finally left the room, Candee and I climbed into our beds. I quickly scanned my new surroundings, and as I closed my eyes, I dreamed of the big day I had ahead of me. Sinking deeply into the cottony soft blanket that engulfed my body, I stared out the window at the half moon, ready and willing to shoot for it. I was very excited to embark on new possibilities, and as I fell asleep to the sound of Candee snoring peacefully, I knew the sky was the limit.

Just as he had promised, Kareem arrived at eleven o'clock to pick us up. I felt weird transforming into a sex kitten so early in the morning. Who in their right mind would be in a strip joint at noon?

When we arrived at the club, we entered through the back and as we passed through the main area, I noticed that the room was packed with men in suits. It was as if a bunch of doctors, lawyers, and executives were having the lunch meeting of their lives and I smelled the wonderful scent of money in the air.

I followed closely behind Peaches as she dashed down the stairs to the basement, to where the dancers' dressing room was. I saw an empty locker and grabbed it, hoping to make it my own, and as I looked around, I was surprised at how nasty the place was. It was a musty box with rusted pipes and peeling walls. There were dingy chairs sparsely scattered throughout and it smelled like a rancid combination of cheap perfume and pussy.

"Unfortunately alotta girls like to steal around here, so make sure you have a strong lock," Peaches warned. I had just sat down on an empty chair in front of the mirror in an effort to get ready for my debut, when that damn Chyna came busting through the door with a bang.

"Bitch, why you in my seat?" she bellowed as she ran up on me and knocked me out of the chair. Off guard and totally taken by surprise, I hit the ground with a thud but instinctively jumped up off the floor and charged her ass with every ounce of force I could muster up inside my one-hundred-pound body. Obviously not thinking that I had it in me, I knocked her ass down with all my might and landed fully on top of her where I began banging her head repeatedly upon the dirty floor. With her braids tangled between my fingers, she tried to defend herself but was clearly no match for me, as I had already pounced on her like an angry tigress defending her young. Both Peaches and Candee tried to break up the fight, getting in between Chyna and me and struggling to keep us on opposite sides of the room. When the smoke cleared, my hair was all over the place and Chyna was missing a few braids.

As she straightened out her clothes, she spat, "This ain't over, bitch! Ya best watch your back!"

Angry and out of sorts, we both knew that I had gotten the best of her, as a long scratch down her right cheek clearly indicated. In response to her threat, I tightly gripped three of her braids and yelled,

"Fuck you! Come get your hair, ya stink ho!"

When I looked around the room, I noticed that all eyes were on me, making me feel a little embarrassed about my display. But I knew what they were thinking. Here I was, all of five feet tall, wearing out this big southern bitch like I was the heavyweight champion of the world.

"All right, ya'all. Show's over! It's time to get paid!" Peaches hollered now, back in business mode.

I took a minute and pulled myself together, shocked that I'd had to whip a bitch's ass after only three minutes on the job. But as if I hadn't just been rolling on the floor, the other girls came up to me and began introducing themselves with handshakes and finger waves as they welcomed me to the club.

"So what are you wearing on stage?" Cheyenne, a pretty olive-complexioned girl with long auburn tresses, asked.

"Well, I brought a g-string and a bra. But I kinda thought they were gonna have costumes here," I replied, realizing that the room didn't have anything in it for the girls other than asbestos poisoning. Everyone laughed at my ignorant assumption.

"Girl, the only thing Vanity gives us for free is a headache!" a girl who introduced herself as Kitty cackled, and the others followed behind her in hysterics.

"Girl, you need some gear. We'll hook you up this time, but you better get your ass to the mall and pick you up some shit as soon as possible," Candee offered, feeling sorry for me.

Like a bunch of older sisters, the girls gathered around and performed magic on my makeup and hair. They then gave me a pair of red vinyl hot pants and a white sequined tube top to put on. Just as they finished up, a knock came at the door, and a fine-looking brotha stuck his head in the door.

"Simone, you're up next!" He smiled, looking me up and down before dipping back out.

"That's Rich," Peaches told me. "He's the deejay."

No sooner had he shut the door when Sparkle, a very dark-skinned chick with long, jet black, Indian-textured hair and the highest cheekbones I had ever seen, told me to watch out for him.

"That's Kareem's nephew and he likes to live a little on the dangerous side," she said with a heavy African accent.

"I'm starting to like danger more and more every day." I smiled, licking my lips and thinking he was fine as hell.

"Well, the dangerous deejay is calling your name to go out on stage. Good luck!" Candee said with a wink. My heart immediately fell to my stomach as my new friends rushed me out the door and up to the stage. I stood there with a huge lump in my throat and waited for the curtains to open. The music blaring through the speakers and bouncing off the walls of the club was 2 Live Crews' "We Want Some Pussy." The music had me pumped and I twirled out into a spin down the main stage and stopped to steady myself at the pole before swinging around it. I slid down the pole facing it with my pussy pressed up against its coolness and spread my thighs open as wide as I could. As I began to internalize the lyrics of the song, I was compelled to dance my heart out. I did a few of my classic ballet moves up against the pole and mixed in a little modern dance with some hip-hop. With each move I made, the guys seemed to go more and more out of control. I knew it was because my dance style was different from what the other girls had to offer, and they were loving a little variation from what they were used to. However, as I got more into the dancing part of my act, I realized that I was forgetting to strip. But that only created an aspect of anticipation, making my already salivating audience that much hungrier. Feeling as though I had made them wait long enough, when my second song started, I ripped my shirt and hot pants off like Houdini, causing the crowd to go absolutely wild.

The energy from the audience created a magnetic surge throughout my body. No longer in control of myself, I inadvertently dropped down in front of a customer who was standing at the edge of the stage and wrapped my legs around his shoulders. My pussy throbbed just inches away from his lips and I had him drooling like a rabid beast. I then grabbed his head and shoved it between my legs and began rubbing my pussy across the top of his bald head, causing the crowd to go absolutely insane. I was so in the zone that I forgot to pick up the money that was piling up on the floor of the stage. When my third song was over, I took a modest bow and ran around the stage to pick up my loot and as I knelt down to scoop up the last of my cash, a fine-looking Asian man leaned in close and whispered, "Next time come a little closer. I would have given you my credit card and the deed to my house."

The rest of the evening went off without a hitch and my momentum continued. My first performance had been nerve-racking and exciting, but I couldn't wait to do it again. Everyone in the club was amazed by my skills and I felt like an overnight sensation. Kareem was so proud of me that he immediately took me under his wing and introduced me to an associate of his by the name of John Moose.

Kareem told me that John, a middle-aged white man, was a big-timer in the oil business and particularly smitten with me. He was a tall man of medium to slender build, and as he gripped his drink tightly, I noticed that there were a few age spots on his hands. Above his lip sat a lengthy, well-groomed, outdated mustache that curled on both ends, which made me giggle. I knew it was a rare thing to see a wealthy white man in a black strip club, especially one who looked like a stereotypical Texas oil millionaire. He smelled of money, which seemed to permeate the nostrils of all the girls in club who began to hover around as if they wanted to turn him upside down and shake all the money and credit cards from his pockets.

When I approached him, he warmly smiled and led me into the Champagne Room. Every girl in the place wanted to find herself within these highly coveted invitation-only four walls, and as we entered, I immediately took a few sips of my bubbly and thanked him.

"Simone, I just wanted to say you looked great dancing out there. You're graceful, stimulating, and very hot. I'd really like to take you with me to Naples, Florida. When will you get some time off?" he asked. Thinking he was just going to ask for a lap dance, I was a little taken aback by his offer, which caused me to blush and reply,

"That's pretty far. I don't know."

"Of course, you'll be paid handsomely for your presence," he promised.

I shrugged. "Well, if Kareem says you're cool, I guess it'll be OK. I will have some free time in a few weeks." I shrugged again.

"Good! Then it's settled. I usually play golf while I'm there. Do you golf?" he questioned.

"No, never," I replied even though I think he already knew the answer.

After about twenty minutes of small talk, I decided to go see if I could make some more money before my shift ended. Thus I gave Mr. Moose a kiss on his cheek and told him to be sure he followed up with that offer to Naples.

"You know where to find me," I winked. "And thanks for the champagne."

As I began to walk away, Mr. Moose gently pulled me back to stuff two hundred-dollar bills into the palm of my hand.

"Now, *you* have a good day, dear." He smiled before releasing me.

I made so much money that night that I decided to work the late shift as well, and by night's end I was totally exhausted. When I had finished changing and gathering up my belongings, Rich, who I had been flirting with all evening, knocked on the door of the dressing room. With his smooth caramel-colored skin, emerald green eyes, and deeply set dimples, I thought he was not only strikingly handsome but also one of the sexiest men I'd ever met.

"Hey, Simone," he said, smiling. "What are you getting in to tonight?"

"Nothing but sleep. I'm beat. It's been an amazing day!" I huffed.

"Why don't you come take a ride with me on my bike?" he said.

While his offer was tempting, I really didn't want to get into any trouble for fraternizing with the staff, being that I had literally just gotten there. After all, I had probably already broken one of Kareem's many rules by kicking Chyna's ass. But Rich was hard to resist. Not only was he fine and cool, but I had never been on a motorcycle before.

"You make it hard for a girl to turn you down. But I think we should meet down the street," I suggested, remembering Kareem's rule about not fraternizing with the staff.

"Meet you on the corner in five!" He grinned, his dimples sinking deeper into his sexy cheeks.

Rich left the dressing area and headed out of the club. I glanced into the cloudy mirror to fix my curls and makeup and then headed out after him a few minutes later. I managed to sneak out without Kareem seeing me and thought about Peaches's earlier warning before I shook her heavily accented words from my mind. When I exited the club, I saw Rich on the corner waiting. Hoping no one would notice, I quickly ran up behind him and hopped on the back of his bike, wrapping my arms around his waist and holding on as tightly as I could.

We glided through the quiet city streets in the wee hours of the morning, the breeze gently smacking my body as we cut through its stillness. I felt euphoric, engulfed in the night air as the sound of the bike's motor hummed loudly in my ears. When we finally stopped, we were in a dark, lush park with lots of grass and trees. Rich pulled off the road and parked his motorcycle out of site and grabbed me by the hand, leading me into a wooded area not far from the road. He stopped among a cluster of large trees and spun me around to lean me up against the trunk of the nearest one. In one swift motion, he began kissing me passionately up and down my neck, groping my tender breasts and sliding his hands beneath my skirt.

However awkward it was, I could feel myself getting wet thanks to his aggression, which was turning me on. We slid down the tree into the grass, grinding up against each other forcefully. I then unbuckled his pants and pulled his zipper down, stroking his dick over his boxers. As he moaned in ecstasy, I licked the throbbing tip and proceeded to give him the blow job of his life. As if I were sucking sap out of one of the surrounding trees, I made sweet love to his caramel manhood. I gently held the base of his cock with both of my hands and stroked it in rhythm with my head bobbing up and down. I made loud slurping sounds with my mouth and let my thick saliva run down his shaft. I could tell by his moans that he was in heaven and my assumption was confirmed when his body jerked wildly several times, ramming his dick farther back into my throat as he held me in place and busted into my mouth. As his cum squirted from its meaty pistol, I smeared it across my lips and enjoyed its milky flavor before he'd calmed down and pulled my head up from between his legs.

"Damn! You give some serious head. I want more," he groaned. "Come home with me tonight so we can finish what we started. I promise to get you back to the house safe and sound, before anyone wakes up."

"You crazy? I'll get into trouble," I laughed, wiping my mouth.

"No you won't. I do this all the time," he assured me with a shrug.

"Well, you are just going to have to wait for this pussy till *I'm* ready to give it!"

Rich looked frustrated and I could tell that he wasn't accustomed to women telling him no.

"Come on then. I'll take you back to the condo," he snapped.

You gotta make them burn for more. I heard Carmen's third rule echo in my mind. If I had any chance of getting Rich off of me, I knew I couldn't give up the pussy right then and there. He was obviously used to getting all the pussy he wanted, when he wanted—so I had to be different to stand out from the others.

I got up off the ground and dusted myself off. After Rich did the same, we walked back to his bike in silence. He had an attitude, but a smile was plastered upon my face. I knew I'd give in to him eventually, but it would be on my terms, in my time, and at my cost.

eleven

wild style

I had never made more money than I made at Club Vanity in all my life. Even the money I had made with George seemed small in comparison to all the loot I was taking in at that club. My biggest moneymaking night was Monday. That was when most of the hip-hop crews and rappers came in. Notorious for showboating and outdoing one another, they'd crack open bottles of expensive champagne all night long and give very generous tips to the girls they liked most.

One particular Monday night, the club was overly crowded and the cash was flowing like Niagara Falls. Rich was doing his thing in the deejay booth and the music was pumping us all up more than usual. There were five sexy dancers on the stage grinding to the beat as anxious customers salivated at the edge of the stage. The vibe was more festive than usual, as there was a large group of drunken horny guys celebrating a bachelor party. The geeky groom had a Heineken in his hand and a line of vodka shots in front of him as he enjoyed his last night as a single man.

"Yo, yo, what up my niggas? Right now coming to the stage are two of the baddest bitches in this muthafucka! Ya'll give it up for tonight's 'Double your pleasure' feature—Simone and Chyna!" Rick yelled out over the mic, catching me off guard.

I instinctively came running up the stairs when I heard my name, and Chyna was already positioned on the stage working her butt off and trying to showboat. I was hesitant to join her because I wasn't in the mood to fight. However, since I had already been announced, I had no choice but to make my way up to the elevated platform. I seductively strutted out onto the stage and approached the shiny silver pole. When I got there, I wrapped my legs around it and gyrated back and forth as if it was a savory pulsating dick. The crowd hollered uncontrollably for me to give them more. The hoots and hollers that resonated through the air gave me an adrenaline rush and I crawled over to the bachelor party to really do my thing. I yanked the funny-looking groom by his tie and dragged him to the front of the stage as everyone in the place went nuts. I aggressively placed him on his back and squatted down above him. Not to be outdone, Chyna ran over to get in on the action. As I contemplated my next move, Chyna ripped off his belt and yanked down his pants. I could feel his boner nudging up against my ass and giggled as I wrapped the leather strap around his neck, sliding my juicy pussy up to his face.

"You can look but not lick," I informed him.

The groom smiled as I flipped him over on all fours and rode him like the dog he was. As I yanked on his belt and smacked his butt, the crowd threw money at me and begged to be next. Of course, this made Chyna jealous, and knowing she had to kick it up a notch, she grabbed a customer's beer out of his hand just as he was turning it up to take a swig and went back over to the groom to bounce her big titties in his face. The groom bit and nibbled on her voluptuous breasts for a few seconds before Chyna placed the beer bottle down onto the floor of the stage. All of a sudden she broke out and did a split on top of the beer bottle with her pussy lips wrapped tightly around its neck. She then proceeded to do a handstand, gripping the bottle with her love muscles before emptying the frosty liquid inside her sugar walls. The men went absolutely insane and the women were in shock. I even had to sit up on the groom's back and watch the bitch in amazement before I got up and conceded defeat.

"Girl, you win this round!" I spat, waving Chyna off. The crowd was still throwing money at us when we left the stage and all I could think was that it sure was too bad we didn't get along. We probably could have made a lot of money together. However, I didn't have much time to think about it as I watched my main competition jet to the Champagne Room, trying to get there before me. That was where all the real ballas hung out. Guys had to pay extra to get in and the girls had to be chosen to enter. Obviously feeling herself and thinking her little pussy trick had gotten her carte blanche, Chyna walked right up to the door and tried to enter.

"Hold on there, Chyna," Big Lurch, the huge security guard, said as he stopped her at the entrance. "There's a private party going on with the rapper Big King. You can't go in right now."

"What the fuck you mean I can't go in? I'm the biggest moneymaking bitch in this place!" Chyna snapped.

"Big King picked out the dancers he wants and you weren't one of 'em. Now go on back out there and work the tables," Big Lurch replied, holding his ground.

Wondering if I was going to get dissed like Chyna, I eased my way on up to Lurch and smiled. He immediately opened the heavy curtains for me and I stepped inside with ease. As Chyna furiously stormed off, I wondered what kind of revenge her jealous ass was going to plot against me.

A cloud of smoke filtered out and the distinct smell of weed wasn't at all subtle. I noticed when I was in there with Mr. Moose that anything was allowed inside the Champagne Room. If all parties were with it, anything went. As the smoke cleared and I saw who was standing in front of me, my breath got stuck in my throat. Rapper Big King stood there with a fat blunt in his hand as he flashed a smile of glittering gold front.

As I stepped deeper into the room, I caught him looking me up and down, licking his lips.

"Yo Shorty, you fine as hell. I saw you on the stage doin' your thang. That's why I told the security dude to let you in. I'm snatching you up for the night!" he said and took my hand, leading me over to the rest of his crew.

Big King's entourage sat on the surrounding couches with butt-naked strippers draped all over them. He found an isolated spot for us a couple of feet from where they were and began trying to impress me, free-styling to the music and rapping about the gold records he had hanging up on the walls of his recording studio. When he finally took a breath, I cut in with a shameless plug for myself.

"Ya know, I sing," I told him. "I would love for you to hear me one day. Maybe I could be your protégée or something."

He laughed, not taking me seriously.

"Maybe the 'or something,'" he chuckled.

"Seriously. If you let me come down to your studio, I promise you won't be disappointed," I assured him as I rubbed up on him.

"How 'bout not disappointing me right now by shaking that ass all in my face?" he requested.

As if my life depended on it, I jumped up and danced my heart out, hoping all the while that the better I danced, the more Big King might want to give me my big break. I shook and gyrated my body with zest, totally hyped about the future while making money in the present, and as the cash continued to endlessly flow, I danced for Big King and his comrades until the place closed.

In an attempt to sober up, I showered and changed before leaving the club, and by the time I made it out onto the street, it was already after four A.M. A few patrons still lingered out in the parking area as I tipsily strolled out onto the street in search of the cab I had called. I looked up and down the lot, as well as out onto the dark street, but did not see my taxi anywhere. I did, however, see Rich straddling his bike and talking to a few of his boys. Figuring he would probably give me a ride if I asked, I went over to him. Before I could initiate conversation, as if he read my mind, Rich tilted his head to the side as his green eyes sparkled with delight.

He smiled. "I told Chyna she could have your cab."

"You told Chyna what?" I asked, now annoyed.

"You don't need the cab, 'cause you and me are gonna hang out and then I'ma drive you home myself."

"Oh yeah?" I smirked. I was still afraid of getting fired but I was more tempted than before to give in to my urges. Rich was cool and I liked his style, which made him that much sexier. I decided to take my chances.

I looked around to see who might be watching and then in an instant, jumped onto the back of his bike once again. Without saying a word, Rich turned on the bike and sped off noisily down the deserted street. We rode for what felt like an hour before he pulled into the parking lot of a one-story flat that had a tacky sign above it that read "Liberty Motel." It looked a little grimy but was evidently good for short stays. As I waited outside on the bike while he went into the office to pay for a room, all sorts of hookers, drag queens, and freaks of the night passed me by as they entered and exited the seedy establishment.

Inside Room 223, as expected, the decor was sorely lacking. The room was decorated the color of dried blood. The tackiest mirrors I had ever seen in my life adorned the ceiling, while the raggedy bed was covered with dull white sheets and an uninviting dingy-looking spread.

"Home sweet home!" Rich announced and headed straight into the bathroom.

I closed the door, disgusted by the dirtiness of the room, but kept going with the flow. I couldn't believe that this classy-looking cat, who I knew made good money at the club, had brought me to such a cheap motel. I had expected a lot more from him but said nothing and sat on the bed waiting for him to come out of the bathroom.

When he finally entered the room, he'd stripped down to his shorts and held a bag of cocaine in his hand. I could tell that he had done a few lines already when he asked,

"You ready to party?"

"I don't do drugs. It's not my thing," I replied.

He laughed. "Oh, a virgin. I like virgins. All right, then. Let's talk."

"About what?"

"You." He smiled. "Tell me about yourself. You from New York, right?"

"Yeah."

"So what you doing down here?"

"Just trying to jump-start my career."

"Career in what? Booty shaking?" He laughed.

"No," I snapped. "Dancing is just a stepping-stone."

"For what? Hooking?" He laughed again, this time more heartily.

"You're a real character, aren't you?" I huffed.

"All right, all right. So go 'head. Tell me. You really wanna be an actress or something, right?" he asked sarcastically

"As a matter a fact, yeah. I act and I rap."

"You rap?" He chuckled as if he didn't believe me.

"Yeah, I *rap*. What's so funny about that?"

"Females don't rap." He huffed, blowing me off. "Most chicks who strip really wanna go to Hollywood or do some other shit. None of 'em ever do, though."

"Well, I'll be the first, then," I assured him.

"How? Do you even know anybody in Hollywood?"

I hesitated before answering. "Well, no."

He smiled. "Well, this might be your lucky day."

"How's that?"

"My boy just happens to be a casting agent out there *and* he knows LL Cool J. Maybe I could hook you up."

"Really?" I asked excitedly.

"Yeah, I think you might have some potential," he said, looking me up and down with lust in his eyes. "We'll talk more about it later. But right now, let's have some fun."

He reached over and shoved his cocaine dipped pinky in my face.

"Come on. Don't knock it 'till you try it. It'll make you feel good, especially while I'm fucking you."

"Who said we were fucking?"

"Will you cut the reindeer games? I know you want me. The way you slobbed my shit told me that. And you wouldn't be here now if you didn't want some. So come on. We both adults. Let loose and taste this!"

Rich placed his finger inside my mouth before pushing me down on the bed and removing my clothes deliberately and skillfully. As he moved in for the kill, all I could think about was meeting his casting agent friend and being thrust into stardom. After he had taken off everything except my panties, Rich dabbed some more of the white powder on the tip of his tongue and stuck it inside my mouth, kissing me deeply until I gave in. Within seconds, my lips and mouth went numb, giving me a sensation that I had never felt before. When we came up for air, Rich trailed a long line of coke between my perky breasts and down my body, stopping right at my thinly shaven pubic hairs. Without warning, he then took in a deep breath and snorted the entire line. When he got to the end, he spread my thighs apart and dove in, eating my moistened pussy like it was cocaine pudding pie.

I quickly became aroused and excited beyond belief. I wanted to ride on his tongue to orgasm. I reached down and grabbed his curly head, pressing my pussy up against his fast-flickering tongue to slow him down. He sucked hungrily on my little erect bud and I tightened my grip on his head with my thighs as I massaged my pulsating clit on his face until I jerked and came in his mouth.

Rich lifted up, wiped the back of his hand across his mouth and spread my legs apart once again before slowly sliding his cock deeply into the crevices of my loins. He fucked me in every way imaginable, flipping me in a variety of positions, each one more stimulating than the last. He then put me in a sixty-nine, pumping his dick in and out of my mouth while he licked every inch of my ass. When he'd had enough of that, he did me doggy style like a Great Dane on a Chihuahua, and in each position his dick remained hard as granite. After over an hour, my pussy walls had gone numb and I realized that Rich was so high that he couldn't cum and that he'd only taken a break to do more coke. Obviously a coke expert, he showed me how to sniff it, smoke it, and eat it. Soon my entire body was frozen and I felt like a spider tangled in its own web. As I lay on the bed looking up at the mirrors on the ceiling, I felt like I was floating outside of my body, watching my own demise as I began tripping out, hallucinating and feeling like someone was going to come and kill us both. As I lay paralyzed, I could feel Rich kneeling over me for about thirty minutes jerking his dick off, dying to cum.

"Ughh! My fuckin' dick is gonna explode!" he yelled before finally busting his nut. I thought I was dreaming, for as he screamed out in agony, only a tiny drop of cum squirted out onto my stomach before he dropped to the bed on top of me like a ton of bricks. After he didn't move for a moment, with every ounce of strength I could muster up, I rolled his limp body off of me. I was scared, but wondered why I felt strong and full of energy. It was such a confusing high. Beside me Rich's eyes had rolled up into his head. Now terrified, I prayed that he wasn't dead, and as I lay on the bed in a panic, I felt like I was going crazy. I pushed and pulled at him, trying everything in my power to get him to stir, to no avail.

"Rich, Rich! We gotta get outta here! They're after us! I need to go back! I don't even know where I am!" I cried. Rich lay still as a two-day-old corpse as the room spun vertically on an invisible axis. I sobbed uncontrollably, wondering how I was going to explain being in a hotel room with a dead man, where we got the coke from, and why I was breaking the rules of the club. As I checked the windows to see if I could slip out of the room unnoticed, Rich scared the shit out of me by sitting up on the dingy sheets and laughing hysterically.

"Ah, you're such a good girl," he said sarcastically. "Come on. Our time is almost up anyway."

I threw the dusty pillow across the room at him, realizing that he had played a horrible joke on me, and with a sigh of relief snapped, "I'm still fucked up."

Finding my behavior to be comedic, Rich cackled like a hyena as he clumsily helped me put my clothes on.

"You really were a virgin," he chuckled.

We left the room and stumbled down the pissy concrete stairs, as Rich held my hand and helped me stay steady. When he dropped me off, it was nine-thirty in the morning and I was still high as a kite and wide awake. With the exception of my fingertips, my body was numb and as he left me standing in front of the condo in a zombielike state, before he sped off into the morning sun, he smiled. "Thanks for letting me bust your cherry!"

twelve

the green door

I had been wondering when Mr. Moose was going to show up at the club again, and as if he knew my schedule, on the last day of my three-week stint, he did. As I completed my final set, I watched from the stage as he entered the club and walked over to the bar. I couldn't wait for the song to end so I could speak to him and remind him of the offer he had made. Jack had yet to call with another gig and I had no clue what I was going to do next. Hanging out in Naples with a rich man seemed like an offer I couldn't refuse.

"Hi, sexy. I've been waiting for you," I said, giving him a peck on the cheek.

"Hello, little darling. You don't have to wait any longer. Are you ready to go to the Sunshine state?" he asked.

"More than ever," I replied, truly not ready to go back to New York.

"I'm going to talk to Kareem and finalize everything. I'll be right back." He smiled. I watched as Mr. Moose disappeared into the crowd and headed to the back of the club where Kareem's office was. I wondered what kind of "deal" they were finalizing without me being in on the negotiations, but figured that as long as I got a free trip, it was all good. A few minutes later, Kareem and Mr. Moose approached me and shook hands.

"Pack your bags, pretty lady. We leave in the mornin'. I'll have a car pick you up and bring you to the airport. We'll be flying on my private jet and I'll meet you at the plane. Be ready to go by six A.M." Mr. Moose grinned.

Without letting me say a word or ask a question, he kissed me good-bye and placed a thick knot of bills into my hand.

"Don't be late," he warned as he walked away.

I gently nodded, put the money in my tip pouch, and watched him walk out of the club into the daylight.

When I entered the dressing room, I excitedly told everybody about the opportunity I had been given and listened as they all offered advice about what I should do and how I should do it. However, I wasn't nearly as interested in what they had to say as I was in taking a couple of hits of coke. Ever since the night I had spent with Rich, cocaine had become a regular part of my diet. I liked the feeling it gave me, and since it was plentiful at the club, I never had to waste my own money buying it.

Although I was bombarded with warnings, I couldn't help but wonder what it might be like to have a powerful man like Mr. Moose fall in love with me. I let myself dream, briefly dismissing my own rule about never taking seriously any man who'd connected themselves to a dollar. But Mr. Moose seemed different. After all, he had already given me money and we had never even touched. He was also taking me away—something no one had ever done before. I honestly believed he thought I was special and I wanted to get to know not only his wallet, but him as well.

When my shift ended, I went to give Rich his tip. But as I reached out to hand him the cash, he tightly pulled me to the side by my arm and barked, "What the fuck are you doing?"

"Huh?" I said, confused by his anger.

"I hear you're going away with that old ass trick tomorrow. You better get your mind right and remember that you my bitch!"

I jerked my arm away from him. "*I'm your bitch?* What the fuck are you talking about?" I exclaimed, shocked by his psychosis. Rich and I had only been together those two times. I had no idea he was thinking that we were in any type of relationship. But then again, the girls did warn me that he was crazy.

"Any bitch I fuck in here is mine. That's the muthafuckin' rule!"

"You don't own me! And what is your problem, anyway? You fuck *all* the bitches in here! Does that mean we all belong to *you*?"

I then threw his tip on the ground and stormed out of the club, leaving him standing in the booth looking stupid. I could hear commotion behind me, as he angrily punched the wall of the booth. Although I really liked Rich, I refused to let him get the best of me or dampen my spirits. I was going to Naples and nothing and no one was going to stop that.

When the limo arrived, I was up and more than ready to go. The shiny black stretch Mercedes-Benz moved quickly through the Atlanta streets and when we got to the airport, I was driven out onto the runway where I was escorted up the steps and on board a sleek private jet. An attractive flight attendant took my bag and showed me to my seat before bringing me a refreshing mimosa. I felt energized as I sat patiently waiting for my sugar daddy.

About twenty minutes had passed before I finally heard his voice, and as he approached my seat with a huge smile on his face, he looked like he had fallen straight off of a western movie set. He wore a ten-gallon hat, thick-heeled spurs, and chaps that flapped quickly when he walked.

"Hi there, pretty darling! You're looking lovely this morning," he complimented.

"Thank you," I replied bashfully.

Mr. Moose sat beside me and strapped himself in, unable to keep his eyes off me. He suddenly grabbed my hand and said, "I'm glad you could make it. I hope you enjoy yourself."

"I'm sure I will," I happily answered, as I felt the jet take off down the runway.

Once we were off the ground and climbing through the clouds, I decided to initiate conversation, as I wanted to get to know my new admirer better.

"So, tell me about yourself," I asked.

"Well darling, what do ya wanna know?"

"Anything . . . everything!" I shrugged.

"Well, I don't know if Kareem told you but I own one of the leading oil companies in this here United States. I'm a pretty good chef. I love fast toys and golf and last but certainly not least, I love beautiful women, like you. Been married eighteen years to the same girl and got three boys ready to take over my empire when I pass on. And that's pretty much it. How about you?"

I gave Mr. Moose a half smile and turned to look out the window to hide my disappointment. He had a family, but as we flew twenty-five thousand feet up in the air, it was obviously far too late to back out of the trip.

"I didn't realize you were a family man," I sighed, knowing our trip would not amount to anything more than just a meaningless sexfest.

"Oh yeah. But that shouldn't worry you, darling. Just look at this as taking a vacation with a close friend," he said as he touched my face and slowly slid his hand down my neck and over my breast to the tip of my nipple.

"I'm going to take care of you. If it's money you're worried about, don't be. I have plenty. Just go with the flow and enjoy yourself. You'll see. I'm a great guy and this is sure to be the start of a wonderful friendship." He continued. I somehow managed to give him a smile before I laid my head down on his shoulder without uttering another word.

The peacefulness of the flight lulled me to sleep, and when I awoke, it was to the thump of the wheels touching down. When I sat up, I stretched and looked out the window. We were in Naples.

We stepped out of the plane into the Florida heat and the humidity gently hit us in the face. The sun was hot and shining brightly and the scent of blooming flowers wafted through the air. A limo waited for us out on the tarmac and the driver whisked us away through the lush swampland en route to the Grand Hotel.

Thirty minutes later, we pulled into the circular drive of the resort. As soon as we stepped out of the limo, my eyes widened. I had never been to such a grand place before. The lobby of the hotel was richly decorated with red carpet leading inside and a huge sparkling chandelier hung above automatic doors. I felt like I had entered the doors of Emerald City. I was ecstatic and could only imagine what luxuries awaited me in the room.

Mr. Moose's assistant checked us in and we were approached by a couple of his colleagues. The four rich old white men wore golfing attire and carried expensive equipment in designer bags as several pretty young blondes adorned their sides. The only brunette and woman of color in the group, I stood out like a sore thumb, especially when one particularly white-bread man patted Mr. Moose on the back and smiled, "John, I see we're in an *exotic* mood this time around."

Mr. Moose grinned like a teenage boy who'd just fucked the head cheerleader. The girls smiled hard, bouncing around and trying to look sexy. They all looked about my age and I suddenly realized that we were all there for the same purpose. After chatting for a few moments, Mr. Moose explained that we still needed to get settled and told them we would meet them on the course in an hour.

When we arrived in the penthouse suite, it was unbelievable. I had never seen a hotel room so romantic, so exquisite, so large, or with such a spectacular view. I wished there would have been a chance for us to connect, but reminded myself that I was there on business. I was with a married man who just wanted to play, so I unpacked my bags and decided to milk the situation for all it was worth.

Before Mr. Moose took a shower, he requested that I put a bikini on beneath my sundress. I did as I was told and when he got out of the shower, he dressed himself in some tacky but probably high-priced golf gear complete with checkered pants and a funny-looking hat. He then grabbed his clubs and we headed out to a private area on the course.

As we pulled up in our little cart, I noticed that all the girls were topless and wearing g-strings as they lined up on the green with clubs in hand, ready to take their shots. The whole thing was a little crazy to me, but I figured that this was just how the mega-rich got down.

"Why don't you join the gang?" Mr. Moose suggested. "I'll give you a seven-hundred-dollar bonus to see those beautiful breasts of yours while you play."

"You're kidding right? I told you I don't know how to play golf," I replied.

Mr. Moose smiled.

"Come, I'll teach you," he offered.

We headed toward the course, and before I knew it, I was in my bikini bottoms and topless like the other girls. As Mr. Moose stood closely behind me, his sagging body pressed up against mine, I could feel his stiff dick as it poked me in the crack of my ass. I giggled and enjoyed the experience, but no matter how I tried, I repeatedly missed hole after hole. No one seemed to care about that, either. They just liked watching me swing and bounce up and down, shaking my tits. Surprisingly, I was actually having a good time as we all drank champagne and pranced around, enjoying all the luxuries the men presented us with. As I came to terms with my role, I cheered when John got the ball in the hole, boosting his ego from 5 to 25. I was actually OK with the entire scene. After all, I had been blessed with a beautiful body and had become quite comfortable putting myself on display.

When the sun finally began to go down and the game was wrapped up, I felt nice from the champagne and a little excited from walking around half naked all day. Having wealthy men stare lustfully at me like they would give me the world made me feel beautiful and desired, even if all they wanted was a good fuck.

After such a sexually charged day, when we got back to our suite, both Moose and I were ready to get it on. Shortly after crossing the threshold, he sat down in one of the plush chairs by the window. Without hesitation, I rushed over and knelt down before him, spreading his crooked legs apart.

"No, no, no. I want to do something a little different. Why don't you go lay on the bed?" He suggested, pulling me up before I could get started.

"Oh, OK." I shrugged and did as I was told. Mr. Moose reached down into a nearby Gucci duffel bag and pulled out a state-of-the-art video camera.

"Wait a minute, I'm not into that!" I snapped, rising from the pillow-top mattress. While I didn't mind getting freaky with the old dude, having it captured on film for others to watch over and over again made me really uncomfortable.

"Relax, little darling. Trust me. It's okay. I don't want to tape us having sex together. I just want to videotape you masturbating so I can watch you after you've gone back home."

I silently looked at him with my brow raised.

"I'll give you thirteen hundred dollars if you let me videotape you playing with your pussy and getting yourself off," he offered.

I hesitated for a moment as I thought about it.

"Will this be for your eyes only?" I asked skeptically.

"Promise. For my private collection. So you can be with me even when you're not."

"When will I get the money?" I asked.

John pulled out his wallet and laid a bunch of hundred-dollar bills on the coffee table. After the impromptu transaction was made, I stepped out of my dress and pulled down my bikini bottoms. I then piled the pillows high up against the headboard, leaned back against them on the bed and spread my legs open. I slowly started rubbing my pussy and spreading my lips apart with my fingers so that he could get a good look at my throbbing clit. I closed my eyes and tried to imagine erotic and nasty thoughts to help get me more excited as I stuck my finger in my mouth before sliding it down to my muffin and circling it around my clit to tease myself, making it swell even more. It felt so good and I was enjoying it so much that I forgot all about the camera.

After about ten minutes, Mr. Moose became so aroused that he couldn't hold the camera steady any longer. Before I could cum, he grunted and busted a nut on himself right in his pants. When he was finished, he got up and went into the bathroom, took a shower and got into the bed, passing out immediately.

As he snored like a hibernating grizzly, I sat wide awake staring at him. I couldn't believe that after all of my anticipation, that was it. The man didn't say one word to me. He didn't hug me, kiss me, or touch me in any way. He just crawled beneath the luxurious duvet, gave me his back, and went to sleep. As I stared blankly at the ceiling, I tried to force myself to do the same before accepting the fact that I had apparently served my purpose for the evening.

Mr. Moose woke early the next morning to head out to the course, leaving me in bed to nurse the sunburn I had gotten from being naked on the green the day before. Needing to recuperate from the hectic schedule I had endured over the past three weeks, I welcomed the opportunity to catch up on some much-needed rest and relaxation, and took advantage of the magnificent spa facility on the premises of the resort.

Feeling good from the royal treatment I had received, that evening I joined Mr. Moose and his friends for supper on a private yacht. It was a beautiful night to be on the ocean. The air was warm and the moon was full. I couldn't believe how romantic it was and wondered if Mr. Moose had ever shared romantic moments like that with his wife.

"What would it be like to be married to a man like that?" I asked myself, wondering if their marriage was built on love or money. Maybe the Mrs. had a little plaything of her own, I reasoned.

After a dinner of exquisite food and drink, Moose was anxious to get back to our suite. I was incredibly horny, as the langostino, oysters, and champagne had created an itch between my legs that desperately needed to be scratched. But as we entered the room, Mr. Moose headed straight for his camera so we could shoot some more video. As much as I wanted to get fucked, it was evident that this man didn't want to touch me. He merely wanted to get off from watching me fuck myself—not participating. So I played with myself once again, spread-eagle as my dripping pussy extended invitation after invitation to his pulsating dick. But he didn't even want to sniff it, and while I was enjoying all the luxuriousness of the environment, I knew the first thing I was going to do when I got back was find someone to douse my sexual fire.

On the second day of my intercourse-free extravaganza, I got a message from Jack offering me four more weeks at Vanity. My stint had ended when I flew off with Mr. Moose and I had thought about what I was going to do when my vacation was up. Since I had enjoyed the money I made and was not particularly anxious to go back to pounding the pavement in New York, his offer was welcomed and accepted.

I arrived back at into the club, five thousand dollars richer, realizing that the game had just begun. As I got ready for my first set, Kareem entered the dressing room with a roar, "Well, if it isn't Miss 'Fuck the Deejay'! Simone, what were you thinking? Don't you know the rules?" he yelled.

I stood there looking at him with a stupid look on my face. Rich had let our secret out of the bag and I was mad as hell.

"He kept pressuring me!" I tried to explain.

Kareem yelled at me at the top of his lungs, making me wonder if this had been the real reason he'd offered me four more weeks, so he could go off on me face-to-face.

"Simone, there's a reason I have the no-fraternizing rule! Rich might be my nephew but he's obsessive when it comes to his women, and like it or not, the deejay is part of your act!"

Kareem sat down and tried to calm himself before continuing. I really didn't know what the big deal was. So what, I broke the rule? Rich broke it, too, and he was the one who'd started it. Had he yelled at his nephew the way he was yelling at me?

"Honestly, Kareem, I had no idea that Rich considered me to be one of 'his women,'" I replied, confused by the entire conversation. How did one insignificant encounter get blown so far out of proportion? If anyone should have been pissed, it should have been me. Never again had Rich mentioned introducing me to his agent friend, which I realized was probably all a lie to get the pussy and the main reason I had fucked him in the first place. I knew I should have waited for the contact before spreading my legs.

"You have a chance to be big, Simone. That's why I asked you back here. Most bitches come here for a couple of weeks then I send them on their merry way. I like to keep shit rotating. But you . . . you got something," Kareem continued after taking a deep breath. "Look, you need to forget about Rich. It fucks up the flow of harmony in the club. Don't mess with him unless you are ready to be his bitch! Do I make myself clear?"

"Yes," I softly replied, trying to understand his backhanded compliments as I breathed a sigh of relief. I actually thought I was about to get fired. He hadn't even yelled at me like that when I kicked Chyna's ass.

"Now get to work. We got a new feature in and you go up after her. Oh and before I forget, Moose said you did a great job in Florida. If you play your cards right, they'll be plenty of cats like Moose."

Kareem left the dressing room and I proceeded to get into costume. Curious about my new competition, once ready, I hurried up into the club to watch the new featured dancer. She was a porn star named Cherokee. A beautiful American Indian princess, Cherokee had deep reddish brown skin and long straight black hair that hung down to her voluptuous ass. She must have been a big star, for as she danced, three huge bodyguards secured each side of the stage protecting her from the salivating clientele.

I watched intently as she pranced back and forth across the stage, shaking her boobs and feeling on her butt and thighs. She wasn't doing much, yet she was scooping up big bucks. This burned me up because I wanted to make top dollar like the features did. I just didn't know how to go about doing it. The girl wasn't putting any effort into making the men empty their wallets, but the bills were flooding the stage like water. I was determined to keep my eyes and ears open, hoping to learn whatever I could about raking in the dough, because I sure as hell was a better dancer and entertainer than she was and deserved to be paid more. The only she thing she had on me was that she was a porn star and I wasn't.

When her set ended, Cherokee blew kisses to the audience as she exited the stage. One of the bodyguards handed her a little white poodle that she snuggled in the crook of her arm as she passed by me and smiled. Ready to collect my money I ran up to the stage and positioned myself right in the center, waiting for my theme song to begin. The crowd went wild, as I was clearly the house star and they had missed me. Evidently the noise and ruckus caught Cherokee's attention because as I started my set, I noticed her standing to the right of the stage, watching and listening as the crowd went crazy for me. After watching for a few minutes, through the smoke I saw Cherokee motion for Kareem to come over to her. I continued to grind my pussy seductively up and down the pole but noticed Cherokee whispering into Kareem ear.

When my set was finally over and I received my usual thunderous ovation, as I left the stage, Kareem whispered in my ear, "Someone wants to meet you. Come with me."

I followed him to the other side of the club, then downstairs to a door with a glittery red star on the front of it. Kareem knocked and a pleasant voice called out, "Please come in."

Kareem opened the door and stood aside to let me enter first. What I saw on the other side made my jaw drop. The room, which had beautiful soft pastel pink walls, was elaborately decorated with a pink leather sofa and fresh flowers in each corner. To the left sat a table covered with a pink linen tablecloth and adorned with fresh fruit, bottled water, and a sterling-silver coffee server. Additionally, there was a crystal Mikasa bowl filled with snacks and a deli platter to its right. A brightly lit smudge-free mirror ran the length of the wall and a shellacked mahogany wood clothing rack held Cherokee's beautiful and sensuous outfits. The room didn't even look like it belonged in the club, and compared to the dirty broom closet where me and the other girls dressed, it was a queen's palace. Sitting in a pink-and-gold chair that resembled a throne, with a long Virginia Slim perched between the pointer and middle fingers on her right hand, sat Cherokee, who was dressed in a beautiful black silk floor-length robe with feathers around the neck and sleeves.

"Simone, meet the legendary Cherokee. Cherokee, this is Simone Young," Kareem stated in a very businesslike manner.

"Hello, Simone." She smiled, extending her hand. "Do you have time to sit and talk?"

"Oh, yes. If it's okay with Kareem," I said, looking at my boss.

"Of course. Anything for Miss Cherokee." Kareem leaned over and kissed the back of her hand before turning to leave. "I'll let you two ladies have your privacy."

As he closed the door, Cherokee smirked. "Men. They're like puppy dogs. They put on all these manly fronts, but for some reason they turn back into little boys when they meet a porn star. It feels good to know I have that kind of power, though. Wouldn't you wanna know what that feels like? I think you have what it takes." Cherokee rose from her chair and stood directly behind me as we stared at our reflection in the mirror, checking out our profiles.

"A porn star? I don't know about all that," I laughed. "That's a pretty big step from dancing, don't you think?" I stated, as I watched this red-boned vixen play with my hair and undress me with her glistening eyes. She then put her hands on my hips and tenderly patted my butt.

"You know how to use this, right? I mean you do fuck, don't you?" she questioned.

"Yeah?" I replied, now showing off. It stroked my ego to know that this famous porn star thought I had what it took to make men powerless.

"Tell me how this sounds to you. What if you got the chance to shoot a few movies? It would get you outta here and make a name for you. Then you could come back and headline, making top dollar and getting a star on *your* dressing room door. You don't belong on the stage dancing for just a few dollars. You'd be able to come and go whenever you pleased and the club would pay you to perform at their venue. Honey, if you're smart, you'll have plenty of powerful men like Kareem following you around, panting after you like a puppy dog!" She laughed.

I turned around to face her, my heart pounding from the picture she painted. I looked deeply into Cherokee's eyes to see if she was for real.

"That sounds tempting and all, but I'll have to think about it," I replied, not really knowing what to say or sure if I was ready to take such a tremendously life-altering step.

Understanding my position, Cherokee smiled. "Of course you should think about it. It would change your life. Here, take this number," she said, handing me a black-and-white business card. "He's a friend of mine in the business. He owns one of the top management companies in New York. Tell him that you come highly recommended by me. With my endorsement, you'll get the royal treatment."

I took the card from her perfectly manicured fingers and tucked it into my garter.

"Well, I better get back out there and work the tables," I said, as I strolled toward the door.

"Stars don't 'work tables,'" Cherokee said matter-of-factly. "But I have a feeling you won't be working them for long."

As I headed back out into the crowded club, I felt like I was walking in the twilight zone. Cherokee was glamorous and spoke the truth. And if the difference in dressing rooms was any indication of what she said, I believed her. After all, she seemed to be living the life I wanted.

I immediately reached into my garter and pulled out the business card Cherokee had given me. In black bold letters, the card read "Aaron Roth, Vice President of E.M.B. Productions." I tucked the card back inside my garter and went back into the club to hustle up some table dances and work the VIP room.

When Cherokee came back out onto the floor, I watched as she made money hand over fist, just by taking Polaroid shots with the customers and signing autographs. She didn't climb up on tables, but if they were willing to pay more, she'd sit on their laps and pose, spreading her coochie for the camera. Customers were lined up in droves to buy a picture of her for thirty bucks a pop. She didn't have to walk around and ask anybody if they wanted a table dance like the rest of us did. Her dances were private and there was a waiting list to get one. Cherokee periodically winked my way as she stayed busy all night in the private VIP room until she was finally whisked away into the night by her three giant bodyguards.

thirteen

porno dreams

When I finally took a day off from the club, I more than needed it. As I chilled out with my housemates, kicking back in the living room of our condo and smoking on a fat blunt, I decided to let the girls in on the career change I was contemplating.

"So, what do ya'll think?" I asked, after giving them the details of my encounter with Cherokee and taking another hit of coke.

"Girl, you are turning into a super freak!" Maria exclaimed, turning on her Latino accent extra hard.

"I think it's cool if that's what you wanna do. Will you give me a part in your movie?" Candee laughed, twirling her honey blond curls around her finger.

Peaches jumped in, "Lemme tell you something, it's not that easy. It may sound all well and fine, but it takes a lot of guts to do something that shit. I was approached a couple of years ago to be in a porn movie with this guy but I chickened out. Don't get me wrong, I'll admit I'm a freak, but I didn't want everybody knowin' my business and judging me. That's a whole 'nuther level of freakation. And once you start that shit, it follows you for the rest of your life!"

Peaches's words made me think. She was right. If I became a porn star, everyone in the world would see me butt-ass naked in positions that I hadn't even seen myself in. Dancing was one thing, but the porn business was taboo. It was a secret society that most chicks didn't have the balls to try for membership in.

"Well, I'm just considering anything that might get my name up in lights," I reasoned.

"*Mamasita,* you do porn movies and you *and* your coochie will be shining!" Maria chimed, causing everyone to laugh.

Ready to catch some more zzz's, I got up off the couch and stretched.

"I'm beat, guys. I think I'm gonna hit the sack," I stated, kissing them all good night and heading off in the direction of my room.

I turned out all the lights except for one dim night-light before eagerly climbing into bed. Sleep, however, eluded me as my mind continued to twist and turn at the thought of taking Cherokee up on her offer. I hadn't gotten the response I'd been looking for from the girls, but I knew that it was ultimately up to me to decide what I was going to do.

As my eyelids grew heavy and I was just about to drift off, I heard a soft knock on the door and Candee and Peaches came tiptoeing in.

"Simone? You asleep? Peaches and I have an idea," Candee whispered from the shadows. I couldn't see the features on her face, but the faint illumination gave her silhouette a glow.

"No, I'm still up," I answered.

"Well, we thought we'd help you out. So you can see if you've got the goods to be a porn actress," Peaches giggled.

"What do you mean by that?" I asked, as they looked at each other with devilish smiles before running over and jumping onto my bed. Candee started taking her tank top off and fondling her own soft perky breasts and hard nipples. In awe, I watched as Peaches undressed and took her panties off, flinging them to the floor.

"If you think you got what it takes to be a porn star, show us your skills," Candee begged.

Even though I had bragged to them a couple of times about my extraordinary seduction skills, the only woman I'd ever fooled around with was Carmen. Figuring that I'd better put my money where my mouth was, I sat up and grabbed Peaches's breasts, stroking them and sucking on her nipples until they were hard as nails. Candee reached for my panties and as she slid the silky garments down, she started feeling me up and kissing my calves, blazing a trail of hot kisses up between my legs and thighs and licking at my clit to give me a little tease.

Getting into it, I lay back on my pillow and grabbed Peaches by the waist, pulling her so she that was straddling above me and kneeling with her pussy over my face. When it brushed my lips, I stuck my tongue out and slithered it across her clit, licking it up and down. I licked the juices off the side of her thighs and pecked at her kitten from front to back a few times before I began to tongue-fuck her. Peaches lost her mind, moaning and rocking her kitty back and forth across my mouth as she begged for me not to stop. Growing more amped every second, I sucked on her clit like I was giving head to a man. Peaches couldn't hold back her orgasm and when she started speeding up her rhythm, I knew she was about to cum.

"Oh my God! I can't take it!" she screamed in delight. Candee's face was still buried between my legs, licking my clit and finger-fucking me with her thumb when Peaches fell over limp onto the sweaty sheets.

When Candee came up for air, she pulled her hand away from my pussy and snapped, "It's about time I had some of this pussy. I been wanting to see what you were working with since the first moment you walked through that door!"

Not wanting to disappoint her, I got up and bent Candee over on all fours before swiftly smacking her on the ass. I then spread her creamy vanilla cheeks until her pink pussy popped open with an invitation for me to come inside. I stuck my tongue up inside her sugar walls as far as I could go, swirling it around, in and out like a serpent. Peaches lay back against the head of the bed, rubbing herself and getting off as she watched us. When I started flicking my tongue across Candee's puckered asshole and rubbing my hand back and forth up against her swollen bud, Candee screamed.

"I'm cumming, please! Don't stop, please, keep going baby, don't stop, yeah, yeah, ahhh," she hollered as she came so hard it squirted out like a geyser. Her juices splashed out all over my face and she collapsed on the bed like a gunshot victim, rolling over on her back as if she were dead. She had stars in her eyes when she looked up at me and moaned, "Wow! Girl, you *are* good! That's all I have to say. Just damn good."

Peaches remained against the headboard of the bed stroking herself as she groggily smiled. "That was the bomb! Shit, you definitely know how to get a girl off, Simone. You have my blessing and if you want, I can write you a reference."

I was happily satisfied and proud that I had lived up to all expectations. I knew right then and there that I could be a force to be reckoned with in the porn industry, and as I drifted off into a peaceful slumber, I knew it was only a matter of time before I saw Cherokee again.

While the money was good at Vanity, I have to admit I was getting tired of the same old routine. The same old cats came in night after night, not offering me any variety, and I was growing tired of the grudge Rich had held against me for going to Florida. He started cutting my songs abruptly and sometimes didn't play the songs I requested as if he were deejaying for his own personal enjoyment instead of for my show. He even went so far as to start messing with Chyna, which I really didn't care about, but there was only so much of his shit I was willing to take. It was obvious to everyone that Rich and Chyna were always purposely trying to piss me off.

One particular night as I pulled up for my shift, Rich drove up on his motorcycle with Chyna on the back all snuggled up. I wanted to throw up but brushed them off, rationalizing to myself that they deserved each other. As I got out of the cab, Chyna jumped off the bike, shot me the finger, and deliberately bumped me as she walked by. Rich followed closely behind her with a smirk on his face and it took all the control I had inside not to jump on both of them and rip their asses to shreds.

Thirty minutes later as I preparing to start my set, I went to the deejay booth to give Rich my music, like I usually did. When I entered the booth, Rich didn't acknowledge my presence, as he was too busy playing with Chyna's big old titties as he changed to the next song. Disgusted by the entire scene, I cleared my throat to let them know that I was standing there.

"Excuse me but here's my music for tonight's sets," I stated with an attitude.

"No more special requests. You dance to what I play or nothing!" Rich snapped.

"I'm not taking this shit anymore! I'm going to talk to Kareem about this!" I barked as I slammed the door to the booth and went to find our boss. I was so angry when I got to his office that I busted right through the door without knocking. To my surprise, I was greeted by the site of Peaches and Candee on top of Kareem's desk, in a sixty-nine position eating each other out. Kareem was standing on the side of the desk behind Peaches palming her ass as he rammed his dick in and out of her pussy.

"What the fuck? Don't you know how to knock?" he growled, startled by my unexpected entrance but not enough to stop pumping. As if I wasn't there, Peaches and Candee paid me no mind and continued right along.

"Oh shit! Sorry! Forget it!" I hastily replied, quickly closing the door and running back down to the dressing room. Maria was inside straightening up the costumes and looked at me like I was from Mars when I began to vent.

"Damn, is everybody in here fuckin' everybody?" I snapped.

"Don't tell me. Kareem's in his office fucking Candee and Peaches, right?" she chuckled.

I looked at her in surprise, stunned at the fact that this was obviously a regular occurrence at the club.

"He keeps a schedule with most of the girls. Surprised you're not on it. I blow him on Saturday and Sunday and Candee and Peaches do him together on Tuesdays and Fridays. Chyna fucks him whenever he wants her to. Yep, baby girl. Everyone in here *is* fucking everyone in here. I don't know why you're so shocked," she snickered.

"Man, this place is wild. He just broke on me the other day about breaking the no-fraternizing rule and now I find out he's fucking damn near every bitch in here!" I spat.

"Like uncle, like nephew . . ." Maria shrugged.

Just then I heard my name being called over the intercom system and left the room to find out what was up. When I entered the main room of the club, Big Lurch stopped me.

"Simone, you and Chyna got a private customer waiting in the VIP room," he informed me.

"Shit! I gotta dance with that bitch again?" I huffed, heading to the Champagne Room. When I arrived, Chyna was already in there wilding out for the private party. I danced my way into the room and of course Chyna was not happy to see me. And although I was sick of her shit, I was determined to make my money. Figuring I would make the best of a fucked-up situation, I decided to make the show interesting so I challenged Chyna to a strip off. Of course, the guys were down for it, egging the two of us on. And as usual, Chyna did her typical nasty, gross, and disgusting moves. But I outshined her with my limber body as I began climbing on our spectators like they were my own personal monkey bars. I swirled my pussy around on their foreheads and shook my ass as I stood over their heads. My body was so lean and my moves were so slick that even Chyna was distracted watching me, forgetting to pick up her money. I did my thing and the money flew at me like I was in a rainstorm. I was finally able to prove that that bitch didn't have anything on me because she wasn't a real dancer. All she had was a big fat ass that looked great when she jiggled and bounced it up and down. But tonight our customers wanted entertainment and that was my specialty. Unable to handle the competition, Chyna made her little money and left the Champagne Room as I continued dancing for the guys and raking in the dough.

When the night was over, I left the VIP room feeling buzzed from adrenaline and champagne. As I headed toward the dressing room to change out of my costume, Chyna strutted up to me in the middle of the club and confronted me yet again.

"Nice dance moves. You musta gone to that *Fame* school or some shit. But I'm the winner in the long run, bitch. After all, I got your man," she snapped all up in my face.

I honestly couldn't have cared less about the fact that she and Rich were fucking, but the fact that she was bold enough to put her finger damn near on the tip of my nose was enough to make me lose it. Unable to contain myself a moment longer, I finally lost my cool and smacked Chyna hard across the face. Refusing to let her get her bearings, as she stumbled back, I jumped on her ass with all fours and there, right in the middle of the club, an all out rumble broke out. Customers did their best to get out of the way as tables flipped over and drinks tumbled onto the floor. Security came running over to pull us apart, but not before I had jabbed her dead in the eye like smooth-ass Sugar Ray Leonard did Roberto Duran at Caesar's Palace.

Kareem must have heard the commotion because he came running out of his office, buckling up his pants and hollering at us at the same time. He was pissed off at the interruption and embarrassed that his two biggest moneymakers were causing such a disturbance just feet away from his stage.

"What the fuck?" he yelled.

After the two burly guards had separated us, I yanked my arm out of Big Lurch's grip and screamed, "I have had enough of this! I don't need this bullshit! I'm outta here!"

I ran down to the dressing room, threw on my clothes, and began to empty out my locker. I violently tossed my clothes and toiletries into my bag and grabbed my costumes from the rack. When I pulled my knapsack from the hook inside my locker, the business card Cherokee had given me fell out onto the floor. I quickly picked it up and hesitated as I asked myself if I was ready to make that call. As I headed toward the door of the dressing room, Kareem almost knocked me over as he entered.

"Simone, I know Chyna's been busting your chops since day one but I thought you were tougher than that. Look, why don't you just take a day or two off? This feud between you two will blow over. I don't want to lose my best dancers over some bullshit!" he pleaded, for the first time, humbling himself.

"I don't think so. I think it's time for me to move on," I replied, refusing to make eye contact.

"You sure?" he asked.

"Positive," I answered, clutching my belongings and giving him a hug.

"Thanks for everything," I continued.

"Vanity's door is always open if you wanna come back," he said.

"Thank you." I smiled, leaving him standing alone in the dingy room.

I decided right then and there that if I ever entered that club again, I'd have a glittery red star on the front of my dressing room door.

fourteen

wishing on an x-star

The annoying sound of my alarm clock woke me the next morning. While Maria and the girls were sad to see me go, they wished me well and made me promise to stay in touch.

I didn't feel sad about leaving Atlanta until they all got together and threw me a huge surprise bash at the club, paid for by Kareem. I was told that my farewell party was the biggest shindig Vanity had ever seen. Even Rich and Chyna were in the house, although they kept their distance. They probably just wanted to make sure I was really leaving. Once back in New York, I decided that I deserved to treat myself and rented a stretch limo to drive me home from the airport. As the black Mercedes navigated through traffic on the Grand Central Parkway, I hit the button to lower the window, letting the humid breeze blow in my face. I was happy and at peace, for I had made it out of Atlanta alive, in one piece, and over ten thousand dollars richer.

As I entered the door of the brownstone, I dropped my bags and dragged my weary body into the living room. I was happy to be home but the place was a mess. Ebony and Jessie had obviously been living like pigs since I'd been gone. Still, I had not realized how much I had missed my house and didn't even get angry. I even decided to clean up the living room and kitchen before taking a hot shower and lugging my bags upstairs to my room.

A little while later, I heard the front door slam downstairs and knew that my best friends were home.

"What the fuck? Who cleaned the house?" I heard Ebony ask.

"Don't look at me. You know I didn't do it. I never clean," I heard Jessie remind her.

I decided to creep downstairs and surprise them and when I entered the living room, I yelled, "Surprise!"

"Oh my God! You're home!" Ebony screamed, running over and giving me a hug.

"Simone, girl, we missed you!" Jessie chimed in.

We all hugged as we jumped up and down in excitement, happy to be together again.

"We didn't know you were coming home! Why didn't you tell us? You look great!" Ebony squealed.

"I'm sorry. Everything has been moving so fast that I didn't have time to call much," I tried to explain.

"Bitch, you *never* called!" Jessie said, playfully shoving me.

"Well, fill us in on everything—and I mean *everything*!" Ebony howled.

We giggled with excitement, eager to fill one another in on what had been happening over the past two months. With a big bag of pretzels and a six-pack of wine coolers, we all went up to my room to exchange stories. I also called Carmen, who rushed right over to get in on the welcome home party.

Like old times, we laughed and gossiped the night away. I couldn't believe how happy they were to have me home, and I hadn't realized how much I had missed them. It felt good to be home with a new opportunity ahead of me and I was excited to find out what lay ahead as I took yet another step closer to my pot of gold.

fifteen

you're the one

It was an incredible feeling for me to wake up in my own bed. I'd had a ton of fun hanging out with my roommates and Carmen the night before, but I had been careful not to tell them about the next phase of my career. I wasn't ready to spill the beans just yet because, while they were all for freely expressing their sexuality, I didn't think they would understand. Plus, I didn't know whether or not it was definite, so I didn't bother sharing until I was completely sure.

I reached out to Mr. Roth as soon as I climbed out of bed, and scheduled a meeting the same day at three o'clock. Since I had some time before my meeting, I decided to do a little shopping first. Thus, I hopped into a cab and headed to the Village. I got out on Christopher Street and walked along the sidewalk checking out the little boutiques and trying to find something cute.

I dipped inside a designer shoe store and purchased a pair of blue velvet pumps with chrome high heels. I knew they would look nice with a spaghetti-strapped blue dress I had hanging in my closet. After I left the shop with my purchase, I continued my leisurely stroll down the street. But as I walked along, I passed by a window displaying condoms in various sizes and colors and dildos shaped like nothing I'd ever imagined. The letters on the storefront read SEX NOVELTY SHOP. At first I resisted going in and continued walking. But curiosity got the best of me and I turned around and pushed open the shaded glass door. Once inside, it felt like I had landed on planet erotica, as there was nothing but rows and rows of sexual paraphernalia as far as my eyes could see. There were racks and shelves filled with porn of all types—hard-core, soft-core, bondage, lesbian, you name it—they had it. On the walls were pinup posters with *Playboy, Hustler,* and *Penthouse* cover models, and all the customers seemed to be engrossed in the centerfolds of dirty magazines. I walked around the store, aware that men were looking my way with nasty thoughts in their minds. I ended up in the lingerie section in the back of the store and picked out a very provocative bra and panty set and headed to the counter to pay, mesmerized by the women on the video boxes and wondering if one day that could ever be me.

I left the store extra-hyped to meet with Cherokee's contact, and by the time I had arrived at the offices of E.M.B. Productions, I knew I was crossing the threshold into a new destiny.

I was led down a corridor by a buxom blonde who introduced herself to me as Cookie. As we strolled down the long hallway, I noticed huge posters of the movies I assumed they had produced, as well as glamour portraits of the adult stars. The women actually looked like real movie stars and I hoped to one day grace the wall alongside them. When we reached the last door, Cookie knocked and a deep voice answered, "Come in."

Cookie stepped aside so I could enter.

"Mr. Roth?" I asked the middle-aged, olive-complexioned man who sat behind the desk. At a glance I noticed that the office didn't look like what I had expected. It was more like a cross between a one-hour photo lab and an accountant's office, although it had exotic memorabilia in every corner. There was also a family portrait of Mr. Roth with what I figured were his wife and two kids.

"Yes. You must be Simone," he replied, rising from his chair and firmly shaking my hand. "Come on in and have a seat," he continued as I smiled and did as I was told. He said nothing at first, as I sat uncomfortably, not knowing exactly what to say.

"Let me take a look at you," he began, breaking the silence. "Would you mind standing up and turning around?"

I did as I was asked and stood up shyly, rotating my body so he could get a good look.

"So, what do you think, Mr. Roth?" I asked, eager to know.

"Aaron. Please, call me Aaron . . ." He hesitated, looking me up and down as if I were a science project.

"Well," he began, "you're a little rough around the edges, but I honestly think you could be a gold mine." I smiled as he motioned for me to sit, happy that he approved of what he saw.

"Little lady, I think you're a rosebud waiting to blossom. With my help, you could be the first ever African-American adult star under contract and probably the biggest black actress this industry has ever seen." He smiled from ear to ear. My eyes lit up like a firecracker on the Fourth of July.

"Cherokee was right. She knows talent when she sees it," he laughed. I began to blush at the thought that I could be so huge.

"So when do we start?" I asked, eager to collect my first paycheck.

"Well, I'm going to offer you a seven-movie deal that will include money to take care your housing needs and money to keep you comfortable for a while. After you've shot the videos, you can start featuring in the clubs and on the road making top dollar. But, I have to warn you, it may sound easy but it isn't. It's actually a pretty tough ride. You gotta be strong. And unfortunately the industry hasn't accepted many black performers, but I'm willing to sign you to a contract and do my part to make sure that your name becomes bigger than life. If you play your cards right, you'll be the first black girl to ever go places that only blondes have been allowed to go."

I stared at him wide-eyed and did my best to take it all in.

"I like what you're saying so far, I think." I smiled.

"Well, how are you living these days? A lot of girls come to me broken and strung out. But I turn them away. I'm a producer, not a counselor. So, do you have your own place on a decent side of town?" he asked.

"Yeah. I live in Harlem with two roommates."

"Well, eventually I'm sure you'll wanna get your own place. But I guess that's OK for now," he stated.

As I listened to his words, I couldn't believe how quickly I was sucked in. While I really didn't know what Mr. Roth saw in me, I was more than ready to work and go for it. I wanted to make his agency proud and didn't want to disappoint him or Cherokee.

"OK, so it's settled. Would you like to get something to eat? It's been a busy day and I haven't had lunch," he offered.

"OK," I agreed.

"There's a nice cafe across the street," he said as he got up from his chair and walked over to the coatrack to grab his jacket.

We headed to a tiny French bistro located directly across from his office where we talked over food and drinks, discovering that we had quite a few things in common. As he picked my brain, we realized that we shared some of the same beliefs about religion and even liked the same types of music.

Aaron laughed at my jokes and shared some of the tricks of the trade. He even told me how he got into the adult-moviemaking business and, needless to say, I was extremely intrigued by his stories. A Jewish man with a little soul, Aaron expressed to me how difficult it was for African-Americans, especially women, to break through in the industry in a way that would make them into mega-stars, explaining how the few who had managed to get in were being taken advantage of.

"Simone, I'll be honest with you. The world may not be ready for some-one like you. But I've been feeling for quite some time that someone should push the envelope and start breaking down these barriers. Now that fate, and Cherokee, has brought you to me, I think that person should be me, and I'm gonna do my best to make you larger than lust."

As our meal neared its end and our emptied plates were cleared from the table, Mr. Roth removed a three-page contract from his ostrich-skin briefcase and handed it to me. As I gave it a brief overview, I saw there were seven movies at three thousand dollars per movie, plus a four-hundred-dollar-a-month stipend for one year. Of course my eyes lit up.

"This sounds pretty good to me," I told him in excitement.

"It is very good, Simone," Mr. Roth assured me. "Actually it's better than good—it's great! In this business, most actors earn only seven hundred and fifty to a thousand dollars per film. Some earn only three hundred bucks—and that's without a contract, a stipend, or management. But if you sign this, you will also make a ton of money in special appearances and danc-ing in the clubs. You're gonna be huge, I tell you, 'cause I'm gonna promote you like you're Marilyn Monroe!"

Although he had me totally gassed about the fame and fortune, I still questioned if I was doing the right thing. Being exposed naked for the world to see scared me, and I honestly didn't know if I could do it. Still, I shrugged off my doubt and picked up the Mont Blanc pen he handed me. I then pro-ceeded to flip to the last page, eagerly scribbling my signature across the dot-ted line. Mr. Roth immediately did the same and we both stood up from the table, sealing the deal with a tight corporate handshake.

"Welcome to E.M.B., Simone Young. I promise to take very good care of you and all your professional business," he said with a smile.

"When do we start?" I asked.

"Soon. Go get some rest and I will get your first script to you tomorrow. It's gonna be great. I have a feeling this is the beginning of something big!" he announced.

By signing the contract with E.M.B Productions, I had crossed the point of no return. Still, I continued to keep it secret from my roommates, which was pretty easy to do since they were preoccupied with their own lives. My only real concern was my mother, who I hadn't spoken to in months. I had avoided her calls until she eventually stopped calling altogether. I knew she would have never approved of my lifestyle, never mind accepting the idea of me being in the porn industry, no matter how much money I was making. Francine Young wanted her daughters to stay in school, go to college, and become doctors or lawyers. If she knew that I was about to become an X-rated film star, she would have had a fatal heart attack. But I was headstrong and determined not to let anyone get in my way. I was nineteen now and legal, which meant that no one could stop me from doing anything I really wanted to do. Still, I missed my mom and decided to call her just to let her know that I was okay. Once I got her on the phone, however, it was the same old thing. She screamed at me before starting to cry, begging me to come home and give up the streets. Unable to take the dramatics, I simply cut her off dead in her tracks, repeated that I was OK and that I loved her, then hung up the phone. I wasn't going to let anything ruin my high. After all, I had money in my pocket and a new job that was going to get me on the path to stardom. So no matter what anyone said, I was jumping in feet first.

With Jessie and Ebony nowhere to be found, anxious to celebrate my pending stardom, I decided to head down to the G Spot in search of creating a little party of my own. I hadn't been to the club in ages, and when I rolled up in the cab, there was a rowdy crowd standing outside. I made my way through the crowd to the front of the rope where I saw Reggie, who had the usual look of stress written all over his face. When I yelled out to him, he noticed me and smiled, walking over to let me through the barricade as he gave me a big hug.

"Hey, Reggie! I missed you! What's going on?" I asked, squeezing him tightly and looking around at the mob scene.

"Let's go inside to the office so we can talk. I need a break, anyway," he suggested. He instructed one of the other security guards to cover him while he was gone and we headed into the club in the direction of Mr. Walton's office. A strange feeling of déjà vu came over me as Reggie unlocked the door to the room. I stepped inside and made myself comfortable in Mr. Walton's chair as my friend sat on the edge of the desk.

"You look like you're about to go nuts! What's up? You okay?" I asked, concerned about my boy.

"Hip-hop night is outta control here. And there's too much violence. Walton doesn't even come on the weekends anymore 'cause of all the threats against him from people who've been banned from the club for bullshit. We even had a few shootouts and it's just crazy. The cops been called down here too many times. So now we had to install metal detectors and make everybody take off their shoes, stick out their tongues, and all that crazy shit," Reggie rambled, as he paced around the office.

"Seems like a lot has changed since I left," I sighed, feeling a little bad for him.

"It has. It's like nobody wants to have fun anymore."

As a friend, I walked over and gave Reggie a tight, encouraging hug, and when we let go, he stepped back and smiled like a cat who had just swallowed a plump and juicy canary.

"Damn, through all the commotion, I didn't notice how good you look! Where have you been? You disappear and reappear out of nowhere, looking like you hit the Lotto. What you been up to?" he asked.

I turned and sat back down in Mr. Walton's chair as I lowered my head humbly before looking up at him with an innocent look on my face.

"Well, Reggie, that's actually one of the reasons I came to see you. I wanted to tell you about my new career," I began. I took a deep breath and hesitated before continuing. While I wasn't ready to tell my girls, I had to tell someone, as it was burning a hole in my tongue. I figured that Reggie would have a more liberal opinion about it, being a man and all.

"I've been working as an exotic dancer and I just signed a contract to star in adult films. I'm going to be a porn star," I announced. Reggie's mouth fell open as my news hit his ears and he stared at me in disbelief.

When he finally found his voice, he angrily began, "Simone, are you crazy? What do you know about making porn movies? Do you know how dangerous that business is?"

Somewhat shocked at his response, I immediately jumped to my own defense.

"Hey, don't you judge me! Don't think I don't know about all the underground shit that comes in and outta this place. And besides, I'm a grown-ass woman! I needed money so I could get out on my own and I found out that men were willing to pay me for my time. So I'm taking advantage of that while I can 'cause you only live once! On top of that, I'm a good dancer and not only am I desirable to men, but to women, too! Why shouldn't I use what I've got while I've got it?" I reasoned.

"Simone, those people just wanna use you. You need to realize that if you go that direction you'll never be happy. You may make money, but you'll find out that what you're doing is gonna follow you around wherever you go. I'm telling you, it's not the way to go if it's fame and fortune that you're really after."

"Look, I tried to do it the so-called right way. I went on a million auditions—shit, that's how I met you. But nothing. And I needed money."

"There's other ways to get money, Simone. You are talented. Why don't you just give it time? Someone will discover you. Why choose to go down the hard road of porn? Hmm? Look, I'm your friend and naturally I only want what's best for you. I just don't want anything bad to happen to you," he reasoned.

"Reggie, you don't understand. I'm good at what I do, and there's a part of me that really likes it. Not to mention the fact that Mr. Roth, the head guy at the agency, says I could be one of the biggest stars in the entertainment industry," I tried to explain.

Reggie laughed.

"You mean in the *porn* industry. Look, Simone. There has never been a porn star to break into Hollywood and there probably never will be. It's too much of a taboo and mainstream America ain't ready for all that!"

"Well, Reggie, maybe I'll be the first!" I snapped, getting up and giving him a sweet peck on the cheek.

"Look, I just wanted to say hello and give you my new number so we can keep in touch. I cherish our friendship and just thought you'd be happy for me. Take care." I smiled as I opened the door to leave.

Morning came with an early knock at the door. I groggily stumbled from my bed and looked out of my window to see who was standing on the stoop.

To my surprise, it was Mr. Roth. Thus, I swiftly grabbed my robe and ran down to answer the door.

"Hey, Mr. Roth, I mean, Aaron. What brings you up here this early Sunday morning? I thought I wouldn't see you till next week," I asked as he stepped across the threshold.

"Good morning, Simone. Sorry to disturb you, but the early bird catches the worm!" he laughed. "I actually came over here to personally deliver your first script. We start shooting on Monday."

"That's in two days!"

"Yes, I know. But I decided we should bang the first one out quickly, so we have something to start promoting. It takes three full days to make a video. So learn your lines. There aren't many so you shouldn't have any problems. A car will be here in the morning to pick you up. Be ready by six A.M. and be sure to rest today so you'll look fresh for the camera."

Without saying good-bye, he dashed out the door and left me standing alone with the script rolled up in my hand. Suddenly, I began to panic. It was fine as long as it was just an idea, but now it was starting to feel very real. According to the script, my first scene was with a man and the second was with a woman. I just hoped my co-stars would be sexy and attractive enough to make the experience a whole lot easier.

I read over the script all day until I knew it inside and out. The sex would come naturally, I hoped, but I really wanted to show off my acting skills if I could. Since there wasn't too much dialogue, I knew I was going to have to make the best of what it did have to offer.

As night fell, for the first time in a really long time, I got down on my knees and said my prayers before jumping into bed. My eyelids became heavy and I was eager to rest, knowing in the back of my mind that I was about to begin my journey to becoming a porn star.

sixteen

lights, camera, and sex

As I tossed and turned in my bed, enjoying the comfort of deep slumber, I heard a muffled yelling outside below my window.

"Simone! Simone, wake up! You're going to be late!" the voice called up from the street. I sat up startled and disoriented from being woken up so abruptly, before I heard Aaron yelling my name once again. I ran over to the open window and stuck my head out.

"OK, OK! I'm coming down!" I replied.

"I've been ringing your bell for ten minutes! Throw on some clothes. You don't want to be late your first day!" he yelled back, with a hint of impatience in his voice. I slammed the window shut and ran down to let him in.

"I overslept," I stated, gaining my consciousness as I opened the door. "Can you wait here while I take a shower? And what about my hair?" I asked, now in a frenzy as I ran around the brownstone grabbing my stuff.

"Take a shower there," Aaron snapped, stopping me in my tracks. "And we have someone who will take care of your makeup and wardrobe."

Upon hearing his words, I halted and took a deep breath. I then went to my room, threw on a pair of jeans and a T-shirt, and ran back downstairs, still stuffing my feet into my shoes and piling my hair up on top of my head in a scrunchie.

"I'm ready," I huffed.

"Good. Trust me, Simone. Everything's going to be fine," Aaron assured me. "You will have to work on your punctuality, though."

All the noise and commotion brought Ebony and Jessie out of their rooms, just as Aaron and I were about to leave. To my surprise, Ebony had a bat in her hand.

"Girl, you need to let somebody know when you have company. I thought we were being robbed or something!" she said as Jessie emerged in her nightshirt and bare feet.

"Oh, sorry we woke you guys up. But I gotta go," I replied.

"Where are you going so early in the morning? And who's the herb?" Jessie nodded her head toward Aaron, covering her mouth as she yawned.

"Good morning, ladies. I apologize for the intrusion. I'm Aaron Roth," he announced as he held out his hand. Ebony cocked her head to the side and gave him attitude.

"Who was talking to you?" she asked, then turned back to me and snapped, "What's up?"

I had to think fast if I wanted to continue with my little secret, since I still hadn't told my roommates about my new career.

"He's just a photographer who's taking shots of me today on the Brooklyn Bridge. We gotta go now so we can catch the early-morning sun," I announced, pushing Aaron on the back of his shoulder toward the door as I avoided looking them in the eyes.

"Yes, that's right. We'd better get going. Nice meeting you charming ladies." Aaron smiled as we headed out the door.

We headed over the bridge into Queens to an underground studio where we would be filming. I didn't pay much attention to how we got there, as everything felt so surreal. My mind was caught up in the zone and I was quiet the entire ride. I had a knot in my stomach and as much as I tried to hide it, I was nervous.

When we arrived at the studio, I was feeling really insecure. Not only did I look a mess but I was about to have sex in front of an audience with people I had never met. Despite trying to psyche myself out, I wasn't feeling sexy at all. In the background of my thoughts I heard Aaron hyping me up and trying to reassure me that everything was going to be great. After a while, his comforting words slowly started to have an effect.

We walked into a bustling arena of people running around setting up. Aaron introduced me to his production crew as they hurried by carrying lights, cameras, and props. I met the cameraman, the boom guy, and the lighting guy. They weren't weird like I'd expected, and if I didn't know any better, I would have thought I was on a regular Hollywood set.

"Let's get you set up in the dressing room," Aaron began. "You'll be sharing it with the other ladies and I'll show you where you can take a shower. Then I'll rush you to wardrobe and makeup."

"OK," I replied.

Aaron walked down the hall as I hurried behind him like Alice following the Mad Hatter to Wonderland. When we finally arrived at the door at the very end of the hall, Aaron knocked and warned, "Ladies, I'm coming in!"

I followed him in and was introduced to the girl I would be working with. Her name was Lucy Kane and she was sitting in a chair fixing her garter belt.

"Lucy, this is your new costar, Simone Young. This is her very first movie, so I want you to go easy on her and be patient. Simone, meet Lucy Kane."

Lucy looked up from strapping her garter to her stockings and spoke with a silky smooth voice.

"Hi, sweetie! We're going to have lots of fun!"

My cheeks turned hot from embarrassment but I managed to keep my cool and said hello in a bashful tone. As I sized up my costar, I noticed all that Lucy was working with. Her breasts were huge—at least triple D's—and her hour-glass figure made me wonder how she could physically stand with such a huge top and bottom—with the tiniest waist I had every seen in the middle.

"Where is Chika?" Aaron asked, glancing at his watch.

"Her usual spot: the bathroom," Lucy replied.

"When she gets out, do me a favor and introduce her to Simone. Then I want you to show her the ropes like a mentor. I have some things I need to take care of on set. I'll be back right before call time," Aaron instructed, and then he was gone.

I looked around the tiny dressing room, searching for a vacant spot I could call my own. There was lingerie thrown on the floor and draped over the chairs. The vanity table was covered with cosmetics and lotions. Lucy finished hooking up her garters and noticed my flustered state.

"Girl, relax! Sit down and take a deep breath. You've got a minute. Chika will be out of the bathroom in a second, then you can shower. She's taking care of something . . . if you know what I mean." She smiled with a wink.

While I wasn't quite sure what she meant by that, I nodded my head anyway.

"So, are you nervous?" Lucy asked, trying to make small talk.

"A little bit." I weakly smiled.

"Have you ever been with a woman before?"

"Yes. But never on camera or in front of an audience."

"Ooh. I love it! Newbies are my specialty! Well, maybe we should warm you up before you go out there. Let me show you some of my dildos."

Lucy hopped up out of her chair and grabbed her bag. She started pulling dildo after dildo out of her bag. She had big ones, black ones, and all sorts of weird-shaped vibrators.

"Now, this one is perfect for breaking in virgins. Not too big, not too small. And looks like it's just right for you!" she said excitedly.

I took the pink love toy from Lucy's hand and sized it up. It was about seven inches long and stiff, but it had some flexibility to it. I smiled as Lucy slapped the artificial penis around in her hand and we both started to giggle. Attempting to break the ice further, Lucy reached out and started to gently fondle my breasts. In response I did the same and tweaked Lucy's nipples between my fingers, slowly lifting her big boobs in my tiny hands, juggling them up and down and getting used to their weight.

"Why don't you lick my nipples?" Lucy whispered.

I did as she asked, leaning in to kiss the side of Lucy's neck before planting a trail of soft kisses down between her cleavage. Without any further hesitation, I slowly started sucking on her plump round nipples before I playfully smacked her breasts together and held them tightly, sucking each one and flicking my tongue in small circles around her areolas. I was becoming quite aroused and my pussy screamed to be set free from my g-string when suddenly the bathroom door swung open and Chika thrust into the room swaying from side to side. I quickly pulled away from Lucy, feeling like we'd just been busted.

"Are you fucked up again?" Lucy peered at Chika with a squint. "Aaron is going to be pissed," she said, shaking her head. "Anyway, this is the new girl Simone. Today is her first day."

"Good luck, kid. This business is fucked up!" Chika slurred. She was a tall and slender beauty with a face as delicate as expensive porcelain. Her long flaming red hair indicated that her ancestors were from Ireland, and through all of her exquisiteness, I could tell that drugs were getting the best of her.

"Oh, shut the hell up. All you know how to do is get fucked up, doing coke and all that other crazy shit you do. Stop trying to scare the poor girl!" Lucy said.

I watched in disbelief as Chika slid down the wall and hit the floor. Lucy ran over to help pick her up as I stood there, not sure of what to do.

"Simone, you should run into the bathroom now and start getting ready. You have to be in makeup soon," Lucy suggested. I grabbed my bag and ran into the bathroom to take a shower while Lucy dragged Chika on her back over to the chair, trying to help her get it together before she had to go on the set. As I walked toward the showers, I heard Aaron banging on the door.

"Chika, you and Rod Jox are up in ten minutes!" he called from the other side. As I walked forward, my attention turned to Chika, whose crystal blue eyes had rolled up into the back of her head. Lucy kept trying to give her water, but Chika knocked her hand away. Clean and damp, I emerged from the bathroom wrapped in a large white towel, just in time to see Chika put on some lipstick at the mirror. As she puckered her lips, she caught me watching and winked at me as she fixed her dress and calmly left the room.

"Wow, she's stunning. She looks like a super model," I said to Lucy.

"Yeah. Too bad she'd rather stay high than keep her money. But all of us aren't like that. Some girls do like to party all the time, though. Chika's one of the partyers."

I walked out of the dressing room in my towel and slippered feet, hoping the makeup people would work their magic on me. In less than an hour, I stepped out of wardrobe looking like an exotic princess, feeling and looking sexy in every way.

As I walked down the hall, I could hear loud moaning coming from the set. Curious, I crept up to the side and hid behind the production crew to check out the scene. Aaron was on the far side of the stage standing behind the cameraman, and before us on a brightly lit platform was Chika in the doggy-style position. Her male costar was riding her like a stallion. He rammed his cock up inside her hard as her pussy dripped with sweetened nectar. I focused in on her coochie, which I thought looked a bit fleshy and loose, but Rod Jox seemed to be loving it. As if no one was watching, he pulled on her hair and bit the back of her neck, pounding his thick tool in and out of her loins. After several minutes of humping, he pulled his cock out and slapped it on her ass a few times. As sweat streamed down Rod's face from exertion, Chika looked extremely bored and didn't show any emotion. Her moans sounded like they were on cue and it was pretty obvious she was faking it. Still unfazed by her lack of enthusiasm, Rod's dick was hard as a rock and it was obvious that he wasn't about to stop until he was ready. With a look of lust on his face, he flipped Chika around and forced her head down onto his dick, but not before he ripped his condom off. He then pulled on her hair and pumped his dick in and out of her mouth with the swiftness of a jackrabbit in heat.

There was no dialogue as the camera zoomed in to catch Rod's overflowing cum pop shot. Chika opened her mouth wide and licked up as many drops as she could catch. Cum dripped from the fake eyelashes that dangled from her eyes, loosened up from all the kinky sweat.

I backed up slowly and tiptoed down the hall, passing the men's dressing room on my way. The door was wide open, so I slowed down and took a peek inside. There was a tall muscular white man with his back turned to me, and while I couldn't see his face, his body looked hot.

"Hi there," I said, trying to get his attention.

When the mystery man turned around, he was everything I could hope for. His jaw was strong and his hair was blond, reminding me of the Marlboro Man as he nursed a can of Budweiser as diligently as a newborn suckling from its mother.

"What's happening, sweet face? I'm Tom Ryder," he began, looking me up and down. "You must be my co-star, Simone," he began.

"Yes." I smiled.

"They didn't tell me you were this delicious!" He smiled, too, making me blush.

"You wanna beer? It makes the ride better," he offered.

"No thanks," I said, declining.

"Well then, I'll have yours," Tom laughed.

"You drink that like it's water," I said as I noticed two six-packs sitting on a nearby table.

"Yeah, well, the juice in here gets the juice in *here* flowing." He grinned, pointing to his bulging crotch. "And on that note, you better get back to your dressing room before we wind up doing our scene right now," he continued with a country drawl, holding up the red-and-silver can and rocking it between his fingers.

"I think you're right. See you on set." I winked, looking forward to having him slay me.

I scooted out of his dressing room, thinking that adult porn stars were out of control and wondering if I would eventually be like that. As the time neared for my debut, butterflies fluttered in my stomach like they were having epileptic seizures and my heart rate elevated as I tried to calm myself. Moments later, Aaron strolled down the hallway and asked, "Are you ready? You and Tom Ryder are on next."

I tried to smile. "As ready as I'll ever be."

"All right. See you in five," he said before hurrying down the hall to summon Tom.

Debating whether or not I should back out, I took my time getting on set. When I finally made my grand entrance, I headed to the stage and sat down on the rickety bed. The sheets felt heated but I realized that the warmth was coming from the bright lights above our heads. Surprisingly, the room temperature relaxed me and I didn't feel as shy as I thought I would. As I lay there, the camera guy and boom man loomed closely in to adjust the equipment, while another six or so crewmen hung around to watch.

The set was cheap-looking and the sheets on the bed were tacky with yellow and blue flowers, which surprised me. For some reason, I had envisioned satin sheets and plenty of sheer flowing curtains. But there was none of that. In fact, the set was very low budget with unrealistic-looking props, which made everything appear cheesy and cheap. As I looked around, I took in the scene and soaked up my surroundings; then, without warning, my costar suddenly came running onto the set and pounced on top of me, catching me completely off guard and knocking me over onto the bed. It wasn't romantic at all and I almost felt attacked as the stench of stale beer reeked from his pores.

"You ready to take a ride on this cowboy?" he snarled.

Speechless, I wondered what other surprises were in store for me.

"Okay, let me set up the scene for you," Aaron began. "Tom will go outside and knock on the door. He's the pizza delivery guy. Simone, when you go to answer the door, he'll ask you if you ordered a pepperoni pie. You'll say yes and pull him inside. Once you close the door, say your next line and then he'll tackle you on the bed. From there, you should start groping him and tearing his clothes off. Just follow Tom's lead. He knows what positions work best. Got it?"

"Yeah. I guess that's pretty easy," I replied hesitantly.

Moments later, Aaron cleared everyone from the set and Tom went behind the fake door to wait for his cue.

"Quiet on the set! Take one, speed, and . . . action!" Aaron yelled before the cameras started rolling.

We ran through our lines so quickly that it was only a matter of seconds before Tom threw the pizza box onto the floor and was all over me. He kissed me passionately, leaving wet smelly saliva all over my body as he undressed me. Right in the doorway of the set, he slid my panties down to my ankles and stuck his tongue in and out of my kitty-kat, licking his way down my legs. He then fingered me as he lapped at my clit with his fat pulsating tongue before I came all over his fingers. Surprised at myself, I blacked out in ecstasy, moaning like a wild animal. I was shocked at how good he felt. Tom definitely knew what he was doing, and like an overzealous sex machine, he picked up my naked body and carried me over to the bed. Following his lead, I did what felt natural and ripped off his tank top before unzipping his pants and yanking them down along with his briefs. His dick was so hard that it popped out and almost smacked me in the face. My eyes lit up and I smiled. It was hearty and big, so I grabbed it with both hands, closed my eyes, and wet my lips before stuffing it into my salivating mouth. From the edge of the bed, I stroked and sucked his dick simultaneously. Tom stood with his hands on his waist, looking down at me and watching as my lips slid up and down his cock, drooling and slurping him like a penis pump. After a few moments, Tom pulled his dick out of my mouth, slid on a condom, and pushed me back onto the bed before pouring a glob of lube on my pussy. I spread my legs apart and played with myself for the camera, inviting him to dive in.

"You ready for my pepperoni?" he asked, sliding the full length of his cock inside me. I couldn't help but scream out loud—he was so big I could hardly breathe. All my senses were focused on my stretched walls. It felt like his dick had taken over, causing my entire body to stiffen up at the intrusion. He began fucking me slowly until I loosened up, and after a couple of minutes, I was taking his wood like a pro. His eyes said he was surprised at how good my skills were as he relished in my flexibility, flipping me in several different positions. In my peripheral, I could tell that the cameraman was having a hard time keeping up with us, and as I soared someplace in between heaven and earth, Tom's dick hit spots and nerves I didn't even know existed, causing my trembling sugar walls to vigorously contract. Tom's body started to shake in response to what he felt from me, indicating that he was also in another zone, and we both would have stayed there if it hadn't been for Aaron's voice breaking our trance yelling directions.

"Pop and cum shot!" Aaron bellowed.

Tom popped his dick out and shot his load all over my stomach before Aaron yelled, "Cut!"

But ignoring the direction, Tom continued to gyrate and grind his dick up against my stomach, obviously not wanting the scene to end and causing Aaron to call him out specifically.

"Tom, I said 'cut'!" he hollered with force.

As Tom lifted his body from mine, covered in a sheen of beer-smelling sweat, he asked, "Did you enjoy the ride?"

I looked up at him in a daze and replied with a sigh of exhaustion, "It was incredible."

Aaron walked up on the set and handed me a towel.

"You were amazing," he told me with a smile. "A true porn star has been born! Cherokee sure knows a star when she sees one! Now go take a shower and a fifteen-minute break. You're up with Lucy Kane next."

I quickly got up and walked off the set, feeling like I had just ridden a virile stallion. After taking a quick shower, I went back to makeup and wardrobe for a touch-up and changed my costume. Feeling pretty, liberated, and confident, I was ready for round two. After getting a quick bite, it wasn't long before I heard Aaron yelling, "Talent on the set!"

Lucy and I hurried down the hall to a set that resembled a bar at some club. The walls were blue with built-in colored lights. A large portable bar prop took up most of the set and a fake palm tree stood in the corner. Red candles were lit on two round tables and a funky-looking multicolored rug was on the floor as two neon signs flashed above the bar on the wall of the backdrop.

"What a cool set," I said aloud, thinking this one was far better than the previous.

"They all look the same to me." Lucy shrugged, unimpressed.

Heading in our direction, Aaron blared through the megaphone, "Crew in position!"

Once he reached us, he began to explain the scene.

"This one's pretty easy. You're both hanging out at the bar and ask the bartender for another drink. After he pours it, you start making out and just glide into the sex," he instructed.

"That's it?" I asked with a chuckle under my breath. It really didn't get much simpler than that.

"That's it." He smiled, leaving us to stand in his usual position beside the cameraman.

I couldn't believe how much money I was getting paid for so little work. It was even easier than stripping.

Sensing my wonder, Lucy responded, "I told you this was a piece of cake."

"Quiet on the set! Take one, speed, and . . . action!" Aaron called from behind the camera.

I got in position and began sipping on my drink as I waited for Lucy to make the first move. Following the script, Lucy asked the bartender for another before setting her glass down on the bar. She then began petting and playing in my hair before I moved in to kiss her on the lips. She gently slid her hand down between my legs and started caressing my thighs. I could feel myself getting wet and made a bold move to stand up and hop up on top of the bar counter. In slow motion, I sat directly in front of Lucy, moving her drink out of the way before propping my feet up on the bar stools on both sides of her, giving everyone a clear view of my clean-shaven coochie. Since I wasn't wearing any panties, like the pro that she was, Lucy didn't need to be told what to do next. She pushed my form-fitting silk dress up around my hips and ate my pussy like it was being served up on a silver platter. She devoured my muff slowly and methodically, strategically running her tongue over every inch of my juicy pussy lips, licking and sucking like I was a tasty sweet lollipop.

I involuntarily squirmed and gyrated my hips up off the bar as I attempted to get deeper into her mouth, moaning and throwing my head back as I rode my orgasm out on Lucy's face. When she finally came up from between my sticky legs, she stuck her tongue down my mouth, allowing me to taste my own pussy juice. After swallowing hard, my costar hopped up on the bar and I grabbed her bodacious boobs, slurping and slapping them up against my face. I then reached for a nearby pink dildo, putting it in my mouth and sucking on it a few times before sharing it with my costar. Stalling for time, I straddled Lucy's hips and slowly kissed her down between her breasts to her belly button. Once I hit the side of her inner thigh, I dove right in without thinking. A natural feeling came over me and I knew exactly what to do.

Within a moment's time, Lucy's eyes rolled back into her head and she was overwhelmed with pleasure. She begged me to stop making her cum. But when I slowed down and pulled the dildo out of Lucy's butterfly and tapped it on her swollen clit, she smiled and caressed my hair like she was in love.

"Cut!" I heard Aaron call from behind and although I wasn't ready to stop, I followed his directions.

"You were hot!" he continued. "Now that's what I call *erotica*! It's a wrap, people!" He smiled, proud of us, proud of his direction, and proud of his movie.

Lucy and I jumped off the bar prop, giggling as Aaron walked up and handed us both soft terry-cloth towels.

"Did you have fun, Simone?" he asked me.

"Yes . . . more than I expected!" I replied.

"Well, you did great. Better than I thought you would, actually. Go shower and I'll drive you home," he offered.

"OK." I smiled, heading off to the dressing room.

I walked down the hall with Lucy, recapping the scene we had just done. We were proud of ourselves and since neither of us had been really ready to end when we did, we decided to take a shower together so that we could finish up. Unbeknownst to me, I suddenly had this overwhelming desire to be with a woman. The Pandora's box had been opened and I would soon learn that I couldn't deny the inviting scent of femininity.

When Aaron pulled up outside my brownstone, he handed me an envelope containing my first payment. I was ecstatic and took the envelope happily, giving my new boss a peck on the cheek before running inside the building.

Although I was feeling on top of the world, I could not believe what I'd just done. I had always been considered a skinny little tomboy and knew that nobody would think I would ever star in a porno flick. Thus, I vowed to keep my new profession a secret as long as I could. Still, I couldn't deny the fact that I loved the attention and that the strong sexual gratification was an extra-added bonus. It was all so invigorating and intoxicating, but I also didn't realize the sacrifice I was making or the consequences I would have to pay down the line for those very feelings. I had put a large price on finding love and stardom, and while the things I was searching for were quite simple, my choices had just catapulted me into a sordid web of complexity.

seventeen

dancing with the devil

Time was moving fast and so was my new X-rated career. When it all began I had panicked about my debut and had also been pretty worried about
how I was going to look on film. Would people really like me? My insecurities had me asking myself if folks would get turned on from watching me and
if they would they think I was sexy. I loved what I was doing but I simply
wasn't ready to have people criticize my skills. Yet as I watched the money
pile up even though my movies weren't even on the market yet, I knew I had
something special. Properly prepping me for the life, over the next several
months, Aaron booked me for photo shoots and feature dancing at places like
the famous Show Girl World on Forty-Second Street in the heart of Times
Square. Needless to say, with all of the indulging I was doing, I quickly became fully acclimated in the world of porn.

As my underground popularity grew, I desperately wanted to share my
secret with someone, but my roomies were always either working or hanging
out with their new boyfriends, leaving me alone and with no one to talk to.
Keeping the secret was starting to stress me out. I tried to relax myself with
weed and these miraculous foot reflexology treatments that my girl Mercedes,
down at my favorite herbal shop, turned me on to, but I still longed to spill
the beans.

Before I knew it, I had seven movies under my hat. My shyness and curiosity had disappeared like the T-Rex, and at the age of nineteen, I was living a lifestyle most could only dream of. I went on shopping sprees almost
every other day and decked the brownstone out with new furniture. I still
had not told Ebony and Jessie the truth about what I was doing, but since I
insisted on paying all the rent, they didn't ask any questions. There was a part
of me, however, that envied my friends and their carefree lives. They had

steady boyfriends, took weekend trips, and worked at jobs that didn't require them to be in character at all times, and as much as I loved the money I was making, I still longed to be in love. But that wasn't my life. No. My life consisted of professional freaks, sex addicts, and lots of cash, and while I enjoyed the cash, it was the other two I could really do without.

Loaded down with bags from Gucci and Bloomingdale's, I kicked my front door closed behind me and dropped my shopping bags onto the kitchen table. It was my first free weekend in a while and I was hoping to spend an evening with my girls just shooting the breeze—maybe drink a little, smoke a little, and order a little Chinese. But a note on a piece of loose-leaf paper greeted me as I headed toward the refrigerator.

"Simone," it said. "We know we were supposed to hang out tonight but Carmen got us a free hookup to go to Virginia Beach. We'll be back on Sunday. Maybe we'll chill next weekend! Love ya! Ebony & Jessie."

Disappointed, I sat down at the kitchen table, annoyed that they had not invited me.

"I like Virginia Beach," I said aloud before realizing that there was nobody around who cared. I slowly took off my heels and rubbed my own feet. As angry as I wanted to be, I couldn't really blame them for not including me. I was never around anymore and had been so busy hanging out with my new porno friends that I'd clearly lost touch with what was going on in my roommates' lives. Given our different hours, we rarely saw one another, and when we did, they had their men strapped to their backs, making the environment not conducive for girl talk. Still, I wasn't about to spend a Friday night alone sulking, so I called some of my new friends and invited them over for an impromptu get-together. After all, I was the party girl now times ten. What was I supposed to do? My roommates were gone and I needed some attention.

After making a few phone calls, I pulled myself together. From my closet, I grabbed a sleek black dress and slid it over my smooth, naked body. Without a bra or panties beneath, I wore a pair of black lace thigh-high stockings with a black lace garter and sexy high heels. Satisfied with how I looked, I went downstairs to prepare for my guests. I ordered food from a local restaurant and sipped on some champagne until it arrived. The alcohol quickly had me buzzed and feeling good, like I didn't have a care in the world. I gave no more thought to the fact that my friends had deserted me, putting them out of my mind as I chased the pot of gold at the end of my sexual rainbow.

Shortly after the food had been delivered and set up, the party porno train arrived. When the doorbell rang, I was shocked to see Rod Jox, Lucy Kane, Chika, Tom Ryder, and a bunch of their friends from the adult industry standing on the other side of my threshold. I immediately became hyped, knowing that I was about to have the time of my life, and actually became glad that my girls had abandoned me for the weekend.

Without warning, Rod bust through the door carrying Chika in his arms. It was obvious that Chika had started partying before she arrived, as her eyes were bloodshot and droopy. Rod dropped her on the couch with a thud and, like he lived there, went straight to the kitchen to make himself a drink. Draped on both sides of Lucy were two sexy half-dressed young guys, crawling on their hands and knees down at her feet. They were oiled up and wearing black leather and silver-studded collars with leashes around their necks as if she was walking them.

"Hello, angel!" Lucy smiled. "These are my loyal pets Bow and Wow. You like?"

I looked down at the men on the floor and laughed, "I hope they're house-trained."

Lucy chuckled and pulled them along with her around the apartment. Tom brought in three hot chicks he had kidnapped from the porno shoot he'd just finished a couple of hours before, and my house was filled with strangers occupying every corner of my living room.

Chatter and laugher resonated throughout the room and someone took it upon themselves to turn on the stereo. As I introduced myself to my guests, I saw Tom pull out a bag of weed and start rolling up a bunch of joints to pass around.

"Fuck that! I got the real goods!" Chika bellowed, now fully alert. She whipped out what must have been about an ounce of coke and when I heard all the "Ooohs!" and "Aaahs," I thought I was in Smurf Village. Chika poured the pure white powder out onto the coffee table and everyone gathered around like mice scurrying for cheese. Skillfully, she made lines for everyone like she was carefully laying cement, and partygoer after partygoer sniffed and snorted away to the beat of hip-hop playing in the background. The entire room was getting higher and hornier by the minute and, having not had any in a while, I sniffed a line or two as I bounced around playing hostess as the party hit its peak. Adding to the entertainment, Rod Jox began to strip and started dancing butt-naked on the kitchen counter holding on to the cabinets while his flaccid dick hung at least eleven inches down from his hairy groin. Within moments, a busty red-haired girl gravitated his way and stood below him in an attempt to suck him off. Her mouth followed his dangling stick as it swung back and forth. When she finally got a firm hold of it, she sucked the hell out of his now-stiff rod. She slurped and deep-throated him until he spurted out his load all over her nose and lips as the creamy liquid oozed down her chin.

Back in the living room, Chika's voice could be heard above everyone's as she chatted a mile a minute. She was totally coked up, sitting on the sofa with her legs spread apart, while some girl licked cocaine off her coochie. The girl seemed to be enjoying the action but Chika wasn't paying her any attention— she was probably so numb she didn't even feel it. From the looks of Chika, it was like the girl wasn't even there as she kept right on talking about the latest MCM purse she had just added to her already overflowing collection. As she continued her conversation with no one in particular, some muscle-bound guy went over and joined in on the scene. With the swiftness of a locomotive, he pulled out his bone-hard cock, poured a line of coke on it and pointed it at Chika. Pausing midsentence, this caught her attention and she stopped talking, immediately wiggling her nose up the shaft of his dick and sniffed away. After she'd snorted every flake of snow, she looked up at him, winked, and deep-throated his dick as if her life depended on it.

Enjoying the crazy scene, I danced my way through the crowd. Strangers grinded up against me, trying to explore my freak limits. Needing to hear my own thoughts for a moment, I ignored them and made my way down the hall to Ebony's room. To my surprise, Tom was standing by the bed, butt-naked except for his cowboy hat and boots and a condom that was tightly strapped on his hard dick. He had the three girls from the porno shoot bent over on the bed moaning as he stuck his cock inside each one of them, one after the other. I silently watched as he slid his dick into the first girl and rode her pussy nice and slow, slapping the ass of the girl to the left hard enough to leave a red mark as the girl on the right waited patiently for her turn. When he pulled out, he rammed his cock up in the second beauty's pussy, speeding up his strokes and pounding her real good. Her moans grew louder and louder, as she backed her ass up banging him back. When Tom finally pulled his hard iron out of her coochie, I could hear the suction pop from her twat, which aroused me to no end. I guess the third girl didn't want to wait any longer because she gently nudged the middle girl out of the way and aggressively reached for Tom's dick herself.

"Hey, it's my turn!" she meowed.

Tom slapped his dick on the girl's butt and gave her what she wanted, fucking her so hard that I wasn't sure if her screams were from pleasure or pain.

"Oh shit!" Tom yelled, his voice sounding strained. In the blink of an eye, he pulled his cock out of her dripping pussy, ripped the condom off, and jerked himself to the finish line. He spurted his jism out onto the middle chick's ass; when the girl to the left turned around so he could jerk off on her breasts, the girl who'd had him first waited on her knees with her mouth open, anxious to catch the last few drops upon her tongue. When he was sure he'd drained the last drop out of his monster, he collapsed on the bed. As they all caught their breath, they finally noticed my presence in the doorway watching and smiled. Wishing I had been in on the action, I nodded back with a calm expression and walked on down the hall.

By the time the clock struck midnight, I was so high, I could barely walk. As the room began to spin, I stopped to lean up against the wall in the hallway to try and get my bearings. My heart pounded quickly and I felt as though it was going to jump out of my chest. I slid down the wall as people just stepped over me and continued to party. A passerby handed me a glass of water and the next thing I knew, someone was pulling me up off the floor and carrying me upstairs to my room. In my dazed state, I could feel the stranger lay me on the bed and close the door. Paralyzed, I listened to the party going on downstairs without me, zooted from the coke and nauseous from the alcohol. Hoping to steal a moment of peace, I had almost closed my eyes when my bedroom door slowly opened and a shadow of a man stood in the doorway. As he walked into the dimly lit room, the moonlight caught his face and I recognized Rod Jox.

"Hey, Rod . . . I had to leave the party for a minute. I think I got a little too fucked up," I tried to explain.

"Yeah. Should I call a doctor to take care of you?" he soothingly asked.

"No no no," I assured him. "I don't need a doctor. I think I just need a minute to rest." I tried to smile through my haze. My head felt like it was about to explode and all I wanted to do was close my eyes with hopes that when I opened them, the pain behind my temples would be gone.

Without a word, Rod eased the door shut and peeled off his clothes before diving into the bed with me ready for action.

"Rod! I can't! I'm really sick!" I squirmed, trying to get out of his grasp. His large muscular hands held me tightly and my small body was no match for his.

"Oh, you want it rough, I see!" he laughed, sounding like Satan himself. The echo of his cackle was amplified in my head and I felt as though I was suddenly falling into the bowels of hell as the pain from his grip on my upper arms told me that I would surely be black and blue when he was finished with me. Although I tried to fight, my body refused to listen to the instructions it received from my brain, and as he ripped my legs as far apart as they would go, I screamed out in pain when he thrust his mammoth-sized dick into my tiny, bone-dry pussy. Out of nowhere, he forcefully bit my nipple as he pounded in and out of my pussy, causing me to scream in anguish. I had never felt so much pain in my life and as I dug my fingernails into his back in a weak effort to defend myself, the warm sensation of blood dripping from my vagina increased my sickness as I began to gag on my own vomit.

"That's it, you sexy bitch!" he barked. "Take it all, you nasty cunt!"

He pounded away inside of me, ripping my insides to shreds as I begged the Lord above to let me pass out so that I would not have to feel the pain any longer. But I guess God was busy, because I remained incredibly alert, unable to close my eyes or escape the wrath that had been thrust upon me. In the blink of an eye, my whole life had been changed forever, and as my defense mechanism kicked in, an out-of-body experience gave me the opportunity to observe my violation from above. I watched intently as tears of terror streamed down my horrified face for what felt like an hour but what must have only been five minutes. I remained stiff as a board as he cut through my flesh like a chain saw until I finally felt his knees shaking, giving me an indication that he was about to bust the mother load. He slapped me across my face, causing my already-battered body even more pain.

As the room closed in on me and my spirit found its way back inside my tattered form, "That's some good ass pussy!" was the last thing I heard before I faded completely into blackness.

The crust on my eyelids made opening them difficult as the morning sun peaked its way through the venetian blinds. As I attempted to lift my body, I received a painful reminder of the previous night's events and was forced to reconsider making a move. I decided to wait a moment before emerging from my position, when I looked over to see Rod passed out beside me with the sheets draped over his tanned butt, the freshness of my scratches clearly evident. He had a tattoo on his back that read NEVER ENOUGH in all caps, and I realized that he probably didn't think he had done anything wrong the night before or else he would have left the scene of the crime like most rapists do.

Sensing that I had awakened, he began to stir.

"Hey . . . what a night, huh?" He smiled, stretching and looking around the room at the clothes and beer bottles spewed across the floor. Unable to respond, I merely faked a smile as he continued, "Well, it's been fun but I gotta go!"

He then jumped up, threw on his clothes, grabbed his belt, and ignored me as his cell phone rang. He answered it on his way out of the room without even saying good-bye.

When I was finally able to garner enough strength to raise my body, I sat there at the end of the bed trying to determine what physical and emotional state I was in. It was weird. I felt violated, abused, used, discarded, and dismissed all at the same time. At least if he was going to rape me and stay the night, the least he could do was say good-bye in the morning.

As I emerged from the bed and reached for my robe in the closet, I experienced excruciating pain permeating every cell of my body. I looked down to see black-and-blue marks covering my legs and hoped they would disappear by the time I filmed my next movie. Embarrassed by the bruises, I threw on a pair of sweatpants and headed downstairs into the living room. There were people everywhere passed out on the couch and floor. I sighed and shook my head, carefully stepping over people I didn't even know before going back upstairs to take a shower. When I grabbed my towel off the rack and swung the shower curtain open to turn on the faucet, I was startled by a guy comatose in the tub. He had an empty bottle of champagne in one hand and his limp dick in the other. Hungover, battered, and boiling with fury, I screamed: "Yo! Get the fuck outta my tub!"

The stranger woke up in a panic, hopped out of the tub, and ran out of the bathroom. Having had enough, I followed him down to the living room and ordered everyone out of my apartment. Groggy faces and bloodshot eyes looked at me like I was crazy, but they all got up and filed out the door. When the last freak left, I slammed the door and leaned my black-and-blue body up against the wall before taking a deep breath. I was unable to control them—tears began to pour from my eyes like never before. I wasn't entirely sure why I was crying but I think I was beginning to realize that the lifestyle I had chosen was no joke. It was a serious game and I wasn't sure I was really ready for it. But even if I wasn't, I knew it was too late to turn back.

The out-of-control, unplanned party at my house was an incredible wake-up call for me. I realized that my life was spinning out of control faster than I could spell relief and I needed the familiar arms of my mother to make me feel better—if only she'd been the comforting type.

While going to Brooklyn to visit my mom sounded like a good idea, it was a whole lot easier said than done. The thought of visiting Francine terrified me, I had deliberately and repeatedly ignored her requests for me to do something constructive with my life. Not to mention the fact that my mother wasn't the easiest woman to go crawling back to. She had her ways and could hold a grudge for life. And although I needed her more than ever, her strict code of right and wrong made me pause and reconsider several times. Still, my spirit told me that the only way I would be able to continue pursuing my future was to find my way home and visit my past.

The ride to Brooklyn seemed to take forever, but that was not quite long enough. At every light, I was tempted to turn back. It had been nearly two years since I had been to my mother's house, and as the black Lincoln Town Car rolled up in front, I noticed that not much had changed. The same faces still peppered the stoops and corners, and even the letters on our mailbox still read "oung" instead of "Young." Nope, nothing had changed but me.

I stepped out of the car and a flood of memories came over me. Hoping to get the most out of my visit, I walked up the steps and rang the bell, trying to let the warm feeling of being home overpower anything painful that might have been lurking in my memory.

I rang the bell twice before I heard my mother come to the door.

"Who is it?" she asked from the other side.

"It's me, Mom," I nervously replied.

In an instant, Mom swung the door open and grabbed me tightly, giving me the biggest hug I had received from her since I was five years old. I did my best to hold back the tears, but I couldn't.

Words could not express how happy I was to see my mother, and I realized how much I had missed her as I reveled in the warmth of her arms. I walked into the house, which looked exactly the same. Mom hadn't changed a thing and, as usual, everything was clean and in its place.

"Come in, baby. Let's go sit in the kitchen and talk," she suggested.

I followed closely behind her and before she could sit down, she gave me the once over and said in awe, "My goodness, Simone! You look like a million bucks! Absolutely beautiful. Well, you always were a beauty. But you look like you hit the lottery. And since I know you didn't, tell me what you have been doing . . ."

I turned to my mother and spoke in a very calm voice, hoping not to evoke an argument five minutes through the door.

"Mom, I didn't come here to get in a fight with you. But I've just missed you so much. You're the only mother I got and I have something to tell you," I began. Mom sat down at the table and looked at me with a raised brow.

"If it's bad, Simone, I don't want to hear it. You know I did the best I could with you and your sister. I just don't understand why you don't want as much for yourselves as I want for you," she sighed.

"Mom, I do want a lot for myself. Always have. I just have a different way of getting it, that's all. There's lots of different ways to be successful, Ma. . . ."

Mom took in a deep breath and gave me a longing look.

"OK, so tell me, what's going on?" she asked.

I hesitated for a moment as I told myself that it wasn't too late to lie. However, I had decided against it, figuring that the truth would eventually come out sooner or later anyway. My career was taking off and it would be impossible to hide it forever.

"Well, Mom. I have a new career and I'm making a lot of money. I'm taking care of myself and I even opened a savings account. I wanna give you things, too, Mom. I wanna take care of you so that maybe you won't have to work so hard anymore. Maybe I can help you open that salon you've always wanted to open," I began.

"How are you making all this money, Simone? Are you dealing drugs or screwing someone who is? Because if you are, I want no part of it," she snapped, waving me off.

"No, Ma. It's nothing illegal," I began. "I'm an exotic dancer, and I'm making adult films."

Mom sat speechless and stunned but not surprised. Her piercing eyes looked straight through me as I noticed a slight jump in the vein above her right temple.

"Simone, you have always had a wild side, so this does not surprise me," she sighed. "You know you're throwing your life away, right?"

Annoyed at her response, I instantly stood up and copped an attitude.

"Look, for once in my life I'm making money and taking care of myself. I finally get the attention I always craved from you and I was hoping that just once—just *once*—you could support me without judging and trying to make me feel bad!"

"Simone, honey, those freaks are only using you for their own selfish needs! Don't you know that all attention is not good attention! Don't be stupid! If you were under eighteen, I'd lock you up right now!" she barked, tossing the dish towel that she was holding onto the countertop.

Upset, I started walking to the front door.

"Well, I'm not. I'm grown and I don't need your permission! I only came by to tell you so you didn't have to hear it from somebody else. I just hoped that for once you could open your arms to me and love me regardless. I know I'm not the perfect daughter you prayed for but I'm still your daughter!" I yelled.

On my heels, Mom followed me to the door and yelled, "Simone, I'm sorry! Is that what you want to hear? Please don't go! This is your home where you'll always be welcome and accepted! Even after they've used you up and spit you out!"

That took the cake. I suddenly regretted ever coming by in the first place. I should have just let her hear about it on the street, let her see me on TV. At that moment I hated Francine Young.

"Thank you, Mom," I cynically snapped on my way out. "Thank you for always loving me unconditionally and for always knowing how to show it!"

The humid Brooklyn air smacked me across my face like a disgruntled lover as I walked down the block trying to erase all the bad words I had just exchanged with the person whose love I wanted most. I knew my career choice was unconventional to say the least, but aren't mothers supposed to love their children no matter what? It didn't matter, though. Regardless of how my mother felt about my life, my big day was coming and no one and nothing could stop it. My movies and magazines were going to hit the street the very next day and my life would be catapulted in the direction of the unknown.

As I traveled back to Harlem, I felt like the walls of life were closing in on me. I was in the final countdown, and in a mere twenty-four hours the whole world would know my secret.

eighteen

party like a "porn star"

I was too anxious Sunday night. The new issue of *Pin Up* magazine hitting the stands had every crevice of my mind totally occupied.

When the sun had finally risen, still in my pajama pants and T-shirt, I ran to the corner newsstand to look for the magazine.

"Do you sell *Pin Up* magazine?" I nervously asked the vendor. Without looking at me, he pointed to the side rack. My breath was caught in my throat as I saw my own image staring back at me. There I was, smack dab on the cover, looking hotter than ever! I could hardly believe it was really me! I looked like a sexy untouchable vixen—not Simone Young, the skinny tomboy from Brooklyn. Without delay, I bought five copies and ran back to my apartment. I immediately called Aaron and left him a message to tell him that I had seen the cover of *Pin Up* and that I was not only happy with it but also with the centerfold spread. Elated, excited, and barely able to contain myself, I then waited for the adult stores to open so I could go by and see if my movie was out on the shelves. And just as Aaron had promised, it was!

When I was done making my rounds, I went downtown to thank Aaron face-to-face. The treats just kept on flowing that day, because when I arrived at his office, he had more good news for me.

"Pack your bags, Simone," he told me. "We're going to Vegas!"

"Oh my God! What for?" I asked, excited.

"Well, I've got a booth at the adult convention and you're scheduled to be there signing autographs for all your fans," he explained.

"Fans? What fans? My movie just came out today!" I replied.

"I know, but I have over twenty thousand preorders ready to go. They think you're hot, kid! And I'm determined to make you hotter!"

"Oh my goodness," I said, totally taken aback. Twenty thousand preorders? For little ol' me?

"What exactly is an adult convention?" I asked, eager to learn more.

"It's the fantabulous world of porn, kid! Buyers, sellers, and X-rated stars all meet there to sell their products and greet their fans. It's the perfect blend of media, industry, and *connoisseurs* . . ." he laughed.

"Wow, who would have thought?"

"They'll also be having the X-rated Adult Awards Show, which, of course, you'll be paid for, too."

I was excited beyond words as the precious sound of opening cash registers echoed in my mind.

"When do we leave?" I asked.

"Tuesday morning. Vegas, here you come!" he announced.

As Aaron gave me the details of my upcoming adventure, I grew more and more comfortable with him handling my career. It was clear that he had a vision for me and a plan to get me not only where I wanted to go, but also where he felt I deserved to be. As I got to know him, I realized that he was an excellent businessman and a great guy with a family that he was very loyal to. I admired him for that and it showed me that he had dedication in his heart—a trait I was quickly learning rarely existed in men. By the time I left his office, I was totally psyched about the trip and one hundred percent sure that Aaron was a person I could trust.

Once back at the brownstone, I was finally ready to sit the girls down and tell them the truth about my new career. They had just gotten back from their trip and I knew it was only a matter of time before they would hear about it. Anyway, news had hit the streets fast and to my surprise, there were a ton of messages waiting for me on my answering machine. I listened to all of them, which basically sounded like, "Hey, Simone! I saw you in a porno magazine! Oh my God, are you crazy? But you do look good. Call me back!"

I giggled, having had no idea that so many of my friends secretly indulged in the world of pornography, making it totally impossible to hide my newfound celebrity. Still, while I was far too terrified to call anyone back, I knew the time had come to drop the bomb on my roomies.

"Hey, Ebony and Jess! Come here! I need to talk to you guys!" I called from my room.

When they finally emerged in my doorway, I took a deep breath and began,

"Okay, I know I been kinda MIA lately, but I'm just gonna give it to you bluntly. . . . You guys are looking at a new porn star diva!" I excitedly announced as I pulled out the magazine and video and yelled, "*Bam!*"

At first they were silent, looking at the magazine and flipping the video box over and over as if they were examining a recently landed unidentified flying object.

"You must be shittin' me. I can't believe it!" Jessie finally replied, breaking the silence.

"What the fuck?" Ebony looked at the box cover and handed it back to me. "You look hot, girl!"

Shock suddenly transformed into disdain and the face of life appeared as Jess spat, "What the fuck were you thinking? Are you crazy?"

"See, *that's* why I didn't say anything to you guys!" I said defensively.

Supportive and connected, Ebony waved Jessie off and leaned over and gave me a hug.

"Well, I told you. I always got your back, and I mean that," she offered.

"Yeah, me, too, I guess . . ." Jess hesitated. "I'm sorry I freaked out on you like that, but, Simone, c'mon, you gotta admit. This is some other shit . . ."

"I know . . ." I shrugged with a chuckle, giving the magazine the once-over again.

"Well, ya better invest in some Trojans or something 'cuz there's gonna be a lot cum flowing your way!" Ebony joked, making a congratulatory toast to my new career with an imaginary champagne flute. "Well, I guess we have to celebrate," she continued.

"OK, I'll call Carmen and see if she wants to come out and party with us tonight," I suggested.

"I don't know about that. She's the one who got you sowing your freaky ass oats in the first place!" Jess added.

I paid her no mind as I walked over to the phone to invite Carmen to my new-career celebration. Now that the cat was finally out of the bag, I could forge full-speed ahead on my starship to stardom, worry-free and able to breathe again.

Carmen and Mercedes arrived at the brownstone one after the other around ten o'clock. As usual, Carmen was already fired up when she got there and looking for her next fix. I had not had a chance to tell her about my new career and was annoyed with Ebony when she took it upon herself to divulge my business.

"So, did you know that your girl is a bona fide deep-throater?" Ebony announced.

It was now one hundred percent official. Everybody knew and there was absolutely nothing I could do about it. So I merely leaned back into the sofa with an innocent look on my face and said nothing.

"What?" Carmen asked.

"Yeah. She's a porn star now. Go 'head. Ask her," Ebony continued.

Carmen gave me a confused look before I gave a gentle nod. There was a moment of silence in the room before Carmen jumped off the sofa like she had hit the lottery.

"I knew it! I knew it! You freaky undercover bitch! And you all thought *I* was the wild one! When it's her ass! *She's* the freak!" she screamed.

"Oh, sit down! You *are* the wild one! My girl Simone here has talent," Jessie said proudly in my defense.

"Talent?! Bitch, I'll show you talent. Spread your legs!" Carmen snapped.

"Come on . . . ya'll shut up! Let's get outta here. I'm ready to party!" I announced, anxious to get to the club and release some energy.

" 'Let's get outta here? I'm ready to party.' Um, helloooo? I just found out that I'm in the presence of a porn star. I want the scoop, *chica*," Mercedes replied, wanting all the details.

"Later, I promise. Right now I wanna party!" I told her.

I grabbed my bag and my girls jumped right into gear like party robots, knowing the routine all too well. We piled out of the brownstone and headed to the club. The Cove and hot sounds of deejay Steven Shock were calling us and, without further adieu, we needed to answer.

When me and my crew got to the club, the doorman let us in without any hesitation. I didn't know if it was because we were all flyy, or because of my new career, but it seemed like every step we took, people were looking at us and whispering. I wondered what was going on but tried not to give it much thought, brushing it off as a simple case of mild paranoia. The dance floor beckoned us as soon as we entered and we immediately gravitated to the large sweaty crowd getting their groove on in the center of the room.

As I moved to the hypnotic sound of the house music that resonated throughout the atmosphere, a short, pudgy-looking guy tapped me on the shoulder and smiled.

"I saw you on the cover of *Pin Up* today."

I was stunned at first. The issue had only hit the stands that day and I was already being recognized?

"You looked good!" he continued before he walked away.

I smiled with a huge lump in my throat and kept dancing with my friends.

After we had danced several songs in a row, we got off the dance floor and caught our breath. As soon as we found an empty booth above the dance floor, a sexy older man came over to our table with a bottle of Dom Pérignon.

"Hello. My name is Robert Pontiero," he began, extending his hand for a shake. "I'm the owner of this establishment and I just wanted to give you and all your beautiful lady friends here a token of my appreciation for coming to my club tonight."

I hesitantly replied, "Thank you."

As he popped the cork, a waiter came over with glasses and began to pour out enough of the foamy liquid for each of us.

"I've seen your work and I think you are fabulous," Mr. Pontiero continued. "If you ever need anything, please, give me a call." He smiled, handed me his card, and kissed the back of my hand before excusing himself.

"Ciao," I sighed with a finger wave, not knowing where the Italian was coming from.

As the expensive bubbly slid over my tongue and down my throat, I was loving the benefits that came with my new career. While we sat in the booth getting juiced up, a guy in a goofy disco angel outfit, equipped with wings, came rolling up to our booth on roller skates and giggling. He put four white tablets on the table, flashed a big smile and skated off.

"Simone, that's Ecstasy," Carmen said. *"Now* we're about to have some real fun."

"What is it?" I squinted, looking at the pills closer.

"The best new drug in the world!" Carmen raved, picking up one and handing it to me. "Split it in half," she instructed as if she was a vet. I did as I was told and gave half to Jessie.

"Bottoms up!" I laughed.

In the matter of minutes, I was flying high. A feeling that I had never felt before came over me, and for no apparent reason, I was instantly horny, feeling sexy and overly aggressive. Acting on my impulses, I started feeling up Carmen, who was totally receptive. Right in front of everyone, we began making out, kissing and touching each other, and wanting to get naked and ready to fuck at any second.

Jarring us back into reality, Jessie interrupted, "Ahh, ladies? I think it's time to get back out to the dance floor, where you chicks can shake it off, huh?"

"Yeah, you right. I'm ready to cruise this joint. Come, my pretty bitches! Let's go hunt!" I exclaimed, now fully taken over by the drug.

We glided through the club like we were in a live music video. In my hazy state, I was the conductor of our party train as my long curly black hair bounced down my back and my tight leather minidress rode up my hips. Every step I took gave any fortunate onlooker a peek of pink lacy panties. But I wasn't the only one in my clique that had something to offer. Ebony was looking cute with her freshly boxed braids, as she suggestively licked on a lollipop and looked for action while Carmen's entire persona screamed *"Fuck me"* as her 34 D's pushed out and begged to be caressed. Jessie, looking like a sexy tomboy with her short and sassy haircut, tempted every eyeball in the place with her form-fitting blue jeans that snugly hugged and accentuated her big juicy heart-shaped ass. The logo on her cut-off T-shirt read DO ME! and that's exactly what every dude in the place looked like they wanted to do.

As we made our way through the crowd, it was evident that we were testosterone magnets, because we couldn't go two steps without some guy grabbing us or trying to talk. While most of the cats were nothing to rave about, there was this one dark-skinned Tyrese-looking brother who passed us by and headed toward the men's room. We all almost broke our necks trying to get his attention, but he never noticed us and continued on his path toward the restroom.

"Ladies, I'm calling first dibs on him! He's mine. I'll be back!" Ebony announced as she walked straight into the men's restroom without hesitation. As I went to grab her, I found myself inside the porcelain room mesmerized at the variation of dicks lined up against the walls pissing in the urinals.

"What's up, baby?" Ebony asked Mr. Chocolate, who was just about to whip his shit out. Every guy in the room turned when they heard a female voice and were clearly shocked to see this cute little mocha-colored chick with braids standing there licking on a lollipop.

"Yo, boo, you looking for me?" one guy asked, stopping his flow of pee long enough to show her his fat dick before resuming his release.

"Nah, baby. Looks good, but not tonight. Tonight I'm looking for the last guy in the row," she replied.

The black Adonis shook his Johnson gently when she said who she was looking for before turning toward her with his ample dick still dangling out of his pants.

"Damn, baby, you want it that bad?" his voice echoed throughout the room.

"What if I do? You gonna give it to me? Looks like you've got enough to share." She smiled.

As if it were a live-action film, the rest of the men looked at him waiting to hear his answer. But Adonis hesitated.

"Damn, nigga. If you don't wanna fuck her, I will!" one greasy-looking guy with dirty blond hair snapped.

"Nah. No thanks. I only want him. But ya'll can watch if you want," Ebony said. No one seemed to notice me standing at the door and I couldn't believe I was watching one of Ebony's weed-smoking escapades right before my very eyes. Now I knew her stories were true.

"Aight, then. Come get this dick," Adonis replied, licking his full lips à la LL Cool J.

My girl walked over to the guy, slammed him up against the tiled wall, dropped to her knees, and proceeded to suck him off like her life depended on it. One guy ran out to tell his friends what was happening so they could get a good view of the show. Dudes came running into the restroom to get a peep of the action as Ebony pumped up and down on her dark brown stick of cocoa, with one hand holding it steady and the other squeezing his balls. In delight, her man slid farther down the wall. Eager to see what else the club had to offer, I eased my way out of the bathroom and made my way back out into the club. The rest of my entourage was on the dance floor jumping up and down and ripping their shirts off. The jungle house beat of "Set It Off" by Kraze was playing and the base in the song reverberated up through the floor, filtering through our hot and horny group. As I spun myself around in circles, the Ecstasy made me feel like I had wings. The crowd on the dance floor was captivated by our little exhibition and all kinds of men were running up to me and my crew hoping to cop a feel on one of our half-exposed tits.

As my clothes clung to my body from perspiration, I searched for Ebony, figuring she had probably finished her business with Adonis. After looking for her for about twenty minutes, I finally spotted her coming out of the men's room with Chocolate man himself. Her hair was a mess and she had cum stains on her T-shirt.

"Hey, girls." She smiled. "This is Shawn. Ain't he hot? I won him in a cee-lo game and he's ours for the night!"

We all smiled as we gave his fine ass the once-over hoping to have some of what our girl experienced before the night was finished.

"Come on, ya'all. Let's get outta here and go over to that after-hours spot the Blue Door!" I suggested, needing a new environment and a new selection of fresh meat.

We headed out of the club with Shawn and about ten other people in tow anxious to get to the next location. When we arrived, me and all of my friends were comped, including the ones I didn't even know. We got high, drank, and partied until the sun came up, not even knowing where the drugs or the liquor was coming from. All I knew was that I had now officially arrived in the world of stardom and I had no intentions of ever turning back.

After such an eventful night, needless to say, I had no strength to get out of bed the next morning. The hangover from the Ecstasy was way more intense than any drug I'd ever tried, but I knew I had to get up and pack for my trip to Vegas. My girls were in just as bad a shape as I was, and when I went to say good-bye to them, no one moved. Thus, when Aaron arrived to pick me up, I simply vacated the premises unnoticed by my friends, stepping over Carmen, who was knocked out on the living room floor. For some unknown reason, my eyes swelled with tears as I drove off in Aaron's car, waving good-bye to the comatose bunch. As we maneuvered through the city streets, I sighed and tried to ignore the massive drug-and-alcohol-induced migraine that throbbed behind my eyes, looking forward to Vegas and to all of my dreams coming true.

nineteen

the land of lust

As hungover and exhausted as I was, I was unable to sleep during the five-and-a-half-hour plane ride to Vegas. The constant chatter of Aaron and his E.M.B. staff had me hyped beyond words and too wired to close my eyes for one second. Needless to say, when we finally landed, I was ready to rock and roll.

Las Vegas was like a different world to me. It was a flashy town with lots of high rollers and I was drawn to the glam. As the shuttle headed to our hotel, I had a smile fixed on my face as I gazed out the window at the bright lights and neon signs. The hotels looked like giant glittering palaces lining the streets. Throngs of people were milling around outside, hoping Lady Luck would be on their side. Tourists were out in droves, snapping pictures and making purchases from the street vendors who were selling everything from roses to pussy. It seemed that anything and everything was available for a price. All you had to do was ask.

When the shuttle pulled up to the opulent Sahara Hotel, a line of beautiful and scantily clad women posed for the paparazzi in the lobby. Reporters hovered and cameras snapped causing a bevy of flickering lights. As our group entered the hotel, I heard a voice screaming out my name. It surprised me that anyone knew who I was, but I didn't turn around as Aaron leaned in closely and whispered, "This is only the beginning."

Once we had checked in, I hung out in the lounge with Aaron, meeting other adult stars and directors before getting ready for the evening's festivities. I was definitely in the right place to mix and mingle with people in the X-rated business, and I couldn't believe how big the industry was. I met conservative, suit-and-tie men who owned porn production and distribution companies, as well as many who did not fit the stereotype of what "porn people" looked like.

After mingling for a while, I decided to go up to my room with hopes of getting some rest before the next day's big event. Still a little hungover, I was exhausted and overwhelmed from the long flight. After showering and changing into something comfortable, I made myself a cup of herbal tea before placing my head snuggly upon the soft down pillow provided by the hotel staff. My eyelids were heavy, and before I knew it I had drifted off into a magnificent state of slumber, dreaming vividly about what was to come.

I was awakened bright and early by the sounds of gentle rapping on the door of my room. Room service had arrived to deliver a scrumptious breakfast sent by Aaron. Famished and well rested, I ate the hardy meal while watching the activity down on the Vegas strip from my window, then I got dressed and waited for Aaron to pick me up. He arrived promptly at nine A.M. As we entered the crowded convention center, I was taken aback by the slew of people who had all come together in the name of pornography. The place was filled with over twenty-five thousand people representing the industry in some form or fashion. There were countless rows of large-, medium-, and smaller-sized booths with different company logos on them, and every booth had male and female actors signing autographs and taking pictures with fans. There were many long lines of people standing and waiting to meet their favorite porn star and I wondered how long my line would be or if I would have a line at all.

As we made our way over to our medium-sized booth, Aaron gave me the lowdown on exactly what I was expected to do.

"Simone, just stand here and smile, sign autographs, and take pictures with your fans," he instructed, handing me a pen. He then hung up a life-sized poster of me, and in less than five minutes, a few people started coming over. At first it was a little slow, but the line steadily grew and I was amazed at how busy my booth was becoming. So was everyone else. Things began moving quickly and I started getting into the groove. Flashes flashed and people begged me to touch them—and not only men, women, too. I even plopped myself down in one guy's lap to take a picture with him. In full porno mode, I was in rare form—feeling bold, beautiful, and desired—taking peek-a-boo shots with whoever asked. Aaron was glad to see the response I was getting from the fans and was happy about the investment he had made in my career. To add icing on the cake, distributors continuously flocked by our booth to place orders. Like a proud papa, Aaron's chest was puffed out as his protégée quickly became the buzz on the exhibit floor.

As I continued to sign my name and give attention to my fans, I couldn't help but notice the largest booth in the convention center, which just happened to be situated directly across from ours. The setup was absolutely gorgeous. It was in the form of a miniature castle, complete with a bridge and mote. Six beautiful girls stood glamorously on the bridge signing autographs and their line was the longest in the exhibit hall.

Even while I was engrossed in my own activities, I couldn't help noticing a man standing on the sidelines of the booth overseeing every move. He looked powerful and was very handsome. I assumed he was the owner of the company. It was clear to all that he was about his business, having no interest in anything other than what was going on at his booth. However, when the crowd started to thin down, the handsome gentleman's eyes met mine and I smiled at him as he started to walk in my direction. For some reason, my nerves kicked in and my stomach started doing flip-flops. But to my disappointment, he walked right past me.

"How have you been doing, Aaron? I see you've found yourself a star," the man began, as he shook my boss's hand and gave him a friendly pat on the back.

"Yes, I do believe I have," Aaron replied with a friendly smirk.

"I'm Harley Foxx, owner of X-Diva Video," the gentleman turned to me and said. "Whatever he is paying you, I will triple it. Think it over and let me know."

He then looked back at Aaron and nodded good-bye before walking back over to his booth with a presidential swagger. The man had presence. And he was sexy, too. Feeling uncomfortable about Mr. Foxx's brazen move, with a tinge of loyalty permeating throughout my psyche, I felt the need to say something to Aaron.

"Is he serious? What an arrogant egomaniac!" I snapped, not really feeling that way at all. I just didn't want Aaron to think I was a traitor.

"No, no . . . Harley is a good guy. And a real power player in this industry. He just comes off like an asshole sometimes. Money can do that to you," Aaron laughed. I was actually relieved at his response, for right at that moment, the powerful presence of Harley Foxx, combined with his arrogance and self-assurance, made me want to do him right in the middle of the convention center.

"Well, he does look big-time." I shrugged.

"He is. And to be honest, I would be a fool to let you turn down his offer. Harley Foxx is at the top of the game. He has what most people in this industry want. Fame and fortune. He's kind of like the Hugh Hefner of the porn world."

"You're actually willing to let me go to another company already? But I haven't even been signed to you six months!" I exclaimed, shocked that Aaron would even consider letting me move on so soon.

"Yes, I know. But E.M.B. is a small company. We could never do for your career what X-Diva Video could."

"Wow, Aaron. That's pretty unselfish of you. You really do care about me," I sighed, getting a little emotional, as no one had ever taken my best interests and placed them before their own.

"Of course, I do," he assured me. "But bigger than that, I think a move to X-Diva Video could be a great thing for both of us."

"How's that?" I asked, with a raised brow.

"Well, I think this is the perfect time for me to become your manager," Aaron suggested. I knew there had to be a catch. People with testosterone never did anything without getting something for themselves.

"For a handsome price, I will release you from E.M.B. if I can be your manager and get you the best deal possible with X-Diva," he continued. But honestly, his suggestion didn't sound half bad. After all, Aaron had found me and it was only right that he climb the ladder of success by my side.

Hearing his words, I looked intently over at the X-Diva booth once again. The crowd in their area was the largest in the entire hall. If I didn't know any better, I would have thought Prince and the Revolution were handing out free records. And as I compared the considerably smaller swarm at our own booth, I experienced a career-defining moment before exclaiming, "You gotta deal!"

Aaron smiled at me in delight. I wondered if the dollar signs in his eyes were as large as the ones in mine.

"Simone, signing with X-Diva will make you a pioneer in the industry. Not only were you the first African-American girl to ever be signed to a contract, but now you will be the first ever to get a contract from a major company. You're about to change the face of this industry!" Aaron exclaimed.

Knowing the magnitude of what it meant for my career, he was more excited than I was. I, on the other hand, was naive and clueless as to what this meant not only for my career but also for my life. Only later would I come to realize the depth of what I was delving into.

As the day progressed, I continued to smile for every camera that flashed before me as I basked in the shine among the glory of lust. When I had signed my final autograph of the day, Aaron suggested we head back to the hotel to get ready for a party that one of his friends was throwing later that night.

Back in the privacy of my own room, I freshened up and put on the sexiest outfit I had packed. I curled my hair, put a shiny gloss on my lips, and sat staring at my own reflection in the mahogany wood–framed mirror. Gone was the little girl who just wanted to be loved and remembered by the world. In her place was a stranger. How did it come to this? I asked myself. When I received no answer, I took a deep breath and closed my eyes for a few seconds to collect myself. When I opened them, I saw a determined young girl who was simply brave enough to go after what she wanted.

"If this is who I am now, so be it. I just have to make sure I do my best at whatever comes my way—and do it with class. I'm a porn star now and proud of it," I said aloud into my reflection.

The front lobby of the Hotel Rio was crowded with beautiful women flaunting their million-dollar assets. There was a bevy of blondes, brunettes, and redheads in alluring outfits, enticing every eye to follow them. You couldn't help but be drawn and sucked in by the sea of lusciousness that seemed to send a whispering invitation to all within view, and it was impossible for me not to get caught up in all the hoopla that I was witnessing. Everyone looked powerful and beautiful in a way like no other. These X-rated stars were probably the most desirable people on the planet, possessing the ability to make you cum just from watching them on screen and now in person. I could feel the moisture and heat rise between my thighs as I navigated through the crowd, just from being in the presence of so much lust.

As I made my way up their version of the red carpet, a tall beautiful buxom blonde blew me a kiss and winked at me as I walked by. I followed closely behind Aaron through the crowded casino and was captivated by the ringing bells and flashing lights of the slot machines. The Rio was a fabulous

and glitzy hotel, lavishly decorated with striking colors and bright illumina-
tions throughout. The way the high rollers threw their money down on the
tables baffled me.

We made our way over to a secluded elevator bank, and when we arrived
on the penthouse floor, the elevator doors opened into a wide hallway packed
with people hanging out and partying. Half-naked girls were running in and
out of the rooms and loud rock music filtered through the atmosphere. Upon
crossing the threshold of the suite, we were immediately greeted by a sexy
strawberry blonde with the biggest, juiciest ass I had ever seen on a white
chick. Aaron leaned in closely and told me that her name was Stacey Storm
and that she was one of the most legendary icons in the adult industry. From
looking at her, I could understand why she was an O.G. in the porn game—
she was that delicious.

"I'm Stacey Strom," she said, turning up her seductive West Coast charm.
"You're quite a beauty. I saw you at the convention, making a big buzz on the
exhibit floor. Maybe we'll get the chance to work together one day. I'd love
to eat you up. You're such a little cutie!"

"Simone Young," I shyly replied with a slight nod.

"Stacey, you bad girl . . . are you trying to scare away my new talent?"
Aaron interjected, interrupting our moment.

"No, of course not, Aaron, dahling. I'm just letting her know what I
want!" she exclaimed, with an exaggerated look of innocence on her face.

Stacey took me by the hand, taking it upon herself to lead me around the
room and introduce me to everyone. After a couple of cocktails, I was back in
my comfort zone, mellow and eager. Stacey was a mega-star in the industry
and here she was being nice and motherly to me, taking me under her wing.
My heart beat quickly and I was completely starstruck and feeling connected
to the people in the room, like I knew them from a past life or something.
But the environment was unlike any I had ever been in before and the magnitude of pure erotic passion that flowed throughout the suite was incredibly
overwhelming. In every corner of the room there seemed to be an orgy going on as the owners and distributors of top companies made national as well
as international deals over cigars and pussy. As they talked business and poli-
tics, naked flesh rubbed up against their bodies and foreign hands slid down
the front of their pants jerking their cocks off, momentarily distracting them.

Still, deals were sealed and money was made in an environment that probably closely resembled the reason Noah was told by God to build his ark.

Not quite ready to jump into the pool of lust just yet, I sat with Aaron to keep him company. I tried to strike up a conversation but it was damn near impossible with what was going on all around me. Aaron seemed numb to it, but I was more than mesmerized by the whole thing, wondering how his wife felt about his job.

Suddenly, Stacey came dancing into the living room suite wearing a red-and-gold belly dancer outfit, swinging her hips from side to side, and clicking miniature tambourines between her fingers. Everyone swarmed around her and started throwing money at her feet. She summoned me to come dance with her but my shyness resurfaced as all eyes glared upon us. However, she wouldn't take no for an answer and pulled me onto the floor, dragging me gently on my back and causing my dress to ride up around my hips, exposing my smooth cocoa-colored thighs and firm legs. Once she got me onto her stage, she flicked her shoe off and planted her foot right between my legs before rubbing my pantiless pussy.

"Don't move! I'm gonna make you cum with just my foot caressing that pretty kitty-kat of yours!" Stacey informed me and the crowd of onlookers.

Our audience watched in silence, waiting for Stacey to turn me, the new girl, out.

"Yeah, right. I'll never cum that way," I defiantly replied, playing into the act.

"Promise me you won't move," she cooed. "Just relax. Pretend there's no one here but you and me."

Stacey rubbed her big toe back and forth across my anxious clit very slowly until I became wet. She then spanked my pussy with her foot, tapping it and spreading my sweet juice all over before gently spreading my lips open with her toes. A warm sensation started to swell in the pit of my belly and I couldn't believe how wet my pussy was getting. I tried to play it cool and stay in control, but Stacey recognized the signs of lust and started rubbing faster and with more friction. I could feel my clit swelling up and started to squirm. Two half-naked sexies joined in the fun and skillfully pinned me down. I fought to get up before I lost all control and succumbed to the building orgasm. Unbeknownst to me, Stacey's foot was like a perfectly sized dick and her toes felt like the tip of a tongue, causing my body to tremble and rock up against her foot. The party spectators cheered her on in voyeuristic delight, and when I couldn't hold back any longer, I screamed as my juices sprayed out uncontrollably upon Stacey's toes.

"Oh my goodness, I'm cummming!" I yelled, to my own surprise.

My orgasm was explosive as my body jerked several times before I crumpled limply on the floor. The audience excitedly applauded Stacey's work, throwing more money at her as her two accomplices released me and planted proud kisses all over my face and neck for getting through their little initiation with flying colors. As a finale, Stacey slowly slid her foot from my pussy, shook the cum off her toes, and started dancing again. Paralyzed, I could do nothing but lay there on floor, relishing in the feeling as pure pleasure and satisfaction flowed throughout my veins.

"Sweetie, you'll soon learn that you can use just about any object at your disposal to bring on an orgasm. But you have to know how to use it. Hang with me and I'll teach you how to master it all." Stacey smiled, her pearly white teeth shining like halogen lamps.

Dumbfounded by the sensations I had just experienced, I gave my new mentor a kiss on the lips and the party went back to getting its freak on. The sideshow was over and I bashfully went back over to sit with my new manager. I had evidently passed the initiation.

"Aaron, I think I've had enough for one evening. She made me cum so hard, I feel like I have no energy left. I'm drained!" I moaned.

"OK. I'll take you back to your room so you can get some shut-eye," he laughed. We said our good-byes to everyone as we made our way to the door.

When we passed Stacey, I humbly stated, "Thank you for the tip, Stacey."

"Oh, that was nothing! There's a ton of tricks for you to learn. You can start by reading my book. And, Aaron, make sure you book a scene for us to do together. I like her. She's a hottie with a lot of pent-up passion, and I think I'm just the one to help her release it." Stacey winked, stroking my cheek before heading back to the party.

As we left the penthouse suite and made our way to the elevator, I was amazed at what I had just experienced, knowing that the scene was one for the history books.

"Aaron, all I can say is wow! This whole experience has been so mind-boggling! I thought I had skills, but these people are no joke!" I exclaimed.

"It's all about mastering your craft, Simone," he replied like a knowl-edgeable professor.

The elevator doors opened ready to carry us back down to the main casino floor. Aaron was right. It was time for me to step up my game, take notes from the best, and create my own niche. I was fully determined to watch, listen, learn, and make the porno industry my oyster.

twenty

triple-x red carpet

After a night of some much-needed beauty sleep, I was ready to shine. The X-rated Adult Awards Show awaited me and I was only too excited to be attending. Wanting to look my very best, I took several hours to slowly prepare myself for the ceremony. By the time Aaron arrived to pick me up, I was a complete vision of loveliness, wearing a beautiful strapless red silk dress that flared at the waist and red silk shoes with satin ribbons that laced up my perfectly toned legs. My simple but elegant accessories consisted of a pearl choker and matching teardrop pearl earrings. My hair was twisted up in an elegant bun with a few stray corkscrew curls cascading down around my impeccably made up face, making me feel more beautiful than I had ever felt before in my life.

When Aaron called from the hotel lobby, I quickly splashed on my perfume, grabbed my red clutch bag, and exited the room feeling like royalty. As I approached the front desk where my new manager stood, his eyes lit up in excitement.

"You look amazing!" he exclaimed.

I smiled, playing coy with him before holding out my hand for him to kiss. He did and stood aside like a perfect gentleman to let me exit the hotel ahead of him, then enter the limo he had hired to drive us to the awards show.

"There will be a lot of people coming at you tonight," Aaron told me. "But all you have to do is smile and look sexy. Remember to promote your movie and you'll do just fine."

"OK, I got it," I nervously replied.

"Why doesn't that sound reassuring to me?" he asked, sensing that something was wrong.

"Well, it's just that all this is so new to me. I just don't wanna lose my cool," I sighed.

"You'll be fine. You're a natural," he soothed.

Our stretch finally rolled up to the venue behind a line of limousines, and I peered out of the tinted window at the land of ultimate erotica. Paparazzi flocked around the limos to get the first shot of whoever was inside.

"You ready, kid?" Aaron winked.

I nodded.

"Then let's go. Your public awaits!" he said.

The driver came around to open the door for me. I took a very deep breath before stepping out of the car. Cameras clicked away and fans screamed my name, sending an incredible adrenaline rush throughout my body. Still not used to the popularity, I was again shocked at the fact that anyone recognized me at all. As I made my way up the red carpet, fans ran up begging me to put my signature on their T-shirts, bodies, or anything they had to offer. I graciously signed a few autographs and glided through, waving to the people along with the other sexy starlets. The entire scene could not have been better if I had scripted it myself.

"You give good red carpet press, Simone," Aaron complimented. "You're learning fast."

I giggled softly and scanned my surroundings. It sure was a sight to see. The women were scantily clad, dressed in miniskirts and see-through gowns showing off their goods. And true to what Aaron had told me when we first met, blondes definitely dominated. If I didn't know better I would have thought it was an award show for the sexiest blonde, there were so many in the place. Platinum blondes, strawberry blondes, honey blondes, dyed blondes, natural blondes—tall ones, short ones, ones with big hair, curly hair, and straight. I even saw a sexy blond midget walk by with a dark Latin hunk at her side. I also noticed that almost every girl in the hall had a man draped over her shoulder or hanging off her arm. And to my surprise, they all knew each other. It was like one big happy family, as they all seemed to reunite with their male or female costars. I, on the other hand, didn't know anyone except Aaron and his staff. Still, I was ready to step it up and throw myself into the pack. I wanted to be recognized and a force to be reckoned with within this exclusive new world, and everything I did was a step closer to that goal.

Thanks to my preconceived notion of the porn world, I was expecting to see and meet the grimiest and greasiest people on the planet. But that simply wasn't the case. Much to my surprise, the people attending the event were actually very respectable-looking. The men were a mix of corporate tycoons, professionals, and working middle class. And while there were a lot of sex kittens throughout, many of the women looked like the average housewife.

As I continued to soak in my surroundings, a man with a press pass hanging around his neck approached me and asked if I would pose for a few shots for his magazine. I quickly obliged and walked over to the wall to smile and pose for his camera. In no time, a flock of press and cameramen surrounded me asking for a little tease. I hesitated and looked over at Aaron, waiting for his approval. When he gave it to me, I turned my back to my public, looked over my shoulder smiling, and unzipped my dress. Everyone went crazy as I then returned to face them, popping my perky titties out of my red dress and shaking them with vigor.

"Woah! Now, that's what I call a moneymaking shot!" one of the paparazzi yelled out.

Some of the girls noticed the commotion and came over to peep out the new girl. Not to be outdone, two of my colleagues burst through the pack to get in on my action as the paparazzi had a field day. I didn't even know the two girls but I didn't mind because they were both smoking hot. One was Asian and the other was an Australian built like an Amazon. They grinded up against me like they'd known me for years, but I didn't mind at all, as the show we were giving had the entire place at our mercy.

When I was finished with the peep show, I tucked my boobs back into my dress and one of the girls helped me zip back up. I got a loud moan from the press, for they were clearly disappointed that the presentation had ended. So to appease them, my new friends pulled up their skirts, turned around and bent over with their butts pressed together, giving onlookers the perfect ass and g-string shot. The paparazzi snapped away, happy to have more flesh shots to sell to the tabloids. I quickly made friends with them and together we dashed off to get drinks. It was important to me to finally make some real friends in the business. Aaron let me go, glad to see that I was getting into the groove of things. But he kept a watchful eye on me while maintaining a slight distance, allowing me to establish myself apart from his shadow. As I hobnobbed with my new pals, a couple of feet away from me at the bar I saw a very corporate-looking gentleman approach Aaron and listened intently as I overheard him say, "Excuse me, Mr. Roth, is it?"

"Please, call me Aaron." My manager smiled as the two shook hands.

"Lyle Foster, producer of the show," the man stated.

"Yes, I know who you are. Pleasure to meet you."

"Aaron, I would love for your new girl to make a stage presentation and give out an award to one of the winners tonight. Do you think she would do it?"

"Of course. She'd be honored."

"Good. Here's the lineup sheet. The highlighted one is hers. Enjoy the show." Lyle smiled, handing Aaron a white piece of paper.

"Thank you, I will, and same to you." Aaron grinned as if he had just hit the jackpot. The men shook hands again and Aaron headed toward me to give me the details of his conversation.

"Hey . . . I'm really having a great time so far and the show hasn't even started yet," I said.

"Well, you're about to have an even better time. This must be your night to shine. The producer of the show wants you to give out the award for Best Actress of the Year."

"Are you serious?" I asked, as if I hadn't heard the conversation.

"Yes. He wants you," Aaron assured me.

I gave my manager a hug and a quick peck on the cheek before he led me to the backstage area, which was a madhouse of organized chaos. The stars were in rare form letting their "diva attitudes" surface as people argued over goodie bags and who they wanted to go out on stage with. Quite a few of them were noticeably tipsy, while others were just flat-out drunk. Many were coked up and horny, judging by the way they were rubbing up on each other. The women seemed more aggressive than the men, as many of the male stars were hanging back in the cut, drinking and waiting for their cue, smacking butts, pinching boobs, and teasing the women as they walked by.

The backstage coordinator was running around like a chicken with his head cut off as a rock and roll band played their funky music on stage preparing the audience for the show that was about to begin. When the show's hosts hit the stage, the crowd went wild. I stood by Aaron on the sidelines and watched the show take off. It was so professionally put together that I felt like I was at the Grammy awards! I could definitely tell that the people in the industry took their business very seriously. Although the categories were best blow job, best girl on girl, best anal input, and things like that, it was evident that this was big business and the awards were given to those who went that extra mile to please an audience.

After waiting at the side of stage awhile, my feet began to scream in pain, reminding me that my footwear was made for glamour and not standing. Sensing my discomfort, the stage coordinator walked up to me and said, "You have a little time before you have to go up. Why don't you go around to the other side of the stage where you can sit down?"

"Oh, thanks. You're a lifesaver," I whispered and hurried over to the other side, sitting down in a folding metal chair to rest my aching feet. I sighed in relief and continued watching the show, still feeling a bit anxious in anticipation of getting my part over with.

Just as I was beginning to get comfortable in my seat, a tall blonde walked up and rudely stood right in front of me, obstructing my view of the stage. All I could see was a pair of long legs wearing black pumps with rhinestone heels and a fluffy blue-fox boa draped around some shoulders. As if she felt the rays from my eyeballs permeating against her spine, the chick suddenly turned around and have me a perfect view of her 34 triple D's.

"Who are you?" she spat, an air of self-glory emanating from her. Speechless and taken aback by her tone of voice, I stared at her blankly like a deer caught in a pair of headlights.

"Don't you see whose name is on that chair?" she continued.

I stayed cool and twisted around to look at the back of the chair. There was no name written on it. It was just a simple metal chair.

"There's no name on this chair and the stage guy told me it would be all right if I sat here," I drily responded.

"Well, in case you didn't know, I am the hostess of this show and I say you're sitting in *my* chair. Now get the fuck up!" she barked.

I instantly felt my body temperature rise, angered at the rudeness this bitch had tossed my way for no reason whatsoever. This Valley Girl obviously had no idea who she was messing with. I might have been in Vegas, but I was still a girl from the 'hood, ready to fuck a bitch up for just looking at me the wrong way. For a moment she took my memory back to Atlanta and that bitch Chyna, but I knew I was playing with a much bigger fire than Kareem and Club Vanity. Figuring that I had much to lose if I jumped on her, I decided to take the high road and just chill. Thus, I relinquished the chair just as the stagehand came running over to tell me that I was up next. Moments later I was walking out onto the glorious black lacquer stage in front of a roaring audience. The echo was loud and the lights were blinding but I followed the cue cards as instructed, adding a little something cute of my own to say right before I opened the envelope.

"And the actress of the year goes to Jackie Jugs!" I finally announced. I picked the award up off the podium as Jackie came running up to accept it. She forcefully snatched the statue from my hand and whipped out a piece of paper to read her speech.

"I wanna thank my parents, my manager, the studio, and, last but not least, I want to thank my fans. Thank you all so much! I had the best fucking time—I mean the best time fucking! And may God bless you all! Stay horny! Porn rules! Rock and roll, dude!" Jackie ranted. Before walking off the stage, she pulled one of her tits out and licked her nipple for the audience, then danced off the stage with me leading the way. The crowd stood and applauded as if they had just seen Princess Diana.

At the end of the show, every star who had won an award was called back out onto the stage to dance. Grabbed by some miscellaneous actor, I was among them, bumping and grinding up on total strangers and having the time of my life. I was sucked in by the glitz and glamour and was totally ready to hand my soul over to the adult industry. As I danced my heart out, I had no idea just how lonely my soul would ultimately become or that I had just stepped into the beginning of a very lustful end.

The show was over but the party was just beginning. I had made a lot of new friends and decided that the after party was the place I needed to be in order to become fully acclimated into this new world. Word spread quickly that there was going to be a big bash, and since the party scene wasn't really his style, Aaron decided to call it a night and headed back to the hotel to rest up. I, on the other hand, had been bitten by the porn bug and headed to the party with my new family of friends.

I jumped into a limo that was like a little self-contained disco, as music pumped loudly and girls hung out of the sunroof, baring their breasts as we cruised down the Vegas strip. I felt liberated as I smoked weed alongside my new comrades and, being the new kid on the block, I was in the hot seat, as everyone in the limo wanted to lick my twat and get to know me better. Sex was like a handshake in that environment and it was obvious that fresh meat excited the veterans of the industry. The only thing that bothered me was the fact that I knew my freshness was temporary.

As we approached the location of the after party, the limo stopped abruptly and cocaine powder went flying all over a busty girl who was wearing a very low-cut black cat suit. Every cokehead in the car shrieked in horror, until one guy was bold and desperate enough to crawl over and run his nose up and down her scantily clad body, snorting it all up. It was pretty funny and everyone laughed heartily. When the driver finally opened the door, we all got out high as kites, straightening up our clothes, and ready to make an entrance into a world of narcotic-tainted lust.

twenty-one

wet hollywood

The party was in full swing when my new friends and I made our grand entrance. Once inside, everyone scattered in different directions. Some went in search of party favors to powder their noses with and others searched for old friends while many looked to make new ones. Since I was new on the scene, I decided to stroll around a bit and check out the surroundings. To my surprise, I again noticed a number of mainstream celebrities in attendance. In fact, it seemed like the later it got, the more the Hollywood players showed up. And they seemed to be popping out of the woodwork. I had no idea that so many so-called regular folk were big fans of porn. Being surrounded by not only porn stars but real Hollywood stars as well had me double starstruck. I was having a visual orgasm of sorts, drinking it up with top comedians, actors, star athletes, and musicians. While I made my way through the party, I spotted several celebrities getting their grooves on over in quiet corners with the award-winning porn stars of the night. There was a lot sucking and fucking going on in the main room, the bathrooms, and even some of the closets. It was actually cool to see the mainstream celebrities mixing and mingling together freely and not hiding. The celebs seemed to know that their secrets and habits were safe in this private environment with these people. I concluded that there was something about porn stars that made people feel comfortable enough to spill all their sexual secrets. After all, how could people who worked in the adult industry be judgmental?

I cruised around the grand bash, eventually making my way out to the pool. There was a huge crowd making a big splash, and although I was lavishly dressed, I wanted to get wet. I slid open the patio door to a wet and wild party scene. PG- and R-rated actors were doing it up with the XXX-rated stars and everyone in the pool seemed to be having the kinkiest time of their lives. On one side of the pool, female porn stars popped out of the water topless, riding the shoulders of different hunks as they engaged in a sexual game of lust-filled beach ball. It was like a tropical zoo filled with the types of beautiful girls that any man would love to cage up.

As I walked around, I passed by a few Hollywood actors who winked at me and tried to flirt. I stayed cool and watched as most of the other girls fell all over themselves trying to be the one to get their attention. I shook my head and chuckled when I spotted Lucy Kane over by one of the tiki bars near the pool.

"Lucy, how are you?" I asked, giving her a big hug.

"Simone! I see you made it out here to the big time. You've been making quite a buzz!" She smiled.

"Yeah, and let me tell you, this has been a very enlightening experience," I said in awe, shaking my head gently from side to side and scanning the premises.

"Well, consider yourself lucky. It takes some girls years to make it to an event like this. Let's sit down and catch up," she suggested, leading me over to some vacant lounge chairs.

We sat and reminisced about our sex scene together in New York, gossiped about the stars and the industry, and watched as guys chased their prey around the pool, ripping bikini tops off and tossing naked chicks into the pool. Interrupting our dialogue, Lucy's cell phone rang and she reached into her purse to answer it.

"Hello?" she sexily cooed into the tiny receiver.

As she engaged in her conversation, I took the opportunity to relax, placing my head back onto my chair and staring up at the heavens. It was a clear night and the stars were brilliant against the backdrop of the dark desert sky. They looked so close that I felt like I could reach out and almost touch one, maneuver it just so, and make all of my wishes come true.

When Lucy hung up her phone, she turned to me with a sly look on her face and asked, "You wanna have some *real* fun?"

"That depends on what you have in mind," I chuckled, knowing that whatever my friend had to offer what going to be crazy.

"Well, I'm dating the basketball player Stephan Manes. Have you heard of him?" she began.

"Yes, of course! He's only the biggest basketball star in the world right now."

"Well, he has a mansion out here in Vegas and he wants me to come over and he told me to bring a friend. He prefers white women, but you're a hottie, so I'm sure he'll adore you. So whaddaya say? You wanna come?"

Would I like to party with a superstar athlete like Stephan Manes? He was only an NBA championship winner with millions of dollars and a body to die for! How could I possibly refuse?

Without hesitation, I left the poolside with Lucy and we made our exit from the party. Although I felt like I was riding on the coattail of my friend, I really didn't care. I knew there would be plenty of time for me to blaze my own trail and build my own little network of friends. That night I was getting the chance to meet the top man in the NBA and boy was I excited.

Lucy's private limo pulled up to a wall of giant steel gates. When the fancy-looking iron opened automatically, the car drove through a garden of brightly colored, impeccably landscaped flowers that led up to the mansion. The driver stopped at the front entrance and opened the door. Leaving me behind, Lucy ran up the stairs and reached for the gold doorknob, pushing open the tallest door I had ever seen. She then summoned me from the car and I cautiously followed. I could tell that my friend had been there many times before, and if I hadn't known any better, I would have thought she lived there.

When we walked in, I felt like I had entered the giant's castle from Jack and the Beanstalk. I'd never seen anything so beautiful and elaborately decorated. It was like a royal palace. Everything glistened and was buffed to perfection, sparkling like a scene straight out of *The Lifestyles of the Rich and Famous*. The front hall was massive and grand, like it had been custom-made for a man seven foot six inches. And when I looked up at the ceiling, my mouth dropped in awe. A huge chandelier hung in the circular foyer made up of what looked like a million crystals. It was encased in gold arms and was absolutely brilliant.

"Follow my lead," Lucy instructed.

As I was told, I followed Lucy up an elaborate staircase whose banister was overlaid in gold. In the distance I could hear music playing, and when we reached the top of the stairs, we turned right and walked across a balcony that overlooked the entrance from where we had just come. When we reached a set of mahogany double doors, Lucy turned the latch and walked right in. Larger than the size of two living rooms, it was definitely the master bedroom suite. To the left of the room was a couch and a cigar table sitting before a window that expanded from the floor to the ceiling. On the other side of the bed was an elegant fireplace and two extra-large black velvet futons that sat upon miscellaneously tossed leopard-skin rugs. The man of the house was laid out on his California king–sized waterbed wearing a black silk robe that lay open exposing his well-cut chest and a pair of sport boxers that fit just right. To complete the scene, on Stephan's feet were a pair of purple and yellow Nike sneakers, reminding us just who the hell he really was; a massive-sized blunt dangled from his succulent lips.

"It's about mutherfuckin' time!" was his greeting. "Come here, baby!" He smiled as Lucy ran over and jumped on top of him.

"Oh, stop your whining, Daddy," she said, chastising him. "Your hot-headed bitch is here now!" She then leaned in and took a shotgun from the joint.

As I observed their interaction, it was clear to me that I was invisible to them, so I stayed that way and stood silently in the doorway. After taking a couple of hits and a few nibbles on each other, they finally noticed me and Stephan extended an invitation for me to join in.

"Come on over here, little one, I don't bite. Hey, I know who you are. I just got your tape in the mail last week," he said, taking another drag on the joint and holding it in. "Nice work," he moaned, sounding constipated.

"Thanks," I replied.

I went over to join them and sat down on the edge of the bed. I felt a little shy, but only because I was once again starstruck. I couldn't believe I was in Stephan Mane's bedroom. But I didn't want to seem like a ditz, so I thought I'd return the compliment.

"I love your work, too," I offered.

"You brought a shy one with you, L. I guess we're going to have to help her loosen up," he laughed.

He jumped up from the bed and walked over to the wet bar on the other side of the room. He poured a few glasses of Merlot and pulled out a cigar box stocked with blue chronic and some pills that I recognized as Ecstasy. We each took a pill, and after one glass of wine, I was ready to let the games begin.

Like a little boy at his eighth birthday party, Stephan chased us around the mansion, grabbing and snatching our clothes off until we were butt-naked. Then he sat on his throne like the king he was, lording over his beautiful sex slaves. We entertained him by dancing and playing with each other, all the while tantalizing him with erotic gestures. Then Lucy gave me a look that said, let's give it to him, so we crawled over to Stephan and spread his long legs open wide enough for us both to fit between them. From the moment I entered the house, I had imagined what his cock looked like, figuring that it must have been massive because his stats said that he wore a size sixteen shoe. When we untied his robe, out it fell, long and fat like a Dominican plantano. My eyes bugged out as it lay slumped over his thick hairy thigh, hanging limply down the side of his leg, not even hard yet. I gave Lucy a look that said, *This is a big one,* then went in for the attack. We both grabbed the hung cock and started cranking it up so we could take a drink. Lucy and I took turns slobbering away. With a serious look on his face, Stephan watched us as we devoured his manhood, all the while puffing on a fat joint. He was loving the way we seemingly fought over his dick, and once it grew to full erection, it seemed like it was the size of my arm. How in the world was I gonna fit this monster of a dick inside my precious sex pocket? I asked myself. Lucy must have read my mind because she got up off the floor and straddled Stephan's legs, facing him. She smothered his face between the jumbo-sized boobs she'd bought and he bit down on her pink nipples before aggressively rubbing her ass. I stopped giving him head to position his dick beneath Lucy's coochie. I manipulated it like a metal joystick, teasing Lucy and getting the head slippery wet. When Lucy couldn't take anymore of the teasing, she rammed herself down on his cock like someone shoving a corkscrew into a bottle top. It was an incredibly tight fit and I watched her pussy slide up and down his weapon, her inner walls massaging and stroking his dick and dousing it in her slippery juices. I stared silently, mesmerized by it all as I stayed on my knees and helped out by pulling Lucy's hips down upon him. I then gently rubbed his balls while Lucy continued to impale herself, observing and eager to taste his perfectly round and heavy nut sack. Stephan moaned from the sensations and begged for me to squeeze and suck more. So, I decided to go a step further, especially since he supposedly preferred white women and I wanted to show him what a black bitch could do. Like the skilled fallatian that I was, I moved in with my slithery tongue and licked the base of his dick as he thrust in and out of my friend's pussy. Feeling really nasty, I even licked the spot between his asshole and the base of his cock, making him spasm. He wiggled uncontrollably, ready to bust, but obviously didn't want to cum yet because he pulled Lucy up off his dick and carried her over to his bed. After throwing her down, he came for me, picking me up and tossing me over his shoulder like a caveman, dropping me beside my friend. He then pulled my hips back so that my ass was in the air, spreading my butt cheeks apart as far as they would go and attempting to stick his dick inside. Never having experienced a back shot of this magnitude in my third hole, it didn't exactly drop right in.

"Damn! You're so fuckin' tight, I can't get in!" he complained.

"Wait, let me get it wet!" I said, down for whatever.

That was Lucy's cue to get her mouth on me again. She slid her tongue up and down my split, starting from my clit and ending at my asshole, getting me nice and lubricated. After a few moments, I was ready to go.

"Here you go, baby. Try it now," I offered, positioning myself for easy entry. Stephan corkscrewed his cock inside my sugar walls as I screamed out from a pain that hurt so good. Relentless in his desire, he continued to push until it was all the way in. After a few slow strokes, I got used to his size and then it was on. Stephan rode me right and I loved every second of it. I could feel that he was about ready to pop but he still wanted to hold his nut so he pulled out of me suddenly and got up off the bed and, with his dick leading the way, went over to the CD player and threw on some Miles Davis. He then lit up another joint and headed down to the kitchen to get a snack.

In a sweaty lust-filled stupor, Lucy and I sipped some wine as we waited for Stephan to return. He came back with his dick swinging from side to side carrying a large bowl of red and green grapes. He jumped back in the sack and we picked up where we'd left off with our free-for-all in between eating and feeding him grapes. When he finally did cum, he came so hard, it was as if he had just won the slam-dunk contest at the All-Star game, then he collapsed in a state of exhaustion. Still needing to climax, Lucy and I gave each other oral pleasure while Stephan lay limply watching. Once we had gotten ours, I fell back into the pillows swirling in a whirlwind of sexual sensations. Lucy cuddled up on Stephan, who seemed to really be feeling her—a flaming redheaded big-silicone-boobed white chick. I silently chuckled at what Lucy had told me about him preferring white women, when he himself was a deep chocolate African-American brotha.

Hey, to each his own, I said to myself.

But the evening didn't end there. After getting our second wind, Lucy and I found ourselves in Stephan's shower, where we engaged in even more uninhibited sex with the sexiest basketball player alive. When we'd finally finished, Stephan was famished and we let ourselves out after he'd collapsed, amid a sea of Trojan wrappers and spent condoms.

Back in the limo, we laughed about the whole night as our X-induced high began to fade. When the limo stopped at my hotel first, I gave Lucy a kiss good night and hugged her tightly.

"I think I'm gonna sign a contract with X-Diva. Why don't you move out here to the West Coast? Maybe we could get a place together," I told her.

"Oooh . . . you lucky dog! Every girl wants to be an X-Diva girl. And you must have read my mind! I've actually been seriously considering moving out here. Now I have a reason! And of course I'll be your roommate! Then I could really teach you the tricks of this *dirty* trade!" She smiled, giving me her number before we parted ways.

I made my way up to my room and called Aaron, asking him to meet me in the hotel restaurant. I showered again, changed, and quickly headed downstairs to get some breakfast. I hadn't slept a wink but was still wired from all the coke and X that I'd consumed the night before. Over a plate of scrambled eggs and sausage, I shamelessly told my manager all about my night and how it felt to meet and fuck an NBA superstar. Intrigued by my words, Aaron was all ears as he listened to my story about my all-night threesome with Stephan Manes.

"Simone, you're playing with big boys now. Be careful and keep it to yourself. Except for me, of course. You can always tell me anything," he warned.

"Well, I don't usually kiss and tell, but I gotta say, this shit is burning a hole in my tongue. How can I not tell at least one person about this? Not even my girls back in New York?"

Aaron smiled at me, shaking his head at my greenness.

"You just told one person—me," he reminded me with a tilt of his head.

We ate our breakfast and Aaron gave me all the details of the deal he had managed to broker for me with X-Diva Video. He had negotiated a contract that would have me do six movies at the rate of six thousand dollars a film and he would get fifteen percent. The company would also pay my rent in

California for one year. I was ecstatic. Not only was I getting a huge pay increase, but I knew that by signing a deal with the top adult entertainment company in the country, my success was unlimited.

"Well, what are we waiting for? Where do I sign?" I asked with excitement.

"We get back to New York tomorrow and I'll take care of the paperwork. Then we'll come out to Hollywood and get you set up."

I smiled. I was more than ready to get back to New York and pack. California awaited me and so did my success.

"You know, Simone, I can't move out here with you, so you'll be on your own. Do you think you can handle that?" Aaron asked me.

"I think so. But Lucy said she's been thinking about making a move out here."

"That's all well and fine, but Lucy's not in your league, Simone. Watch your back with her. There's a lot of jealousy in this business and sometimes it gets vicious. This is a pretty sneaky town with a lot of smiling faces that mean you no good. So promise me that you'll be careful."

"I will," I promised.

"I'm always a phone call away and I'll be taking care of your career and image from the East Coast."

While I appreciated Aaron's words of warning and wisdom, as I finished my meal, all I could really see were the dollar signs and bright lights dancing in my head like sugarplums on Christmas Eve.

twenty-two

bang on the beat

My flight from Vegas was a smooth ride with the only turbulence being the erotic aftershocks I continued to feel from the convention. As I gazed out of the airplane window, I felt incredible. My trip had gone better than planned. I had made a huge buzz at the convention and everyone knew that I was indeed a rising star. But I had gotten so caught up in Vegas that I had neglected to call my roommates, who I knew would have a few harsh words for me when I returned to Harlem. Still, I couldn't wait to see them just the same.

Bumper-to-bumper traffic across the Triboro Bridge made the ride back to Harlem long and uncomfortable, but the cab finally exited on 135th Street and I was home. As short as it had been, my trip had changed me mind, body, and soul. I felt as if I was evolving into a super sex goddess, but I was also losing control. The logical and sensible side of me knew that sometimes fantasies were meant to remain just that.

When the cab rolled up to my brownstone, I jumped out, grabbed my bags, and went inside, smiling and feeling like a real diva. I unlocked the door and slowly stuck my head in. Ebony and Jessie were both asleep on the sofa in front of the TV.

"Simone? Is that you?" I heard Ebony ask as I closed and locked the front door, pulling my bags inside and walking into the living room.

"Hey, what's up?" I smiled.

Ebony got up and gave me a hug and kiss as Jessie woke up yawning. When she saw me, she, too, stood up stretching and offered an embrace.

"You deserve to be spanked, young lady! You didn't call and we were worried about you!" Ebony scolded me.

"I'm sorry, you guys. I was just so busy. I'm gonna get a cell phone this week. Promise," I told them. "But I did remember to bring you both something."

My roomies smiled with anticipation as I pulled their gifts out of my bag and handed them over.

"I just picked up something cute at the hotel gift shop." I smiled.

Ebony opened her gift first and pulled out a snowball with the Vegas skyline in it. She shook it up, stared inside the globe, and shrugged.

"A snowball? You couldn't bring me back a big dick? Or at least a big dick *inside* the snowball?!"

We laughed as Jessie opened hers. Always the grateful one, Jess unwrapped her box and pulled out a magic kit.

"Cool. I always wanted one of these. Now I can play a few tricks on my tricks!" she joked. The laughter continued as they begged for details of my excursion, which I eagerly shared, forgetting all about Aaron's warning of discretion. My girls listened carefully as I provided them with almost every sordid detail of my wild and wet adventure, except the part about me moving to Hollywood to do movies for X-Diva Video. That, I wasn't so eager to spring on them just yet.

I spent the better part of the day settling in and catching up with my roommates. Ebony was dating that guy she had met at the Cove who she'd turned into her personal sex slave, making him do scandalous and nasty things to her in public places. Jessie, who was still working her nine to five, had dumped her last boyfriend but was still getting her freak on. She had started hanging out in underground swingers clubs down on the Lower East Side of Manhattan and had become pretty addicted to playing sex games with strange couples. I, on the other hand, was just glad to be relaxing in my own bed.

As the sun went down and I began to drift off to sleep, I heard a soft tap on my bedroom door.

"Hey, sorry if I woke you," Ebony peeked inside and said.

"Nah, it's OK. I wasn't asleep yet," I replied.

"Listen, my man Shawn is friends with this hip-hop producer and we're going to his studio. I know you're still trying to make connects in the music business, so do you wanna come? I hear he's pretty good."

I immediately perked up at the *p* word and my interest was peaked.

"Did you say producer?" I questioned.

Ebony smiled.

"I guess that's a yes. Get ready. He'll be here in a thirty minutes."

I was geeked, even though I was tired. I knew I needed to get some rest but I didn't want to miss the opportunity to meet someone who might be able to help me. Maybe I could finally show my other talents to the world and make money and fame in a more socially acceptable way. I knew I would eventually have to stop lying on my back. My newfound fame and fortune was a temporary thing that would soon fade away once my youth and beauty had deteriorated. Thus, retiring from the porn industry and collecting a pension was never an option. Plus I wanted more. I wanted the gratification and satisfaction that came from being a real triple threat. So ignoring how tired my body was, I jumped at the chance to break into a more accepted genre of the entertainment industry.

Ready in no time, I sat anxiously downstairs waiting on the sofa looking so dazzling that no one would have ever guessed that I had just returned from a hot and heavy time in Vegas less than twelve hours ago. When Shawn arrived, we all dashed outside, climbed into his ride, and headed to a high-tech midtown Manhattan recording studio.

Upon entering the place, I immediately took notice of this fine guy who was headed our way. The closer he got, the more I wanted to drop to my knees. He was a dreamy thug love fantasy sporting a blue velour sweat suit, with gold and diamonds shining brightly around his neck, and a blinding multicarat diamond stud in his ear. He wore a platinum diamond-encrusted Concord watch and was holding a bottle of champagne, walking around like he knew he was the shit. Taking a closer look at his face, I recognized him as J Cash, one of the dopest hip-hop producers to ever grace a studio. J Cash had produced nearly half of the hip-hop records on the radio and had made superstars out of mediocre rappers. I had seen him on the cover of *The Source* magazine more times than I could count and his thug-next-door good-looks always had me yearning to taste him. As he stood before me, my physical desire for him increased, and although I knew he was someone who could definitely make me a star if he wanted to, I also found myself wanting him on a level other than business.

"What up, my nigga! Glad to see ya made it. I see you brought your girl—and who do we have here? You brought a new hottie wit ya! I'm J Cash, What's your name, Ma?" Dream thug announced with a presence that screamed ultimate street royalty. I was speechless.

"Wait a minute," he continued. "I know who you are. You're that new porn chick everyone's talking about. I *know* you ain't shy! Not wit those moves I seen you working wit!" he cackled. "Now come on and let me introduce you to my crew. They're fans of yours!"

J Cash grabbed my hand and walked me down the hallway to studio A, busting through the door and announcing our entrance.

"What up, fools? My nigga Shawn D. is in the house with his girl, and I think ya'all might know her friend. This is Simone. They're my guests, so make them feel at home." J smiled.

I could barely believe what I was seeing. Having never been in a recording studio before, I had no idea they got down like that. There were three thug-looking guys sitting around the studio. Each of them had a stripper grinding on his lap as they foamed at the mouth. Needless to say, there was very little recording going on in the recording booth, and as my girls and I made eye contact, we couldn't help but giggle.

"They're on a little break," J informed us.

The guys looked up and nodded my way as I stood at the door and tried to play it cool. J told us all to take a seat as he positioned himself at the engineering board. While I couldn't seem to keep my eyes off the women dancing and taking off their g-strings, as if they were boring paintings on the wall, J started mixing down his beats, not paying the groupies any mind. He was busy working, running the tracks back over and over again before pressing the intercom button on the board.

"You ready, dog?" he asked a grizzly-looking dude who was standing in front of the microphone in the booth.

I broke out of my trance and turned around to face the glass box.

"Who's that?" I asked, suddenly interested in music again.

"That's my new artist, Bone. He's the next big star in the rap game."

Bone yelled over the mic, "Yo, Cash man. I think I need some inspiration up in this muthafucka!"

"Aight, I got you, man." J turned around and snapped his finger. "Ladies, go take care of Bone."

Two of the girls jumped up and walked into the recording booth and started tongue-kissing him and rubbing on his body. An exotic Asian chick got down on her knees and unzipped Bone's baggy jeans, pulling his dick out to bless him lovely. I stared at the scene before me, standing up to get a better look. I watched as she stroked him with her hand and simultaneously sucked him off. Behind him stood a brown sugar girl with her bare breasts pressed up against his back, twisting his nipples between her fingers. She had taken his shirt off and thrown it on the floor and as Bone started to shake, he let out a loud groan.

"Augghh!" came through the speakers loudly and clearly as he came all over the girl's face before dropping to the floor on his knees.

"Yo, thanks, dog," he moaned, unable to say much more.

My knuckles turned white from the tight grip I had on the board as I felt like I had busted a nut on myself. When my eyes met J's, I whispered with a chuckle, "Wow, I had no idea what all went into making a hit song."

J laughed and leaned in close.

"Come with me." He smiled. "I want to show you something." He took me by the hand and walked me out of the studio, leaving the others to continue on with their own party.

"Where are we going?" I asked as he dragged me down the hall.

"Somewhere a little more private," he said with a gleam in his eye. We finally approached a nondescript door at the end of the corridor; he opened it but it was dark inside. I got a little nervous until he flicked the lights on. We were standing in a bathroom. I looked at J Cash and softly giggled. That was his cue and he took it, slamming me up against the tiled wall, kissing me and biting down my neck. My heart raced as I realized he wanted me and I silently prayed that he would want to explore my talents as much as he wanted to explore my body.

In one swift motion, he raised my skirt up over my hips and ripped at my stockings, trying to get his fingers inside my juicy pussy. J had me so excited that I could barely breathe. I wanted him to ram his dick up inside of me so badly as we tore at each other's clothes, trying to find the skin that was hidden beneath. I took it upon myself to slide down the wall, pulling at his boxers on my way down. His perfectly sized dick was rock hard and ready. I looked up at him and slowly rolled my tongue around the head of his manhood before wrapping my anxious lips around him and swallowing the head deeply inside my mouth. His eyes rolled back up into his head as I sucked it slowly before speeding up and twisting my tongue around as I slurped and sucked, using every muscle in my mouth to make him drop to his knees. Desperate to be inside of me, J grabbed the back of my head and pulled me off his dick as saliva dripped out the sides of my heart-shaped mouth.

"Bend over the sink, baby," he instructed. "I wanna introduce myself to you!" J reached in his pants for a condom, ripped open the wrapper with his teeth, and slid it over his massive piece of meat.

When he entered my sugar walls I moaned so loudly that my mating call echoed off the walls. I wondered if we could be heard outside in the hall, but was too engrossed in lust to give a damn.

"Don't stop!" I begged as he began to slow his momentum. I was hungry for him and showed him by taking over and backing up on him and slamming my ass into his dick, almost knocking him over.

He tightly grabbed on to my hips and pounded me with conviction as my face smashed forcefully up against the mirror. In the heat of our desire, I could feel J's perspiration dripping all over my back as he ached to bust inside the warmth of my tight walls.

"Damn, baby! I'm about to cum!" he screamed like a coyote caught in a trap.

He then pulled out, ripped his condom off, and busted a nut all over my lower spine. In the silence that followed, my face was in the sink as he fell back against the wall and slid down to the floor holding his exhausted dick in his hands.

We both started to laugh before I turned around and leaned up against the sink. I wanted to ask him to produce a track for me right then and there, but decided that wasn't the time or place. I didn't want him to think that was the reason I had fucked him. I was ready to give him my pussy the moment I met him. I knew I had to get him to a place where he could appreciate and see my other talents.

After we'd straightened out our clothes, I quickly fixed myself up in the mirror. Of course, I didn't want to look like I'd just been fucking. I preferred to be a private freak and wanted to appear like the good girl in public. But I assumed that everyone figured we were somewhere in a room wilding out. That was probably his M.O., and I knew I wasn't the first and would not be the last.

Once back in the studio, J Cash went right back into producer mode. He seemed to forget that I was there and *shhhed* me every time I tried to say anything to him. When I tried to sit beside him at the board, he sent me back over to the sofa like I was some groupie trying to steal his beats. If I didn't know any better, I would have thought our episode in the bathroom had been a figment of my imagination. At one point a busty redbone made her way over to him and gave him head while he was adjusting the levels on the song. Suddenly feeling like a used piece of meat, I rolled my eyes and sat back watching him punch the moneymaking buttons on the board as old girl slobbed him off real good. Jessie and Shawn cuddled up on the couch watching him work his musical magic.

"Boo, we're gonna roll. You ready?" Jessie leaned over and whispered in my ear after the song wrapped.

"Yeah," I replied.

"Yo, J, we out, dog. Catch up wit you later, aight?" Shawn stated as he headed out of the studio door. J didn't even turn around. He just threw up a peace sign and kept working.

As I left the room, I instantly labeled him as rude, walking out without even bothering to say good-bye myself. As we got into the elevator, Jessie asked me if I had enjoyed myself, and with a huff, I snapped, "J Cash is an asshole . . ."

"He may be, but my dog got mad beats!" Shawn bragged.

"Fuck his beats. He ain't the only producer in this world, ya know," I spat.

"Do I taste a little saltiness, Simone?" Jess asked with a chuckle. I waved her off as if she was imagining things, and when the elevator doors opened, we ditched Shawn outside at the curb and headed back uptown to our humble abode.

twenty-three

the pawn of desire

I awoke the next morning to the sound of my roommates arguing. In the distance I could hear Jessie screaming at Ebony about drinking all the orange juice, and thanks to the previous night's events, I was tired and not in the mood for the noise. Aggravated and annoyed, I stormed downstairs and got in between the girls, pissed that they had woken me out of a perfect sleep.

"Can you two stop fighting? It's just orange juice!" I barked, looking at Ebony, who was standing before me holding an empty carton in her hand and looking furious as Jess maintained a smart-ass look on her face, devoid of any remorse.

"Listen, guys. I think it's time I tell you that I don't have much time left to spend with you, so can we please live peacefully and have fun?" I earnestly requested.

"What do you mean you don't have much time? You sick or something?" Ebony asked with concern.

"Yeah, what are you talking about?" Jessie added.

I looked down at the floor, suddenly becoming mad at myself for springing my departure on them that way.

"I'm moving to California," I explained. "I was offered a deal that I couldn't refuse."

My girls stood silently in shock before Ebony dropped the empty juice carton on the floor and walked out of the kitchen. Finally breaking the stillness, Jess tried to soothe me by saying, "Don't mind her, girl. You know how she feels about you. You're the leader of this pack. If you leave, who's gonna lead now? Carmen's too crazy and a flake most of the time. Plus, she really only cares about herself. But I know you gotta do what's right for you. We're not your responsibility. So don't you worry about us. We'll be fine. I think it's cool that you're getting to follow your dreams. And Ebony? Once she gets over the shock, she'll be happy for you. I know she will."

I hugged my girl tighter than ever and with gratitude said, "That's the true love I was looking for. Thanks, Jess."

We made ourselves breakfast and sat down at the kitchen table to a meal of toast, eggs, and ham, laughing and talking about what had happened the night before.

"I'll never fuck another music producer again," I huffed. "Okay, I'm lying . . ."

We were cackling like hens in a barnyard when Ebony walked in and sat down at the table beside us. With tears in her eyes, she turned to face us, interrupting our humor-filled conversation.

"I'm sorry," she began. "I'm really happy for you, Simone. But you bitches know I don't like change."

Jessie and I looked at each other before cracking a smile and reaching across the table for hugs, as tears streamed down all of our faces.

"Are we all friends again now?" Jess asked.

"Yes," Ebony and I sang in unison.

As we cleared the table and made plans for my last few days in New York, the phone rang. Jessie answered it and handed me the receiver, telling me that it was Aaron.

"Hey Aaron, what's up?" I said, adjusting the device to my ear.

"Hey Simone. I hope you're all packed and ready to head out west. The contracts are here and waiting for your John Hancock. X-Diva wants to shoot your first movie next week, so I booked your flight for Monday morning," he told me.

"That soon, huh?"

"Yep. I told you. Those X-Diva boys don't play around."

"OK. I'll come down to the office today and sign the contracts."

"Excellent. Also, I gotta call from a friend. He wanted to know if you were available tonight. His client, Jason Kool, is performing at Radio City and has invited you to come to the show. Do you wanna go?"

At the mention of Jason Kool's name, my mouth instantly fell open. Jason Kool was one of the most famous R&B singers of all times—not one of those little one-hit wonders I would have expected to be lusting after me.

No, Jason made beautiful love songs and had a squeaky clean positive image. Who would have thought that he would be interested in anything that had to do with me, never mind the porn industry.

"Of course I wanna go!" I replied.

After receiving the details from Aaron, I hung up, gassed at what was in store for the night. I told my girls what was up and headed down to the Village to shop. I needed a new dress—something elegant, sexy, and most of all classy. Jason Kool was an A-lister who kept company with other A-listers, and by the end of that night, I wanted to be one, too.

The night air was cooler than I had expected and I reminded myself that summer was almost over. As I entered the historic hall and approached the will-call booth, a man walked up to me and asked if I was Simone Young. When I confirmed that I was, he informed me that he was the head of Jason's security and that Jason was waiting for me backstage. I followed the man to the backstage area and into a private lounge that was connected to Jason's dressing room. As soon as I entered the lounge, Jason came walking out of his dressing room smoking a cigarette. He was extremely tall and looked stunning in a pale yellow suit with a dark blue tie and matching handkerchief in his breast pocket. He looked rich and suave in every way and when he got close enough to me, he took hold of my left hand and gently kissed it, sending a rapid surge of electricity up my spine.

"You are the apple of my eye," he cooed, openly admiring my assets. I felt like my legs were going to buckle as his melodious voice suddenly made me giddy and girlishly shy.

"Hello. It's very nice to meet you." I bashfully smiled.

"Sit down and relax. Would you like a drink?" he offered.

"Yes, thank you," I replied, pulling out and dusting off the manners my mother had taught me many years ago. Paul ordered one of his crew to fetch me a glass of wine as I took a seat on a nearby plush cream-colored leather sofa.

"After the ten o'clock show, we'll talk," he promised.

Jason Kool was charming and fluid as he walked around the lounge mingling with the other guests. When the second show was about to start, he turned around and winked at me before putting his cigarette out and heading out onto the stage. Once again the crowd roared for him, and without hesitation, he erupted into one of his velvety smooth hit songs. As I watched his extraordinary talent from backstage, I compared his silky voice to that of a beautiful cherub. It amazed me how, despite the fact that he appeared to be a chain smoker, he was able to hit every note crisply and clearly, an indication that his voice was indeed a gift from God.

After an hour of pure musical enchantment, Jason finished his set as the audience threw roses on the stage. Obliging their request for an encore, Jason fed his fans one more song before exiting the stage. Waiting for him was his assistant with a towel and lit cigarette in hand, as well as an unlimited quality of adoration from those of us in the green room.

As he passed by me, he told me he would be right back. To be honest, I couldn't tell if he was flirting with me or just being nice. After all, he was such a gentleman and I was just honored that he knew my name and had asked me to be his guest. When he finally emerged from his private dressing room in a dark navy blue suit with a platinum-colored tie and a handkerchief in his pocket, I took a deep breath and tried to remember a time when I had been in the company of someone more charismatic. I couldn't.

"Did you enjoy the show?" he asked, his voice smooth as Häagen-Dazs vanilla ice cream.

I smiled. "Yes, I loved it. You were great. Thank you so much for inviting me."

I shook his hand and he held on tightly, unwilling to release me.

"Do you have to leave so soon? I was hoping you would join me for a late dinner."

"Well, OK." I shrugged, figuring it would be rude to decline.

"Great, then it's settled. We'll go to this fancy place I'm sure you'll like. A few of my friends will be coming along also, but you can ride with me and my publicist in the limo."

I smiled and waited as he gathered up his friends. We then dashed out the back door of the Music Hall and into a waiting stretch limo. Fans waited out on the curb with hopes of getting autographs and pictures but Jason merely waved them good-bye as we piled into the car. He was mine for the night, but I wasn't quite sure what I wanted to do with him—or what he wanted to do with me, for that matter.

As we entered the upscale Park Avenue eatery, all eyes were on us. Jason, his publicist, four other miscellaneous people, and I sat down to a delicious dinner of lobster and other delicacies as everyone praised him for a fabulous performance. Although their words were true, the ass-kissing from all around the table was overwhelming and I chuckled to myself, wondering what kind of egomaniac he was behind closed doors because of all the brownnosing he got on a daily basis.

I sat quietly nibbling at my food, joining in the conversation only when I was spoken to directly. Still unable to figure out why I was there at all, I just went with the flow. As the dinner neared its end I grew tired of networking and needed to get back to the house to start my packing. After dessert and cappuccino, we all left the restaurant and said our good-byes, and as I stepped off the curb into the street to flag down a cab, Paul stopped me.

"Why don't you let me take you home? My limo can drop you off and it would give me a chance to get to know you a little better," he proposed.

Flattered that he was willing to go out of his way for me, I accepted the offer and climbed into the back of the limousine. But as the car started to pull off, I noticed Jason's demeanor begin to change. In an instant, he ripped the tie from around his neck and began to speak in a heavier tone of voice.

"Damn, I'm glad that bullshit's over," he snapped, turning to me. "So what's up, sexy?" he asked with a sleazy look in his eye. "I've seen your flicks and you fuck real well. Truth be told, I'm your biggest fan. So why don't you come over here and give me some of that mind-blowing shit you give so well?"

I was shocked and disturbed by his sudden transformation. The perfect gentleman he had been a minute ago had suddenly turned into a sleaze-bucket thug in a thousand-dollar suit who may as well have been puffing on a blunt beneath a low-pulled baseball cap.

"Excuse me?" I asked, with a tilt of my head.

"Come on, bitch. Cut the fucking games," he instructed. He then proceeded to pull down his zipper and start jerking off right in front of me. Angered by his disrespect and audacity, I became furious. Yes, I had performed in X-rated movies, but did that automatically mean that I was down for whatever, whenever, and with whomever as long as they whipped out a dick?

"Are you fuckin' serious! Put your damn dick back in your pants!" I spat at him, disgusted. Without thinking, I tried to open the door of the moving vehicle, determined to remove myself from the situation. Luckily the driver was the only one who could release the locks or else I might have rolled out onto 78th and Broadway as we moved through the streets at forty miles an hour.

Like a madman, Jason jumped to the side of the limo where I was sitting and forcefully grabbed the top of my head, tangling his fingers in my hair and shoving me down onto his bulging crotch in an attempt to force me to give him a blow job.

"Get off me!" I screamed, tears suddenly streaming down my heavily made up face. As if my life depended on it, I screamed, punched, kicked, and twisted my body trying to break free of his grasp, but Jason Kool was determined to get what he wanted and the louder I screamed, the tighter he held on, refusing to let me go.

As I saw the partition rise, I took that as an indication that the limo driver wanted absolutely no part of what was happening in the cabin of the car. But I screamed louder, hoping to evoke some sort of consciousness from the chauffeur. After smacking me all in the face with his ample-sized dick, Paul suddenly decided to push me away and I hit the left panel of the car with a thud. After collecting myself, slightly disoriented, I scrambled to the farthest corner of the car. Terrified and trapped, I glared at him, seething with fury from the other side of the black leather seat. A crazed look in his eye told me that he wanted to bust me in the head, but remembering his own celebrity, decided against it, probably not willing to deal with the backlash of negative publicity that would have surely come from such a deed.

"You ain't no *real* porn star!" he snapped as he fixed his clothes.

"Fuck you, you sick bastard!" I yelled, trembling. "Let me outta here!" I banged forcefully on the tinted window. Obviously jarring him back into reality, like Mr. Hyde turning back into the doctor who created him, Jason suddenly settled down and began speaking in the voice that I had heard when I first arrived to his dressing room.

"Simone, I'm sorry! I just thought you wanted to have a little fun! I didn't mean to frighten you!" he begged.

Not listening to his sorry excuse for an apology, I violently banged on the partition. Thank goodness the car began to slow and when it finally came to a stop, I jumped out and hightailed it up the dark city street, damn near breaking the heel on my Gucci stiletto.

"Simone! Come back! I apologize! I swear! Please come back!" Jason called from behind. Refusing to return, I ran until I couldn't run anymore. When exhaustion had finally gotten the best of me, I came to a halt and looked around in a daze. I stood alone huffing and puffing on the sidewalk, trembling with anger and fury. Jason Kool was not the gentleman his romantic heartfelt songs had led his fans to believe him to be. He was a fraud, a fake, a wolf in sheep's clothing. I would have expected that kind of behavior from the rappers, but never from a smooth and mellow R&B crooner. How could this man pretend to be so sweet, then treat me like a piece of common streetwalking trash when no one was around to witness it? Was that the way the world saw me?

As much as I wanted to, I knew that if I reported the incident to the police, my profession as well as every indiscretion I had ever made in my life would become front-page news. His people would try to discredit me and who would believe the word of a porn star above the word of one of the top R&B singers in the world? It was my word against his and it was clear that I didn't even have an ally in the driver. Once again, I was on my own and like everybody else before him, Jason Kool would get away with hurting me.

When I finally arrived home, I was glad the house was empty, as I was in no mood to explain the state I was in. My makeup was smeared, my dress was torn, and Ebony and Jess would never understand my decision not to go to the police. I figured I was better off keeping the entire ordeal to myself.

As my head ached and my body throbbed with pain, I dragged myself upstairs and took a long hot shower. The water was borderline scalding but I needed it that way to wash off the disgusting stench of Jason's cologne and the feeling of his dirty hands all over my body. When I finally emerged from the stall, I crawled into bed and cried myself to sleep.

twenty-four

i'm an x-diva girl

California was calling my name and I was more than ready to answer. By the time I boarded my flight to L.A., I was one hundred percent prepared for whatever the West Coast had in store for me. The six-hour flight seemed shortened by all the daydreaming I did. What would it be like to be an X-Diva Girl? What would it do for my career? Would it be everything I imagined? Questions flooded my mind but they could only be answered by the experiences that awaited me.

Lucy picked me up at the airport and we headed back to her apartment. The free spirit that she was, after the convention, Lucy had decided to move straight to L.A., so while my contract had X-Diva paying my first year's rent, it was up to me to find, furnish, and secure a place of my own. So when Lucy offered me her guest room until I found my own apartment, not wanting to incur the cost of a pricey hotel, I eagerly took her up on her offer. Plus, I figured it would be cool to live with somebody who was already familiar with not only California but the industry as well.

As I rode shotgun in Lucy's Honda Accord, I was happy to be in Hollywood and Lucy was overjoyed to see me. Dying to taste me, she kept dropping subtle hints but I paid her no mind. I was there with a one-track mind and that was to get buck wild for the camera and for the camera only.

"So, girl, you wanna party tonight?" my friend asked as she pulled into the narrow parking lot of her apartment complex.

"Nah, I don't think so. I been partying a lot lately. My girls at home showed to me a real good time before I left. So now all I wanna do is rest and get ready for my shoot tomorrow. I really just wanna relax," I answered with a yawn.

"Oh, don't be a party pooper! I'm having a few friends over tonight!" Lucy said, trying to convince me.

"Girl, you are so wild," I laughed. "But you're gonna have to count me out of this one."

Lucy cut her eyes at me and turned off the car. I quickly got my bags out of the trunk and went straight up to Lucy's tiny but cozy two-bedroom apartment. Fatigue had finally caught up to me and all I wanted to do was take a hot shower and hit the sack. I had no desire to hang out with Lucy and her friends and figured there would be plenty of time for partying once I was settled in.

Shortly after I was fresh and clean, like a sack of potatoes, I tossed myself across the firm full-sized bed and sighed. I closed my eyes, hoping to rest for a quick second before unpacking, and as I drifted off into a quick nap, my cell phone rang and startled me.

"Hello?" I asked into the mouthpiece.

It was Sharla from the office of X-Diva giving me my call time for the shoot the next morning. It suddenly began to dawn on me that I was going to be the star of the film. Before I had only been a supporting character but this time I was going to be front and center. Of course this made me excited and nervous, but as I listened to Sharla tell me they would be sending a limo for me in the morning, I knew I had hit the big time. Excitement flowed through my veins and I could not wait to hit the set at X-Diva, which I imagined would be fabulous and extravagant in every way.

As I tried to relax, loud noise and music caused me to peek my head out the bedroom door. Lucy's party was about to be in full swing and the doorbell was ringing nonstop. While part of me wanted to go out and join the festivities, another part of me craved peace and quiet. Determined to do my best on the set the next day, I knew it was important for me to get my beauty rest so that I would look optimal on camera. Doing my best to ignore the gala going on a few feet away from where I was trying to rest, I set my alarm for six A.M. I then reached for my soft cotton blanket, wrapped it around my body, and plopped down on the bed, shoving my head beneath a pillow to stifle the loud music that was playing and purring my name. It was difficult to fall asleep with lustful laughter so close by, and I could tell that the party was a booming success. However, I forced myself to sleep, knowing that my career depended on the success of my first film, which could very well be my last if I did not make the best possible impression.

The limo was on time and waiting for me when I came downstairs at seven A.M. It was white, fabulous, and brand new. The driver stood by the door in a crisp black uniform with a matching hat and quickly opened the door as I neared it, and while he wasn't particularly friendly, he drove like he was on a mission.

As I made myself comfortable on the white leather seats, I gazed out of the window taking in the sights like a tourist. There was a fire burning in my eyes and I was anxious to meet the costars I'd picked out from the photos in the company-casting album. They were all beautiful, but I wondered what kind of personalities they had. Would they be nice? Or would they be jealous, insecure assholes like the many I had already encountered?

I tried to keep an open mind and an optimistic attitude. After all, I was finally in Hollywood, the place where dreams came true, and I really had no reason not to be happy. I was living a life that many only dreamed about and was extremely grateful. The limo cruised down Sunset Boulevard and made a right turn, heading up a mountain. The road we traveled was narrow and steep and I became nervous. The limo came to a stop at a huge modern ranch-style mansion that overlooked Los Angeles. The driver came around to open the door for me and I hesitated before getting out. When I spotted a large film crew coming out of the front door of the enormous house, I took a deep breath, got out, and carried my bag up to the front door and walked in. I was amazed at the beauty of the structure, which was elaborately decorated by someone with obvious exquisite taste.

"This is incredible!" I dropped my bag at the door and scanned the mammoth-sized room. It was airy and bright with a grand staircase that lead upstairs. To the left was the living room, which was decorated with exquisite mahogany furniture. In the center of the space was a beautiful brick fireplace trimmed with gold. White fur skin rugs were thrown across pearl marble floors and I wondered how the softness would feel beneath my naked body. Soft and inviting drapery hung from the floor-to-ceiling windows adorned with imported chantilly lace that seductively whispered my name. Instinctively, I walked over and ran my fingers gently through the fabric as I looked out of the window at the lush green lawn and blooming shrubbery. I had been under the impression that I would be shooting in a studio like I had done in New York. However, I was quickly learning that I was in a very different place now, and I heard a voice in my head say, "Toto, I don't think we're in Kansas anymore."

"You must be Simone," a voice behind me stated.

"Yes?" I politely smiled.

"Hello. My name is Peter Jones. I direct most of X-Diva's movies and you, my dear, are now an X-Diva girl, so welcome aboard!"

"Thank you. I'm real excited to be here."

"Well good, because today is going to be a long one and your enthusiasm will be needed. So let's get you into makeup and introduce you to the cast and crew."

Peter had a stagehand carry my duffel bag while he gave me a tour of the six-bedroom estate. As we walked though the house, I imagined doing my scenes on fancy canopy beds and on the fur rugs that were tossed throughout the rooms. In such gorgeous and romantic surroundings, I knew I could give an astounding performance. The crew seemed nice, and without further adieu, I asked Peter if he could show me to the makeup room. I was now excited and ready to perform.

We entered a spacious room on the far end of the left wing. The walls were covered with mirrors and bright lights, which enabled a reflection to be viewed from every angle. There were plush leather swivel chairs mounted in front of countertops that were covered with curling irons and cosmetics. At the back of the room were several racks of sexy clothes and shoes just waiting to be put on. It was nothing like the dressing rooms I was used to, and I expected to come of out there looking more beautiful than ever.

"This is our wonderful makeup artist, Jenny," Peter said, introducing us. "She knows how to make you look like a million bucks. And this is Sheena, one of your costars," he said as he turned to the sexy long-legged bleached blonde with a pretty flower tattoo running down the side of her leg. She had on a shear blue teddy and her high cheekbones accented her ice blue eyes. She had a look about her that was cold and devious and I could tell that the girl was all about her business. I could also tell that she was definitely investing the capital she made from her coochie fund in precious stones, as her neck and ears were decorated with more carats than Bugs Bunny's rabbit hole.

"Everyone, this is our new X-Diva girl, Simone Young. Treat her nice," Peter announced before he hurried off and left us to get ready.

Sheena was in the styling chair getting the final touches put on her face.

As she sat there shining with pure California beauty, she paid no attention to me and seemingly ignored my presence.

"You gals get younger and younger every day," Jenny said with a smile. "But you're cute. Have a seat and I'll be right with you."

I nodded gently and took a seat in the chair next to my coworker. It was hard not to check Sheena out from the corner of my eye, for she looked like a flawless life-sized Barbie doll, so perfect in every way that she almost didn't look real. She must have felt the rays from my observation because she finally decided to address me.

"So . . ." she began, not turning her head to face me but looking at me in the mirror. "You're new to the game, aren't you?"

"Yes, um, well, I've done a few movies in New York," I stuttered.

"Oh yeah?" she replied, clearly unimpressed. "Well, you're an X-Diva girl now. All that New York shit is nothing compared to what you're gonna be doing here."

I said nothing but desperately wanted to defend Aaron and his company. I wanted to tell Miss California Beach Barbie to get off her high X-Diva horse and respect us girls in the game who had worked at other studios. But I didn't. I didn't want to cause trouble so soon without having made myself an asset first. Still, I had to wonder why these X-Diva girls came off like divas. Was I going to end up acting like that, too? I asked myself.

"Well, since you're new to all of this, let me give you five valuable tips. One, always use vitamin E oil on your vagina. It soothes the skin and helps with irritation and tearing. Two, always douche in between each scene. You gotta keep it clean, baby. Three, master a sex trick. Your fans will love you for it. Four, don't get to know your costars before you have sex on camera. They may turn you off and then it'll be hard for you to be convincing. And five, always look like your having a good time—even if the guy is pounding you into the ground." Sheena smiled as she jumped up out of her chair and winked. "Well, good luck, and I'll see you later on set," she continued as she strutted out of the dressing room leaving me speechless. Maybe she wasn't such a bitch after all.

"Sheena's a pro. Been at this a long time. You'd do well to listen to the advice she gave you. She can be a little harsh sometimes but she has a huge fan base," Jenny said.

"I bet," I said with a raised brow, remembering the perfect vision of blond-haired loveliness that had dominated the convention. Judging from the booths, blondes were clearly most popular.

I scooted back in the chair and let Jenny start working her magic. I closed my eyes as she wiped my face down with an astringent-soaked cotton ball. She began applying eye shadow when a guy walked in the room, bumped into Jenny, knocking her off balance, and reached over my shoulders to squeeze my boobs. Startled, I jumped out of the chair and spun around with venom in my eyes.

"What the fuck do you think you're doing?" I yelled.

Standing there to defiantly face me was a sexy light-skinned guy with a Walkman on his head blaring so loudly that I could clearly hear through his headphones the sounds of Too-Short as he rapped about cars riding by with booming systems. But as if he had done nothing wrong, the guy just stood there bopping his head and smiling at me.

"Sorry, I couldn't hear you, baby. Did you say something?" he asked innocently, removing the headphones from his ears.

"Are you crazy? You don't fucking know me like that!" I spat.

"Easy, baby. You *definitely* need to loosen up a bit 'cause I'm about to be fucking you in like fifteen minutes. I'm Jason Stud and by tomorrow this time, I'll definitely *know you like that*." He laughed.

Looking at the incredible bulge in his pants, I suddenly recognized him from the company casting album. Thus, I suddenly felt stupid and a little embarrassed, yelling at my costar like that.

"I'm sorry," I chuckled. "Forgive me. I forgot where I was for a moment. Nice to meet you, Jason. I'm Simone Young." I smiled, offering him a big hug that he eagerly accepted.

Just then Peter walked in and said, "Good, you two have met. I'll need you both in ten minutes. And save that magic for your scene."

Jenny finished my makeup and hurried me into wardrobe. Moments later I was being led down the grand staircase and walking through the elaborate living room and out the front door. I didn't know where I was being taken but willingly followed. We walked around the side of the mansion through a garden of yellow tulips and other colorful flowers. Then we came upon a small clearing with a huge tree at the edge of the woods where a camera crew was set up and ready to go.

"I thought we were shooting inside the mansion," I stated, freezing in my tracks.

"Not this scene. This one is taking place outside. We generally shoot the outdoor scenes first so we can catch the brightest sunlight. Is there a problem?" Peter questioned.

"Nah, man, there's no problem. I can fuck anywhere." Jason shrugged.

"Simone?" Peter turned to me and asked, looking for my answer. Not wanting to seem unprofessional, I perked up as I told myself that I had now truly made the transition from amateur to professional. Still I wondered if people flying by in airplanes would be able to see us before telling myself that that would be impossible.

"No, no . . . no problem. I'm ready!" I replied.

"Grrrrrrreat!" Peter responded like Tony the Tiger.

"So here's how the scene plays out," he continued. "I need you two to give me some foreplay by the trunk of the tree. Then I want you both to climb up on that first big branch there and fuck in the doggy-style position. Jason, when you're ready to pop your load, pull out and do it on her back. Okay? Places, everybody!"

"I'm having sex in a tree? What the fuck am I now, a raccoon?" I asked myself. Still, I went and got into position by the colossal-sized piece of wood. I trembled with nervousness but knew that I had to prove I was worthy of being an X-Diva Girl and that meant I had to build a reputation for being the best. So I pulled myself together, just as Peter yelled:

"Action!"

Jason dove right in and started kissing me as we stood under the tree. In one swift motion, he ripped off his shirt, revealing an inviting six-pack stomach for the camera. He then pulled my top up, giving the camera a peak at my erect nipples before he began sucking on my tender brown flesh. I moaned, giving in to his seduction as I unzipped his pants and stuck my hand down his shorts to caress his love muscle. I ran my hands up and down his muscular chest and through his thick black hair while he licked and teased my areolas. His caramel-colored skin felt smooth and his athletic body was firm and hard beneath my grip. When I was ready to devour him, I reached back down into his pants and unfolded his beast of a cock. My eyes lit up with desire as I stroked his cock and watched it grow hard beneath my tender touch.

As my hands slid up and down his meat, he began to pulsate. Wanting to last, he backed up from me and leaned me up against the rough bark of the tree, slowly pulling down my g-string and pushing up my tight miniskirt. He then dropped to his knees and spread my legs open, swirling his tongue between my swollen pussy lips. As I moaned with pleasure, the camera zoomed in to catch Jason's oral techniques and then a close-up of the ecstasy on my face. My temples throbbed so furiously that I felt like my head was going to explode. In a moment's time, I came so hard that I slumped down the tree, its jagged surface scraping my bare back. Before I could hit the grass, Jason caught me and picked me up, placing me on top of his shoulders. My knees shook uncontrollably but Jason held me up close to the tree and I used all of my strength to reach for the biggest branch and climbed on. My mind swirled a mile a minute as I could not believe that, like an animal in the wild, I was about to have sex in a damn tree! Although the branch was bald, as if it had been sanded down for a smoother surface, I felt like I was performing in a National Geographic television special. My costar effortlessly climbed up behind me, like he was as used to fucking in trees as much as he was used to fucking in beds.

Positioning ourselves before the camera, I hugged the wide branch with my thighs and wrapped my arms around it, tooting my ass up in the air like I was a jockey on a horse waiting for the gates to open. Jason didn't waste any time as he hopped on and rode me so hard that he shook the leaves from the tree. He didn't even seem to care about the fact that his knees were getting scratched and cut up from the friction, and while my knees were pretty much in the same condition, I was enjoying the pain that came along with the pleasure. Jason's big cock hit my spot, making me quiver with each and every stroke.

Peter motioned for the cameras to zoom in, as he could probably tell that Jason was about to cum and he wanted to make sure he got the pop shot.

"Jason, you ready to cum?" Peter called.

"Yeah, man! I'm ready to unload!" Jason grunted.

Jason stroked his dick inside my slippery pussy at such a rapid pace that I thought any second we would burst into flames. When he finally grunted and pulled his dick out, he began to ferociously jerk himself off until creamy white cum shot out like a bullet escaping a 357 all over my back. As we came down from our sexual high, Jason's thick semen dripped down off the side of the branch into the grass below. He then slapped his slightly deflated cock up against my butt and shook the rest of it out. Visibly shaken and wobbly, Jason pulled me into his arms to soothe and steady me.

"Cut!" Peter yelled. "That was great! Magnificent! Time for lunch, everyone! The crew eats first!"

The production assistant brought over a robe and towels. Jason jumped down off the branch and helped me down. My body was limp and Jason walked alongside me toward the mansion.

Back at the house, I went straight to the shower and followed the tips Sheena had given me. By the time I got out of the shower and got dressed, everyone was already eating. Starved from the workout I'd just had, I found a place at the table next to Peter. After filling myself with a healthy portion of leafy vegetables and grilled chicken, I retired back to one of the secluded rooms in the right wing of the house. I had one more scene to do before my job was done and needed to rest up to ensure an optimal performance.

When my second casting call came some two hours later, I was more than ready to hit the set. It was a boy-girl and girl-girl scene in the kitchen and I was hyped. Although I couldn't believe I was having a threesome with total strangers, I knew it would be so arousing.

Soon I was before the camera once again, its lens following my every move. The scene was just as wet, wild, and kinky as the first and I went all out to prove my sexual prowess. In the heat of so much fiery passion and lust, I became an animal, navigating on primal instinct and focused on nothing but unmitigated sexual gratification as if the continuity of my species depended on me.

By the time Peter yelled "Cut!" once again, both my body and mind were completely worn out. As I rode in silence back to Lucy's apartment, I could not wait to shower again and drown my body in vitamin E oil. My coochie ached with pain and as I grabbed my bag and headed upstairs, I'm sure I was walking like I had been ridden by a bull from behind. And in a way, I felt like it. I was proud of myself, though. I had definitely done my thing and proven myself worthy of being an X-Diva Girl.

twenty-five

sunset strip me

As I rested in my room spread eagle, allowing my coochie to cool off and reading the latest issue of *The Source* magazine, a gentle knock at the door jarred me out of the article I was deeply engrossed in about Tupac. Before I could ask who it was, Lucy stuck her head in and smiled.

"Hey, girl. You look like shit. The first day is always rough on the gem, though. You'll be fine. . . . Anyway, listen . . . Stephan just called and he wants you to call him."

I was surprised. Why would he want me to call him? Wasn't he Lucy's man? And anyway, I was in no condition to wrestle with his hung-like-a-horse ass.

"Well, here's his number," Lucy continued, handing me a number scribbled on the back of a card before leaving the room.

When I had finished my article, I called Stephan and was shocked when he asked if he could see me, and only me, again. With slight hesitation, I agreed, telling him that I would be available later that night, upon which he told me that he would send a car for me around nine o'clock.

As if she'd been listening at the door, Lucy immediately stuck her head back in and asked, "So, what did he say?"

"He wanted to know if I could come over tonight," I replied, deliberately not making eye contact.

"Oooh, tonight's not good. I already have plans. What about tomorrow?" Lucy asked.

"Well, he didn't exactly ask for *us* . . ." I stuttered. "He, um, kinda asked for me to come alone."

"He kinda asked for you to come *alone*?" Lucy repeated with a huff. There was an awkward silence between us as I put down the magazine and pretended to be busy gathering up my clothes to do laundry. But before I knew it, Lucy had exited the room, slamming the door with such force that I saw a paint chip fall from the ceiling. Although I like her a lot, if I had to choose between the two, Stephan Manes had a higher position on my Richter scale. He was a millionaire superstar mega-athlete and I considered that to be far more valuable to me than my friendship with one of my porn star colleagues. After all, she wasn't even an X-Diva girl. . . .

Since I had already gathered up my dirty clothes as a diversion to Lucy's conversation, I figured I should go ahead and do my laundry. I didn't really want to be in the house anyway, as you could cut the tension with a knife.

As I entered the laundry room in the sublevel of the complex, I saw that there was another person in the room.

"Hi," I said as I walked past her.

Startled that I had spoken to her, she politely replied in a shy voice, "Hello."

She was cute in an "I go to Bible class five days a week" kind of way; the kind of girl my momma would have loved—and opposite from me in every way imaginable.

"What's your name?" I asked her as I began unloading my soiled clothing into the machine.

"Martha Nash. I live in four-B," she answered with a squint, in a "Why are you talking to me? Can't you see I'm doing my laundry?" kind of way.

"Oh! You live right upstairs from me!" I smiled, ignoring her hesitation to converse.

"Yeah, I know. I hear you and your friends partying all the time." She smirked, like she already had the goods on me, leading me to believe that she wasn't as innocent as she came off.

"You should come by sometime," I told her as I added detergent to my load and started the machine.

"Oh, no thanks," she said. "I think I know what kind of people you all are and, sorry, I don't swing that way."

"And what kind of people is *that*?" I asked with a laugh. I wanted to get huffy, but she was so innocent, I just couldn't seem to get angry with her.

"The freaky kind," she snapped, then turned her back to me as if she wanted no part of me, like some of my promiscuity would jump off onto her if she made eye contact with me too long.

"Well, I was just trying to be neighborly," I replied with a shrug.

Martha unloaded her wet garments into the nearest empty dryer in silence. We did not make eye contact as the sounds of the spinning, washing, and drying devices provided background music. I wished I had brought my magazine to keep me occupied, as the awkwardness was overwhelming. However, I did not want to pressure "Miss Praise the Lawd" into having a conversation with me that she probably did not want to have.

"Are you a porn star, too?" Martha asked, finally breaking the silence. "There's a few of them living in this building. Had I'd known, I would never have moved here."

"Yes, I am," I replied. "And proud of it."

"That's an interesting thing to be proud of. Most folks are proud of their kids or their alma mater or something like that," she said as she rolled her eyes.

"Well, I'm not *most folk*." I smirked as I checked my watch. If I left right then, I would have just enough time to pick out a sexy outfit before Stephan's car picked me up. I could always come back down and get the clothes after they were dry.

"Well, you know where I live if you ever want to stop by and chat," I offered, knowing she wouldn't.

"I don't think so." Martha shrugged.

I laughed at her unwillingness to befriend me before saying good-bye and heading back upstairs to get ready to see what Stephan Manes had to offer me.

In an effort to become more familiar with my new town, I began checking out the nightlife in Hollywood almost every night with Stephan on my arm. He was a bona fide party animal. My newfound celebrity afforded me opportunities to hang out with rock stars and the Hollywood elite. People I never would have dreamed I would know were suddenly inviting me to exclusive parties at their Beverly Hills homes. Life as an X-Diva Girl had me floating on cloud nine. The powers that be were happy with my acting skills and loved me for my humble attitude. I was X-Diva's new star and cranking out movies so fast that they offered me a new contract before my first one was fulfilled. My future was looking very bright and they weren't about to risk another company snatching me away. All in all, I simply loved California. My career was going great and I was spending time with Stephan Manes on a regular basis. For a brotha who preferred white girls, he sure was taking care of all of my needs. Of course, my relationship with him only created more tension with Lucy. I knew my days in Lucy's apartment were numbered. Stephan had stopped taking Lucy's calls, and although I had not told her how much I was seeing him, somehow she knew. Tension was building daily between us and I knew it was only a matter of time before the shit hit the fan.

"I think it's time you found yourself someplace else to live, bitch!" Lucy said as she burst into my bedroom early one morning. As I sat in front of my vanity mirror applying a thin layer of foundation, I looked at her like she was crazy.

"Lucy, does this have to do with me seeing Stephan?" I calmly asked her, trying to diffuse the situation. Ignoring my attempt, Lucy walked over to where I sat and up got in my face.

"OK, I think you better get out of my face," I snapped, rising from the table and leaving the room. Hot on my heels, Lucy was right behind me, following me so closely that I could feel the warmth of her alcohol-tainted breath.

"Fuck you!" she screamed, spitting in my face.

Feeling her saliva hit the side of my cheek brought out a rage in me I thought no longer existed. Out of nowhere, I reared back and punched my now ex-friend in the face. We started to rumble on the floor, falling through the unlocked door and out into the hallway of the apartment complex. As we continued to do damage to one another, our nosy neighbors came out of their apartments to check out the Jerry Springer–like show we were putting on. In the distance I heard some cheers for Lucy, while others chanted my name. But no one dared to step in between the brawl for fear of getting knocked out themselves.

All of a sudden, just as I was about to rip the last track of weave from Lucy's head, Martha, the girl from the laundry room, ran up and tried to separate us. When she pulled us apart, Lucy ran back inside the apartment, slamming the door with a thud and locking me out. As I tried to gather myself, Martha shooed away our nosy audience.

"Why don't you come up to my apartment and sit for a while and try and relax. I'll make you some tea," she offered. In my tattered and wrinkled clothing, I followed my neighbor up to apartment 4B. Upon entering, I realized that Martha's place represented her well. It was practical and simple—like her.

It was decorated in earthy colors with artwork that was conservative and traditional. There was no hint of sexuality or erotica. In fact, she had the largest framed poster of the "Footsteps" poem I had ever seen in my life hanging directly above her checkered slip-covered sofa.

Unlike our initial meeting, this time Martha was full of conversation. She took it upon herself to let me know how degrading pornography was and how I was selling myself short as a woman.

"So many women have died before us so that we could have the same rights as men and not belittle ourselves by allowing others to violate our bodies," she preached. As she talked a mile a minute, I suddenly had the feeling that I was back in Brooklyn listening to my mother lecture me. Still, I listened intently, as I never had one of my own peers really break it down to me the way she was.

Validating my assumption, Martha was heavily into her church and attended Bible study, although not five days a week. I actually like listening to her and she listened to me, too, as I tried to get her to understand that it wasn't right to judge people by how they made their living. By the end of our conversation, Martha was open to my suggestions and promised me she would work on being a little more open-minded if I would at least *consider* looking into another profession.

"But I don't know what else I would do," I sighed, not even sure if I had anything else I was good at. I knew I could rap, but that dream seemed to be getting farther and farther away from me.

"Well, at least think about it. You're a young girl, Simone. You have your whole life ahead of you," Martha stated with conviction.

"I hear what you're saying. And not for nuthin', but maybe I can share some of my beauty tips with you. I know there's a sexy girl inside there somewhere," I laughed.

Martha blushed, lowering her head bashfully. As the afternoon progressed, we talked for hours over pot after pot of brewed herbal tea. By the time the sun went down, I had a feeling that Martha Nash and I were going to add a lot to each other's lives.

Hoping that the situation would cool itself off between me and Lucy, I jumped at Martha's offer to stay in her guest room for a few days. Martha actually turned out to be a really cool person. We hung out doing innocent girly things and she helped me in my apartment hunt. I liked being around her because we did normal everyday things that didn't involve sex. With Martha, I was a regular person. She liked me and accepted me for who I was without further judgment, and no one had ever really treated me that way before. Of course, Jessie and Ebony loved who I was, but they were on the verge of cracking themselves, so how could they really judge me? Martha on the other hand was the first friend I had who was living a righteous life, minus the promiscuity and gold digging. She actually had me wanting to live that way . . . kinda.

After a couple of days, I began to feel bad about what had transpired between Lucy and me. After all, she had been the first person in the porn industry to really take me under her wing and befriend me. I actually started feeling bad about betraying her. Wanting to make peace, I finally decided to go back to the apartment and apologize. When I arrived at the door, to my surprise, it was ajar and the apartment was empty. Everything from the furniture to the curtains had been removed. With a panic attack brewing, I ran to my room. Everything was gone except for a single dress hanging in the closet that Lucy had given me and that was cut to shreds. I then ran into Lucy's room and it was all cleared out as well. After telling myself that we had not been robbed, I realized that Lucy had up and left with all my shit. The panic attack now taking over, I felt like I was going to die. Lucy had disappeared in the wind with everything I had worked so hard to obtain. Once again someone had gotten over on me. I wanted to find Lucy and kill her with my bare hands, but knew that would be virtually impossible. Lucy was a smart hustler and had probably been planning the heist from the moment she'd given me Stephan's number. I thought back to all the stories she'd told me when she was drunk about the different people she'd swindled and conned. I never thought there was any truth to them, but now I realized she was probably somewhere sipping on a glass of Moët telling somebody about what she'd done to me.

Dismayed and distraught, I had no idea what I was going to do. I had lost everything that I had worked so hard for just because of one bitter jealous-ass bitch.

twenty-six

where is the love?

Just to spite Lucy, I continued seeing Stephan, now with a vengeance. I hoped I would eventually run into her but that never did happen. It was like she knew I was looking for her and had vanished into thin air. On the flip side, I definitely enjoyed Stephan's company and the sex was great at first. However, I soon realized that he had a tendency to be jealous and possessive. Sometimes it was understandable, being that so many of his NBA teammates tried to secretly get at me. One of them, Russell Howard, was relentless in his efforts to snatch me away from Stephan. But I simply wasn't interested. He was so bold that eventually he and Stephan got into a physical altercation at a charity event in San Francisco that Stephan had flown me to. Of course the press had a field day with the situation, blowing it even further out of proportion. Soon after the incident, Stephan started to become distant and aloof when it came to our relationship. He would sometimes rant and rave for hours on end about how if I ever touched any of his teammates, he would never deal with me again. In bed, he started turning his back on me, ignoring the fact that I needed his attention. And when I would try and reach for him, he would shoo me off.

One night in particular, Stephan came in from a game and passed out as soon as his head hit the pillow. I knew that he had been having some trouble on the court and that the fans were starting to turn on him. Our relationship was starting to become stale and routine and the only thing left for us to do was fuck. Outside of the bedroom, he was no longer giving me the companionship I wanted. It was like we couldn't go anywhere without the press being all up in our faces. On top of that, he didn't want anyone to know that he was dating a porn star so we were constantly running from the paparazzi. Deep down that hurt me a lot. I couldn't understand why it was so bad to be seen with me. After all, I wasn't the first adult actress he had been with. After awhile, being with him was starting to bring me down.

As the sunlight crept through the window and I found myself experiencing yet another sleepless, lonely night I looked over at Stephan snoring in bed beside me and a single tear slowly slipped down my cheek. We had barely spoken in days and he would often stay out until four A.M. without so much as giving me a call. It was like he just didn't care about anything anymore. But I did. I wasn't a quitter and he wasn't all that I had going for me. I was trailblazing my way through the porn industry like a windstorm, breaking racial barriers and gracing the covers of magazines that other African-American actresses could only dream of. I was also becoming a smart business lady. I refused to be treated any differently from any of the white actresses at X-Diva—not even those who had been in the industry longer. I wanted to be treated like a diva and have the same opportunities as the rest of them, and this was the first time in my life that I was demanding and getting the respect I deserved. Although I had become famous doing something society considered taboo, I was going to make the best of it and ride with the fame I had been given. I still yearned to be a big mainstream star but I felt like I was getting lost in the land of deception and desires. I wanted the world to see the real me. God had given me many talents and I wanted to prove to the world that I wasn't just another pretty face who spread her legs for money.

Back at Martha's crib, I was finding it difficult to shake the funk I was in. I hadn't heard from Stephan in days. He hadn't returned any of my calls, and I suddenly realized how Lucy must have felt. Not willing to give a man that much power, I figured that if Stephan didn't want to satisfy my needs, then I would go out and find someone who would.

It took much doing but I was finally able to convince Martha to go with me to an X-Diva party. After I assured her that it would not be a room full of orgies and that there would be other guests not affiliated with the world of porn, she hesitantly agreed.

We entered the party looking flawlessly beautiful and all eyes were upon us. Martha even cleaned up good enough to catch a few glances. The place was wall-to-wall celebrities. A-listers from the film and music business were hanging around the bar and in the VIP booths. As I made my way through the crowd, I went up to most of them and said hello. The house music was pumping and I went out to the floor hoping to dance my unpleasant memories of Stephan away.

Pulling me from the dance floor and out of my zone, Martha made me walk with her to the bathroom. Along the way, we ran into Gee Dog, one of the most popular black porn stars in the business. Barely noticing me, he stared my friend in the eyes and smiled, licking his sexy lips as he approached her. Then he casually handed her his card and went strolling off into the crowd. The look on Martha's face said she was flattered and hooked. She shoved the card into her purse and went into the bathroom without saying a word. I didn't say anything either, hoping she would ignore the advance and keep it moving. Martha was clearly no match for a porn star and Gee Dog was totally out of her church-girl league.

We handled our business and left the bathroom. Gee Dog must have been keeping an eye out, because he quickly headed back over to us. I knew what was on his mind and wanted to warn my friend. I felt like I had to protect her, being that she was so innocent and unplucked, but just as I was about to administer a word of caution, Gee Dog walked up to her and whispered in her ear, "Can I get you a drink?"

Martha was stunned and nodded. I knew she didn't think of herself as pretty or sexy and was thrilled that he even noticed her. She gave me a look that begged for my approval and I shrugged, hoping she would be OK. She was a grown woman, and although I wanted to protect her, I felt she was long overdue for a little bit of fun. As they walked over to the crowded bar and ordered, I gave Martha the thumbs-up. I could tell that the sexual energy in the room was seeping into her body and that she was starting to feel horny. As I walked off into the crowd, I saw the freak lurking inside my friend dying to get out. I just hoped that I hadn't opened up a can of worms that she would ultimately regret releasing.

As I did my best to navigate through the crowd, I was nearly knocked over by a broad-shouldered man wearing a Yankees baseball cap tipped down low to his nose. He wasn't looking where he was going but after our collision, he lifted his head.

"Excuse me," he said, now focusing on me. "Damn, you are stunning!"

As my eyes met his, I couldn't believe whose face I was staring into. Max

Ford, the legendary actor who had been in over fifty major films, was one of the sexiest white men in Hollywood.

"You're not so bad yourself," I said with a grin.

"Well, you'd better be careful. I may be more dangerous than I look." He slyly smiled.

"I happen to like danger," I replied with a raised brow.

"Well, I like girls who like danger," he laughed. "And what might your name be?"

"Simone Young. I'm one of the X-Diva girls."

Max took a small step back and looked at me more closely.

"Oh yeah. Now I recognize you. I've seen your work. I'm a huge fan of X-Diva."

As he talked a mile a minute and smiled from ear to ear, I could see white powdery residue at the edges of his nostrils. After he downed another glass of brown juice, he said, "What do you say we get out of here? We could go to my house and talk. I promise to be a gentleman."

"You must be kidding, right?" I laughed. "I've heard about you." I waved my index finger in his face.

"And what exactly have you heard?"

"I heard that you can get *pretty* crazy!"

"Well, if you don't believe everything you've heard about me, I won't believe everything I've heard about you. . . ."

"Everything you've heard about *me*? What could you possibly have heard about me?" I skeptically asked.

"Ut eh eh . . . I don't like to gossip . . ."

"You're a character . . ." I laughed.

"C'mon. You have my word. I won't harm you in any way. I just wanna talk. Get to know you a little bit."

I knew I could handle myself, so I agreed. I was curious to see who he really was and anxious to find out if the stories I had heard about him were true.

"OK, but let me tell my friend that I'm leaving," I said.

I dipped through the crowd to find Martha. When I finally did, I explained to her where I was going and kissed her good-bye after she told me that she would be fine catching a cab home. I had a feeling my friend wanted to get into something at the party and my early departure would give her carte blanche to do so.

Outside the club, I found Max was waiting for me beside his gleaming black Porsche. He opened the door for me to get in and once I was snugly buckled in the passenger seat, he pulled off. We cruised down the shoreline to his house, which was set out on a bluff, facing the ocean. It was an art deco mansion tucked behind a private gate with looming surveillance cameras everywhere to ensure the utmost security.

The place was as remarkable on the inside as it was on the out. Every room looked like a scene from a *Lifestyles of the Rich and Famous* episode. The living room was decorated in rich pearly white and there was a billiard room that was designed like an old Western saloon. Portraits of famous sports figures hung on the walls of the game room, and the entire theme of the place screamed "bachelor pad" with video games and large television monitors in every room and corner.

After I had made myself comfortable in the living area, Max walked over to the bar and poured some cocaine out onto the counter.

"You're too cute to be in the porn business. You look like you could have done more with your life," he said matter-of-factly.

"Like you?" I sarcastically replied, eyeballing the pure white powder sitting on the countertop. Max lifted his head up from snorting the line of snowy dust.

"You're right. I'm no angel," he chuckled.

We both laughed at the validity of that statement as Max went over to the wine rack and uncorked a bottle of expensive red wine. As the blow kicked in, Max talked fluidly about his life and the scandals that he was tired of fighting. He even mentioned that he was trying to find his spiritual side and wanted to get his life in order. I wondered if he realized that he was spilling his guts to a complete stranger, but I could somehow feel his pain. I sat silently and listened to him while he poured his heart out to me, finding it difficult to believe this was the same guy the gossip columns wrote so many negative things about. The sensitive side of me understood that he had made some poor choices, but I could also see that he wanted and needed the help of a real friend.

After finishing the entire bottle of wine, we moved into the bedroom and talked some more as the big screen of the TV glared back at us. I felt buzzed and giddy, but even in his speeded state, Max was still smooth. As the sun began to rise, I realized that he never even tried to touch me.

"I didn't bring you here to have sex with you. But if you'd like to crash here, you can," he offered.

"Thank you. I think I will. I'm about to pass out," I replied, doing my best not to nod off.

"I enjoyed talking to you. This has been different for me. Every woman I bring back here, I have sex with. A few times I might have even done a little too much coke, and flipped out on a couple. You'd think I'd get sick of seeing the inside of a jail cell," he chuckled somewhat sarcastically.

"I understand your pain more than you think I do," I sighed.

Without another word, we both removed our clothes and climbed into bed beside each other, falling asleep the instant our heads hit the pillow. Several hours later, we awoke to the scent of our own flesh, which lured us into each other's arms and caused the inevitable. Out of comfort, curiosity, and convenience, we made passionate love as friends who both needed to feel the warmth of someone who cared.

When he dropped me off at Martha's apartment, Max smiled and kissed me gently on the cheek as a child does his favorite aunt.

"I had a wonderful time. I'll never forget you."

"Will I see you again?" I asked, already knowing the answer. Men like him were never looking for anything long term.

"Maybe in passing, but other than that, I don't think so." He shook his head. "I'm trying to turn my life around, remember?"

I got out of the car and he winked at me before speeding off into the early morning. I felt sad that he didn't think he could turn his life around and still be my friend.

As I walked into the apartment, I thought intently about Max. Here was this big Hollywood actor with more money than God, miserable as the day was long and refusing to face his fears. Although he had the love of millions of fans who enjoyed his work, he clearly didn't have control of his life. But these people didn't know the real him. I, on the other hand, felt honored to be given the opportunity to be there for him when he needed someone to talk to. After hearing his pain, no longer did his stardom impress me. In fact, it humanized him, removed the glamour and made me feel sorry for him. It also left one thing in my mind—that nothing was ever what it seemed and everyone needed of love. Little did he know, but Max Ford and I were much more alike than different.

twenty-seven

the lost spirit

The pages on the calendar turned quickly as my days turned into weeks and my weeks turned into months. Before I knew it, I had been an X-Diva girl living a very comfortable life in California for almost a year. With Lucy gone, I decided to take over her apartment and make it my own. I was doing well but life was bittersweet. As my popularity as a porn star continued to increase, I had an increasingly difficult time making the transition into mainstream. It seemed that the only roles I was being called for were those requiring a sexy vixen gyrating in the background of some usually less talented persona. I even got offered roles to play myself, but nothing that was ever close to pulling out my true theatrical side. As far as my personal life was concerned, I continued to come up empty there as well. I explored relationships with both men and women but they never turned into anything long lasting. No one wanted to get serious with a porn star and it always became obvious that I was simply a passing fantasy only to be discarded after the desire had been fulfilled. They were all very willing to play, but they were never willing to stay. Although I wasn't aging much physically, each day brought me new wisdom and I began to grow tired of the life. As I moved into veteran status, I was no longer a teenager curious about my sexuality. Nor was I the sex machine that the business had dutifully trained me to be. On top of that, it seemed that my professional life was slowly blurring into my personal. At work, I had to follow two extremely important rules: think like a machine and leave your emotions at home. It became more and more difficult to turn these rules on and off for the camera as each day went by. I constantly tried to remind myself about the difference between love and lust, but that, too, was no easy task. People outside of the industry couldn't seem to get it and people inside seemed to get it too much. Like most of my colleagues, I had dated a few of my X-rated costars, but that never worked out, either. Ecstasy and alcohol had become a part of my daily diet and there were times when I could not decipher fact from fiction. On top of that, the vigorous weekly/monthly AIDs testing began to take a toll on my psyche as well. I eventually decided that I wanted and *needed* so much more. I'd had enough of the vicious cycle that the porn industry offered and was truly ready to step out into the real world. I had my own dreams and fantasies, and to make them come true, I was going to have to make the decision to leave the business.

Officially deciding to hang up my g-string and break my contract with X-Diva was difficult. Being that I had another two years on our agreement, I knew Mr. Foxx would be disappointed by my choice, but he always seemed like a guy with a heart when he regularly announced to us actors that whenever we decided to leave the life, he would support that decision. That being the case, I was very surprised at his reaction to me turning in my resignation.

"You want to break your contract?" he said, his dark, beady eyes glaring at me with disdain.

"Yes," I stuttered, suddenly nervous.

"You have nearly two more years on your contract, Simone," he replied with a slight shake of his head. He no longer looked in my direction, but began sifting through unopened mail sitting on his desk.

"I know, but you always told us that when we were ready to stop, we could," I stated, reminding him of his own offer.

"Everybody knows I don't mean that shit. That's why we have contracts. There has never been an X-Diva Girl to break a contract. It just doesn't happen. X-Diva chooses not to renew contracts. Actors don't break them."

"Well, I guess I'll be the first." I halfway smiled.

"Do you think this is a joke, Simone?" he questioned.

"No, no. Mr. Foxx, please, I'm twenty-one years old and I wanna start taking my life more seriously. I'm ready to retire from the adult business. I wanna explore other avenues in my life. Can you blame me for that?"

"It's not about blame, Simone," Mr. Foxx began. He looked me up and down and hesitated for a minute before continuing. "And twenty-one is the prime age for this business."

"It's the prime age for other things, too," I replied, now more confident in my decision.

"Well, it's your life. Go live it," Foxx said.

"I'm not looking to become Halle Berry or anybody else for that matter, Mr. Foxx. I'm just looking to become the best Simone Young I can be. And I can't be that here," I solemnly stated as I rose from the chair and exited his plush million-dollar office. My heart beat fast and it took all the strength I had within to keep the tears from falling. As I made my way out of the building that housed X-Diva's swanky corporate offices, a sense of determination took over. As the smooth California breeze flowed through my soft bouncy hair, I knew I had something to prove—not only to Mr. Foxx, but also to myself and the world.

In a matter of days, much to my delight, I received a FedEx package containing my release from X-Diva. While I was happy to be free, the bittersweet reality hit me that I was going to need some money to subsidize my new hustle. With no more films scheduled on my calendar, I knew my small savings would be depleted in a matter of months if I didn't get another job soon. I immediately reached out to Aaron with hopes that he might help me get some feature spots. Although not happy about my decision, he agreed, but with all the partying and shopping I was used to doing, I knew I had to find something on my own as well. I wasn't as prepared as I could have been for my exodus from the adult film industry. Still, I knew I would ultimately be fine. I was a survivor.

Thanks to the name I had built with X-Diva, Aaron was able to secure several gigs for me as an exotic feature at different clubs across the country. As long as I didn't have to fuck anybody, I was fine with that and took the jobs with the intention of carving my path to the mainstream in the forefront of my mind.

As the winter months slowed down my bookings, I took a job at a spot that had private peeping booths. Much to my surprise, the pay was great and I made a ton of money. The way it would work was that men would slip their loot into a tiny slot on the wall and then a privacy partition would rise, exposing me in all my glory sitting behind a glass playing with my pussy. The customer could then pick up a telephone receiver that was mounted on the wall and I would do the same. From there the john would tell me want he wanted me to do so that he could bust a nut. It was a lovely working relationship and I never had to feel the dirty hands or smell the putrid breath of any perverted strangers. I worked seven hours a day helping customer after customer get off. When they finally finished their business, the custodian would come in and clean the cum stains from the glass and mop up the floor. While some of the johns came unprepared, others wore women's panties or adult-sized diapers to conceal the embarrassment of leaving their sinful spillage of fluids behind. The best part about the whole thing was that the customer only had ten minutes to get his nut off before the screen went back down and my pussy faded into blackness. Of course, if they wanted more they had to put additional money in the slot. Sometimes a dude would be in there for hours, pumping more money into the slot than I could count. It was a splendid situation and I loved the security of the glass because I didn't have to worry about any unwanted groping. While I will admit that it was pretty kinky, it paid the bills.

After several months of making a killing touring the strip clubs and working the peep booths, I had enough cash to pack up my belongings and move into a little house on Venice Beach that I'd had my eye on for a while. Without the money from X-Diva, maintaining Lucy's apartment quickly became a hassle and with my change in lifestyle, the tiny one-bedroom cottage overlooking the Pacific Ocean suited me better.

As I spent the afternoon packing up my belongings for my move, a soft knock came at the front door. When I opened it, I was surprised to see my friend Martha, who I hadn't seen in a while.

"Oh my God!" I exclaimed, grabbing Martha and giving her a big hug. Happy to see each other, we bounced up and down with excitement.

"You look great!" Martha replied, admiring my beauty.

"And look at you!" I smiled, turning her around where she stood. "You sure don't look like the same girl who used to quote Bible verses!"

Martha wore a sexy and revealing low-cut yellow halter top that displayed her ample naturally perky 36 C's for the world to admire. The color looked nice against her caramel-colored skin, as her tight jeans caressed the other curves of her body.

"I know. A lot has changed," she stated pensively.

"Tell me about it," I sighed.

"No, really. I've got something to tell you that's totally gonna freak you out."

"What?" I asked with a hint of worry.

"Well," she began, "since you've been out there touring, I've started a new career."

"OK?" I stated, wanting more. Martha was a bright girl, so her going into a new moneymaking venture wasn't necessarily a shock to me.

She hesitated. "I'm in the porn business now."

My eyes damn near jumped out of my head and I dropped to my bed and faked a heart attack.

"Martha, are you crazy? Aren't you the one who kept telling me how much I needed to let it go? How did this happen?" I exclaimed.

"Well," she began, pacing back and forth and failing to make eye contact with me. "Remember the X-Diva party you took me to? Well, remember the guy Gee Dog I met? Anyway, he's my boyfriend now and we do sex scenes together."

I looked at my friend with bewilderment, wondering what on earth Gee Dog had done to Martha to turn her out. I never would have believed it in a million years had she not been standing there telling me herself.

"I never thought I would do something like this but, girl, I have to be honest, I really enjoy it," she continued with a chuckle.

Martha studied me closely as my expression changed from shocked to more shocked.

"I know it seems sudden and I know my momma is gonna kill me if she ever finds out, but Simone, I'm having the time of my life! I feel so alive and free!" she bellowed, spinning herself around in a circle with her hands reaching toward the heavens like Julie Andrews in *The Sound of Music*. As I watched her twirl with happiness, I covered my face with my hands and vigorously shook my head.

"Martha, you have no idea what you are getting yourself into. I'm telling you from experience that this business is an emotional roller coaster that never ends, and it follows you forever. Are you sure you're ready for that?" I asked softly, now sounding like those who had warned me.

"Ready or not, here I come," she laughed as if it were all one big joke.

"So what do they call you?" I questioned, still shaking my head.

"Tina Cherry! Gee came up with it because he popped mine!" she said proudly.

"Popped your what?" I asked, confused and taken aback by her excitement.

"My cherry, *silly*!"

I looked at Martha with a raised brow for a moment in silence before we both fell out laughing. I had to admit, if it wasn't so damned pathetic, and if I didn't already know what kind of heartache she was in for, it would have been pretty funny.

"Well, Miss Cherry, I guess there really is a freak in everybody." I shrugged and continued my packing. After all, what could I really have done to stop her? I wasn't her mother, and even if I was, Martha was a grown-ass woman and had made her own decision. All I could do was warn her. Some people just had to learn the hard way.

"You're right, Simone. And I thank you for teaching me to be more open-minded. Now I know never to judge anyone ever again." She smiled.

"Well, since I'm retired, if you need a manager, lemme know."

We laughed as I listened to Martha's first encounter with Gee Dog at the X-Diva party I had taken her to. It seemed that while I was making my mental connection with Max Ford, my girl Martha was getting her back dug out in a coat closet by Gee Dog himself.

As I placed item after item into a medium-sized brown box, Martha suddenly took notice of what was going on and quickly scanned the room.

"Hey, what are you doing? You leaving?" she questioned.

"As a matter of fact, I am. I finally made enough money to move down to Venice Beach into this cute beach house I've had my eye on."

"Wow, I'm going to miss you. You're my only friend around here. I was kinda hoping that we'd start hanging out again and you'd give me some of your porn star tips."

"Well, it's not like I'm moving to Japan. You can always come and visit. And we'll still hang."

"OK, I'm gonna hold you to that." She smiled as she started wrapping some dishes up in newspaper in an effort to help me pack.

"Well, we definitely should celebrate your retirement and your new house," Martha suggested, placing a cushioned glass into the box.

"OK, what do you wanna do?"

"Well, I hear there's this party tonight for the Black Music Convention. Why don't we hang out there and make it sort of a private going-away bash for you?"

"Sounds good to me!" I exclaimed, happy for the invitation.

Hours later, dolled up and looking delectable, we jumped into Martha's red Mustang and went to the music convention's after party. By the time we got to the private club, the party was in full swing. We walked around checking out the place and tried to blend in with the crowd as I noticed that a lot of people were staring at me. At mainstream events I often caused more than a few whispers.

"Isn't she a porn star?" I heard someone ask.

While their expressions said plenty, I did my best to ignore them. Some, however, were brave enough to come up and shake my hand, which made me feel good because I loved having fans. I just hoped that my porno fans would follow me into mainstream.

"Let's get something to wet our tongues," Martha suggested, wanting to get loose.

Not in the mood to drink, I declined her offer and sat down in a high-backed chair as I watched Martha head off to the bar. She strutted over to the Formica counter and ordered. I watched silently as my former-Bible-toting friend flirted with guys and searched for some poor soul to fuck the shit out of, as the look in her eye said she was looking for action.

After she made her way back to me, like an animal in heat, Martha sat down and crossed her legs, flipping her skirt up high enough to give a peek at her naked butt cheeks. In a matter of seconds, her victim headed toward her. Martha smiled at him and slowly slid her fingers down between her braless breasts before subtly disconnecting the first button of her blouse.

"Why don't you come with me? I've got something nice to show you," she said without wasting any time.

The sexy stranger, an extremely well-cooked piece of meat, responded in a deep sexy voice. "No problem. But do you mind if I bring my friend along?"

Martha checked out the man walking up beside him. He didn't look like an American but was definitely hot.

"I think I can handle that." She smiled, looking him up and down.

"My man is from Nigeria and I wanna show him a good time while he's visiting," Dark Cocoa informed us. The sexy foreigner slowly rocked back and forth with his hands firmly planted on his broad hip bones, grinning and undressing us with his eyes. I said nothing, although I assumed they wanted me to participate in the encounter, which I had no interest in doing. I was, however, curious to see Martha in action.

"Follow me, boys. You got a car?" she asked, rising from her seat.

The sexy stranger nodded, eagerly groping for the set of keys in his pocket. With Martha leading the way, we all followed her out to the parking lot, where Deep Cocoa took over and led the way to a hunter green Escalade.

As we climbed in, the African guy turned his attention toward me and questioned with a raise brow, "Why you so quiet?"

"I'm not participating tonight," I informed him. "I'm just the audience."

"Ooh, I like dat . . . you're what they call 'a voyeur,'" he moaned with a heavy Nigerian accent.

We all jumped into the backseat of the massive vehicle. The smell of new leather permeated the cabin as Martha told the African guy to pull out his dick. Once he followed her order, she climbed over in between the seats to sink his colossal penis down her throat. His friend watched from the side as he slowly removed his tie and suit jacket. He then pulled his shirt up from out his pants and lowered his zipper before pulling his dick out to warm it up for her. As she continued to suck his friend off, Dark Cocoa turned to me and asked, "You sure you don't want none of this?"

"I told you, I'm the audience," I reminded him with a wink.

"Awww, you don't know what you're missing," he replied as he moved over and began slapping his long black tool on Martha's ass while simultaneously lifting her skirt up around her hips. He grabbed his wallet for a condom and slipped it on in one swift motion as his African pal tightly gripped the back of the leather seat. My girl sucked the hell out of his cock—slobbing it down and jerking him off like a skilled professional. One would never have guessed that she was so new to the game.

Dark Cocoa positioned himself behind her as he squatted down between the back and front seats before ramming his cock up inside of her. Although I wasn't participating, the sound of sweaty flesh slapping against the leather turned me on as I watched Martha's sloshy wet pussy drip foamy white cream out onto the floor of the cabin.

"Yeah, baby! You like that dick, don't ya? Suck that *Coming to America* cock for Big Daddy Shaka Zulu!" Africa moaned. I wanted to laugh, as his accent sounded so funny saying such words, but I held it in and continued to focus on the live action taking place before me.

Martha fucked and sucked away like a veteran, seemingly unable to get enough of the meaty stuff and cumming multiple times before the African guy screamed out in painful pleasure.

"Oh my God! Me gonna cum!" he spastically cried, pulling his cock from Martha's mouth and squirting his load out like a well-decorated warrior from the Zulu nation. Once it had all been released, he tried to stand up and bumped his head on the roof, spilling his cum into Martha's hair and down her back. With a thud, he dropped back onto the seat with a wide grin on his face.

Although his buddy was spent, Dark Cocoa continued to pound my friend with his thick and meaty wood as he slapped and wiggled her ass with zest. She squeezed her butt cheeks and contracted her love muscle, forcing him to pull his dick out and bust his cum inside the condom. When he was done, he pulled the rubber off, tied it up in a knot and disposed of it out the window.

The air smelled like a sour combination of ass and leather and we were all sweating from the sensational animalistic sexfest that had just occurred in a tight and confined space. Martha pulled her skirt down and spun around, falling between the African guy's legs on the floor.

"Wow, that was good. What's your name?" he asked between breaths.

Martha buttoned up her shirt and pulled herself together. She then grabbed my arm, opened up the truck door, and stepped out.

"Not knowing my name adds mystery to the fuck. Bye, boys! It was fun!" She smiled before skipping off, heading back into the party without a backward glance.

As we headed up the walkway back to the club, I looked at my friend with new eyes. She showed me a side of her I never thought existed and I was amazed. I didn't know how much hanging out with her I would do in the future, now that she was a bona fide freak, but she sure made for a wild time that night.

Once inside, Martha headed off to find her next conquest. She tried to get me to be her sidekick once again, but I declined, having participated in enough risqué activity for one night. I decided to head to the lounge area where I found a nice plush chair. Sitting directly across from me on a couch was an average-looking bookworm type of guy—not too handsome, but not ugly, either. I noticed him because he was gazing at me, and although he was definitely not my type, I found his attention flattering. Since I tended to attract mostly bad boys, I figured a nice, normal intellectual kind of guy would be a good change of pace. I blushed and hoped that he would get up the nerve to talk to me. And he did.

"Hi, my name is Derek Wells. I must say, you are very beautiful," he stated charmingly once he'd made his way over to me.

"Thank you. I'm Simone." I smiled, extending my hand for a shake.

"Yes, I know." He winked.

"OK," I replied, realizing that he must have seen my work. I suddenly felt shy but wanted to keep the conversation going. "So, what do you do?" I asked him, hoping he would turn out to be more than just one of my fans.

"That's a typical L.A. question," he said with a smile. "I'm actually a film director. My first movie hits the theaters in two months."

"Wow, that's pretty cool. You must be excited," I replied, impressed. I had never met an actual mainstream Hollywood director before.

"Yeah. So how about you? Are you still doing adult movies?"

"No, I retired. It was time to move on."

"Can you act?"

"As a matter of fact, I can."

Derek looked at me with a raised brow, indicating that this would be my first opportunity to prove myself outside of the adult genre.

"Would you like you accompany me on a date sometime?"

"Sure, of course," I stuttered, caught off guard. I couldn't remember the last time a man had asked me out on a regular date, and I was excited at the prospect of having a normal relationship. I gave Derek my number and told him to call me. I didn't want to seem too anxious or talk his ear off, so I decided to make my exit and leave him yearning for more.

As I strolled off to find my freaky friend, thoughts of making Derek my boyfriend entered my mind. He was just what I was looking for. Normal, smart, and average—just the kind of guy I needed in my life. Or so I thought.

while it was
s. I mush it was you
—holdin' out... But
t, I'm ready to fall.
w, find that person w
you?

I've actually ben th
home for a little m
up with you guys fo
to just get
ck into my
to me!
go. Time for

Love you
Since

twenty-eight

a home for the heart

I was up the next morning bright and early in anticipation of my big move. I made myself a cup of coffee and waited for the movers to arrive. Everything was boxed up and ready to be hauled out. As I started my new life, there was so much I wanted to leave behind.

I gazed out the window of the condo, sipping a bit of my brew, thinking deeply about the events that had transpired over the past year or so. My life had been a whirlwind of fun since I had gotten to L.A., but now it was time for me to get serious. I had considerably decreased my drug and alcohol intake and was determined to ultimately kick the habit a hundred percent. In my head I was detailing a list of things to do when the sound of my ringing cell startled me and snatched me back into reality.

"Hello?" I asked into the receiver.

"Hi there. It's Derek. How are you today?" he asked. His voice was smooth as butter.

I smiled at the melodious sound and replied, "It's getting better by the minute."

"Are you free tonight? I would love to take you to a movie. There's a new film out that I really wanna see. I hear it's great."

"A movie sounds nice. I'm moving into my new place today, right now in fact. But we could probably make a late show."

"Sounds good. Where should I pick you up?"

I gave Derek the directions to my new beach house but was forced to cut the conversation short when the movers knocked on the door. As I watched them take out box after box until there was none left, I eagerly anticipated my date later that night with my new friend. Once the place was completely bare, I took one last look around and shut off the light before picking up my personal luggage and following the movers. I was glad to be leaving—the ghost of Lucy Kane still haunted me. Besides, I was ready for the next phase of my life.

With the sun in my face and the wind in my hair, I cruised up the perfectly smooth freeway in my candy-apple red Mercedes 500 SL on my way to Venice Beach.

The house was a charming logwood cabin right on the ocean with a breathtaking view. By the time I arrived, the movers were there, ready and waiting to unload. I quickly let them in and in no time they were finished and out the door.

When I'd finished getting dressed, I decided to wait for Derek outside on my porch. The stars were out and the sky was mesmerizing. It was the perfect night for a first date, and when he pulled up in his silver BMW, I was more than ready for our night out on the town.

"Good evening, Simone. You look great!" He smiled, exiting the sports car with a single red rose in hand. I smiled and thanked him as I gently sniffed the velvety soft petals of the flower before getting into the passenger's side. He was a perfect gentleman and was making quite an impression. We made the last showing at the theater and watched the remake of a classic drama about a man who had been in a coma for years and somehow became conscious again, living a new life in a new world. The film inspired me and somewhat mirrored what was happening in my own life. We shared a large box of popcorn and watched the flick in the back of the near-empty theater. I couldn't resist messing around with him a little in the dark, and his khaki pants didn't hide his growing boner. As if I didn't know what I was doing, I would accidentally brush my hand across his crotch as I reached for the popcorn or passed him the large drink we shared. To my delight, he stayed hard the entire movie.

When the credits began to roll and Derek stood up, with a noticeable bulge in his pants, he immediately invited me back to his house in Bel Aire. I eagerly accepted his invitation and drove with him to his beautiful modern-style home. When he opened the door and ushered me into his home, I looked around the grand but empty space. There had to be about twelve rooms in total, but all of them were bare without a single stitch of furniture.

"Where's your furniture?" I laughed.

"I just moved in three months ago and I've been taking my time fixing the place up. I think I need to find a decorator. But never mind that. I have the essentials. Come with me upstairs," he replied.

We walked up a doublewide staircase to the master bedroom. To my surprise, it was the only furnished room in the house. I assumed that was what he meant by "essentials." The room didn't even look like it belonged in the house. The bed was royal, fit for a king. The linens were made of the finest fabric and seemed to call my name as I stood in the doorway. A Bose stereo and a small television sat upon a plush white rug and there were scripts scattered all over the room.

"I see you like to keep things simple. I like that." I winked, sitting down on the floor in front of his stereo. I picked up a nearby CD of an artist by the name of George Howard, whom I had never heard of. I popped in the disk and pressed play, and out came the sensuous sounds of a beautiful and melodious saxophone, tickling my ears and my fancy.

"Would you like something to drink?" he asked.

"Do you have any red wine?"

"Absolutely."

I was at ease and relaxed as I waited for Derek to come back with my drink. He quickly returned with two glasses in one hand, a bottle of Pahlmeyer Napa Valley red wine in the other, and a romantic look in his eyes.

"You know, you're one of my fantasy girls. Forgive me . . . I know you must hear that all the time. It's just that I admire your strength and courage. It takes a lot to do what you used to do," he began.

"Well, that's all in my past now. I'm looking toward the future." I smiled, taking my glass from his hand.

"Good. I'm sure you have a lot more to offer to the world than that."

His realness and warmth made me feel comfortable, and the more wine I drank, the more I opened up my heart and soul to him. He was the first man to really seem interested in what I had to say, and as he listened intently to my words, I was falling in love with him by the second. He also shared his story with me and told me how big he was hoping his movie was going to be one day.

"Just make sure you stay humble," I warned, knowing so many who had gotten swooped up and sucked into the Hollywood way of life. "I've been around many rising stars and when fame hit they turned into monsters."

"Oh, I'll never forget where I came from. It's just not in me to be like that," he assured me.

As the night wore on, Derek showed me the script of what he was going to be working on next. I was impressed with his writing, and it made him even sexier. As we went through each page, I could feel the sexual tension rising in the room. As badly as my body wanted to feel him inside, I began to wonder if we should wait a little before having sex. Derek and I had connected on a mental level and I didn't know if having sex with him too soon would ruin that. With these thoughts in mind, I refused to make the first move. A total gentleman, at first Derek initiated nothing and we continued just listening to music. I actually thought I was safe, until he got up the nerve to take our party to the next level.

"Would you like to get in the Jacuzzi with me?" he asked, avoiding direct eye contact.

"Hmm, do you promise to be a good boy?" I said jokingly.

Derek hesitated, then said, "Do I have to?" sounding like an eight-year-old. And just like that, he had me, dammit.

"No," I told him, looking him in the eye. "You don't have to be a good boy."

Derek smiled and stood, pulling me up off the floor with him. He took me by the hand and led me into his oversized bathroom. Like the rest of the house, it was sparsely furnished, with the exception of several scented candles that were strategically placed along the corners of the tub. I slowly peeled off my clothes as he prepared the water, spellbound by the sight of my naked body. I could tell that it was the first time he had ever been with a girl like me, and while I was grateful for the adoration, I secretly hoped he was not just fulfilling the ultimate dream of making love to a porn star.

Once the water was ready, I dipped down into the deep porcelain basin and invited my host to join me.

"What are you waiting for? Come on in. The water's nice," I cooed.

In a little bit of a Steve Urkel kind of way, Derek overcame his shyness and removed his clothes, joining me in the hot bubbling water. Unable to contain myself any longer, I decided to make it easy for him and went for it. Like a panther stalking my prey, I moved over to him and wrapped my arms around his neck.

"Umm, your body feels good. It's so soft," he moaned as my nakedness brushed up against his. Caught in the moment, Derek made a move to kiss me. Without thinking, I turned my head, forcing him to plant his lips on my cheek instead of my mouth.

"No kisses?" he questioned with a surprised tone.

"No, no, nothing like that. It's just that a kiss is the way to my heart, and hearts get broken," I softly explained.

"I won't break your heart, Simone," he whispered before kissing me passionately. The electricity of the kiss not only had me slippery and wet between my legs, but also thrust me into the deep and scary web of love. Submerged in soapsuds, our bodies morphed into one as our tongues waltzed to the beat of the Jacuzzi's churning motor. When we finally came up for air, Derek blew away the bubbles that hid my pussy before lifting up my hips so that he could brush the rest of them clear. He wanted to see all of my kitten, up close and personal. He licked my coochie and sucked on my clit until it beamed like polished silverware as my head rested up against the side of the Jacuzzi. I'd never had a guy eat my pussy for so long or so dutifully—or so well. His soft, pointy, rapid licks made me cum over and over again, creating a pain in my abdomen and causing me to splash as I jerked up and down in orgasm. By the time he entered me, my feet and hands were wrinkled from being in the water so long, and my legs trembled and weakened from the assault Derek's tongue put upon my womanhood.

When he was ready, Derek pulled me close to him so that I straddled his body and eased me down onto his throbbing muscle. My slippery pussy filled up with his hard dick as he grabbed my perky titties and massaged them with his tongue, licking my nipples as I impaled myself gently up and down on his wood. Derek made slow, raw love to me in the Jacuzzi until we were both satisfied beyond our wildest dreams. When he finally skeeted his load of cum out into the water, I teasingly splashed him as he came down from his orgasmic high.

By the time we made it to his bed, we were both drained. Upon the smooth sheets Derek wrapped me in his arms, lulling me to sleep. It all seemed too good to be true and I was in heaven. Could it be that I had finally met the man of my dreams? Was it possible that an intelligent black man with aspirations and goals living a simple life could actually adore me? As I drifted off into a peaceful slumber, I smiled as I grasped on to more hope than I had ever been able to grasp in my entire life.

My romance with Derek Wells went full steam ahead over the next few weeks. We spent a lot of time together, going to the movies and out to dinner. We took long walks along the beach, learning each other inside and out, and I began spending less and less time at my beach house. We had become a couple and would even make time to see each other no matter how busy we were. Whether it was making love on a rainy night under a full moon in Miami, or getting down on the hood of the car in L.A., we had a romantic and sexual chemistry that just wouldn't quit.

Derek made me feel special and safe when we were together, and my feelings were growing for him, but I didn't dare say anything, for I was afraid that talking about it would jinx it. When he unexpectedly asked me if I would attend his movie premiere party with him, I knew he felt the same way about me.

The night of Derek's movie premier had finally arrived and, as usual, he was on time to pick me up. He arrived in a black limousine and we got to the premiere in time to make a grand entrance on the red carpet. I could see the streets were jammed and I got a little nervous. As the car pulled up in front of the theater, I grabbed Derek's hand before the driver could open the door.

"Derek, are you sure you want me here with you?" I asked.

"Stop being silly. Come on. Of course I do," he replied.

As we exited the car we were blinded by hundreds of flashing bulbs, which created a magnificent light show before our eyes. Derek smiled proudly with me on his arm as we strolled down the red carpet like Hollywood royalty. After the viewing, we headed over to the Palladium for the after party.

The celebration was amazing and the entire cast partied alongside Hollywood's most elite. Derek's movie was a success and I was so proud to be on his arm.

The event was a huge success and while I was having a great time, as the evening progressed, people began pulling Derek in every direction, causing me to eventually lose him in the crowd. I could tell he was enjoying every second of his newfound fame but was hurt that I had quickly become a shadow to him. As I aimlessly navigated through the party alone, I realized that I was losing him to fame in just one night. Two hours into the party and I was stunned at how my boyfriend was changing right before my very eyes. To make matters worse,

I had to ignore the looks on the faces of so many who whispered about Derek arriving with a porn queen on his arm. It seemed as if my presence had made him the ultimate stud for the night, as every woman in the room wanted to get to know him better.

When I was finally able to grab his attention for a moment, I discreetly pulled him aside.

"I'm getting tired, babe. I'm ready to leave," I said, hoping he would try to stop me.

"Oh, OK. I didn't even know you were still here. I got caught up. Why don't you let the limo take you back and I'll call you when I can?" he suggested, not even looking at me. Hurt and insulted, I glared at him. He was flanked by groupies as if he hadn't even come with a date. Without a word, I stormed off and left the party, taking the limo back to Venice Beach alone.

As the car drove through the smog-filled night, tears streamed down my cheeks. I could not believe the record time it took for the fame demon to jump into Derek's soul and possess him. I knew he was a good guy, but he was crazy to get hit with the bug so quickly. Damn, at least let the film hit the theaters first!

The ride home was long and depressing. The fairy-tale beginning of what promised to be a wonderful evening was ending in a nightmare. When I arrived home, I quickly realized that my house was not the only thing that was empty.

twenty-nine

humble hustler

Several days had passed and I received no call from Derek. I dared not call him, afraid that his response would only hurt me more. I figured he was probably busy living the Hollywood life with all its perks and privileges. His movie had been released and he was receiving wonderful reviews from every A-list critic in Tinseltown. That being the case, I knew he wouldn't be coming back down to earth anytime soon.

Deep down in my heart, I knew that what we had was over and I refused to allow myself to dwell on what was lost. Although I had to stay focused, my quest for love was my one true weakness, and unfortunately, it had been another one-way street where Derek was concerned. Thus, I decided to put all my energy into achieving my goals, placing love and romance on the back burner for good.

Thinking that a change of scenery would do me some good, I reached out to Ebony and Jessie with hopes of crashing in my old room in New York for a while. Of course, they were only too thrilled to have me back in the brownstone. So without further adieu, I bought a one-way ticket on American Airlines and headed home.

When my plane landed at Kennedy Airport, my spirits were high even though my heart was still broken. However, I wasn't about to let that stop me. Although we had gotten off to a rocky start, J Cash was the only person I had ever met who could actually do something with the demo I had managed to make in a little rinky-dink studio in Beverly Hills. It wasn't much, but it was enough to show him that I had skills and I was determined to get him to hear it.

As soon as I got home, I got Jess to con her man into giving me J's number and nervously called him up. I didn't know what to expect, since he had done the Dr. Jekyll/Mr. Hyde thing on me when we first met, but to my surprise, he greeted me with a pretty warm reception. Time had passed and I knew he'd probably seen me blowing up the porn industry and was probably thinking we could flip another episode like the last, but I had something else in mind.

Without hesitation, I dropped my unpacked bags in my bedroom and headed to J's studio. When I arrived, I was surprised by the scene. No longer were there groupies or homies hanging around ready to engage in a sexual fiasco. The mood was serene and work-oriented with just an engineer and J Cash creating at the mixing board.

"So, what's been up?" he asked, hugging me tightly. "You still look good—on and off the big screen. So, you wanna do a sequel?" he chuckled with a wink, referring to our first encounter.

"Thanks, J. But that's not why I'm here," I responded with a serious tone in my voice.

"Aight, what's on your mind?" he asked, leaning back into his chair.

My heart pounded a mile a minute and my nerves had me feeling like I should forget the whole thing. Still, something inside of me said that I could not give up without trying. So I decided to just go for it. With all the pride I had left in the world on my sleeve, I looked J dead in the eye and gave it to him straight.

"Listen, I could fuck you and suck you but that's not what I came here to do," I told him. J looked at me with a raised brow as he listened to my words without responding.

"I want you to check out my demo. I can really flow, which you will see if you take the time to listen to it. No joke. It's been rough trying to find someone who will give me a chance to blow up in the mainstream world. But you seem like a visionary, so I figured, what do I have to lose?" I continued. I held my breath, waiting to get shot down, but held on to the slightest inkling of hope. After about thirty seconds of staring at the tape, J looked me up and down and winked.

"Aight. I'ma give you a shot, and if you're wack, you'll get the fuck outta here and never come back unless you ready to gimme some of that shit you gave me before. *But* . . . if you're hot, I'll never ask you for no pussy again. Deal?" he propositioned.

Impressed by his realness, I chuckled and replied, "Deal."

I placed the tape on the side of the board for him to pop into the deck, but he waved me off with an attitude.

"Fuck the demo. Take your ass into the booth and kick me a freestyle over this beat I just made," he said.

My eyes lit up and my heart really started pounding. Here was my chance to audition live for one of the top producers in the game and there was no way I was going to mess it up.

Without a word, I practically ran into the booth and threw the headphones on. J started the track, and off the top of my head, I busted the best flow I could muster. The expression on J's face was that of surprise as he put his blunt out in a nearby ashtray and stood up to pay closer attention.

"I can bounce to the East, I can bounce to the West, I gets these boys bouncing like they whips on these breasts! What's next on the roster? Whatever . . . it's gonna cost ya!" I continued rhyming my heart out with strong sexy lyrics that seemed to roll off my tongue like warm butter. When he had had enough, J ordered the engineer to stop the track and pressed the button on the intercom to tell me to come out of the booth.

"Yo," J softly began as if he was in awe. "That was some of the dopest shit I heard in a minute. I had no idea you could rhyme!"

"You were too busy trying to get me to spit cum, not rhymes," I laughed.

"I ain't know," he chuckled. "But now that I do, paper before pussy. I say we work on putting out a single first and if it hits like I think it will, then we'll record a full album and get paid, baby!"

I could finally breathe and was unable to stop myself from jumping up and down with joy. I hugged J tightly before he told me to come back the next day in business mode. For the next few weeks we worked in J's studio every other day. He had me in somewhat of a hip-hop boot camp of sorts. Being around him brought out a new work ethic, as he was a slave driver and hard as hell on me.

"I don't want nobody questioning your musical talent based on your other, um, 'talents'!" he would yell as he pushed me harder than he pushed his other artists.

I would often roll my eyes at him and wonder if he was making me suffer because I wasn't fucking him anymore, but truth be told, by the time my single was released, my skills had tremendously increased and I was ready for the fierce competition of the rap game. My single got great reviews and I was prompted to sign a record deal with J Cash's company, Hit Records. But the reception of my audience varied. While some in the hip-hop community was in an uproar to see a porn star cross over into mainstream, others welcomed me with open arms. Many loved my tenacity and "I don't give a fuck" attitude. My name was even mentioned in the verses of some of the hottest rappers to ever grace the mic. But I remained honest, humble, and sweet, and by the time my album dropped, I was hosting popular music video shows and making guest appearances on daytime TV. In my mind, I was finally a hit and was happy to bask in the luxury and glory of it all.

After an extensive promotional tour, I was so exhausted that I thought I was going to collapse. Since the brownstone in Harlem was always party central, I desperately wanted to head back to my house in Venice Beach for some rest and relaxation. And since I didn't want to be alone, on a whim, I decided to bring Ebony, Jessie, and Carmen along with me to give them a mini vacation. It was the least I could do, for they had been my most enthusiastic supporters.

Of course, they were gassed and excited about going to Cali, and as we exited LAX I bellowed, "Mothers and wives, keep your eyes on your boys 'cause three of the horniest girls in America are now on your shores!"

As we hustled through the humid air, the California smog hit me in the face, but I was on top of the world. My new career was just beginning with an album produced by one of the hottest producers in the game on one of *the* most successful hip-hop labels of all times. I had my best friends by my side, a pocketful of cash, and I was finally living my mainstream dream. Life was good and I was living proof that it ain't where you from, it's where you at.

thirty

tricky love

As my career steadied and my music caught on with the masses, on the surface it appeared as though I was living on top of the world. The reality of it all, however, was that I was lonely. Whenever I came home after traveling or a long day of work, I yearned for true companionship. I tried to date but kept coming across sharks and barracudas that bit with meaningless passion. Having stopped doing drugs, reality hit and it wasn't pretty. On the upside, it seemed that rap music was finally collaborating with the porn industry. Anyone watching the top-ten hip-hop music videos on BET could plainly see that. Being thrust into the environment presented me with the opportunity to date a few rappers, but while I seemed to have a lot in common with them, there were no real love connections made. Still, I was honored to get so much love from the hip-hop community, even though most of them wanted more from me than just sixteen bars on a track. Surprisingly, though, they seemed to have as much respect for my craft as I had for theirs. Most of them were good guys who naturally possessed incredible sex appeal that could not be denied or ignored. That being the case, there were definitely times when I couldn't resist some of their requests, indulging them in fantasies that sometimes even made me blush. But obeying the code of the streets and knowing the rules and regulations of the game, I knew not to suck and tell. Some of the guys were so kinky, no one would have ever believed me if I did decide to dish the dirt. But while they were fun for the moment, deep down inside, when I was all alone in my little beach house, I knew these escapades were slowly stripping my soul. None of the encounters ever turned into true love and with all that I had experienced and accomplished, I still yearned to find my soul mate.

A full moon glistened outside my window, pulling me from my sofa and begging me to enjoy its heavenly illumination. Bored with nothing to do, I hopped into my car and took a ride down the Pacific Coast Highway. I wanted to enjoy the perfect evening, even if I had to do it alone. And since my girls had gone back to the Big Apple, there I was once again all by my lonely.

As my stomach began to growl, I realized that I had not eaten and pulled over to this quaint little family restaurant for a quick bite. It was pretty busy for such a small establishment. Instead of waiting for a table, I glided over to the bar, sat on the only empty stool that was available, and requested a menu. I ordered a few appetizers, then noticed a distinguished-looking gentleman in a black pin-striped suit and silver Versace tie sitting to my left. I tried to ignore him but I could feel his eyes burning a hole through the side of my face.

"Are you waiting for someone?" he finally asked.

"Do I *look* like I'm waiting for someone?" I sarcastically snapped, not in the mood for yet another meaningless encounter.

"Sorry to bother you," he replied, quickly catching on to the fact that I didn't want to chat.

Feeling a little badly that I had been rude for no reason, I decided to change my tone and continue the conversation.

"I'm sorry. I didn't mean to be rude. I'm not in the best of moods tonight. My name is Simone and, no, I'm not waiting for anyone," I slightly smiled.

"David Gold," he announced as we shook hands.

"So what's the reason for your foul mood? What's his name?" he teased.

"No," I chuckled. "There is no 'what's his name.' "

"Well, you're definitely a beautiful woman. And I'm sure deep down inside you know what you want. Maybe you just don't know how to go about getting it."

I looked at him, amazed at his insight. Was I that easy to read or was my loneliness just that obvious?

"You're right. I do know what I want. And I haven't got a clue about how to get it."

"Well, what is it that you want?" he asked.

"You really wanna know?"

"Absolutely," he said.

"Well, it's like this: I'm tired of casual dating, I'm ready to settle down, get married, and raise a family. But it seems those things keep eluding me. I just can't find the right person to do it with." I was suddenly mad at myself for confiding in a complete stranger. But I needed someone to talk to and David listened as I threw all of my emotional baggage on the bar. When I finally came up for air, he soothingly smiled.

"You're not alone," he said. "The whole world is looking for love. It's the stuff most great songs are made of, and no matter how much money you have or how good you look, we're all looking for that one person who will love us unconditionally. No?"

I shook my head in agreement before he continued.

"Take me, for example," he continued. "I'm a successful real-estate broker, some might even call me a tycoon. I'm not a bad-looking fellow. Smart. And I have everything I could every dream of—except a special woman to share it with."

I was surprised by his words. Men like him had their pick of the litter. After all, who wouldn't want to marry a rich, handsome real-estate tycoon?

"You're telling me you're single? What's wrong with you? Violent? Drink too much?" I questioned with a raised brow, looking him up and down.

"Nothing is wrong with me. Like you, I simply haven't met the right person yet. That was, until you walked up and sat down beside me. And I have to tell you, I know who you are and you could definitely be the one." He smiled.

I smirked at him, now turned off by the fact that he was nothing more than another one of my shallow, hard-up, and horny fans.

"How could you say something like that? You don't know anything about me," I snapped as my original attitude suddenly returned.

"Maybe not. But sometimes in life you catch a feeling from a higher power. After all, I'm a 'now' kind of guy, which means that according to what you're saying, you're the type of woman I'm looking for."

"A 'now' guy? What's that?"

"I'm a man who's ready to commit *now*."

I was flattered but skeptical. Could this sexy young Caucasian man be trying to sweep me off my feet? I had never envisioned my knight in shining armor to look like him, but I knew love had no color barriers, and I was open to the idea of trying something new.

"Well, you'd definitely have to show and prove. . . ." I informed him.

"And if you let me, I will!"

I tried my best to brush off his proposal, but in the back of my brain I was open to giving him a chance. The hopeless romantic that I was could not help feeling optimistic.

"I'm actually here on business and I'm leaving in the morning," he explained.

"Where are you from?"

"Fort Lauderdale, but that's only a short plane ride away. I would love for you to come visit me in Florida. I would fly you out first class and that's the only way you would ever fly with me."

"That sounds nice, but we'll have to see," I hesitantly stated.

"I don't want to rush you, so maybe we should just go with the flow and get to know each other slowly."

"I'd like that."

With impeccably manicured fingers, David handed me his card and told me what time he'd be back in Fort Lauderdale.

"Call me anytime after that," he instructed, taking charge of the situation.

I took the last sip of my drink, finished my mini quesadillas, and said good-bye to David Gold before gracefully walking out the door of the restaurant. I hopped into my car and sped off down the freeway with the promise of love and longing in my heart once again. I was mesmerized by David's charm, and while I couldn't believe this was happening to me again, I couldn't deny my excitement. I kept asking God if he could be the one. He seemed perfect—mature and flawless. From his words, he appeared to want the same things I did. He was also way easy on the eyes, with a nurturing soul about him—and oh how I needed to be nurtured!

I was awakened by the chirp of mating birds outside my window. The bright sun blinded me and I could hear the television still blaring from the living room. I got up, turned off the tube, and shooed the birds away. After all, if I wasn't getting any, then nobody was getting any. I then went straight into my Jacuzzi in an effort to soak my fears away. I had not done an appearance in almost two weeks, but my video was in regular rotation on the nation's hottest video show. As I waited for J to give me the word on when we would be going back into the studio to cut some new material, I enjoyed my downtime, filling it with an attempt to become more grounded emotionally and spiritually.

Since our meeting, David had been on my mind a lot. I didn't call him immediately, for I did not want to seem too eager and scare him off. But after letting four days pass, I figured it was time to make my move. After my soak in the Jacuzzi, I threw on my robe and slippers and pulled out his card. I hesitated for a moment as I practiced my opening line before taking a deep breath and dialing.

"Hello?" he finally answered, his voice deep and sexy.

"Hello, David. It's Simone, the girl you met at—"

"How could I forget?" he interrupted. "I've been waiting for you to call."

"Yeah right," I replied. "You must have a ton of women calling you all the time."

"You're the only one who matters now."

I chuckled at his charm and asked, "So what are you doing?"

"Well, I'm in my Ferrari driving down the beach and I wish you where here riding beside me."

"That would be nice," I agreed.

"Yeah, I have to take her out for a ride every now and then to keep her engine happy. But she's not my usual car of choice. I usually drive one of the Bentleys."

"So, you're into cars."

"No, I'm into you."

I giggled as his words made me feel girlish and desired, but I was wary of his demeanor and wondered how many other women were currently caught in his web. In an effort to feel him out and get to know him better, we talked for about an hour. To my surprise, we had a lot in common. It was almost scary. He felt eerily familiar to me, like we had met in another life or something. Although he seemed wise beyond his years, I learned that he was only twenty-nine years old and had obtained his millions by age twenty-five. I was impressed by his intellect and intrigued by the charm that resonated throughout the conversation. He was witty and smart and funny and kind. He made his own rules and danced to the beat of a drum that he had created especially for himself. By the time our conversation was over, I was falling for him fast, drawn to his mind and the memory of his masculine beauty. I wanted him and I hadn't even touched him yet; our mental lovemaking gave me a new kind of desire.

Over the next forty-eight hours, we must have spoken at least twenty times. There was no denying that I was hooked on the routine of it, and every time the phone rang, I prayed that it was him. After a few weeks of phone calls and lengthy conversations, he asked me if I was ready to come to Fort Lauderdale for a visit. Of course I immediately said yes, anxiously packed my luggage, and headed to the airport within hours of his invitation. It was weird how I felt like I knew him inside and out, and we had only laid eyes on each other once. And while I was already madly in love with him, I knew I had to keep my cool. Men like David got scared away easily. I knew I had to play my cards right if I wanted to be a lasting fixture in his life.

The weather in Fort Lauderdale was warm and humid. It was difficult for me to relax during the flight, as my anxiety seemed to grow stronger by the minute. When I arrived at baggage claim, I saw a man holding up a sign with my name on it. I was disappointed that David hadn't come to meet me but was quickly told by this personal chauffeur that he was waiting in the car.

After retrieving my luggage, I was led to a long white limo where I saw David standing with a bouquet of red roses in hand. Throwing caution to the wind, I immediately ran over to him and gave him a big hug and a kiss. As I had hoped, our chemistry was instant.

We drove along the freeway and I felt like I was in a dream that I didn't want to wake up from. David was warm and inviting, creating a comfort in me that I had never experienced before. I silently prayed that it was true love and not just another fling as I battled the demons in my head and tried to relax and go with the flow.

David's home suited him perfectly. It was an enormous villa with a lush, colorful, and impeccably manicured lawn situated along the Florida coastline. It was lavishly but delicately decorated in a manner that appeared to have taken a great amount of effort and skill. While I wanted to enjoy him in private, as the sun began to descend, David suggested we go out for dinner. After I had freshened up, however, we found ourselves sitting on his incredible California king–sized bed talking once again about life and purpose. As the conversation continued, we could both feel the sexual chemistry mounting in the room, and before we knew it, we had attacked each other with the zest and vigor that had been brewing since our initial telephone conversation. Forgetting our hunger, like untamed animals we ripped off each other's clothing, devouring and tasting each other's flesh and releasing a bevy of sexual peaks and orgasms. When we were done pleasuring each other, we fell back onto the bed in a sheen of sweat and uncontrollable laughter.

"I've never felt anything like that before! You're amazing! You're definitely the one," David sighed as he gazed at me with a look of deep passion and love in his eyes. "I'm going to make you mine, Simone Young," he promised.

As he rose from the bed and went into the bathroom to take a shower, I lay speechless, reveling in the afterglow of our unbelievable lovemaking. I was in heaven, feeling loved, secure, and desired by an intelligent man who had made me feel like a child on Christmas Day.

When David returned fresh and clean, he plopped down on the bed beside me and took my hand in his. We continued our conversation, opening up about all our darkest secrets and deepest fears and divulging all the things that made us who we were. The fact that we were from different cultures was not an issue, as we were clearly a match.

We spent the rest of the evening enjoying the warm Florida breeze and a delectable meal at an exclusive Italian restaurant. I really felt like Cinderella. My only fear was that my coach would turn back into a pumpkin at midnight.

The next seven days were unbelievable. David showed me his town like a skilled tour guide. We went to the hottest clubs and restaurants, and in the malls and designer boutiques, he spared no expense, buying me new clothes and shoes and dazzling me with the finer things in life. Our match seemed like it was made in heaven and for the first time ever, I felt truly complete.

As one of Florida's most well-known and influential businessmen, David had the movers and shakers of Fort Lauderdale wrapped around his fingers. When I was with him, others whispered with envy, wishing they were in my shoes. Every waking moment, David effortlessly made me feel like a princess and, more than anything, I wanted to become his queen.

The radiant sunshine blazed its way through the enormous bedroom window as David and I caught our breath after making passionate love. As he deeply inhaled, he pulled me into his arms and held me tightly.

"Why don't you stay a while longer?" he suggested.

I smiled.

"I would love to," I replied.

"Good, because I think I'm falling in love," he said, gently kissing my forehead. As the words flowed from his lips and hit my ears, my heart skipped a beat and butterflies fluttered madly in my stomach. I didn't know what to say and feared that saying it back to him would chase him off. We laid in silence, wrapped in each other's arms as we dozed back off to sleep.

When we woke up a few hours later, we enjoyed another vacationlike day. *What would it be like if this was my life every day?* I asked myself.

David's home was like a five-star resort with maids and butlers on hand to cater to our every whim. They cooked, cleaned, and never let us lift a finger to do anything that was not enjoyable. Yet while I was having the time of my life, I knew I had to find out what was going on back in the real world.

When I finally checked my answering machine at home, there were at least a dozen messages from Aaron, each with growing intensity, as he demanded to know my whereabouts. I hesitantly called him back, knowing that he was going to give me a tongue-lashing.

"Aaron?" I cautiously began.

"Simone!" he bellowed. "Where the hell have you been? I've been trying to reach you! You don't answer your phone! You don't return my calls! What the hell is going on with you?"

"I'm so sorry but I've been out of town. I'm in Fort Lauderdale."

"You're in Fort Lauderdale? Doing what? Never mind that. I have work for you—that is, if you're still interested in having a career!" he snapped.

"No, no, no. Of course I am! I'm just going to be here a little bit longer. Just a couple more days and I'll be back in business," I assured him.

"Simone, you have a career to tend to," he sighed, tired of my antics.

"Just one more week and I'll be ready to roll, Aaron. I promise," I begged.

"I hope so," he huffed. "If not, I'll have no choice but to give your gigs to one of the other girls," he warned.

"I promise, Aaron. I promise . . ."

Although I had told Aaron one more week, a month went by and I was still in Fort Lauderdale. David was showering me with gifts and saying all the right words. Eventually I had to explain to him that I had rent to pay and a career to get back to, but he wasn't hearing it. He didn't want me going anywhere and especially not back to stripping.

With Aaron leaving frantic messages, I knew it was past time for me to go. I gingerly approached David one sunny afternoon while he was sitting out by the pool working on his laptop. He looked so handsome, typing away on some important matter when I crept up behind him and planted a tender kiss on the nape of his neck. Startled, he took me in his arms and wrapped me around into his lap.

"David, we need to talk," I began, looking into his deep blue eyes. "Baby, I don't want to leave but I have to get back to my career and my life."

"Don't worry about your life, Simone. Your life is with me. I'm taking care of you now," he replied, fluffing my statement off with a slight wave.

"Well, that's easy for you to say," I chuckled. "But when I left I was in the middle of building my own empire."

David immediately stopped hugging me and gazed at me with an annoyed look. His eyes, which had just been the color of clear Caribbean waters, were now the shade of a stormy sky just before midnight.

"Simone, you're mine. That means you represent me. I'm not about to allow you to go out there and take your clothes off in front of strangers. And as far as your little musical hobby, you don't need to do that anymore, either. I will take care of all your needs," he snapped in a very aggressive tone that I had never heard before.

"David, I never told you that I was going to give up my career," I said. "I can't just lie around here all day, 'representing you.' . . . I need to work. I *want* to work!"

"Then do something charitable. I have plenty of foundations you can head up if you need something to occupy your time," he replied, now pushing me from his lap and turning his attention back to his computer.

"David, I'm not looking to be taken care of. I'm just looking to be loved."

"And you are. Be glad I can afford to take care of you as well. The fact of the matter is that all you need is me. You can lean on me. That's what I'm here for."

The tap of his fingers against the keyboard of his laptap echoed in my ears like a bullhorn. I finally had a man who truly wanted to keep me to himself and I was fighting it. As I watched David become engrossed once again in the work before him, I relished in the promises he made to secure my future. While he was truly my knight in shining armor, I secretly wondered how much of myself I would have to abandon in order for him to continue loving me.

As each day turned into the next, I began to see changes in David. While everything seemed wonderful and amazing from the outside, a closer peek showed that David was a controlling workaholic who wouldn't let me out of his sight. He refused to let me go out without him and had one of his bodyguards follow me around when he was away. On top of that, he didn't like any of the people I had met, and made it quite clear that I should either keep to myself or find friends he approved of. While it was flattering at first, as the weeks went by, David's possessiveness and jealousy started to make me feel a little creepy. When my mobile phone mysteriously came up missing, I knew something was definitely not normal or healthy about the situation. While I had hopes that my cell would be found, David assured me that it was gone forever and presented me with a brand-new state-of-the-art device two hours later—minus all the phone numbers that I had logged into my original phone's memory. Little did I realize, he was slowly cutting me off from everything and everyone I was familiar with. I tried to convince myself that I was being paranoid, but deep down inside I knew that my friends, family, and all the connections I had made throughout the course of my career were slowly and strategically being removed from my life.

It was a cloudy Sunday morning the day David walked into the kitchen and asked me to stay in Fort Lauderdale permanently. Tropical showers had just watered the earth and I could feel the cool damp breeze blowing through the slightly opened patio door as I prepared a light snack.

"I think it's time that you move in with me, Simone. Going back to Venice Beach would be pointless when you're here most of the time," he said, sitting at the breakfast bar.

I thought I had been waiting to hear those words fall from David's lips, and when they finally did, I was elated, overjoyed, but slightly apprehensive.

"I'd love to live here with you, David." I grinned before running over and hugging him tightly.

Desperately wanting it to work, I did a complete 180-degree turnaround, transforming myself from sexy porn star diva into a happy homemaker—cooking, cleaning, and doing laundry. Hoping to see an extra sparkle in his eye, I even put his T-shirts on hangers and ironed his boxers. Although we had a maid, I wanted to do for my man personally and was committed to giving everything I had to our relationship. I was so grateful for all that he had given me that it was my pleasure to please him. Two weeks later, when I thought I couldn't get any happier, David decided out of the blue to take our relationship to yet another level.

"Let's go house hunting," he suggested.

"House hunting? But David, this is a wonderful house. It's everything a girl could want!" I replied.

"Yeah, but it's mine. I want us to live in a house that's *ours*. One that you can decorate to suit your needs and taste."

I could not believe my ears. Each time I thought David was as good as he could get, he'd do something to make me feel that he was even better. His lavish gifts and insurmountable consideration were enough to make me ignore his periodic jealous and possessive outbursts.

We spent an entire Saturday looking at beautiful estates, ultimately deciding on a dreamy eight-bedroom home with the most beautiful landscaping I had ever seen in my life.

"Do you like it?" David asked, knowing from my excitement that I did.

"Yes, I love it!" I exclaimed.

David made the Realtor an offer right on the spot as I looked around and dreamed of our kids running down the hallways and sliding down the staircase banister. I was so excited about our life together and all the amazing things the future would have to offer.

We moved into our new house within two weeks and, at first, things were absolutely amazing. I had officially left my old life behind and was basking in the new one that being David Gold's woman afforded me. I took the project of making our house a home very seriously and carefully picked out each piece of furniture, paying close attention to every detail. Unfortunately, as our new home became more and more personalized, David began working out of town frequently and things slowly began to change. He started getting home after four A.M. almost every night. Soon the wining and dining stopped and he was never around long enough for us to spend any time together. Thus, I was often left alone, keeping myself busy by decorating and watching far too much television.

Although the signs were there, I was clearly in denial. I had convinced myself that David had to put in long hours to maintain our lifestyle because the thought of him cheating on me was just too much for me to handle. In an effort to get back what we once had, I went all out to please him. Although we had servants, I cleaned the house and went out of my way to cook his favorite meals, hoping to get back some of what we were losing. Sadly, as the days passed, I got lonelier by the minute. Even though we were living in the same house, I had become a shadow to him. Still, when it was time to make love, David was very passionate, which confused me all the more. I just couldn't figure out what was going on with him. Was I on my way out or not? It was just so hard to tell. I became concerned when women started calling the house asking for him. When questioned, David just brushed it off as business. I wanted so much to believe him that I did not confront him. Since he was still introducing me as his fiancée, I simply told myself that I was overreacting and that this was what came with being the girlfriend of a multimillionaire. Still, I knew I would eventually have to talk to him about how I was feeling before I went insane. I guess I was just scared to know the truth, because the truth was probably going to set me free.

thirty-one

i'm burning up

As each day passed, my relationship with David became more and more strained. He began regularly picking fights with me over the tiniest things, making my life so stressful that I felt like I was about to have a nervous breakdown. One afternoon, after David went off on one of his tirades for over an hour, unable to take him yelling at me anymore, I grabbed my keys and hightailed it out the house. With rage in his eyes, hot on my heels, David chased me out to the driveway, furiously banging on the car window and pulling the handle of the door to try and yank me out. I shuffled around with the keys in a panic, trying to find the right one to start the car. When I finally got the engine revved up, he kicked the side of the vehicle as hard as he could before I was able to speed out of the driveway. My heart was beating so fast I thought my chest was going to explode. As I drove up the freeway, I realized that while I had a full tank of gas, my pockets were completely empty. Half of my mind told me to keep driving until I couldn't drive any farther. But the other half told me to go back to David and do everything I could to make him fall back in love with me again.

Following my first thought, I found myself on the shores of Miami Beach. The ocean waves seemed to whisper my name, so I parked and got out of the car to walk along the powdery sand. The sun was setting and I felt overwhelmed with sadness. If I couldn't go back to David, I had no idea what I was going to do. I had abandoned my career, and Aaron was so through with me, he wouldn't even take my calls. I had lost contact with everyone who cared anything about me and I wondered if they would accept me back if I went crawling with my tail between my legs.

"Excuse me. Are you Simone Young?" a stranger asked, breaking my deep train of thought.

I didn't look the person in the eye as I didn't want him to see that I had been crying.

"I've seen your work. I think you're an amazing woman," the man continued.

"Thanks," I mumbled, hoping he would go away. I wasn't in the mood for small talk, especially not with one of my fans.

Ignoring my desire for solitude, the man continued.

"Are you OK?" he asked.

"I really don't mean to be rude but I'm not in the mood to chat," I replied.

"OK, but whatever it is that's bothering you, in time, it will pass. You're too beautiful to be here looking like a lost puppy, although a very cute puppy," he laughed obviously trying to make me follow suit.

"Thanks," I replied, cracking a slow smile.

"Are you flirting with me?" he joked.

"Hell no!" I answered with a chuckle. "Believe me—I'm not on the market. I already have a man who's driving me crazy! That's why I'm out here . . . trying to get away from him!"

"Oh . . . affairs of the heart. The most painful kind. How long have you been married?" he asked.

"Oh, we're not married."

"Then leave him and never look back."

His advice sounded logical—after all, I wasn't David's wife and we had no children. We shared nothing and I really could have walked away and never seen him again. But to me, it just didn't seem that simple.

"It's not that easy," I sighed. "I love him."

"But don't you love yourself?" the stranger asked. I didn't answer him out loud, but his words echoed throughout my mind.

"Don't you love yourself?" I heard his voice say again—once alone and once in unison with me.

"Eric Niles," the stranger confidently stated as he held out his hand to shake mine. Not sure why, I laughed heartily. It seemed I was always meeting men when I least needed to. Too bad they usually turned out to be the wrong man for me.

Eric was handsome with deep dark eyes and a brilliant white smile. He stood about five feet eleven with strong broad shoulders and arms that indicated some occasional weight lifting. They weren't too big and they weren't too small—they were just perfect to hold someone tightly on a stormy winter night. His conversation told me that he was a cool and down-to-earth guy and I definitely needed someone I could talk to at that moment. We sat silently watching the brilliant rays of the setting sun as it reflected off the surface of the deep blue sea. My heart had regained its normal pace, and as the waves swished against the shore, I became relaxed and at ease. Eric seemed to know a lot and was wise as he spoke about love and relationships. I eagerly listened to his experiences and the lessons he had learned, and I shared with him what was going on between me and David, feeling as though it would be safe to confide in someone I would probably never see again.

Once the sun had fully set and darkness blanketed the miles of sand, the breeze kicked up and Eric gently placed his jacket over my bare shoulders.

"Would you like to go across the street and get a bite to eat? I'm feeling kinda hungry," he offered.

I was embarrassed to tell my new friend that I had run out of the house without my wallet.

"Don't worry. My treat. But I'm not a billionaire. I'm just an average guy with a nine-to-five, so don't order an appetizer," he laughed.

We strolled off the beach and over to a nearby restaurant. As we entered the trendy eatery, the sound of calypso music resonated throughout the atmosphere as the waitstaff danced around the tables clad in brilliantly colored carnival-like costumes.

Over a feast with a Caribbean accent, I learned all about my new friend. He was single but hoped to have lots of children one day. He worked in an art gallery in the Dumbo section of Brooklyn and was visiting Florida on business, scouting locations for his boss, who was interested in opening a gallery down here. He claimed to have had only two girlfriends in his adult life—one of whom he had just broken up with. He was a self-proclaimed loner but enjoyed traveling and I was relieved to hear that he was as normal as could be.

Before I realized it, hours had passed and the clock read one A.M. I had to get home before David sent out the cavalry to retrieve me.

"Eric, I've had an amazing night. But I really have to get going," I told him.

"I understand," he sighed, taking a sip of his rum punch. "Will I ever see you again?"

"I'd like that," I hesitantly replied as we jotted down our cell phone numbers on nearby napkins.

As I headed toward the door of the restaurant, I looked back at Eric and waved with a smile. While I didn't want to leave, I knew I was vulnerable and the last thing I wanted to do was fall into the arms of a complete stranger because I had been so neglected by the man who was supposed to love me.

The drive back to the house accelerated my heartbeat once again. When I opened the front door, I was relieved that David wasn't home. A bit dehydrated from the rum punch I'd had at the restaurant, I walked into the kitchen to get a glass of water. To my surprise, on the marble countertop was a vase filled with a beautiful bouquet of long-stemmed red roses and a few hundred-dollar bills attached to a note: "Baby, I had to go out of town on business. I'm sorry about the fight. I promise I will do right by you when I get home. I love you and I hope you're there waiting for me when I return."

My heart melted from the tender words, but I knew it was just another plot to win me back. He always knew the right things to say to keep me riding the roller coaster we called our relationship.

I picked up the flowers and deeply inhaled their sweet aroma. While my logical side was not entirely convinced by the charming words he had written, my emotional side wanted to believe things were going to be different.

That night, I cuddled up alone in our bed and yearned to see David walk through the door. But after three days went by and he still had not returned, I began to worry. He had not called or answered his phone, but my concern ceased when our maid said that he had finally phoned and said he was fine.

After five days of not knowing where David was, I decided that I wasn't going to sit around waiting any longer. My boredom had gotten the best of me and I decided to call Eric with hopes that he would be available for conversation.

"Hey Eric, are you still in town? I know you said you'd be here for two weeks but—"

"I'm still here," he interrupted. "Are you calling to kidnap me?"

"Yeah, basically," I chuckled.

"Where's your man?"

"I haven't seen him in almost a week," I confessed.

"OK, well how about a movie?" he suggested.

That sounded cool, but I really wanted to go back to his hotel and just lie with him. I missed being in a man's arms and longed to be held. I knew Eric had way too much respect for our friendship to mess it up by making a move on me, so I knew I would have to be the aggressor.

"Why don't I pick you up at your hotel?" I suggested.

There was a slight pause on the phone before Eric replied.

"Simone, I don't think that's a good idea. I don't want you thinking I'm being your friend just so I can fuck you."

"Eric, I want to come to your hotel just to chill—not to have sex . . . trust me."

After a bit more coaxing, I was on my way to the Alexander Hotel on Miami Beach. Once there, I tossed myself across the modest bed and turned on the television with the remote control.

"Oh no, no, no. Get up!" Eric nervously instructed, gently tugging at my arm. I scooted out of his grasp and rolled away from his reach.

"Eric! Sit down . . . relax! I don't bite!" I assured him. Eric released his grasp and sat down in a chair by the window.

"Simone, I'm not playing your little game," he snapped in a serious tone.

A little taken aback by his response, I couldn't understand why he had rejected me. I could feel our chemistry but I could also see that he clearly wasn't about to go there.

"Simone, I think you're a brilliant woman and I definitely like you. But I'm not about to get involved with you while you're still involved with someone else. I really don't understand why you're still with your man, but since you are, I'm going to respect that," he reasoned.

"I have faith that he will change," I sighed, now snapping myself back into reality. "He's young and rich. He just needs to grow up a little."

"If you feel that way, then why are you trying to get me in bed?"

I didn't know what to say because I really didn't have an answer. I didn't want to tell him that I was just horny and looking for someone to give me the affection that David hadn't been. I didn't want to tell him that I was lonely. I was too embarrassed to admit to any of that.

"No matter how much you want him to, Simone, men like that never change. He's a player and you're his ultimate prize. He bought you just like he bought those cars in his driveway. You can't put a price on everything, ya know. Especially not love."

That said, Eric got up from the chair and handed me my bag.

"Come on," he continued. "You need to go home. He'll expect you to be there whenever he decides to return. Just like his Ferrari."

Although I was hurt and insulted by Eric's words, I knew he was right. And while I hadn't told him why I was really there trying to seduce him, he knew the deal. When I got up from the bed, I tried to give him a hug but he pulled away. We rode down in the elevator in silence and Eric gave the valet the ticket for my car.

As we waited for the guy to bring it around, Eric turned to me and said, "I may not have the riches, but my heart is pure and filled with good intentions. With me you will learn how to stand on your own two feet and take control of your life. I would treat you like a queen. That should be enough."

I sighed, embarrassed and touched as I looked him in his sweet adoring eyes and smiled.

"Eric, you are a sweet and honest man and I'm so lucky to have you as a friend." My car was pulled before us and I quickly leaned in to kiss him on his lips before jumping into my ride.

Back at the house, David seemed to be waiting for me on the front steps. I could see him standing there as I parked the car, and as I approached him, he extended his arms to me.

"Baby, there you are! Where have you been?! I see you got the flowers." He gleefully smiled.

Happy to see that he was in a good mood, I let the fact that I had not heard from him in nearly a week go right out the window. I had planned to curse him out and rant and rave about his disappearing act, but when I laid eyes on him, I could not help but rush into his arms. I had missed him. Eager to reciprocate, David picked me up and carried me inside the house. He laid me down on the white leather sofa and kissed me passionately, stimulating all kinds of sensations throughout my body. When he whispered in my ear that he had given the staff the evening off, we stripped off our clothes and David commenced to biting my neck and nibbling on my nipples as I vigorously stroked his cock. Without warning, he then grabbed me by my hips and picked me up, slamming me down onto his rock-hard dick. He pumped his rod up in me until I was drenched in my own orgasmic juices, whispering sweet nothings into my ear as he wrapped his hand around my neck, lightly choking me while we continued to fuck. He knew that turned me on, and as he kept hitting me in the right spot, I came hard. It had been a while for me and my cream oozed from my sugar walls coating his stiffness. Without a word, he proceeded to pull me off his ramrod and pushed my head down, inviting me to suck him off and taste my own nectar on his dick. I inhaled every inch of his manhood until I felt him ready to burst. Unwilling to do so just yet, David grabbed his dick and jerked off into my mouth as I dutifully swallowed his entire load. He jerked a few times as his semen spurted out from his fat nut sacks and I lay there on the sofa finger-fucking myself to keep my honey pot warm. I took a deep breath and wanted to recover quickly so that I could be ready for more. When I was, David tore up my pussy for what felt like hours, right there on the living room floor. When I was thoroughly satisfied, I began to doze off in an orgasm-induced euphoric state, only to be interrupted by David, who had reached over into his jacket pocket and pulled out a little blue box.

"This is for you, baby," he calmly offered, handing me the tiny package.

Now wide awake, I quickly sat up and opened the box. Inside was a platinum five-carat diamond ring gleaming back at me so brightly that I needed to grab my Christian Dior shades just to examine it.

"This is to show you that I promise to love you forever and treat you right. This is my promise ring to you, Simone," David explained.

A little disappointed that he had not actually asked me to marry him, my heart still fluttered with excitement as I jumped into his arms and kissed him all over. I then lay back, stared at the enormous rock he had just given me, and envisioned the wedding day that I hoped would soon follow. However, before we could truly celebrate taking our love to yet another level, David got up and began to dress.

"Okay, baby. That was amazing, as always. All those movies you did really perfected your skills," he laughed. Not knowing whether to take his statement as a compliment or an insult, I gave him a confused look but said nothing.

"I gotta go to work," he continued as he kissed me good-bye and headed out the door.

"At this hour?" I asked, observing how late it was. No sooner had I completed my question than I heard the engine start on David's Jaguar. Now speechless, I honestly didn't know what to think or how to feel. Was I just programmed to accept his bullshit? Alone and in awe, I lay silently on the living room floor basking in my own bodily fluids as I heard David speed away in his car. As quickly as he had secured our future, he had vanished—again. Was the ring just a meaningless trinket to keep me quiet and in place? As its luster and brilliance stared back at me from my left hand, I knew that it was.

Still basking somewhat in the fantasy of having a life with David, I stopped taking Eric's calls. I needed to get my head together and didn't want to drag him into my confusion. I loved David and wanted to give him a chance to prove that he loved me, too. For some reason, I had convinced myself that he wouldn't have given me a ring if he hadn't planned on making things better between us. When I finally did speak to Eric, I requested that he meet me at the place where we'd first met. I wanted to talk to him face-to-face. I arrived first and noticed that the backdrop of the colorful sky was reminiscent of our first encounter. When he finally got there, I looked him in the eye and explained that I wanted to give my relationship with David one last try.

"I love him, Eric. I have to give it all I've got and I don't want to hurt you in the process," I explained.

"You love him or you love the lifestyle, Simone? Because from where I sit, he's done nothing to deserve your love other than give you things," Eric snapped.

"Eric, that's not fair!" I defended. "I know I've complained a lot about David, but we did have some really great times before things went sour. Since he gave me this ring I'm hoping that means he's committed to getting things back to where they were in the beginning."

"I really wish you would open your eyes. Maybe one day you will. I only hope for your sake it's not too late."

There was a pause in our conversation before he continued.

"I'm going back to New York. I wish you the best."

Eric turned to walk away and as I watched him from behind, a single tear slowly fell down my cheek. I knew I had broken his heart, but I had never made him any promises. Still I cried because there was a part of me that knew I was letting something very special get away.

I took a moment to get myself together and dry my eyes. I didn't want to look upset when I got back to the house, so I shook it off, wiped my tears, and jumped into my Mercedes to head home. I told David that I was going to get a manicure and pedicure, hoping to give myself enough time to meet with

Eric. However, our talk had taken less time than I thought it would and when I returned home a little earlier than expected, I pulled up into the driveway and noticed a mini red-and-white BMW sitting in the circular driveway. I figured David was having some sort of business meeting but when I dashed inside, I didn't hear any activity coming from his office.

Still clueless, I walked up the grand staircase to the master bedroom when the sounds of lust touched my ears and caused me to stop just outside the door. Assuming he must have been watching one of my movies like he usually did, I entered the room ready to give him the live version of what he was viewing on the tube. To my surprise and dismay, however, the sight I saw made my heart stop. David was fucking a thick chocolate chick with a huge ass and droopy titties in our bed while a sexy Latina was lying on her back getting her pussy licked by the big bootied girl. My man was so engrossed in her pussy that he didn't even notice me standing in the doorway. Speechless, I watched as he slammed in and out of the freakish chick raw, before pulling out and cumming all over her back. It wasn't until he happily smeared his luv cream around on her butt and grinned that he noticed my presence.

"Oh shit!" he exclaimed, tossing the Spanish chick so hard that she hit the floor with a thump.

The sight of me had everyone in the room caught up in a drug-induced stupor. I scanned the area and noticed a pile of cocaine on the nightstand alongside an ashtray piled high with partially smoked blunts. Without thinking, I blacked out and ran over to attack everyone in the vicinity. Titties and asses flapped everywhere as they tried to dodge my blows and get out of the path of my wrath. The chicks somehow managed to get past me as I assaulted David and just as I was about to hit him in the head with a heavy Mikasa crystal paperweight, I came to my senses, dropped it on the floor, and ran from the room down to my car. Again I found myself hysterically fumbling to start the vehicle, not knowing where I was headed as I was slightly blinded by the sheet of tears that covered my eyes. Unbeknownst to me, I found myself at the Alexander Hotel searching for Eric. He was now the only real friend I had and I needed him more than ever. But when I arrived at the front desk and asked the receptionist to ring his room, I was told that he had already checked out.

thirty-two

feel the fire

I spent the night in my car remembering the connection I had made and lost with Eric. I couldn't believe I had let him walk out of my life, only to find out just how big of a master liar and manipulator David truly was.

As the sun rose in the morning and the seagulls swooped down on the white sand to gather breakfast, I headed back home to face my so-called man. Anger and disdain had had a chance to marinate overnight and all I wanted to do was beat the shit out of him on sight. Not wanting to be dragged off to jail, I had to remind myself to keep my cool.

As I approached the door of the mansion, I took a deep breath and walked in. The house was as still as a cemetery. I crept around and finally found signs of life in David's office. When I stuck my head through the massive door, I saw him sitting on the couch naked from the waist down, watching one of my movies. He gazed at my image giving head to another chick as he stroked the shaft of his dick, an empty bottle of Moët nearby. Sensing my presence, he quickly turned off the TV.

"Ahh, you keep busting me. Luck's been bad lately," he moaned, obviously drunk.

"*Luck's been bad lately*?" I repeated with disgust.

He groveled toward me on his hands and knees, his half-erect dick swinging from side to side.

"Baby, I'm so sorry. Please forgive me," he begged. "I have a problem," he continued. "I didn't want to have to tell you but I'm a sex addict. I thought I could settle down, especially with you being a porn star and all. I thought that would do it. But it didn't. I do love you, though. And I need you. So please don't leave me. I can change. I know I can—with time and with you by my side," he pathetically sobbed as he blew his rotten stale breath in my face. As much as I had wanted to pummel him into the floor, I suddenly felt sorry for him. No longer was he the strong, confident real-estate tycoon I had fallen head over heals for. As he reeked of musty alcohol, he seemed no better than the poor pathetic bums and junkies I had left behind on the streets of New York.

What kind of crazy fucked-up luck do I have? I asked myself. Of all the men on the planet, what were the odds of me falling in love with a bona fide clinical freak?

As I listened to his begging, total shock took over and I couldn't believe what was happening. In an instant, my entire life had come tumbling down. Unable to control myself, I began to cry. David tried to comfort me but I wouldn't let him as I kicked and screamed to be released from his grasp. Everything had been so perfect, or so I thought. How could things have changed so quickly—or had they always been that way and I had just been too blind to see it?

"Do you really think that after all that's happened I can just stay here and continue to live with you? I can't! It's over! I'm not about to stay here and play house with your lying, cheating ass!" I yelled.

"You can't leave me, Simone! Maybe we just need some time. A few weeks. Yeah, that's what we need. If we can't work it out after that I promise I'll take care of you until you get back on your feet. Just don't say you're leaving me for good," he begged.

"I can't believe this!" I bawled. "How could you do this to me?"

"I'm so sorry," he tried to soothe as he moved in closer. I pulled back, refusing to allow him to touch me. The sight of him repulsed me, and I could not get out of my mind the image of him in bed with the two freaks.

"I'm going home," I snapped, my voice cold and icy. I then walked out of the room and left David sitting alone in his office. As the sounds of my own lust echoed from behind, I ran upstairs to prepare for my departure. Still sobbing, I packed as much as I could. I had to get out of there. And while I didn't know what lay ahead of me, I definitely knew what I had to leave behind.

Back in California, my very empty beach house looked almost abandoned. I took a deep breath as I looked around and thanked God that I was finally home. Most of my things had been moved into David's place. My house no longer felt like a home. My once cozy, warm abode now possessed a cold and impersonal feeling. Cobwebs occupied corners that had not been touched in months and the place was a dusty mess. The past year of my life quickly flashed before my eyes. I could still envision the images of happy times with David and I knew it would be an adjustment to get back into my old routine. I also knew that I had no other choice but to leave.

During my first week back home, claiming to miss me, David called every day. He wanted to know what I was doing and whether I was spending time with another man. It was clear that he really didn't understand how much I loved him. To keep myself from going crazy, I spent a lot of time with Martha, sometimes forcing myself to ignore David's relentless calls to my cell phone. Then one day the calls suddenly stopped. I knew it was for the better and when I heard through the grapevine that he was dating a stripper from Club Rolex, I knew retreating back to Cali had been the best decision. My sources told me that the girl was an official freakazoid queen who let him fuck her in every hole on her body while she ran through his money like water. Although I should not have been surprised, I had secretly hoped that the distance would make him realize how much he loved me, forcing him to come running back to make things right. But instead I was heartbroken and let down once again. My heart bled profusely from the wound of yet another abandonment, and as each moment passed, I regretted letting Eric go.

As if things were not bad enough, my downward spiral plunged even deeper the morning I read the front page of the *Venice Sun*. I was heading for a cup of coffee at a nearby beachfront cafe when I caught a glance of my old friend turned enemy, Lucy Kane, on the cover of the morning paper. In big big letters, the headline seemed to scream: "Sex Star Slain."

According to the story, Lucy's naked corpse, strangled and beaten beyond recognition, had been discovered in the trunk of a stolen late-model sedan. Her face had been so disfigured that she had to be identified by her dental records. The autopsy proved that she had a large quantity of cocaine and alcohol in her blood, had been sexually assaulted, and was about three months pregnant. There were no suspects.

The article caused me to make a beeline from the coffee shop to puke in a nearby garbage can. Tears slid down my face, as I not only wept for Lucy but for myself. My emotions ran the gamut, from angry to sad, from disgusted to scared.

Was this the only ending stories like ours could have? I wondered. Could that have been me? And while Lucy and I had had our differences, by no means did I feel that she deserved to go out that way. No human being deserved to be killed and discarded like a two-day-old piece of trash. Not even Lucy Kane. She was still someone's daughter, and I could only imagine what her mother must have been going through. If I didn't get a grip, was a scene like that in Francine Young's future?

Overcome by my own dismay, with hopes of escaping my reality, I jumped in my car and drove to the nearest liquor store to get a few bottles of wine. When I arrived back home with my stash, I pulled all the curtains closed and began drinking. In a drunken stupor, I called Martha and eventually passed out with the telephone tightly gripped in my hand.

"Simone! Simone, get up!" I heard a vacuumlike voice ricochet off the walls of my brain. I opened my glazed, shiny, and hungover eyes.

"Martha . . ." I giggled with a slur before passing out once again.

When I finally came to, it took me a moment to realize that I was at Martha's house. I had no idea how I had gotten there and wondered if it was all just a bad dream. However, from my throbbing headache I knew everything had been very real.

"What am I going to do with you?" my friend gazed at me with sadness as she gently shook her head.

"Did you hear what happened to Lucy?" I asked—my voice raspy, my throat still burning from the sting of the previous night's alcohol binge.

"Yes. It's terrible," Martha sadly replied.

"That could have been you or me, ya know . . ." I warned her. "What we do . . . it makes people dehumanize us. Makes them think they can chew us up and spit us out whenever they get ready."

"Simone, Lucy was a special case. You know that. Please don't start freaking out. I mean, what happened to her is fucked up and all, but you and I both know she was crazy . . . God rest her soul."

"You know something, Marth? When I think about it, maybe Lucy's better off than we are."

"Maybe . . ." she sighed, finally shedding a tear.

The loss of David, Eric, and now Lucy was just too much for me to handle. Although I refused to admit it, the news of her death had thrust me into a zombielike state, and while my eyes were open, I was actually walking around like the living dead. In an attempt to keep myself busy and fend off negative emotions, I partied harder and harder until I could eventually feel myself slipping back into my old ways. I began drinking and hanging out every night. In an effort not to think about my life or Lucy's untimely demise, I hit the strip clubs, medicating myself with anything I could get my hands on.

One particular evening, all alone, I popped a few bottles of champagne in the VIP lounge of Lou's Rendezvous. I got a lap dance and as I watched the girls do their thing on stage, I couldn't help but notice how tired and bored they looked. Of course, I could relate, and I wondered if they were secretly experiencing the same sorrows and pains that I had when I was swinging around that pole, searching for something more than forever being labeled a stripper and a porn queen. I also wondered how many of them would end up like my colleague—raped, battered, and stuffed in a trunk like a worn-out Michelin tire.

Breaking my train of thought, one of the dancers jumped off the stage and walked over to my table.

"Hey, Mama. You wanna dance?" the buxom hottie sexily cooed. She was an attractive sistah who's flesh was tight and firm but who's eyes said she had seen things over the years that had shaped her in the most precarious of ways.

"No thanks. I'm done," I sighed.

"Hey, ain't you Simone Young?" she asked, now in her regular voice. I nodded my head as if to say yes, but failed to make eye contact.

"Girl, you look like you just lost your best friend. You okay?" she asked, now helping herself to the seat beside me.

"Yeah, yeah. I'm fine, thanks." I shrugged, hoping she would go away. But as she got up to leave, I gently grabbed her arm and confessed, "Actually, I'm not fine. My life is falling apart. I'm searching for something I just can't seem to find and my whole existence seems pointless."

"Man problems," she stated more than asked. "We all have 'em," she continued. "Ya love him?

"I did. . . ."

"Well, don't you love yourself?"

There was that question again—the same question Eric had asked me the first day we met.

"Yes, I do love myself. I just don't make the best choices when it comes to men," I defended.

"Boo, lemme tell you a little somethin' about the people with testosterone. I been stripping nineteen years and I ain't never met no man worthy of my heart. Once you can remember that, you'll be fine. In my opinion, they all got game. I hear there's good ones out there, but they ain't never came to Cali," she chuckled.

"I met a good one . . . once," I sighed, looking off into the distance.

"Well, what you doing here then?"

She was right. What *was* I doing there?

"Well, if I was you and I met a good man, I'd hold on to him and never let him go. This lifestyle is for the lonely. Ain't nothin' at the end of this rainbow but dirt. You can keep searchin' for that pot of gold if you want to . . . but I'm tellin' ya, it don't exist. Ya hear about what happened to that porno chick?" she asked, referring to Lucy. I nodded my head as if to say yes before she softly chuckled and she stood up.

"That's how most of us end up—strung out or six feet under. Sometimes both. Don't let that be you. I got one more year before I retire. Then I ain't never gonna see the inside of another one of these joints again," she assured me with a wink.

"But I was one of the smart ones. They don't make 'em like me no more. Naaaa . . . this new generation is insane. I got a nest egg and a plan. Ain't never touched no drugs and ain't never fuck no customers. In nineteen years. To know true love is to know yourself—your own value and your worth. You have to start at the beginning and learn from your past. That's the only way you won't be a fuck-up in the future. Remember my words. I may shake my ass for a living but I ain't no dummy." She winked. "Well, I gotta go do what I do—three hundred and sixty-three days and counting, girl. You might be one of the first one of us to make it to the mainstream. You gotta gift."

"Thanks for your words of wisdom," I said with a slow smile.

"Now, if I could only practice what I preach, maybe I wouldn't still be shakin' my ass for these bustas!" she snapped as she strutted off into the smoky distance, flirting with her loyal salivating customers along the way.

As I watched her sashay on to continue her work, goose bumps rose on my skin and I was hit with a major revelation. The mysterious stripper had been an angel in disguise. Her wise words had pierced my brain and touched my heart—a heart that whispered Eric's name.

As if a lightning bolt had jolted me from my seat, I jumped up and hightailed it out of the club in search of what I had mindlessly abandoned.

Back at Martha's apartment, as if my life depended on it, I threw my things together, determined to get to the airport.

"Simone, what's going on?" Martha questioned, standing in the doorway of her guestroom.

With a lump in my throat I replied, "I'm going to find Eric."

"Eric! But you don't even know where he lives, *remember*? And besides, I thought you guys hadn't spoken since you were in Fort Lauderdale."

"We haven't," I stated, still gathering up my stuff.

"Simone, that man could be living on the moon by now. Have you been smoking?"

"No," I snapped, not interested in her attempt to discourage my mission.

"You can't run off to New York in search of some guy! How do you even know he still wants you? You could be setting yourself up to get hurt again!"

"I know the name of the gallery where he works, so I'll start there. I'll find him. I have to believe that. I can't end up like Lucy. There's got to be more to my life than . . ." I looked around and spat, *"This!"*

"Simone, I told you that what happened to Lucy ain't gonna happen to you!"

"How can I be sure? Look, I been running from men like Eric all my life—men who are capable of love. But not anymore. I *know* that man loves me and I want the chance to have a life with him. I don't wanna end up stuffed in a trunk with a dead fetus in my stomach!" I exclaimed with conviction.

"I think you're finally losing it, Simone."

"Maybe. But I have to at least try to find him. I know he's just an average guy and not some rich flashy millionaire tycoon. But maybe that's what I need. He's the only man who ever made me feel like I could have the world. And when I find him, I'm gonna make him feel the same way!"

I clicked my suitcase shut and gave Martha a big hug and kiss.

"Girl, you got heart. Good luck! Just promise me you won't give up on your dream. You have a lot of talent and it would be a sin to let it go to waste," she whispered in my ear.

"Don't worry, I won't. I have to show the world that I'm a true entertainer. I gotta keep knocking down those doors. I still have something to prove," I assured her.

"And when you do, maybe one day you can write a book. Just make sure Halle Berry plays me!"

We laughed heartily as I grabbed my bags and hugged my friend one more time.

"Thank you for loving me unconditionally." I smiled as I headed out the door. I held back my tears as I jumped into a taxi and headed to the airport. Part of me thought I was crazy for searching for the unknown. The Big Apple was huge. How was I going to find Eric Niles among the millions? But as I waved good-bye to Martha for the last time, I felt an uncanny sense of peace. Although I knew the name of the gallery, I was actually clueless as to how I was going to find him. Still, somehow I felt like I was on the right path. Somehow I believed that I was finally going to have a happy ending.

I was suddenly zapped back into reality and brought down from my high when I was forced to fork over an arm and a leg for a last-minute ticket to New York. I tried not to let the cost bother me too much as I dialed 411 in an effort to obtain the number to the gallery where Eric had told me he worked. With time to spare before my flight boarded, I repeatedly called but there was no answer. Looking at the time, I figured that since it was before business hours, I would call again once I arrived.

All the weeks of physical and emotional exhaustion came crashing down on me, and when I nestled down in my seat, I quickly passed out. I didn't open my eyes until I felt the wheels touch down in New York. With a yawn and a stretch, I told myself that I had so much to look forward to—a new life, a new love, and a new destiny.

thirty-three

it takes two

Immediately upon my arrival back in New York, I called directory assistance and got the address for the Sea Gallery. My heart pounded a mile a minute as I rode in silence to the trendy section of Soho. When the yellow cab pulled up at the location, I was distressed to find an abandoned storefront with a FOR SALE sign on the doors. I jumped out of the taxi with tears streaming down my cheeks and ran over to the glass. With all my might, I banged on it with my fists, ultimately slamming my head against the pane in agony. Interrupting my fury, the turban-clad driver honked at me from behind. The meter was still running and he wanted his money. When I got hold of my emotions, I reentered the car and requested to be driven back to Harlem. With a blank and distant look on my face, I sat puffy-eyed and silent in the backseat as we cruised up the FDR Drive.

What am I going to do now? I asked myself.

Eric's cell phone had been disconnected and the only lead I'd had on his whereabouts had turned up empty.

Luck's been bad lately. I heard David's drunken voice echo in my head. The way things had been going for me, if it hadn't been for bad luck, I would have had none.

My return to Harlem was bittersweet. While I had clearly missed my girls and just the spirit of the city that never slept, things had done a lot of changing around the brownstone since I'd run off to Cali in search of fame and fortune. Ebony had moved out and in with a guy she had been seeing for a while. Carmen had gotten knocked up by a man twice her age—an old G from her neighborhood who was more like her daddy than her man. Nevertheless, she was determined to be the mother she'd never had, and at seven months' pregnant and 210 pounds, she was in no condition to run the streets with me. I was proud of her, though. She was excited about becoming a mother and I was excited for her. I only hoped that once the baby was born, she didn't turn back into her old self. Jessie, on the other hand, had quit her job and was on the ho stroll stronger than ever. Since Ebony left, Jess had been paying all the bills in the brownstone, and with the constant flow of miscellaneous dudes coming in and out of the place, I had to wonder if she was running some sort of brothel. I never knew who or what I'd run into coming out of the bathroom at three in the morning and eventually became so uncomfortable with the situation that I was forced to put a lock on my bedroom door. The place was also a filthy mess, with clothing, dishes, and garbage left scattered for days on end, only to be tidied if I chose to tackle the task. Always the most conservative of our crew, Jess had done a one-eighty and was now doing a lot of drugs, causing me to become concerned about her well-being. I knew we had prided ourselves on being wild and free back in the day, but it seemed that my girl was taking the mind-set to a whole new level. Worried, I tried to talk to her about what she was doing but was met with a violent defense.

"I *know* the *porn star* ain't suddenly catch a case of morals!" she venomously spat, causing me to retreat.

It wasn't long before I realized that it would be best if I moved out. But with little money saved, my options were limited.

As I lay awake listening to the shameless sounds of my roommate getting slain by two guys on the living room floor, I told myself that I had no choice but to go crawling back to Aaron with hopes that he would take pity on me and get me some work in my old field. We had not spoken since Lucy's funeral, and even then the conversation had been strained. Thus, I knew he would be apprehensive about helping me.

"I don't know, Simone," he began with a shrug once I'd gotten up the nerve to call him. "You burned a lot of bridges walking out on the business like you did. Plus, I don't know if you're cut out for this anymore. Only the strong survive in this business, and Lucy's death hit you pretty hard. I don't know if you're emotionally stable enough to do this again."

"I'm fine, Aaron. I need to work. My record sales didn't do what the company was expecting and I don't have any other way to make money right now," I groveled.

"All right . . ." He hesitated. "Gimme a coupla days and I'll see what I can do."

The days turned into weeks and the weeks turned into almost a month. As the holidays passed and a new year was upon me, things had gotten pretty grim. Money was scarce and I had to sell a lot of my designer stuff just so I could eat and keep up with my half of the rent. Depression had set in and I spent most of my waking hours locked up in my room sleeping or watching dysfunctional trailer trash on poorly choreographed talk shows. I tried on my own to secure some dancing gigs, but as every interview turned up empty, I began to wonder if I had been blacklisted by the industry. I eventually began losing weight and was unable to afford my costly beauty regimen. With all that was going on, reconnecting with Eric became the last thing on my mind. Although I considered it, I had convinced myself that going home to my mother was not a viable option. I didn't want to feel lower than I already did, and facing Francine Young would have done nothing but remind me how much of a failure I truly was. Hearing a bunch of "I told you sos" would have only made me feel worse.

Then one day Aaron called. Since I'd left his agency, he had made quite a name for himself in the porn industry, representing some of the most sought-after women in the business. He needed a last-minute replacement for a film entitled *The Dicks of Hazard*. The pay would be eight thousand dollars with the option for a sequel if the first one did well. I would be working with one of the most popular and well-endowed African-American actors in the industry, Donnie Cobra, and would receive costar billing. Aaron had even worked it out for the opening credits to read "The Return of the Insatiable Simone Young." As I listened to him reveal the details of the project, my stomach tightened and I could feel the bile sour as it churned its way through my large intestine. It was the ugliest form of déjà vu. Here I was once again being offered another porn gig by Aaron Roth. With all the milestones I thought I had reached in my career, I was right back at the beginning.

"I'll do it," I wryly replied when he finished his spiel.

" 'I'll do it'?" he dryly mimicked. "That's all you have to say? *I'll do it?* No 'Thank you, Aaron, you're a lifesaver!' No 'Aaron, you're the best'? Just a nonchalant, ungrateful 'I'll do it'? Honestly, Simone, you could at least *sound* excited. You're getting a second chance, kid. This could be the beginning of your comeback. Don't screw it up again!" he snapped before hanging up the phone on me. With the receiver still in hand, like a zombie I walked to the bathroom, buried my head in the commode, and proceeded to regurgitate the Cheddar cheese omelet I'd eaten for breakfast. If I hadn't been afraid of dying, I would have killed myself right there on the spot. Instead, I figured it would be better to punish myself by continuing to live.

September 1992

"Come on, Simone! Get into it!" the director screamed.

Is it that obvious that I don't wanna be here? I asked myself. I thought I was doing my best to focus on the massive chocolate dick that was sliding across my tongue. If only I could get that freakin' song out of my head!

"How did you get here?"

There it went again!

"Cut! Cut! Cut!" Manolo bellowed as he angrily threw his silver megaphone to the ground. Out of my peripheral view I could see his portly five-foot frame storming in my direction with clenched fists.

"Simone!" he snarled. "What the hell do you think you're doing?!"

I looked up from my costar's rock-hard member in confusion, releasing it from my jaws and giving my attention to the director from hell.

"Wha–what's wrong?" I asked.

" 'What's wrong?' " he sarcastically repeated, leaning in close enough for me to inhale the stench of his cappuccino-and-nicotine-laden breath. I blankly gazed at him in silence as he engaged in a bona fide temper tantrum.

"Miss Young, do you know my ex-wife? Are you a part of her nasty little conspiracy to ruin my career?" Manolo inquired, his eyes beady and squinting with speculation.

"I don't know what you're talking about, I'm—"

"Shhhh," he interrupted. "Say nothing. Listen . . . Your body language. Your face. Everything screams that your head is somewhere else. You looked forced! Scared! Like I've kidnapped you and forced you into sexual slavery in some Third World country! I can't have this! Where's Simone Young the Porn Star?!" he yelled.

"How did you get here?"

There it went again.

The more that song swirled through my mind, the more difficult it became to focus on my job. The tune became unbearable in my head, and Manolo's image appeared blurry through my Hennessy-altered vision. A lightning bolt flashed behind his silhouette and I had an out-of-body experience as my life passed before my eyes. In the glowing distance, I suddenly saw the image of myself on my yellow tricycle—a pretty little caramel-colored girl with neatly braided pigtails adorned with pink satin ribbons. In a swift View-Master click, I saw my eighth-grade graduation. How I had loved that purple dress my mom had bought me in Macy's! Then the sight of my sister tightly gripping a hypothermic needle and shoving it into her pulsating vein turned the scrapbook ugly before cutting to my mom as she put her hand up to my face and caressed my cheek with her thumb.

"My sweet Simone. You are very pretty, but you need an education to go along with your looks. Looks don't last," she warned.

Then all of a sudden, as if I were looking through a homemade animated flipbook, I saw the faces of Carmen and George,

Reggie and Mr. Walton,

Wellington and Jack,

Kareem and Chyna,

Cherokee and Aaron,

Rod Jox,

Mr. Foxx and Lucy Kane,

J Cash and Jason Kool,

Martha,

Derek Wells,

David,

and Eric . . .

all morph into one. It was a subliminal re-creation of Michael Jackson's *Black or White* video starring the characters from my life. My limbs became numb and hot as my heartbeat accelerated, threatening to give out on me. When Deborah Cox finally stopped singing that now horrific melody, I replied, "The end."

Like a creature from the infamous horror film *Dawn of the Dead*, I rose from the now-flaccid penis that lingered beneath me and walked off the set. In the distance, I could still hear Manolo yelling—in English, in Italian, and then in some unrecognizable dialect. On autopilot, I grabbed my white terry-cloth robe from my personalized chair, slipped my arms into its sleeves, and headed down the corridor, out the front door of the studio, and onto the street, where I robotically flagged down the first taxi I saw.

I don't remember telling the driver where to go, but before I knew it, the car was pulling up before my mother's house. In a hypnotic trance, I handed the cabbie a fifty-dollar bill, got out of the car, rang the doorbell, and waited with weakened knees. I could barely support my own weight, and when the door finally opened, I fell limply into her arms. My entire world had finally come spiraling down upon me and I could no longer contain myself. As I collapsed to the floor, like the pillar of strength I always knew she was, Francine caught me, pulling me across the threshold like a weightless feather. Salty tears of relief poured from my eyes, but my heart knew that it was safe. When I needed her most, my mother was there to remind me that I was finally home, where I belonged and needed to be.